the
space
between
us

For the real Bhima
and the millions like her

ACKNOWLEDGMENTS

As always, this book was made possible by the love, encourage-ment, and support of all my friends and family. Although you are too numerous to name, I hope you know who you are and what a vital role you play in my life.

As always, a special thanks, Noshir and Homai Umrigar, for your constant prayers, good wishes, and kind words. Thank you, Eustatha Kavouras, for your unflagging support and encouragement.

Thank you, Arkady Lerner, for restoring my hands; thank you, Sarah Willis, for your great generosity in reading the manuscript and for your invaluable suggestions; thank you, Mary Grimm, for your optimism, which saw me through dark days. Marly Rusoff, thank you for your faith in me. This book would not have been pos-sible without all your help.

the

space

between

us

PROLOGUE

The thin woman in the green sari stood on the slippery rocks and gazed at the dark waters around her. The warm wind loosened strands of her scanty hair, pulling them out of her bun. Behind her, the sounds of the city were muted, shushed into silence by the steady lapping of the water around her bare feet. Other than the crabs that she heard and felt scuttling around the rocks, she was all alone here—alone with the murmuring sea and the distant moon, stretched thin as a smile in the nighttime sky. Even her hands were empty, now that she had unclenched them and released her helium-filled cargo, watching until the last of the balloons had been swallowed up the darkness of the Bombay night. Her hands were empty now, as empty as her heart, which itself was a coconut shell with its meat scooped out.

Balancing gingerly on the rocks, feeling the rising water tonguing her feet, the woman raised her face to the inky sky for an answer. Behind her was the lost city and a life that at this very moment, felt fictitious, and unreal. Ahead of her was the barely visible seam where the sea met the sky. She could scramble over these rocks, climb over the cement wall, and reenter the world; partake again & the mad, throbbing, erratic pulse of the city. Or she could walk into the waiting sea, let it seduce her, overwhelm her with its intimate whisperings.

She looked to the sky again, searching for an answer. But the only thing she could hear was the habitual beating of her own dutiful heart . . .

BOOK ONE

1

Although it is dawn, inside Bhima's heart it is dusk.

Rolling onto her left side on the thin cotton mattress on the floor, she sits up abruptly, as she does every morning. She lifts one bony hand over her head in a yawn and a stretch, and a strong, mildewy smell wafts from her armpit and assails her nostrils. For an idle moment she sits at the edge of the mattress with her callused feet flat on the mud floor, her knees bent, and her head resting on her folded arms. In that time she is almost at rest, her mind thankfully blank and empty of the trials that await her today and the next day and the next . . . To prolong this state of mindless grace, she reaches absently for the tin of chewing tobacco that she keeps by her bedside. She pushes a wad into her mouth, so that it protrudes out of her fleshless face like a cricket ball.

Bhima's idyll is short-lived. In the faint, delicate light of a new day, she makes out Maya's silhouette as she stirs on mattress on the far left side of their hut. The girl is mumbling in her sleep, making soft, whimpering sounds, and despite herself, Bhima feels her heart soften and dissolve, the way it used to when she breast-fed Maya's mother, Pooja, all those years ago. Propelled by Maya's puppylike sounds, Bhima gets up with a grunt from the mattress and makes her way to where her granddaughter lies asleep. But in the second that it takes to cross the small hut, something shifts in Bhima's heart, so that the milky, maternal feeling from a moment ago is replaced by that hard, merciless feeling of rage that has lived within her since several weeks ago. She stands towering over the sleeping girl, who is now snoring softly, blissfully unaware of the pinpoint anger in her grandmother's eyes as she stares at the slight swell of Maya's belly.

One swift kick, Bhima says to herself, one swift kick to the belly, followed by another and another, and it will all be over. Look at her sleeping there, like a shameless whore, as if she has not a care in the world. As if she has not turned my life upside down. Bhima's right foot twitches with anticipation; the muscles in her calf tense as she lifts her foot a few inches off the ground. It would be so easy. And compared to what some other grandmother might do to Maya—a quick shove down an open well, a kerosene can and a match, a sale to a brothel—this would be so humane. This way, Maya would live, would continue going to college and chose a life different from what Bhima had always known. That was how it was supposed to be, how it had been, until this dumb cow of a girl, this girl with the big heart and, now, a big belly, went and got herself pregnant.

Maya lets out a sudden loud snort, and Bhima's poised foot drops to the floor. She crouches down next to the sleeping girl to shake her by the shoulders and wake her up. When Maya was still going to college, Bhima allowed her to sleep in as late as possible, made gaajar halwa for her every Sunday, gave her the biggest portions of dinner every night. If Serabai ever gave Bhima a treat—a Cadbury's chocolate, say, or that white candy with pistachios that came from Iran—she'd save it to bring it home for Maya, though, truth to tell, Serabai usually gave her a portion for Maya anyway. But ever since Bhima has learned of her granddaughter's shame, she has been waking the girl up early. For the last several Sundays there has been no gaajar halwa, and Maya has not asked for her favorite dessert. Earlier this week, Bhima even ordered the girl to stand in line to fill their two pots at the communal tap. Maya had protested at that, her hand unconsciously rubbing her belly, but Bhima had looked away and said the people in the basti would soon enough find out about her dishonor anyway, so why hide it?

Maya rolls over in her sleep, so that her face is inches away from where Bhima is squatting. Her young, fat hand finds Bhima's thin, crumpled one, and she nestles against it, holding it between her chin and her chest. A single strand of drool falls on Bhima's captive hand. The older woman feels herself soften. Maya has been like this from the time she was a baby—needy, affectionate, trusting. Despite all the sorrow she has experienced in her young life, Maya has not lost her softness and innocence. With her other free hand, Bhima strokes the girl's lush, silky hair, so different from her own scanty hair.

The sound of a transistor radio playing faintly invades the room, and Bhima swears under her breath. Usually, by the time Jaiprakash turns his radio on, she is already in line at the water tap. That means she is late this morning. Serabai will be livid. This stupid, lazy girl has delayed her. Bhima pulls her hand brusquely away from Maya, not caring whether the movement wakes her up. But the girl sleeps on. Bhima jumps to her feet, and as she does, her left hip lets out a loud pop. She stands still for a moment, waiting for the wave of pain that follows the pop, but today is a good day. No pain.

Bhima picks up the two copper pots and opens the front door. She bends so that she can exit from the low door and then shuts it behind her. She does not want the lewd young men who live in the slum to leer at her sleeping granddaughter as they pass by. One of them is probably the father of the baby . . . She shakes her head to clear the dark, snakelike thoughts that invade it.

Bhima's bowels move and she clucks her tongue. Now she'll have to make her way to the communal bathroom before she goes to the tap, and the line will be even longer. Usually, she tries to control her bowels until she gets to Serabai's house, with its real toilets. Still, it's early enough that the conditions shouldn't be too bad. A few hours later and there will hardly be room to walk between the tidy piles of shit that the residents of the slum leave on the mud floor of the communal toilet. After all these years, the flies and the stink still make Bhima's stomach turn. The slum residents have taken to paying the Harijan woman who lives at the far end of the slum colony to collect their piles each night. Bhima sees her sometimes, crouching on the floor as she sweeps the pancakes of shit with her broom into a wicker basket that's lined with newspaper. Occasionally, their eyes meet, and Bhima makes a point to smile at her. Unlike most of the residents of the slums, Bhima does not consider herself superior to the poor woman.

Bhima finishes her business and makes her way to the tap. She groans as she sees the long line, winding its way past the black, disheveled looking huts with their patched, tin roofs. The morning light makes the squalor of the slum colony even more noticeable. The open drains with their dank, pungent smell, the dark rows of slanting hutments, the gaunt, openmouthed men who lounge around in drunken stupors—all of it looks worse in the clear light of the new day. Despite herself, Bhima's mind goes back to the old days when she lived with her husband, Gopal, and their two children in a chawl, where water gurgled through the tap in her kitchen and they shared the toilet with only two other families.

Bhima is about to join the end of the water tap line when Bibi spots her. "Ae, Bhima mausi," she says. "Come over here, na. For you only I've been holding a reservation here."

Bhima smiles in gratitude. Bibi is a fat, asthmatic woman who moved into the slum two years ago and immediately adopted Bhima as her older aunt. Whereas Bhima is silent and reserved, Bibi is loud and flashy. Nobody can stay angry at Bibi for too long—her willingness to help, her good-natured ribbing of old and young, have made her one of the slum colony's most popular residents.

Now Bhima makes her way to where Bibi is standing. "Here," Bibi says, taking one of Bhima's pots from her, despite the fact that she's carrying two of her own. "Get in here."

The man behind them feels compelled to protest. "Ho, Bibi, this is not the Deccan Express, where you have reservations for a first-class bogey," he grumbles. "Nobody is allowed to jump the queue like this."

Bhima feels her face flush, but Bibi holds out a restraining hand and whirls around to face her detractor. "Wah, wah," she says loudly. "Mr. Deccan Express here is worried about people jumping the line. But in one-two hours straight, while Bhima mausi is hard at work, he'll be headed for the local bootlegger's joint. And if there's a shortage of liquor today, God forbid, let's see then whether he jumps the line or not." The crowd around them snickers.

The man shuffles his feet. "Okay, now, Bibi, no need for personal attacks," he mumbles.

Bibi's voice gets even louder. "Arre, bhaisahib, who's attacking you personally? All I'm saying is, you are obviously a man of leisure, a man of great personal wealth. If you wish to spend your days at the bootlegger's shop, that's your concern. But poor Bhima here, she doesn't have a fine husband like you to support her. We all know how well you support your wife. So anyway, Bhima mausi has to go to work on time. And I didn't think a gentleman like you would mind if she filled her pots before you did."

The crowd is whooping with delight now. "Ae, Bibi, you are too much, yaar. Tops, just tops," a young layabout says.

"Who needs nuclear weapons?" someone else says. "I tell you, yaar, they should just unleash Bibi in Kashmir. The snows will melt from the fire in her tongue."

"Wait, wait, I have it," says Mohan, the seventeen-year-old who lives in the hut diagonally across from Bibi's. "A perfect song for the occasion. Here it is:

Forget the atom bomb, India said
Our new weapon leaves Pakistan dead
Just like she did Mr. Deccan Express
Bibi will leave you an utter mess.

Another man, whom Bhima doesn't know, slaps Mohan on the back. "Arre, ustad, you are too much. Our slum's own court poet. With your movie star looks, you should be writing and singing your own songs. Imagine, the physique of a Sanjay Dutt and the voice of a Mohammad Rafi. On Filmfare awards night, there would be no other winners, I tell you."

Despite herself, Bhima smiles. "Okay, you altoo-faltoos," Bibi says with a grin. "Leave us alone now."

By the time Bhima reaches her hut, Maya is up and has tea brewing on the Primus stove. As the girl adds the mint leaves to the boiling water, Bhima's stomach growls. The two stand outside their hut and quickly brush their teeth. Maya uses a toothbrush, but Bhima simply takes the tooth powder on her index finger and rubs vigorously on her remaining teeth. They spit into the open drain that rolls past their home. Quickly, efficiently, Bhima dips a plastic cup into one of the copper pots and washes herself through her clothes. Her face burns as she notices the man in the opposite hut staring at her as she puts a hand under her blouse to wash her armpits. Shameless badmaash, she mutters to herself. Acting as if he has no mother or sister.

When Bhima reenters the hut, Maya pours the tea into two glasses. They sit on their haunches, facing each other, blowing on the hot tea and dipping a loaf of bread into the brew. "Good tea," Bhima says. It is the first she has spoken to Maya this morning. Then, as if the girl's look of gratitude is too much for her to bear, she adds, "Seems like at least something I've taught you has stayed with you."

Maya flinches, and the guarded, wary look returns to her face. Noticing the look makes Bhima feel repentant but strangely satisfied. She is gripped by the need to draw more blood.

"So what will you do all day today?"

Maya shrugs.

The shrug infuriates Bhima. "Oh, that's right, memsahib is no longer going to college, I forgot," she says, addressing the walls. "No, now she will just sit around like a queen all day, feeding herself and her—her bastard baby, while her poor grandmother slaves in someone's home. All so that she can feed the demon that's growing in her granddaughter's belly."

If it's blood she wanted, she has it. Maya moans as she pulls herself up from the floor and moves to the farthest corner of the small room. She leans lightly on the tin wall, her hands around her belly, and sobs to herself.

Bhima wants to take the sobbing girl to her bosom, to hold and caress her the way she used to when Maya was a child, to forgive her and to ask for her forgiveness. But she can't. If it were just anger that she was feeling, she could've scaled that wall and reached out to her grandchild. But the anger is only the beginning of it. Behind the anger is fear, fear as endless and vast and gray as the Arabian Sea, fear for this stupid, innocent, pregnant girl who stands sobbing before her, and for this unborn baby who will come into the world to a mother who is a child herself and to a grandmother who is old and tired to her very bones, a grandmother who is tired of loss, of loving and losing, who cannot bear the thought of one more loss and of one more person to love.

So she stares numbly at the weeping girl, willing her heart not to take in the arrows of her sobbing. "Even tears are a luxury," she says, but she is unsure if she's spoken out loud or to herself. "I envy you your tears."

When she next speaks, she does so consciously. "If you feel well enough, stop by Serabai's house later. She keeps asking about you."

But even through her tears, Maya shakes her head no. "I told you, Ma-ma," she says. "I don't leave the house all day while you are gone."

Bhima gives up. "Okay, then, sit at home while your old grandmother works all day," she says, as she rises to her feet. "Fatten your baby with my blood."

"Ma-ma, please," Maya sobs, placing her hands over her ears, the way she used to when she was little.

Bhima pulls the door shut behind her. She wants to slam it but controls herself. No need for anyone in the basti to know their family problems. They will know about the disgrace Maya has brought upon herself soon enough, and then they will attack her like vultures. No point in hastening that day.

As she begins her walk toward Serabai's house, a cool morning breeze leans into Bhima, and she shivers against it. She can tell from the angle of the sun that she's late. Serabai will be anxious to know what transpired yesterday. She picks up her pace.

2

Sera Dubash glances at the basket of onions hanging near the window and then at the large kitchen clock. Late again. Bhima is late again. She really needs to talk to Bhima about this daily tardiness. After all, she, Sera, is responsible for packing Dinaz's and Viraf's lunches on time each morning, and she needs Bhima here to help her. Yesterday, both children left for work ten minutes later than they should have because their lunches were not ready. Sera had to plead with Viraf not to speed, to drive with care, to remember that his wife was expecting their first baby. "Yah, yah, Mamma." Viraf had smiled, giving Sera a quick peck on the cheek. "We all know that Dinaz's tummy has the words Handle with Care tattooed on it."

Remembering her daughter's pregnancy makes Sera think of Maya, and she feels a wave of remorse at her earlier resolution to chastise Bhima. Poor Bhima, she thinks. As if life has not been hard enough, now even her granddaughter has to add to her woes. Who would have guessed that a good girl like Maya could be up to such mischief? She wonders what happened at Maya's college yesterday, and her impatience to find out the latest news from Bhima makes her glance at the clock again.

Sera sighs. If there's one thing she hates, it's chopping onions, but if the children's omelets are to be made in time, she'd better get down to the task. No telling when Bhima may show up today.

She reaches for a medium-sized onion, and by the time she has peeled the translucent skin, her eyes begin to water. She reaches for the biggest knife in the drawer. Better to get the task over with as quickly as possible. Years ago, Feroz had come up behind her as she worked in the kitchen and said, "My God, Sera. You chop onions like you're chopping heads. Such vehemence."

"I'd rather chop heads than onions," she'd replied. "I'd probably cry less." And Feroz had laughed. That was in the old days, before she lost her ability to make Feroz laugh.

Sera hears Viraf's whistling tunelessly in his bedroom, and the sound makes her smile. She can imagine her young, handsome son-in-law standing before the full-length mirror, adjusting his tie, running a careless hand through his thick hair. There is something wonderful about the sound of a man getting ready to face the day, Sera thinks. Unlike Feroz, Viraf is noisy and makes his presence felt. He drops his hairbrush and murmurs a soft "Damn"; he sings old Beatles songs in the shower; he gargles vigorously while brushing his teeth; he yells to Dinaz for a new bottle of shampoo; he walks noisily into the kitchen with shaving cream on his face and a towel around his waist. Feroz had lived like a thief in his own house, getting fully dressed in the bathroom before he emerged and then walking out of the bedroom without a second look in the mirror.

Sera cracks two eggs, beats them in a bowl, and adds onions, garlic, cilantro, and a pinch of chili powder to the mix. The mixture sizzles as it touches the hot oil in the frying pan. One down, one more omelet to go. She wonders whether she should make two more omelets for herself and Bhima, but the thought of chopping more onions gives her pause. Maybe she will make garlic omelets for the two of them. She reaches for the bread box and then remembers: no starch. This all-protein diet that both Viraf and Dinaz are on makes planning lunch difficult. She looks in the fridge to see what else to pack for the children.

"God, Mummy, thanks so much. I wish you'd told me, though—I could've chopped the onions for you," Dinaz says, walking into the kitchen.

"And gone to work smelling like a Parsi restaurant?" Sera smiles. "No, if you really want to help me, tell me what else to pack for you, deekra. One egg is just not enough . . ."

"It's more than enough. Really."

"Arre, Dinaz, one egg may be enough for you but not for you hubby, beta," Sera says. "I mean, this is a grown man, who works hard at a demanding job."

Dinaz makes a face. "Oh yah, only your beloved son-in-law works hard, the poor thing. Your useless daughter, on the other hand, kills flies all day at work."

"Now, Dinaz, I only said . . ."

Sera hears Viraf's footsteps and smells the Old Spice before she sees him. "Corrr-ect," Viraf says as he enters the kitchen. "Mamma is cent percent correct. Chalo, at least there's one person at home who appreciates me and how hard I work to support my family and my child to be."

Dinaz hits him hard on his arm. "Shut up, yaar. A spoiled brat, that's what Mummy's made you, that's all. Promotion time we'll see who gets the bigger raise." Her smile takes the sting out of her words.

Viraf shrugs and rolls his eyes. "That's because she has an unfair advantage, Mamma. That poor Mr. Dalal is so bewitched by my lovely wife's looks and figure, how can he refuse her anything? Turns into a pudding every time he has to address her. And next to these feminine wiles, what chance does a poor, decent, simple man like me—with a face like a custard apple—what chance do I stand?"

The two women laugh. "Look at him, Mummy. Fishing for more compliments," Dinaz says.

Sera smiles as the couple head back into their bedroom to finish dressing. She is so glad that the trouble that had flared like a match between them a few months ago seems to have died down. From the day Viraf and Dinaz moved in with her after Feroz's death, she had vowed never to interfere in their marriage. After all, who knew better than she how poisonous an interfering mother-in-law can be to a marriage? But still, it had been hard to keep her mouth shut when she noticed the thin lines that had formed around Dinaz's pale, narrow face. She had to bite down on her tongue when Viraf snapped at his pregnant wife at the dinner table or said something so sarcastic that it took Dinaz a moment to look up from her plate, needing that pause to collect her composure, to arrange her face into a blank mask. How well Sera knew that look. How many times had she willed her eyes not to fill with tears at one of Feroz's snubs, not to allow her mother-in-law, Banu, the satisfaction of knowing that her son had drawn blood. At least Viraf doesn't beat her, she would console herself and then hate herself for the weakness of that thought, for having lowered her standards so much that lack of physical abuse had become her definition of a good marriage. She wanted so much more than that for her only child.

Now, looking at Dinaz's retreating form, Sera smiles in quiet satisfaction. Whatever trouble had blown between the children like a dark wind, they had resolved it. Viraf and Dinaz once again had the bantering, teasing relationship they'd always had, the one that told Sera they were friends first and husband and wife second. Even in the early days with Feroz, when he looked at her as if she were a star that had dropped from heaven, she had never known the casual, egalitarian spontaneity that her daughter shared with her husband. In the early days, Feroz had been gallant, courteous, loving even— but always formal. For instance, if she entered the room while he was brushing his teeth or cutting his toenails, he would shoo her away. "This is private business," he'd say. "You don't need to see me at my worst."

When Dinaz yells at her from the other room, it takes Sera a minute to place her daughter's voice. "Are the poras wrapped and ready, Mummy?" Dinaz asks.

"Almost," she replies, reaching for the aluminum foil that Viraf had brought back from his last trip to America.

The doorbell rings, and Sera heaves a sigh of relief. Bhima.

Sera opens the door to Bhima, and one look at her wan, sallow face tells her that yesterday's mission was a failure. She raises one eyebrow questioningly, and in answer, Bhima shakes her head slowly from side to side. This is what Sera appreciates most about Bhima— this unspoken language, this intimacy that has developed between them over the years. That same connection now makes her realize that Bhima wants to wait until the children have left for work before telling her what happened yesterday. And she is glad, because, truth be told, she does not want to involve her pregnant daughter in Maya's trials, does not want the shadow of Maya's unfortunate circumstances to fall over the happiness of Dinaz's pregnancy.

"I'm sorry, Serabai," Bhima is now saying. "The line at the water tap was longer than usual today."

Despite herself, Sera can't keep her earlier irritation from showing. "No great harm done," she says in a voice that sounds tight even to herself. "I just had to make the children's omelets myself. Can't have them be late for work."

Before Bhima can reply, they hear Viraf in the other room. "Dinaz," he yells. "Have you seen my red tie? The one you got me for my birthday last year?"

"God, you're such a baby," Dinaz replies, but even at this distance the two older women can hear the smile in her voice. "It's a wonder you even knew how to chew your food before you met me. How did you ever manage, I wonder?"

"Badly," comes the prompt reply. "I wore mismatched socks to work. And as for feeding myself, didn't you notice the bib I was wearing when you first met me?"

Bhima shakes her head. "That Viraf baba," she says. "Always has something to say. Makes the house seem festive just by his presence, like every day is Holi or Diwali or something."

Sera nods. And knows immediately what Bhima has left unsaid: Not like the old days, when Feroz was alive and she and Bhima had to tiptoe around, afraid of his explosive silences and his explosive temper. When the house felt tomblike, encased in silence, a silence that prevented her from reaching out to others, from sharing her darkest secret with even her closest friends. When Bhima was the only one who knew, the only one who felt the dampness of the pillowcase after long nights of shedding hot tears, the only one who heard the muffled sounds coming from her and Feroz's bedroom . . .

Sera shakes her head impatiently, to clear out the cobwebs of the past. Here I am wallowing in ancient history while poor Bhima has her hands full with her current situation, she thinks. What a self-centered, foolish woman I've become.

"Come on," she says to Bhima. "Your tea is ready. Drink that and then get started on the dishes."

3

Bhima is in the kitchen, washing the dishes from last night's dinner. Sera watches as her hands, dark and thin as the branches of a tree, fly over the pots and pans, scrubbing them until they sparkle like the noonday sun. Try as she might, she can never get the pots to shine the way Bhima does.

Viraf wanders in, adjusting his tie. "That's it," he says to no one in particular. "Next month, I'm buying a dishwasher. No point in poor Bhima slogging like this."

Bhima looks up in gratitude, but before she can say a word, Sera speaks up. "Go, go," she says. "My Bhima can put your fancy dishwashers to shame. Not even a foreign-made machine can leave dishes as clean as Bhima can. Save your money, deekra."

. . . And give it to me instead, Bhima thinks to herself, and then, afraid that one of them will read her mind, she busies herself by concentrating on one particular food spot. Also, she needs a few seconds to fume. Sometimes she can't figure Serabai out. On the one hand, it makes her flush with pride when Serabai calls her "my Bhima" and talks about her proprietarily. On the other hand, she always seems to be doing things that undercut Bhima's interests. Like refusing Viraf baba's offer to buy a dishwasher. How nice it would be not to run her arthritic hands in water all day long. Bending over the sink to scrub the dishes has also begun to hurt her back, so that, at the end of the day, it sometimes takes half the walk home before she can straighten up. But how to tell Serabai all this? And this morning, making her feel guilty because she had to fix omelets for her own daughter and son-in-law. So what if she hates chopping onions? Does she, Bhima, enjoy squatting to shit in a communal room? But she does it because there is no other choice. Compared with that humiliation, chopping onions feels as easy as cutting a cake.

Her anger spent, Bhima's sense of fair play and her stout affection for the Dubash family take over. Oh, you ungrateful woman, she chides herself. And who looked after you when you had the malaria? Was it your ghost of a husband? Who gave you money just yesterday, so you could take a cab to Maya's college? Was it your spread-her-legs granddaughter? No, it was this same woman whose salt you eat, who you are thinking ugly thoughts about. Shame on you.

Remembering her trip to Maya's college makes Bhima glance involuntarily at the clock in the kitchen. A few more minutes and Viraf baba and Dinaz baby will be gone. Then she and Serabai can sip a cup of tea and talk. She knows that Sera is impatient to hear details about what transpired yesterday, and this realization makes Bhima's throat tighten with emotion and gratitude. At least someone else cares about her pregnant brat of a granddaughter as much as she does. It is Serabai's generosity that has made Maya's education possible, and if Serabai now feels betrayed by Maya's treachery, if she feels her investment in the girl's future has come up dry, it is to her credit that she has never spoken of her disappointment to Bhima. From the first time that Bhima had confided the terrible, calamitous news, Sera had been concerned, anxious, and ready to help. "Of course she will have to have an abortion," Sera had said immediately. "There's no other way out. Maya is too bright, too intelligent to ruin her life by becoming a mother at seventeen. I'll take care of the details, Bhima, you don't have to worry about all that stuff. You have your hands full with enough other troubles, I know."

But for reasons she still didn't understand, Bhima had hesitated. Perhaps she had unwittingly taken her cue from Maya, who had stiffened the first time Bhima mentioned an abortion. And then there was this: the unspoken, perhaps unacknowledged hope that the child's father would step forward to assume his responsibility and do the right thing. That the curtain of anonymity, of secrecy, would part to reveal an anxious but honorable young man, frightened but eager to face up to this new challenge, to marry and build a life with the woman who would bear his first child. Yes, seventeen would be young for Maya to deliver a child, and marriage would certainly destroy her dreams of getting a B.Com. in accounting and becoming a bookkeeper at a good firm. The bright path that had rolled out before Maya when she became the first person in Bhima's family to go to college—the good job that would inevitably await her, thanks to Dinaz's and Viraf's influence and business contacts, the escape from the menial, backbreaking labor that had marred the lives of her mother and her mother before her—that path would shrivel up, that much was certain. But—and here Bhima had allowed herself a freckle of hope—perhaps another path would open up. If only Maya would reveal the identity of the father of the baby. In her mind, Bhima saw her darling granddaughter fat and content, busy in a kitchen with sparkling stainless steel pots and pans, frying puris for a rambunctious, dark-haired son and a father who came home each evening from his white-collar job.

She had been so excited when, after weeks of cajoling, begging, and threats, Maya had finally revealed the identity of the father earlier this week. Ashok Malhotra. "I go to college with him," she had sobbed. "He's in my class. Are you satisfied, Ma? Now that you've beaten his name out of me? Now leave me alone, please."

Bhima was satisfied. At last, she had a name to put on the shad-

owy figure who haunted her dreams and nightmares. Ashok Malhotra. A fellow student, who attended the same college that Maya did.
She had wanted to probe more, to find out when they'd had the opportunity to have sex. But here Maya froze up, stubbornly ignoring
Bhima's other questions, staring into the distance with the new,
cowlike expression she had developed in her pregnancy. And suddenly Bhima had decided that she didn't want to know too many of
the sordid details. What difference did the how and where make
now? At least she had gotten the girl to part with her biggest secret,
to reveal the name of the young man who had brought so much
worry into their lives. And she, Bhima, knew where to find him. It
was up to her to do the rest. Maya was just a silly, immature girl,
with no idea of how the yawning pit of fate would swallow her up
if she went ahead and had this child without a father to support the
two of them. It was up to Bhima to act as her advocate, to do what
Maya was incapable of doing—to make this Ashok Malhotra take
responsibility for what he had wrought, to appeal to his sense of
honor. To make him understand that her Maya would be a garland
around his neck and not a chain.

"I'll pay the cab fare to her college," Sera had said upon learning
the identity of the child's father. "You go meet with him, Bhima.
See what his intentions are. See if this Ashok fellow is even worthy
of our Maya or if he's just some out-for-a-good-time lout. I pray for
your sake that he has good moral character."

It was the first time she had ever traveled to Maya's college alone.
The only other time Bhima had visited the building, Sera had accompanied her and Maya. The three of them had stood in the long
line to complete the admission process, and it was Sera who had
spoken to the rude clerk when he had barked an order to Maya;
Sera who had pulled herself up to her full height and looked down

her long, straight, impervious Parsi nose and told the man, in her best clipped, convent-school accent, to kindly watch who he was speaking to, that this child he was treating so badly was probably the brightest student they would ever be lucky enough to have at this college. Under her haughty, upper-class gaze, the clerk had withered and offered a flurry of apologies. "Sorry, madam. No insult intended. What to do, madam, so much work we are burdened by. Please to forgive."

Now, Bhima sought out the clerk's office. Sure enough, the man was sitting at his desk, scowling at some forms in front of him. She approached him tentatively. "Excuse, please?"

The man did not look up. "What?" he said brusquely.

"I'm looking for a student, please? Can you help me find him?"

There was a second's silence as the man finished scribbling on the piece of paper in front of him. Then, "And your relations with the student?"

Bhima was flustered. "Ah. I'm his . . . that is, no relations. I am just wanting to see him."

The clerk must have caught her discomfort, because now he looked up at her with his small, gleaming, piglike eyes. "No relations, eh?" he said loudly, for the benefit of his co-workers. "Perhaps you are hoping to start some relations with a young college boy, hah?" His colleagues snickered while Bhima stared at the floor, unsure of what to do next. Remembering how Serabai had once put this impudent man in his place with a few well-chosen words, Bhima wished, not for the first time, that she had been educated herself. A white-hot fury burned in her. All night long she had braced herself for her encounter with Ashok Malhotra. She had lain awake, stiff with tension and anticipation. She had rehearsed her words, fought with herself about whether to threaten or cajole, attack or appeal. On the way here in the cab, she had been like a boiling pot on Serabai's new Bajaj stove, her emotions ready to spill over. And now this rude thug was blocking her from even finding Ashok, was batting her around idly, automatically, simply to amuse himself. He was toying with her in the same detached, half-bored way that the stray cats who prowled the slum did the mice they got hold of. Bhima felt her resolution and determination trickle away from her.

Another clerk, a woman who appeared to be in her twenties, came to her defense. "Ignore these menfolks, mausi," she said, leaving her desk and walking toward Bhima. "They have nothing better to do, obviously. Tell me, who are you looking for?"

Bhima smiled at her in gratitude. As always, she automatically covered her mouth as she smiled, to hide the two missing teeth. "Thank you, daughter. I'm looking for one Ashok Malhotra."

At the mention of the name, a strange thing happened, Bhima noticed. The four clerks in the office all smiled. "Arre, mausi, why didn't you say first only that you're looking for our Prince Ashok?" asked the male clerk. "Wait, I'll have someone personally escort you to him. He's most likely in his palace, entertaining his court."

Bhima looked confusedly from him to the woman clerk. Watching her face, the man grinned. "The canteen," he explained happily. "That's where Prince Ashok holds his darbar. You can pay your respects to him there." He rang a bell on his desk, and seconds later, a surly-looking peon appeared. "Ae, Suresh," the clerk said. "This fine lady is here to see our Ashok. Walk her to the canteen, would you?"

The canteen smelled of cigarettes and fried foods. It was a loud, cavernous room, filled with smoke and the din of students talking and arguing with each other. Young, dark-skinned boys in khaki pants ran around taking orders and serving steaming glasses of tea. The middle-class students barely looked up to acknowledge the presence of the boys who brought the plates of samosas and masala dosas to their tables, except to occasionally to complain that the tea had grown cold while they had waited for their food. The older male students, especially if there was a woman with them, frequently accompanied their complaints with a friendly but nevertheless hard whack on their young servers' heads. In an age-old, timeless ritual, the boys grinned after getting hit, rubbing their heads and feebly protesting that they were bringing the food out as quickly as the cook prepared it. "What to do, sahib? So busy-busy it is today." The reward for such endearing servility was a slightly larger tip.

"There he is," Suresh said, pointing to a thin man in a dark blue kurta and faded blue jeans. "The one sitting on the right. That's Ashok." Although there were three other boys at the table, even at this distance Bhima could tell that Ashok was the leader of the group. She turned to say something to Suresh, but he was gone, leaving her to walk up to the boy by herself.

The four occupants of the table looked up curiously when she approached and stood silently staring at the father of her great-grandchild. "Yes?" one of the boys said finally. "May we help you?" The others giggled.

Bhima decided she liked the young man sitting in front of her. Emboldened by this discovery, she said, "Are you Ashok? Ashok Malhotra?"

The boy half-rose from his seat. "Namaste," he said. "And you are?"

"I am needing to talk with you." Glancing at the others, "Privately."

Ashok looked surprised. "Er, well, sure, sure." He looked at his companions pointedly, and they reluctantly rose to relinquish their seats to the bony, severe-looking woman who stood in front of them. "Boy, Ashok, your harem of women just keeps growing," one of them said in a whisper, but Bhima heard him and winced. For the first time it occurred to her that this handsome, popular boy might have girlfriends other than Maya.

She shook her head fiercely to dismiss that treacherous thought. Seeing the gesture, Ashok smiled. "Too many flies in this canteen," he said apologetically.

The gentleness of his smile emboldened Bhima, gave her voice. "I'm Maya Phedke's grandmother," she began.

4

They are sitting in the dining room, sipping tea, Sera out of the blue-gray mug Dinaz had bought for her from Cottage Industries, Bhima out of the stainless steel glass that is kept aside for her in the Dubash household. As usual, Sera sits on a chair at the table while Bhima squats on her haunches on the floor nearby. When Dinaz was younger, she used to prod her mother about the injustice of Bhima not being allowed to sit on the couch or a chair and having to use her own separate utensils, instead of the ones the rest of the family used. "You tell all your friends that Bhima is like a family member, that you couldn't live without her," the teenage Dinaz would rail. "And yet she's not good enough to sit at the table with us. And you and Daddy are always taking about those high-caste Hindus burning Harijans and how wrong that is. But in your own house, you have these caste differences, too. What hypocrisy, Mummy."

"Now, Dinaz," Sera would say mildly. "I think there's a slight difference between burning a Harijan and not allowing Bhima to use our glasses. Besides, have you ever noticed the foul odor of the tobacco she chews all day long? Do you want her lips to touch our glasses?"

"But it's not just that, Mummy, and you know it. Okay, if it's because of the tobacco, why won't you let her sit on the sofa or chairs? Or does Bhima have tobacco on her backside, also?"

"Dinaz." Sera was genuinely shocked. "Watch your language, please. You know Daddy would have a fit if he came home one day and found Bhima reclining on the sofa." Despite themselves, both women giggled at the image, at the look of horror on Feroz's face. But Dinaz was not done yet. "It's probably a moot point anyway. As if poor Bhima ever has a minute to sit down and rest in this house."

Sera raised her right eyebrow. "Speaking of which, I heard you inciting Bhima the other day to ask for a raise. Listen, Dinaz, no matter what you think, you belong to this family, not Bhima's. I think when all is said and done, the Dubash family treats its servants better than almost anybody else we know. Money does not grow on trees, darling. Your daddy works very hard for everything we have. It's not right of you to turn Bhima against him. Remember, charity begins at home."

Now, watching Bhima sip at her tea, Sera shifts uncomfortably in her chair. Since Feroz's death, she has occasionally toyed with the idea of asking Bhima to join her at the table. Sure, some of her friends would be scandalized at first, and the next time a servant in the building asked her mistress for a raise, the woman would automatically blame Sera Dubash for setting a bad example. "Sera has made that Bhima sit on her head, not just on her sofa," the neighbor would say. "Next thing you know, these servants will be forming a trade union."

But surely all that would blow over. And really, what difference did it make to her what the neighbors said? It is not their salt she eats, and now that Feroz is dead, she feels free from the fear that had haunted her for so many years—that they would gossip about her marriage. Or worse: that the sharp-eyed ones among them would notice the occasional bruises that clothes and makeup couldn't hide and they would pity her, would tsk-tsk behind her back. Now that Feroz is dead, she no longer has to fear their pity.

And yet . . . The thought of Bhima sitting on her furniture repulses her. The thought makes her stiffen, the same way she had tensed the day she caught her daughter, then fifteen, giving Bhima an affectionate hug. Watching that hug, Sera had been seared by conflicting emotions—pride and awe at the casual ease with which Dinaz had broken an unspoken taboo, but also a feeling of revulsion, so that she had had to suppress the urge to order her daughter to go wash her hands. Which is surprising, Sera now thinks to herself, recalling the incident. She herself had on numerous occasions declared that Bhima was one of the cleanest people she knew. "Bhima wouldn't know deodorant from chopsticks, but I tell you, I have never so much as smelled this woman," Sera had once told her friend Mani. "I don't know how she does it, given the lack of privacy and the lack of running water in her slum. But she does." And ever since Sera had known her, Bhima had taken a fifteen-minute break at 4:00 P.M. to wash her face with the soap that she kept in her own soap dish in the kitchen, to pour Pond's talcum powder under her armpits, and to tidy up her hair, which had grown increasingly scant over the years. Her daily ministrations compelled Sera, who then became aware of her own sour-smelling body, to stop whatever it was she was doing and freshen up.

But despite all this, there is this reluctance, this resistance to let Bhima use the furniture. As they sit in companionable silence sipping their tea, Sera tries to justify her prejudice. Part of it is the damn tobacco she chews all day, she thinks to herself. It just makes me feel sick and dirties everything else about her. Also, having seen where she lives, I can imagine the conditions in the slum—what kind of water she uses to bathe in and, well, how effectively she is able to clean her nether regions.

Lost in her own hot, guilty thoughts, Sera realizes she has missed part of what Bhima has said.

"Oi, Bhima, say the last part again. Sorry. I didn't hear you properly."

Bhima sighs impatiently. And starts her story again.

"I'm Maya Phedke's grandmother," Bhima declared.

Ashok Malhotra looked at her expectantly, blinking rapidly. He leaned forward when she didn't say anything else. "Yes?" he said.

The two of them stared at each other in silence, as if each one was expecting the other to continue talking. Finally, Ashok reacted. "I'm sorry . . . am I expected to . . . I mean, do I know this Maya lady?"

Bhima's voice wavered. "Maya," she said, as if describing her granddaughter to a stranger. "She's a second-year student. Long hair. Tall, with light skin." She stopped, paralyzed by the incongruity of having to remind this uncaring brute what the woman he'd impregnated looked like.

Ashok sailed to her rescue. "Oh, Maya," he said happily. "Of course I know Maya. I guess I never knew her last name, though. Sorry."

Bhima stared at the handsome face in front of her. Not a flicker of guilt or worry on it, she marveled. And what was with these children of today? They had relations with each other without learning each other's last names? In her time, knowing a person's family name mattered more than knowing their first name. After all, it was the family name that told you all you needed to know—what caste the person belonged to, where they came from, who their ancestors were, what their occupation was, and what their khandaan, their family background was like. And here was this boy blithely acknowledging that he hadn't bothered to learn Maya's last name.

"Anyway, how is Maya?" Ashok continued. "Come to think of it, I haven't seen her in many-many days." His face suddenly darkened. "She's okay, isn't she, aunty?"

Bhima shook her head. "She is not. Maya is not all right."

"Oh no," Ashok cried. "What is it, malaria or something? Two of my friends have it right now. But listen, tell Maya not to worry. I'll pass on all my class notes to her. In fact, that will be an incentive for me to stop bunking classes and spend my time in the lecture halls instead of in this stupid canteen." He smiled his dazzling smile.

For the first time it occurred to Bhima that behind Ashok's handsome, clean-shaven face, there hid the brain of an imbecile. Was this boy really half-brained? Or was he deliberately acting dumb, trying to appear innocent and deflect responsibility? Ah, so that was it. The more Bhima stared at Ashok Malhotra's wide-eyed, open face, the more she understood the game he was playing.

Well, she would not let him get away with it. That was the reason she was here, in this strange, unfamiliar environment, to claw at this young man's denials and make him face up to his responsibility. Bhima leaned forward in her seat. "It's not malaria, beta," she said, willing her voice to remain steady. "You know exactly what is wrong with Maya."

Ashok blinked. "I . . . I do?" he said.

There was another silence as they stared at each other. Then, Bhima shook her head impatiently. This boy was not making this easy at all. He could afford to sit here in this canteen playing his games all day, but she could not. She was old and tired and had the long ride back home and dinner to cook when she got there. Besides, there would be a scene when Maya found out about her visit to her college. There would be tears, recriminations, and Maya would look at her with her big eyes and say, "How could you do this, Ma? I trusted you with my secret." As if a pile of books had struck her on her head, Bhima suddenly felt her sixty-five years land with a thud. Every bone in her body sang out its woes, every gray hair twanged its misery, each muscle quivered and trembled with pain. She eyed the smooth-skinned, dark-haired boy with bitter envy. She took in his clean fingernails, his starched kurta, the well-trimmed hair. She noticed the glow of youth and health on his face, the white, unbroken teeth, the unblemished, unwrinkled hands. This boy had all the time in the world. Prince Ashok they had called him, and it was true. This boy could spend, no, could squander time as if it was a devalued, worthless currency. While she, Bhima, had to hoard time, had to make each second of her day count, this boy could rake his hands aimlessly through time, spend it like ten-paisa coins.

Some of the cheated fury she was feeling must have shown on her face, because Ashok Malhotra was looking at her in alarm. "Aunty, are you all right?" he said. "Would you like a Limca or something?"

"Listen, Ashok, I have no time for this. I'm an old woman, not many years left. If for no other reason, take pity on my years and don't play games with me. This is not easy for me either, beta."

The expression on the boy's face changed. Removing his elbows from the Formica table, he sat back in his seat, so as to put as much distance as he could between himself and Bhima. "I am Ashok Malhotra," he said carefully. "Are you sure I'm the Ashok you're looking for?"

Bhima let out a sigh that sounded more like a hiss. "Look, baba. I know everything. No need to pretend with me. Maya has told me everything. I'm not here to blame anybody. I just want to—"

"What? Maya has told you what?"

Finally, they were getting somewhere. "Ashok, Maya is pregnant. She is not sick with malaria. She is pregnant."

Ashok gasped. "Pregnant? That's impossible. I mean, aunty, I'm shocked."

Bhima's voice was gentle now. "I know, beta. We all are. This is not the life I had in mind for my grandchild. Still, who knows the mysterious ways in which God works? Maybe—"

"No, I mean, Maya of all people. I didn't know her well, but I really respected her. I always thought she was a sensible girl, not like some of the other girls I know."

Bhima stared at him openmouthed. This boy was something else. Shameless. Sitting in front of her, talking about the other girls he knew. Did this mean that he had made other girls pregnant also? That there were—God forbid—other little baby Ashok Malhotras running around? A wave of despair and grief struck her.

Still, she had to try. For Maya's sake, she had to make this boy forget about all his other girlfriends. "What's past is past," she said. "The question is, what will happen next?"

Ashok shrugged. Seeing the shrug, Bhima gripped the edge of the pink table to keep her hand from flying up to his face. Her Maya was in serious trouble, and all this philandering, impudent son of a whore could do was shrug at her problems.

"Listen to me," she said, not even waiting for the anger to drain out of her voice now. "I know everything. Maya has told me everything. About you and her. And if you're going to be a father, then the least you can—"

"What? What?" Ashok had risen to his feet, and there was a new note in his voice. "What did you say?"

So he hadn't known. Noticing the quizzical looks the other students were throwing their way, Bhima cursed herself for not having chosen a more private place to break the news to him. "Hey, Ashok, is everything okay, yaar?" called out one of the boys whom Bhima had earlier displaced from Ashok's table.

Ashok's face was white and his chest was heaving. Inexplicably, Bhima felt a sudden urge to giggle. The scandalized boy in front of her was acting as melodramatic and outraged as one of those Hindi film actresses whose virtue had been called into question. But then she noticed the hateful look that he was casting her way, and her laughter died an aborted death inside her. "Beta, sit down," she pleaded. "This is hard, I know, but—"

"Did she say that?" he hissed. "Did she say that I was the father of her baby?"

Unable to meet his eye, Bhima shook her head yes.

"The damn liar. The damn, dirty, filthy liar. How dare she? Bleddy slut. Whore. Just goes to show, you can't trust a woman. Ever."

It took Bhima a second to realize he was talking about Maya. And in that moment she knew—she wouldn't want Ashok Malhotra for a son-in-law if he were the last person alive. For a split second she saw into the future and saw the consequences of that realization, saw the shredded innards of a dream. There would be no kitchen with shiny pots and pans for Maya, no loving husband who would provide her with all the fine things that she, Bhima, never could. Instead, there would be an abortion and a lifetime of furtive shame and secrets. But even that was preferable to forcing this foulmouthed creature to marry Maya. Serabai was always reading out loud newspaper stories about bride burnings and dowry deaths. Bhima shuddered. Some of the things these men did to their wives, you wouldn't wish on your worst enemy. Say what you wanted about Gopal, even when the alcohol had turned her husband into a hollow man, he had never insulted her with the kind of language this young devil had just used toward Maya.

The realization that she did not want Ashok Malhotra to be part of their family set Bhima free. "Shut your mouth, you. Don't you ever talk about my girl in this way. Remember, even if I'm dead, I'll come back from my grave to chop off your tongue. My Maya is a good girl, worth ten of you. It took a filthy animal like you to corrupt her. As for asking you to marry her and make an honest woman out of her, I must have been—"

"Marry her? Make an honest woman out of her?" There was a hysterical note in Ashok's voice. "Arre, bhagwan, am I going out of my mind or what? Listen, old woman, I barely know your grand-daughter. In all these years, I've spoken to her only five or six times and that, too, with other friends around, God is my witness."

Bhima was about to protest, but the wild look in Ashok's eyes silenced her. "This is a plot by my enemies, I can feel it," he said, looking around the room. "It's those Progressive Student Union bastards who have put you up to this. I know it. Bleddy, degenerate lefties. Always trying to discredit us RJS people. All those liberal PSU whores with their talk about secularism and shit. And their ef-feminate socialist 'comrades' who pant after them like dogs in heat. Even then, I never thought they'd stoop this low."

"Beta, I came here to talk about Maya and nothing else—"

"Never would've guessed Maya was one of them," Ashok said in a voice so low Bhima could barely hear him. "But no matter. She cannot harm my reputation. Everybody in college knows I'm an RJS man and that we believe in purity and chastity before marriage. Even some of the Christian students have secretly told me that al-though they don't agree with the RJS's goal of a Hindu nation, they respect many of its teachings. Of course, they'd never admit that in public. Too scared of the Muslim fanatics, I suppose. Anyway, in the RJS we are taught to respect our Hindu women, even fallen women, like Maya. But we also believe in fighting back. We must fight back when someone assails our reputation." He glared at Bhima.

One of Ashok's cohorts walked up to the table. "What's up, boss?" he said, glancing at Bhima. "The old dame bothering you? We can take care of the problem, one, two, three."

But Ashok shooed him away. "No, no, no. I can handle this one myself."

"Chamcha." Bhima snorted to herself, looking at the other boy's retreating back.

But the truth was, she was done here. Ashok Malhotra's stout defense of his character, the mad, paranoid gleam in his eye, his obvious contempt for Maya, and his not-so-veiled threats had vanquished Bhima completely, so that she felt herself folding like a deck of cards. There was nothing left to say, no real reason for her to be here any longer. She had failed spectacularly in her mission, failed so badly that she questioned its goal. "I'm sorry to have upset you," she said quietly. "I hope you can forgive me, beta. I'm just a foolish, stupid woman. If nothing else, take pity on these gray hairs and forget about this conversation. My family"—and here her voice broke—"will never trouble you again. Please find it in your heart to forgive me."

The canteen seemed to have grown twice as long in the time she'd been there. She walked out unsteadily, keeping her eyes to the ground, willing her ears not to pick up the hushed whispers and giggles that followed her. Her feet ached where the rubber slippers she was wearing rubbed against her skin.

The cabdriver was a young, gregarious fellow who clearly wanted to talk, but Bhima was in no mood for conversation. She stared out of the window as the cab flew past the dilapidated buildings and construction projects. Even the spray of the Arabian Sea, as they drove past it, failed to revive her, nor did the sight of its brown-gray water, which usually made her heart lurch with joy.

She went over her conversation with Ashok in her mind, trying to pinpoint the precise moment when it ran away from her like a herd of mad elephants, the exact moment when her heart broke and the future fell apart in front of her disbelieving eyes.

Also, the exact moment when she began to believe Ashok Malhotra's innocence. Because there was no doubt in her mind that the boy had told the truth. And that it was Maya—Maya, the granddaughter whom she had rescued from death's door; Maya, who had come to her as an orphan and grown up to be an intelligent, ambitious, young woman; Maya, the only flesh-and-blood family member she still had near her; Maya, who had been the sole bright spot in Bhima's bleak life; Maya, who was to make up for all of Bhima's own unrealized hopes and aborted dreams, who was the golden focal point of all of Bhima's fantasies and daydreams—it was Maya who had lied to her. It was Maya who had betrayed her. (But shouldn't she be used to betrayals by now?) Maya who had embarrassed and humiliated her. (But shouldn't she be an old hand at humiliation by now?) Maya who, it seemed, was intent on stuffing misery, like hard, cotton pillows, under Bhima's head. (And why, after all, should Maya be any different from the rest of her family?)

Bhima let the cab drop her off five minutes away from the basti. She did not want her neighbors to speculate on the reasons why she had taken a cab home. And today she was also in no mood to feel the sting of their envy. Many of them, she knew, were envious of her good fortune at working for someone like Serabai. "Ae, Bhima mausi," Bibi often told her. "I'm just waiting until your Maya gets a tip-top job and you can retire. Then, I'm going to go work for your Serabai. I want to come home with Cadbury's chocolate for my babies, also. That Gujarati woman I work for is such a kanjoos, if she gives me one extra grain of salt one month, I swear she tries to take something out of my pay next month."

Bhima walked quickly, anxious to be home. The straps of her rubber chappals dug into her feet, but she was too lost in her thoughts to notice the pain. If not Ashok Malhotra, who was the father of Maya's baby? And truth be told, did it even matter? Because the fact was, it was probably one of the louts from the slum who had impregnated Maya. It may even have been the insolent man who lived across from them and didn't have the decency to look away when they performed their daily toiletries. Bhima's face flushed at the thought. No, an abortion was the only way. The confrontation with Ashok Malhotra had taken the fight out of her. She could not imagine going through this with another suspect. And there was no guarantee that that shameless girl would give her the right information this time either. Bhima's cheeks burned with anger at Maya's deception. Her right hand twitched in anticipation of the stinging slaps that she wanted to deliver to Maya's face. She picked up her pace.

But as she approached the basti, a strange reluctance to enter her gloomy hut gripped her. She noticed again how shabby and disassembled the tin-and-cardboard structures looked, more like a giant bird's nest put together by a flock of drunken crows than like a place where human beings lived. She lifted her sari with her right hand to prevent its hem from touching the brown, murky, stagnant water on the ground. With her left hand, she shooed away the flies that swarmed around her. As always, she felt the helpless despair that gripped her when she entered the slum. But today that despair had teeth marks on it. She felt a raw, naked hatred for Maya. Crazy, stupid girl had thoughtlessly thrown away her future like an old newspaper. She, too, would live in this filthy slum now, condemned to live out her days in the same way that she, Bhima, had. And the shadow of her aborted child would follow her always. This close she had come to leaving this place and making something of her life. But the family curse was obviously on her also, hanging over her head like an open claw. The curse that had left Maya an orphan at seven would leave her childless at seventeen.

Of course, if she, Bhima, had not made such a scene at Maya's college today, there may have been some way the girl could have gone back there. She could have had the abortion, stayed home to rest for a few days, and then quietly started classes again. If any of her classmates asked, she could've said she had—what was it that Ashok Malhotra had said his friends had?—malaria. Nobody would've had to know. But the moment her granddaughter had mentioned Ashok Malhotra's name, some strange, irrational optimism had seized Bhima. The vision of the kitchen with the sparkling pots had captured her imagination. It was as if the devil had toyed with her, had infected her with a dangerous hopefulness, had enticed her all the way to Maya's college, dancing ahead of her, pointing the way to Ashok Malhotra's table, where grief and ridicule awaited her like a hot, steaming plate of battatawadas. Guilt ran up Bhima's tired limbs like a radioactive dye. She had un-wittingly destroyed her grandchild's future. Whatever mistake Maya had made could've been corrected. But what Bhima had done—shared her family shame with a stranger, sullied Maya's honor before a self-righteous, pious fool, disclosed her secret to God knows how many prying, curious ears—that damage could not be undone. She had stripped her child naked in that large, bright, crowded canteen, exposed her to the darts of their gossip and careless talk.

Perhaps it was the guilt that made her turn on Maya as soon as the girl opened the door. Gripping the right slipper, which had made a deep, bloody groove into her foot, Bhima waited until Maya shut the rickety door. Then, before she could walk away, Bhima struck out at the pregnant Maya, whose very face now made her sick with grief. "Come here, you shameless, lying girl," she panted. "Take this, and this, and this. Come here, I want to obliterate you, never want to see your lying face again."

Trying to deflect the blows, Maya's hands instinctively flew to protect her abdomen. She swirled around, so that most of Bhima's blows landed on her back. "No, Ma-ma," she whimpered once, and then she fell quiet, wincing silently each time another blow landed.

Her silence infuriated Bhima. She wanted to draw blood, yes, but more, she wanted to draw Maya's tears, as if the tears would baptize them both, purify them, wash them clean of thisevil that had wormed its way into their lives. "Say something," she demanded. Then, in the rhythm of the blows, "Say . . . something . . . Beg . . .

forgiveness . . . you demon child . . . you . . . mistake of your mother's womb." But it was Bhima who was close to tears instead, the events of the day having caught up with her—the humiliation and the exhaustion, the cheated, helpless outrage of having been lied to by her own grandchild and, now, her horror at her own uncontrolled behavior.

The ache in her forearms made her stop. Maya crouched on the floor, looking at her with big, fearful eyes. Her look broke Bhima's heart, made her want to take that young, trembling body and cover it in kisses with the same urgency that she had covered it in blows a minute ago, but she steeled her heart. It was this very same leniency that had allowed Maya to stray in the first place.

"Ashok Malhotra," she spat out. "Father of your bastard child, hah? Arre, a loose woman like you would have to take nine births to land a decent, God-fearing, religious boy like him."

Maya stared at her. "How do you know Ashok is religious?" she asked.

"I met him. I went to your college today to make him a marriage proposal." Bhima laughed bitterly, shaking her head at her earlier naïveté.

"You did what?" Hysteria made Maya's voice loud. "You did what, Ma?"

Bhima forced herself to keep her gaze on her granddaughter's face. "It's your fault. Or do you tell so many lies that you have forgotten what you told me about him? Anyway, it's really my fault. Imagine, believing the word of a fornicator."

Maya winced. "Stop being so cruel, Ma-ma, I beg you. You can beat me with your chappals or a stick, pour gasoline on me and burn me alive, I don't mind. But don't beat me with your words."

"Me beat you? Beta, wait till you see how this cruel world beats you up when the news of your pregnancy gets around. You know how Yasmeen, the Muslim woman in the next basti, wears the pur-dah? Well, you won't need one. Your shame will act as your veil."

"And now you have spread my shame like manure, all through my college," Maya said bitterly. "I know that Ashok. I never fell for his Hare Rama stuff. I've seen how he likes to gossip, especially about girls he doesn't like. And he is such a bigmouth, it's like he was born with a loudspeaker in his throat. The whole college prob-ably knows already."

Bhima gulped the guilt that tasted like sour milk in her mouth. "You should've thought of that before you falsely implicated him. Before you looked in my eyes and told a lie."

"You forced me to," Maya said, and for a second, there was a flash of the old, spirited Maya. "You hounded me and hounded me, and so I said the first, most improbable name that came to my mind. What does it matter who the father is, Ma-ma? The fact is that the baby is growing in *my* stomach, not his. That makes it my curse and my blessing, no one else's . . ."

"Blessing? You refer to that—that thing—growing in your stomach as a blessing? Have you gone mad, girl? Or are you plotting on killing off your old grandma so that you can inherit this palace that we live in?"

Maya put one tentative hand on Bhima's thin arm. "Don't talk of dying, Ma-ma. You are all I have in this world."

So this is how a heart breaks, Bhima thought. This is how cold, how delicate, how exquisite it feels, like the high-pitched violin note on the classical music records that Serabai played. Bhima wanted to hug Maya and kill her, to rescue her and destroy her, all in the same explosive moment.

"All right," she said gruffly. "Don't act like Meena Kumari in some Hindi picture. Go start the stove. The growling of my stomach will soon even scare the rats away."

Maya made to turn away, but Bhima drew her back. "Listen up, girl," she said. "Tomorrow I'll talk to Serabai about taking you to an abortion doctor. Too much time has already past."

5

As Sera waits for the elevator, she wonders if it is safe to leave Bhima alone at home. She has never seen Bhima look so old, so tired, so—what is the word?—*defeated* as she did today. Not even when Gopal had left and taken with him the most precious thing in Bhima's life. Oh, Bhima had been scared then, no question about that, but she knew she was still responsible for Pooja, and that responsibility toward her daughter had emboldened her, kept her from falling apart. No, Gopal may have broken Bhima's back, but Maya had broken her spirit. Ashok Malhotra, indeed. Sera tries to muster up some anger toward Maya but finds that she can't. She tries to picture Maya as she is today—wary, corrupted, defensive, manipulative—but all she can recall is the shy, scared, tiny seven-year-old in the red ruffled dress and golden slippers who had stood before her and Feroz, all the time gripping her grandmother's hand. Bhima had just returned from Delhi with her grandchild, having traveled all night by train, and Sera could see the dark circles around the little girl's eyes. An orphan girl, painfully thin, who Sera won over by giving her three pieces of Cadbury's milk chocolate day after day. Who, two months after Bhima began to bring her to the Dubashs' residence with her while she worked, one day surprised and delighted Sera by saying in English, "Where my chocolate?" It was on that day, or soon after, that Sera decided this was an intelligent child and worthy of a life different from what her grandmother could give her. And that she, Sera, would assume responsibility for Maya's education.

Sera steps into the elevator and spots Mrs. Madan, the fifth-floor neighbor. "Kem che, Sera?" the woman says. "Long time, no see, dear."

"Oh, I've been fine," Sera says. "And you?" She regrets the question as soon as it leaves her lips.

Mrs. Madan sighs. "Chalta hai, chalta hai," she says. "Life goes on. The arthritis is getting worse. See this thumb? See how swollen and red it is, like a big, fat tomato? Baap re, you can't imagine the pain. Still, what cannot be cured must be endured, as my dearly departed Praful used to say. But I tell you, Sera, that's because he never had a migraine headache. Sometimes they are so bad that I can't open my eyes, even. Thank God my servant knows exactly what to do for me then. She's been with me a long time, you know. Not as long as your Bhima, of course. That is truly exceptional, I have to say. No wonder you treat her like a family member. My Praful always used to say that you've made that woman sit on your head, if you don't mind my saying so. But these men, they are hard at heart, no? Not softhearted like us women. I always say, 'Sera will be rewarded in heaven for the way she treats that Bhima.' "

"Heaven has nothing to do with it." Sera begins. "Bhima is a decent person and a good worker—"

"Oh, I know, I know. That's exactly what I tell everybody. No, you are softhearted like me, Sera. See how you go every day to check on your old mother-in-law? Don't think I don't notice, even though I am almost blind because of my cataracts. You may not go to the agyari as often as some of us, but you are religious in your own way, I know. Chalo, time for me to go pick up my prescription. Doctor says I should go for a walk every day, but I tell you, the footpaths are so bad in Bombay today, I'm afraid to step out of the house. Open manholes and construction pits everywhere."

That Mehru Madan is an idiot, Sera thinks as the two women part ways. Confused theology, confused medical facts, confused brain. She remembers that Feroz used to refer to Mehru as Old Scrambled Brain, and the thought makes her smile.

She is still smiling as she gets into the elevator in Banu Dubash's building. The liftman notices her smile and grins back. "Salaam, memsahib," he says. She nods curtly, annoyed that he has caught her in an unguarded moment.

"Second floor," she says, although she is aware that the man knows perfectly well which floor Banu Dubash's apartment is on.

The Monster is lying on her bed, her long but scanty hair tossed like a mane around her pillow. She is asleep when Sera turns the key to the front door and lets herself into the apartment. The familiar smell of Tata's eau de cologne and rubbing alcohol assails her nostrils as soon as she walks in through the door. As always, the heavy curtains are drawn shut because the Monster likes her lair to be dark at all times. The old apartment smells musty, and Sera feels a moment's claustrophobia, so that she fights to resist the urge to part the faded curtains and fling open the windows to let in much needed air and sunlight. As always, her critical eye is drawn to the drab, dirty walls with the peeling paint, and she thinks of how much she would love to have a crew of workers come in and paint these ancient walls a bright color. As far as she can recall, this house has never seen a new coat of paint since she came here as a young—well, not so young—bride, all those years ago. She shudders involuntarily at the memory of those miserable years when she lived in the Monster's home. Thank God she had the gumption to leave and Providence provided her with her own home. Not that living alone with Feroz was Paradise. But still. She would've jumped off the balcony of this house years ago if she'd continued to live with her in-laws.

The day nurse, Edna, is dozing in the large armchair in the right-hand corner of the room, where the Monster lies sleeping, her rhythmic snores filling the space with a dull music. Sera first sees Edna through her reflection in the full-length mirror that makes up one of the panels of the mahogany cupboard that sits next to the Monster's bed. The second panel features a vertical painting of a forest scene—there are giraffes and elephants and fawns. The huge wardrobe had fascinated Sera when she first saw it. The Dubash household had been filled with antique furniture in those days—a carved, mahogany dining room table that could seat twelve, two coffee tables with marble tops, a four-poster bed made of solid teak.

Sera clears her throat deliberately, and the sound startles Edna into wakefulness. "Oh, hello, madam," she stammers as she leaps to her feet. "I didn't hear—Banu aunty was sleeping after her morning sponge, so I—"

"It's okay," Sera says curtly. "So, everything is all right? The night went well?"

"Mostly well, madam. She had one loose motion last night, at about two in the morning." Edna catches the expression on Sera's face and is immediately remorseful. "I . . . I'm sorry, madam. I just thought you'd want to know. Some families want to know every detail about their patient, you know."

Sera takes in the dark, bony, tired face, the frayed edges of the white nurse's cap, the faint outline of a brown stain on the worn-out uniform, and suddenly feels a rush of pity and remorse. "No, no, that's good. We do want to know what's going on with her. Now, Edna, how about if you make us both a nice cup of tea? I'll straighten up a bit in here while you make us a hot-pot cup of Brooke Bond."

Her reward is an unexpectedly joyous smile, as clear as the sky outside. "Okay, madam," Edna says. "I'll make a pot of tea—how you Parsis say?—fattaa-faat. Maybe Banu aunty will like some tea also."

As if she knows that they are talking about her, the old woman stirs in her bed. For the umpteenth time Sera marvels at her mother-in-law's prescience. During the years that Sera lived in this home, she had truly believed that Banu had three extra eyes bored into the back of her head. No matter how discreetly she and Feroz tried to argue about something, no matter how low Sera tried to keep her voice during one of their fights, Banu always seemed to know exactly what had transpired in their room.

Once, she had tried telling Feroz this. "Do you see how your mother looks at me whenever we have a fight? What does she do, spy on us or something? I try so hard to hide our problems from her, but she seems to know each time there's trouble between us."

"Are you on your menses?"

"What?"

"Are you having your period?" Feroz repeated. "Because that's when you get hysterical and paranoid like this, thinking people are spying on you. Next you'll be like those stupid Americans, believing in UFOs and all."

She stared at her husband in silence, more hurt by his dismissal of her concerns than she felt she had the right to be. "Okay, Feroz," she said finally. "Keep making fun of me."

"Well, if you made sense, I wouldn't have to, my dear. Acting as if my mother has nothing better to do than to waste her time watching you."

When Edna leaves the room, Sera resists the urge to follow her into the kitchen. Even after all these years and despite Banu's current helpless, paralyzed state, she is still uneasy when she is alone with her mother-in-law. The bad memories of the past chatter in her ears, like those monkeys in the trees of Khandala. There are too many ghosts in here, and despite the ghostly, half-dead remains of the paralyzed old woman lying on the bed in front of Sera, the dead she most remembers and mourns is the young woman who lies buried in this house. With what hopes that newlywed woman had come into her in-laws' house. With what fervor she had been pursued and seduced by the man who became her husband, who had brought her into that house like she was precious cargo, a fragile piece of bone china. What brightness, what radiance there had been in those days, as if someone had perched an extra sun in the Bombay sky. She and Feroz had been golden then, not young exactly, but that had made their luster all the more dazzling, because it had been hard-won and unexpected. They had found each other at a time when neither had expected to.

She can hear the nurse setting the teacups down on the kitchen counter. "Tea's almost ready, madam," Edna sings from the kitchen. "One garma-garam cup of chai coming up."

Sera doesn't answer, afraid of waking the old woman up. Better to let sleeping dogs lie, she thinks and then feels a twinge of guilt at comparing her mother-in-law to a dog. Still, she is enjoying her moment of privacy and escape from Banu's watchful eyes. Despite the fact that the stroke had rendered Banu helpless and bedridden, despite the fact that she could barely speak, the old woman's beady eyes usually followed Sera across the room, watching her every movement, much as she used to in the early days of Sera's marriage.

Now, taking comfort in the fact that Banu is still asleep and that her darting eyes are shut tight, Sera tiptoes up to the old woman. Banu sleeps with her mouth open, breathing loudly, every third breath released in a loud, guttural snore. A thick trickle of drool wends its way from her mouth onto her pillow. The sight makes Sera ill. Despite the fact that she stops in every day to check on her mother-in-law, Sera can never control the nauseated, closed-in feeling that hits her when she is in this house. She stares at Banu, takes in the shriveled, mousy woman lying in the bed that seems to have grown around her, and reaches deep within herself to pull up a strand of pity but comes up empty-handed. Or rather, she pulls up an endless cord of rope, like the rope used to lower the buckets into the wells at Parsi fire temples. Into the rope are woven bitterness and resentment. The rope feels black and charred in her hands, burnt by her simmering fury. After all these years, she, Sera Dubash, loyal friend, loving mother, benevolent employer, helpful neighbor, generous patron of the arts, cannot forgive this shell of a woman who lies before her. She is both ashamed and strangely exhilarated by the thought.

Sera's eyes fall on the large oil painting of her father-in-law, Freddy Dubash, that hangs above Banu's bed. Freddy looks uncharacteristically serious in the painting, but the sight of his beloved parrot, Polly, perched on his right shoulder, makes Sera smile. If the early days of her marriage had been a dark coal mine, Freddy was the single beam of light that shone from the miner's helmet. He was the reason she had not lost her way completely.

Sera smiles involuntarily, the way she always does when she thinks of her father-in-law. Gazing at Freddy's bald head and familiar face, she remembers the first time she met him—and of course, the ever-present Polly. Three months after they'd started dating, Feroz had invited Sera to his parents' home on a Sunday afternoon. Freddy Dubash, one of Bombay's most successful lawyers, had walked into the living room in a red, embroidered bathrobe with a parrot perched on his shoulder.

"I'm Farokh Dubash," he said. "The Boy Wonder's father. But everyone calls me Freddy."

"Nice to meet you," Sera murmured.

"Feroz tells me you like classical music," Freddy said. "Is that so?"

"My father and I have been going to music concerts at Homi Bhabha since I was seven," Sera said simply. "He's a big music fan."

Freddy turned to his parrot. "Polly, we have a new friend. Shake hands with a fellow music lover. Come on. Shake hands."

And sure enough, the bird lifted a scrawny claw and held it out. Sera turned toward Feroz uncertainly, not knowing what to do. He looked bemused. "Yah, go ahead, shake that animal's hand," he said wearily. "Then your initiation into this crazy family will be complete."

Banu was fussing around, looking embarrassed. "Really, Freddy," she began, but Sera moved toward Freddy with her hand outstretched. "How do you do?" Polly said, when Sera brought her hand up to his claw. Noticing the look of surprise on her face, the others began to laugh. "It's my husband's little trick," Banu said, her voice tinged with embarrassment and pride. "Took him weeks to teach Polly to do that."

"Weeks, my foot," Freddy said. "He learned it in a matter of days. That's because parrots are birds with uncommon intelligence," he told Sera. "Much smarter than dogs, if you ask me."

"Yes, yes, Daddy, you taught Polly this trick in a matter of hours," Feroz said indulgently. "Minutes, even. After all, this damn bird is more intelligent than your own son. Polly is really the son my father never had," he added, turning to Sera. She thought she heard a trace of bitterness in Feroz's voice, but his face was smiling.

But Freddy ignored his son. "Polly likes you," he said to Sera. "Like me, he can spot a classical music lover miles away."

Why did Freddy pappa have to die before the Monster did, Sera thinks, not for the first time. After all these years, she still thinks of the eccentric, good-hearted Freddy as her savior, the man who rescued her from this hellish house.

Banu groans in her sleep, as if she is tormented by her own thoughts and dreams. For a split second her eyes fly open, but they are unfocused and the next second she is snoring again. Still, Sera knows that the old woman will be awake any minute now. She can hear Edna balancing the two cups of tea, getting ready to enter the room. She looks around quickly, guiltily. Edna is almost in the room when Sera bends toward the sleeping woman, as if to caress her forehead. She casts a last, furtive look around before her hand changes its trajectory. Her open palm narrows, so that her thumb and index finger come together like tweezers.

Just as Edna enters the room, Sera takes Banu's soft, droopy, lifeless cheek between her fingers and pinches her. Hard. Her heart pounds in her chest. She waits for the old woman to wake up with a scream even as she knows that Banu's paralyzed face hasn't felt her harsh rebuke. Banu sleeps on, lost in her own fetid world of dreams. Remorse and shame at her juvenile behavior trickle into Sera's veins like gray smoke. Still, she knows she will perform the same ritual again, tomorrow. It is her only way of chalking up a minor victory for the idealistic, hopeful girl who lies buried inside this graveyard of a house.

Her guilt makes Sera reach into her purse and pull out a hundred-rupee bill. "This is for your children," she tells Edna. "Buy them some chocolates on your way home today."

6

hyam, the pockmark-faced neighbor who lives on the other side of the open drain, stops Bhima as she is about to enter her hut. "Namaste, mausi," he says. "Long day today?"

Bhima nods. "Every day is a long day when you're working," she replies. Then, remembering that Shyam lost his job two months ago, she smiles ruefully, to make sure he does not read any hint of chastisement into her reply.

But her neighbor does not seem offended. "Hahji," he says. "Right you are. So, Bhima mausi, are you going to attend our meeting with the corporator tomorrow afternoon?"

"What meeting?" Bhima asks, but even before she finishes asking, she remembers. Bibi had told her a few days ago that the slum dwellers had managed to secure a meeting with one of the municipality big shots, who was to tour the slum. Among the many demands, the slum residents were asking the city to install a few more water taps. "Hah, yes, I remember now," she says to Shyam before the man can answer. "Someone had mentioned something. But what to do, Shyam, I have to be at work at my mistress's place. If I don't work, I don't eat."

Shyam winces, and Bhima curses herself for her insensitivity. "Yes, mausi, I know what you are saying," he says, his voice thick with irony. "For the sake of this whorish stomach, one must do anything and everything. But the welfare of this slum is also a worthy cause, no? Surely your mistress can give you a few hours off."

Bhima feels cornered. Her earlier sympathy for Shyam corrodes into resentment. She is tired, drained, and she is eager to step inside her little hut and shut the door upon the world. Her throat tickles in anticipation of a hot cup of sweet, milky tea, which she hopes the girl Maya has remembered to prepare. She does not want to waste any more time with this unemployed fool. "My mistress needs me," she says sharply. "As for the slum, that's why we have you menfolks—to take care of our needs and to talk and debate with the big bosses. I'm just a poor, illiterate woman, only good for chopping onions and using a broom. And speaking of onions, I have to cook dinner for myself and my granddaughter. So, with your permission, I'll take your leave."

She has one hand on her door when the sound of Maya's name on Shyam's tongue stops her. "Oh, by the way," he says, and even in the dying light of the day, she can see that his mouth is twisted into a simmering cruelty. "Speaking of Maya . . . My Rehka went over to your house earlier today. We were out of sugar, and the missus asked Rehka to run over and borrow some. We've been noticing Maya doesn't leave for college these days, so the missus was sure someone would be home."

Bhima feels her stomach muscles clench. Something is coming, and she is sure it isn't good. "What's this got to do with Maya?" she says and does not try to keep the sharpness out of her voice.

"Slow down, slow down, mausi." Shyam's voice slithers like a snake through the gathering darkness. "I'm telling you, na? What I'm trying to say is my little Rehka entered your place only to find your Maya throwing up in a corner and holding her belly. And when my Rehku tried to help, your Maya turned on her like a viper and chased her away. Now is this any way to treat someone living next door to you in a basti?"

"I'll talk to Maya," Bhima says. "She's had the flu for many days, poor girl."

"Flu, is it?" The voice is even smoother now. "Strange kind of flu, to linger this long. Some of the folks in the basti are saying she's been throwing up for a month or two now. Still, what with the flies and rats and dirty water in this slum, anything is possible, I suppose."

Bhima resists the urge to claw at his pockmarked face. Instead, she says in a calm, measured voice, "Send Rehka over, Shyam. I'll let her have some sugar."

Shyam brightens immediately. His transformation reminds Bhima of the cobra at Mahalati temple, who lowers his hood as soon as the high priest puts a silver bowl of milk before him. "Bhima mausi. I knew I could count on you." She grins. "Once I get a job, I intend to repay all my debts. The child will be over in a few minutes."

Bhima waits until Rehka has left with the half cup of sugar before she turns to Maya. Her eyes sweep across the small room. She notices that her granddaughter has not made her the much-anticipated cup of tea. "What did you do today?" she asks, and the tightness in her voice is a warning.

"Nothing," the girl replies cautiously.

"Nothing," Bhima repeats to the air. "The big-bellied princess lay around all day doing nothing."

Maya's face is as flat as a table but her eyes are welling with tears. But Bhima is not satisfied. "Did you hear what that badmaash Shyam was saying to me about you?" she hisses.

"Leave me alone, Ma," Maya says. "I'm not feeling well." Her voice is as brittle as a clay pot.

Bhima opens her mouth to respond and then closes it. The girl really does look sick.

"Come on," she says gruffly. "You lie down for a few minutes while I make dinner."

As if she has detected the shift in her grandmother's tone, a light comes into Maya's eyes. "I can help, Ma-ma," she says. "You must be tired."

This girl is like an eager-to-please dog, Bhima marvels. Wary when you kick her, but the minute you stop the kicking, her tail wags again. "Okay then, chop up two onions," she says. "And put the rice to boil. I'll cook a vegetable for dinner."

Crouching near the stove next to her granddaughter, Bhima hears Maya's stomach growl. "Did you eat today?" she asks sharply.

"Yes. No. I mean, I tried." Maya looks miserable. "For lunch, I craved a hard-boiled egg. But there were no eggs at home and I—I didn't feel like going to the shop down the lane. So I tried eating a chappati instead. But it just made me sick."

Remembering the omelet Serabai had made for her earlier today, Bhima feels her heart twist with shame. "Silly girl," she scolds. "Lazy you are getting. What, you can't walk to the corner to buy an egg?"

Suddenly, without explanation, Maya bursts into tears. "Walk to the corner? Sometimes I wish I could just walk out of this room and keep walking until my feet turn into wings. Go somewhere where nobody knows me, where a hundred prying eyes are not following me. You don't know what it's like to sit here all day with the door shut, hearing the sounds of the outside world, hearing doors slam, children playing games, the women in the basti talking, and wondering if they're gossiping about me. I feel like a prisoner, but then I ask myself, Who is my jailer? I am my own jailer. I don't know which is darker, Ma-ma—this room with no electricity or the veil of shame that hangs over me."

This is the first time Bhima has seen Maya cry since the pregnancy began. Her granddaughter's sobs are landing on Bhima's chest like fists, but still, she is glad. Let the girl cry. Let her repent for what she has done. She puts a plate of food before the weeping girl, resolutely looking away from the tears that fall into Maya's rice. "Eat," she grunts. "A girl in your condition must eat."

After dinner, Bhima reaches for the tobacco tin and stuffs a wad into her mouth. Chewing slowly, she gazes at her granddaughter. "Hear me," she says. "People are talking. And you can't hide your shame in this room forever. Soon, even your salwar-khamez won't be able to hide your belly. Already, too much time has passed. We need to get you to the doctor soon."

To her great surprise, Maya does not fight her. "I'll go," she says. "I just have one condition—I want Serabai to go to the hospital with me instead of you."

Bhima is surprised at how much this rejection stings. To cover up her feelings, she says gruffly, "Serabai has a hajaar things to do more important than taking a shameless girl to an abortion doctor. I would be too embarrassed to ask her. Anyway, this is our family matter. Why do you want to involve that poor woman? Hasn't she done you enough favors already?"

Maya looks tired. "Just ask her. I know she won't say no. I beg you, Ma-ma." Then, seeing the stubborn look on her grandmother's face, she adds, "You know they'll take better care of me if someone like her is with me. I want this to go as well as possible."

Bhima flushes. She remembers the day Gopal had lain desperately ill and neglected in the government hospital. Sera and Feroz Dubash had stridden in like movie stars and made sure that he got the best care. Maya is right. Rich, confident, and well-spoken, Serabai has a way of making doors open like a magician. Bhima resolves to speak to her in the morning.

Lying on her thin cotton mattress that night, Bhima replays the conversation with Shyam. She has managed to defang the serpent for now, has purchased his silence with a cup of sugar. But for how long? Shyam is not the sharpest of men. If he has noticed Maya's morning illness, surely it has come to the attention of the eagle-eyed women with the paan-stained teeth and gossiping tongues who populate the slum colony. Are they keeping silent out of respect for her, Bhima? If so, how long will the silence hold? Or is she simply the last to know? Are rumors flying around the slum like black kites and is she too stupid and ignorant to know about them? After all, she has no real friends in this basti. Ever since she moved out of her two-room apartment in the chawl where she and Gopal lived and descended into this hell, she has carried herself in a manner that suggests she is not from here. That is one of the reasons she has no interest in attending their stupid meetings with this corporator or that. Even with five more water taps, the slum will still be a slum. And she had been used to something better than this. She knows that her aloof manner makes her a target for her neighbors' recriminations, but she doesn't care. If not for her own sake, then for Maya's, she has to believe that their life here is temporary. Sometimes, while she is stepping over an open gutter or shooing away the flies when squatting to take a shit, it is hard to believe that. But she had clung to that belief, at least until the day she came home and found Maya crouching on the floor, a pool of vomit next to her. When the vomiting hadn't stopped three days later, she had dragged her granddaughter to Dr. Premchand's clinic, thinking it was an acute case of stomach flu or food poisoning. Instead, she had found out that Maya was pregnant.

Thinking about the slum makes Bhima think of her apartment in the chawl, her lost kingdom, and she feels the old, familiar yearning for what she has left behind.

Gopal. It's funny, but she has thought more about her husband since Maya's pregnancy than in all the years before. She had thought that she had gotten used to the loneliness of her life, that she had accepted the numb spot on her heart, as if a doctor had sprayed it with ether. But perhaps the sting of Maya's betrayal has salted the sting of an earlier betrayal. Perhaps it is that, right now, she needs a man to help her navigate these murky waters that her thoughtless granddaughter has led them both into. Or perhaps it is that time doesn't heal wounds at all, perhaps that is the biggest lie of them all, and instead what happens is that each wound penetrates the body deeper and deeper until one day you find that the sheer geography of your bones—the angle of your head, the jutting of your hips, the sharpness of your shoulders, as well as the luster of your eyes, the texture of your skin, the openness of your smile—has collapsed under the weight of your griefs.

Gopal. If she closes her eyes for a moment, she can still hear the tring-tring of his bicycle bell on the day he had launched his strange, earnest courtship of her, when she was twenty and all of life stretched out like a green garden before her.

She had met him for the first time the previous day, at her best friend Sujata's wedding. Now, she was waiting for the number 5 bus to take her to the home of Dinu Shroff, the woman she worked for. Bhima leaned against the railing of the bus stop and shut her tired eyes. They had gotten home so late from Sujata's wedding that she had slept for barely five hours. She had dozed off for a minute when she heard the clanging of a bicycle bell. "Wake up, wake up," an unfamiliar voice said. "Or else the sleep monsters will be tempted to kidnap you away."

Bhima opened her eyes and then immediately shut them when she saw Gopal's face before her. It was Sujata's cousin, that impudent idiot who had winked at her and asked her to dance with him yesterday, as if she was a girl from a bad family. Oh, Bhagwan, let him be gone when I open my eyes again, she prayed.

Her prayers went unanswered. When she opened her eyes, he was still grinning and perched on his bicycle. "Namaste," he said. "I was compelled to wake you up. Any more beauty sleep and your beauty would blind even the sun."

Bhima groaned. "Please keep your khata jokes to yourself," she replied. "I'm in no mood for this."

"In no mood for jokes? Now that's a sad state of affairs, my Bhima. I suppose it's my duty, then, to bring you back in the mood."

How did he know her name? Before she could ask, the man in line ahead of her turned around and spoke to her. "Is this ruffian bothering you, miss?"

Immediately, Gopal spoke up. "Ae, mind your own business, yaar. Coming between a man and his betrothed, for no good reason. Private family mammala this is, understand?"

The man wilted under Gopal's stern stare. "Okay, sorry. I just was trying to—"

"Trying-frying, nothing." Gopal pressed home his advantage. "That's the trouble with our Bombay, too many people interfering in other people's private matters." And as the man turned away, he winked at Bhima.

She looked away from him and saw a red single-decker BEST bus approaching. It was a number 5. She would be rid of this pest in less than a minute.

This early in the day, the bus was half empty. Bhima knew that within an hour the bus would be so crowded that people would be spilling out of the open doorway and it would be hard to find even room to gain a foothold while boarding it. But at this time, she had her choice of seats, and she made her way to a window seat in the front. She untied the knot at the tip of her sari to remove the coins to pay for the ticket.

The next second, she nearly jumped out of her skin as a hand gripped the metal bars on her window. For a second she thought it was someone from the outside trying to steal her bus money. But it was Gopal, on his bike, pedaling furiously to keep up with the bus, one hand on the metal bar, the other gripping his handlebar.

"You fool," she hissed. "Do you want to get killed?"

In reply, he sang to her. "Mere sapono ke rani kab aayegi tu?" The queen of my dreams, when will you arrive? He had a strong, deep voice, and the more he pedaled alongside the bus, the louder it got.

In an effort to dissuade his mad cycling, Bhima moved away from the window and toward the aisle. But at the next stop, more people got in, and she was forced to shift back toward the window. Out of the corner of her eye she noticed how expertly Gopal weaved in and around the mad Bombay traffic, never once letting go his grip on the metal bar. If he was concerned about the bus lurching to a stop and throwing him off his bike, it was not apparent in his confident, loose grip on the bar.

Gopal was still singing the same song, and finally, the man sitting behind her spoke up. "Arre, yaar, don't you know any other songs? If you're going to serenade the lady, you better have more than one song on your hit list."

Gopal obliged by launching into another song, this one filled with double meanings and innuendos. Now several of the passengers got into the fun, throwing out requests his way. Bhima gritted her teeth. This Gopal was just too much. Her fingers itched for the broom that she used at Dinubai's house. She would smack that stupid grin off his face if she had that jharoo with her.

Her irritation and embarrassment almost caused her to miss her stop. "Wait, wait," she yelled to the conductor. "This is my stop."

As she got off, she waited for the bus to leave so that she could confront Gopal and tell him these shenanigans had to stop. To her chagrin, she saw him pedaling away, alongside the bus. As if he knew she was watching, he raised his right hand in a wave. The coward, she thought. Knew I'd give him some vim-zim, so he takes off.

The next day, he was back. But this time he stood perched on his bicycle across the street from the bus stop, too far for her to give him a piece of her mind. She did her best to keep her eyes from straying toward him, but each time she did catch his eye, he clenched his heart dramatically. Idiot, she thought. I wish the next time he holds his chest he has a heart attack and falls off his cycle. The next minute, she stiffened with remorse at the wickedness of her thoughts.

She was thankful when the bus arrived. She took her usual seat, and five seconds later there was the familiar hand gripping the metal bar. This time, she did not jump out of her seat in shock but felt a mild tremor of surprise and irritation at his audacity. She had truly believed he would leave her alone today. The queen of my dreams, when will you arrive? The familiar tune started up again. And again, the skillful weaving and bobbing in and out of traffic. The other passengers, many of whom caught the same bus daily, tittered. "Arre, bhenji," her would-be rescuer from yesterday called from across the aisle. "Why don't you say yes to your man and put him out of his misery? Taking his life in his own hands, he is, for your sake." Bhima fixed a baleful stare at him, and the man went back to reading his newspaper, muttering to himself about the wily ways of the fairer sex.

For the next three weeks, Gopal followed the same routine.

Some days he would wait for her on the other side of the street and pedal furiously across four lanes of traffic to catch up with her bus when it arrived. Other times, he would greet her with the tring-tring of his bicycle bell and circle around the bus stop until she felt dizzy. The only difference between the first day of this strange courtship and the days that followed was that he no longer spoke to her. But the impudent grin, the daredevil tricks on the bike while they waited for the bus to arrive, and the joyful serenading remained unchanged. As did the fact that he rode off alongside the bus after it had deposited Bhima a few streets from her mistress's house. Bhima longed to talk to him, to ask for some explanation for his mad behavior, but the presence of the other passengers silenced her.

One day during those three weeks, Bhima arrived at the bus stop and noticed immediately that Gopal was not there. Her mind told her to breathe a sigh of relief even as her body experienced a disappointed lurch and feeling of letdown. Apparently, her fellow travelers had experienced the same thing. "The young fellow's missing today," an elderly gentleman in a white kurta and dhoti said. "Wonder if he's all right."

A lethargic feeling came over Bhima as she entered the bus. The seven stops to Dinubai's house will take forever without the distraction provided by Gopal, she thought, surprising herself. She looked at the empty, lonely metal bar with something approaching wistfulness, missing the brown hand with coarse dark hair that usually gripped that bar. As the bus lurched forward, she glanced backward—only to see Gopal pedaling furiously to catch up. The next minute the hand was resting triumphantly on the bar. "Hello, my queen," the familiar voice said. "Almost missed you today by oversleeping."

"Look, it's our young hero," the elderly gentleman cried, and there was a scattering of applause from the regulars. "By hook or by crook, he has made it."

The applause irritated Bhima. Idiots, she thought. Encouraging him to be a fool. But she could not dislodge the small feeling of pleasure that settled in her bones at the sight of Gopal riding alongside her.

Then, at the end of the three weeks, Gopal disappeared. Every morning Bhima looked for him as she arrived at the bus stop, both dreading and anticipating the tinkle of his bicycle horn, the cheeky look on his face as he glanced at her while singing an ever-expanding repertoire of songs. Each day she boarded the bus and—as much as she hated herself for doing it—looked back to see if she could spot the familiar cycle. At times, when she saw a boy on the streets who resembled Gopal, Bhima's heart would lurch with joy, and on the inevitable downbeat, when her heart settled back into its usual rhythm, she would scold herself for her stupidity. Some days, when she was sure nobody was looking, she held the metal bar lightly with her own long fingers, pretending she could still feel the warmth from Gopal's hand.

But Gopal was gone. She had scared him away with her stony demeanor, had turned his interest into indifference. Bhima imagined him in a different part of the city, wooing a different girl with a different song. The thought made her chop the onions with so much vigor that Dinubai looked at her with curiosity and asked her if she was feeling all right. She looked up to face her mistress with eyes brimming with tears. "Everything's okay, bai," she said. "These onions are garma-garam, that's all. Making my eyes water."

But Bhima needn't have worried. Sujata and her new husband, Sushil, came over with a marriage proposal. Although Gopal was Sujata's cousin, it was Sushil who did most of the talking. "Gopal does not have any immediate family in Bombay to speak for him," Sushil explained to Prithviraj, Bhima's father. "His mother lives in the village, and his father—may God grant him rest—is dead. So I bring this proposal on behalf of Gopal's older brother. But we can vouch for his character as well as his capacity for hard work. He has a good, steady factory job, makes good money. Your Bhima will not lack for anything, ji. Oh, and one other thing—Gopal has specifically told me to mention that he will neither expect nor want any dowry."

Prithviraj tried to not let his delight show. "I will consult with my family and respond in a few days," he said. "But I will say this— just having a proposal come from a family as good as this pleases me. After all, Sujata grew up before our eyes. I pray that my Bhima finds a husband as worthy as you, Sushil."

They were married a month later in a simple ceremony in stark contrast to the glitter that had surrounded Sujata's wedding a few months earlier. During the wedding ceremony, Gopal looked as subdued and terrified as Bhima felt. There was no trace of the smart-alecky youth who had pursued her with such intensity. But as soon as she was alone for the first time with her new husband, as soon as he had lifted the pallov of the sari from her face as they sat perched on their wedding bed, the old, irrepressible Gopal staged a comeback. Staring into her eyes, a crooked smile on his face, he began tunelessly to whistle the song with which he had first serenaded her. The queen of my dreams, when will you arrive? Encouraged by her giggles, the whistling grew louder, until it gave way to humming. She giggled some more as he nuzzled her chin and tickled her belly. "Stop it," she whispered helplessly. "You crazy man."

With a leap, Gopal sprang up and stood on the bed. He raised both hands above his head like a triumphant boxer. "Yes, I am a crazy man, the crazy head of the household," he declared, modulating his voice, so that the relatives who were inevitably eavesdropping outside their bedroom door couldn't hear him. "And you are a crazy woman for having married this crazy man. But oh, my Bhima, we are going to have so much fun the rest of our lives.

You just wait, woman, I am going to treat you like the queen that you are."

Thinking of her wedding night, of Gopal's broken promise, Bhima stirs restlessly. She knows she must try to sleep, but her mind feels feverish as it races through the crowded hallways of the past. Beside her, Maya snores softly and occasionally murmurs in her sleep. Instinctively, Bhima responds with this new emotion that she's grown familiar with ever since she learned of Maya's pregnancy—a combination of unbearable protectiveness and strong irritability. Hearing her grandchild's snores and murmurs, Bhima wants to smother her with a pillow as well as take her in her arms and rock her all night. She wants to preserve the innocence that lets Maya sleep her childlike sleep; she wants to destroy that innocence much as the baby growing in Maya's womb has destroyed Bhima's peace of mind. It scares her sometimes, how effortlessly both feelings seem to reside inside her heart, how she has grown to love and hate Maya, how a singular strand of love now has fear weaved into it. How she has come to see her own flesh and blood as her betrayer.

But you should be used to betrayals by now, you old woman, she says to herself. You, of all people. Why should this wisp of a girl owe you more than your husband did? Look what he did to you. Stole your life away from you, didn't he? And you've forgiven him, haven't you? No, not forgiven, but you've made your peace with it, no? So why not do the same with this poor, stupid girl?

Straining her eyes to see Maya's outline in the dark, Bhima answers her own question. The situation with Gopal belongs to the past, and like a used wedding sari, she can fold it and tuck it away in a dark corner. But Maya is the present (once, she had also been the future, but no point in thinking about that now). A red-hot, pulsating dot is growing in her womb, throbbing with life and energy. Unsanctified by a priest, conceived under the veil of shame, unwanted by the world, that thing growing in Maya's body has the power to destroy both of them. But before it can do that, before it can wail its grievances to the world, before it can wave its tiny fist at them, they have to destroy it.

A solitary crow caws, and Bhima groans. It is 3:00 A.M., she guesses. In a few hours, it will be time to get up, and she has not even slept for a full hour yet. Soon it will be dawn.

7

It is Saturday morning, and Bhima is late again. Despite her pregnancy, Dinaz has woken up early today to help Sera prepare breakfast. Dinaz knows how much her mother hates chopping onions and cilantro, and since both ingredients are necessary in making Viraf's favorite breakfast dish of akuri—scrambled eggs with chili powder, onions, garlic, and other spices—she has taken on the unpleasant task. Sera glances at her daughter and, as always, feels a sense of awe at how wonderful Dinaz has turned out. If for no other reason, she cannot regret her marriage to Feroz because of what that marriage produced. It's funny, she thinks, Feroz and I were both such flawed people. And yet look at what we made together—one of the nicest people I know, and I'd feel that way even if she wasn't my only child. It makes you believe in evolution or God or miracles or something. The endurance of the human spirit, maybe.

Sera glances at the clock. She worries that this tardiness is becoming a habit with Bhima. I can't have this, she says to herself. I know she's burdened with Maya and all, but after all, she has obligations here also. Unbidden, Feroz's voice plays in her head: "Treating that woman as if she's a family member. Servants have to be kept in their place, I tell you. One of these days I'll come home to find you waiting on Bhima."

As if she has read her mother's mind, Dinaz raises a hand to block Sera's view of the clock. "God, Mummy, stop looking at that clock. It's Saturday; even if Bhima is late one day, so what? She's a human being too, you know."

It always amuses Sera how, when it comes to Bhima, Dinaz instinctively plays the role that she, Sera, did with Feroz. And how she paradoxically takes on Feroz's part. "One day would be okay," she now says. "But this is getting to be too much. After all, there's no point in having a servant if I'm going to end up doing all the work."

If Sera expects sympathy, Dinaz's words give that illusion a quick burial. She thumps her mother on the back. "A little housework never killed anybody," she intones. "It's good for your arthritis—keeps the joints limber. Anyway, Bhima is older than you—she needs her rest more than you do."

Despite herself, Sera smiles. Sometimes she forgets that before Dinaz switched to management at her father's insistence, she was studying to be a social worker. But no matter how successful Dinaz is becoming in her new profession, the old sense of fair play, the thirst for justice, is still ever-present. As for Bhima, she is Dinaz's blind spot. From the time she was a little girl, Dinaz had never been able to tolerate one unkind word about Bhima. "That woman is brainwashing our only child under your very nose," Feroz had once railed at Sera. "And you—you are too complacent and stupid to even notice. Dinaz talks nicer to Bhima then she does to her own daddy." And Sera had bit her tongue and not stated the obvious— that Dinaz saw more of Bhima than she did of Feroz and was treated with more kindness by the servant than by her own father.

Viraf wanders into the kitchen, still in his pajamas. Without being asked, he removes three plates and sets them on the dining table. "Bhima, Bhima, Bhima, that's all I hear these days," he grumbles. "I swear, nobody else's name comes up as much in our house anymore."

"And what's wrong with that?" Dinaz asks immediately. "After all, the poor woman is in trouble."

"Ouch. Didn't think I was going to eat my own head for breakfast this morning," Viraf says. "No, nothing wrong with talking about Bhima's woe, my dear. What I have problems with is that, after all these endless conversations, nothing has been done."

"And what do you propose we do, Mr. Management, sir?" Dinaz asks, the smile on her face softening her words.

Viraf does not smile back. "What has to be done is obvious," he says. "Maya needs to have an abortion, and the sooner it is done, the better off she will be. I'm just surprised that we've waited all this time, actually."

Although she knows that her son-in-law means well, that he has Bhima's interests at heart, something inside Sera bristles at Viraf's proprietarial use of *we,* and the casual way in which he mentions the abortion. Just like a man, she thinks. As if getting rid of a child is as easy as taking a shit. She flushes at the crudity of her own thoughts.

Viraf speaks into the vacuum his words have created. "Well, I can tell from the silence that I've taken a real popular position," he says sarcastically. "But I'm afraid the time for delicacy and beating around the bush is over, ladies. Look, we have to be practical about this. Maya has gone and gotten herself pregnant. And if we sit by and do nothing, we're just prolonging her misery. Seems to me an abortion is the only practical thing to do."

"You're right," Dinaz says as she dishes out the akuri from the frying pan onto their plates. "I know you're right, sweetu." She interrupts herself. "Mummy, should I leave some of this for Bhima?"

"She fasts on Saturdays," Sera reminds her. Seeing Viraf's quizzical look, she adds, "Some saint's day or the other."

"Speaking of Bhima," Viraf says. "She better show up soon if she wants a lift to the vegetable market. I'm not going to be late for my cricket game because of her."

Dinaz and Sera smile. Viraf is crazy about cricket, they know. Every Saturday he doffs his white uniform and drives to a maidan to play a game with his old friends. He has been playing with this team since his first year in college. "You better give your teammates fair warning," Dinaz now says. "After the baby is born, your cricket-playing days are over."

Viraf looks so dismayed that both women burst out laughing. "My God, look at his face," Dinaz says. "You'd think I'd told him he can never eat or drink again."

"Cricket is the food of life," Viraf says dramatically. "It is not a game, it's a way of life. The most elegant, graceful sport there is. And anyway, who knows? If it is a son, I'll take him with me as soon as he can walk."

"Great, so we have another generation of sports fanatic to deal with. No thanks, baba. My son's going to be a reader and a thinker."

"You better be careful what you say, woman. I will not let you turn my boy into a sissy," Viraf says playfully. "I tell you, if technology allowed, I would get the doctors to implant a chip in your belly so that my son would be born with a cricket ball in his hand."

Dinaz turns to her mother. "See how wonderful your darling son-in-law is? Talks about implanting chips in my belly like I'm a damn cow or something."

Sera rises from the table with a smile. "Children, children," she says. "What nonsense you talk."

"Wait, don't get up yet," Dinaz says. "We should resolve this Bhima mammala today." She turns to Viraf. "Sweetu, can you call Rusi when you get back from the cricket game? I know he's not a gyno, but he'll be able to recommend someone, correct?"

"Bhima can take her to the government hospital," Sera says automatically.

"Come on, Mummy. You know what butchers those doctors are

at those free hospitals. And seeing a young, unmarried girl who is pregnant . . ." Dinaz shudders.

Viraf grimaces. "Okay, okay, I'll phone Rusi and get a recommendation. Now, can we change this sordid subject, please? This talk is making me lose my breakfast."

The two women exchange a quick glance. "Viraf's correct," Sera says. "The breakfast table is not the place for such talk." She smiles at her son-in-law appeasingly.

Viraf smiles back. "Besides, it's so depressing talking about abortions and all when Dinaz is—when we are—pregnant. You know? It's like every time I want to just be happy about our good fortune, I feel forced to think about Maya's misfortune."

Dinaz immediately sets down her fork and leans over to kiss her husband on the cheek. "I'm sorry, janu," she says. "I feel the same way, too. Sorry for being so insensitive."

Viraf reaches over to where Dinaz is sitting next to him and links his right index finger to her left. They hold hands through the rest of their breakfast, and seeing them, Sera feels a happiness so sharp and tight, it's like a pain in her chest. It's worth it, she thinks. All the misery with Feroz is worth it because it has brought me to this moment. My daughter has the marriage I never did. And I brought her to this point. I did. I. Screwed-up, flawed, stupid old me.

All her life, Sera has heard a million stories about how a tormented daughter-in-law turned into a shrewish mother-in-law when it was her turn. As if it is some kind of hazing ritual, she thinks. But even now, the scars of her time in Banu Dubash's house are still too fresh for her ever to play such a role in her children's lives. Ever since Viraf and Dinaz moved in with her after Feroz's death, she has done her level best to give them all the privacy they need. What's that strange word the Americans use? Space. She has given them space. And she has held her tongue. At times, it has not been easy, especially when Viraf and Dinaz have had one of their fights. Then the urge to intervene, to say a reconciliatory word, has been great. Somehow, she finds it easy to forgive Viraf, to overlook his eccentricities. But the desire to pull Dinaz aside, to whisper to her that she is wrong, to remind her that an obedient wife rules her husband, to urge her to go back into their room and make up with Viraf, is so strong at such times that she practically has to sit on her hands and staple her mouth shut, to force herself to stay out of their business. That had been her promise to Dinaz when the children offered to move in with her. "I will make sure you two will not be saddled with an interfering mother-in-law."

"Oh, Mummy, we're not concerned about that," Dinaz had replied.

Sera had shaken her head impatiently. "I know what I'm talking about, deekra," she'd said. "The two of you have not been married for all that long. Your marriage is still developing. I know that everything sounds easy and possible now, but living with someone else, especially a person from another generation, is hard. Believe me. I know what I'm talking about."

The first fight with Banu had occurred less than two weeks after Sera and Feroz had returned from their honeymoon. "Feroz, deekra, can you come in here for a minute?" Banu called from her bedroom when Feroz got in from work that evening. He made a face at Sera, who had come to the front door to greet him, squeezed her arm, and went to see his mother.

When he walked into their bedroom a half hour later, he looked embarrassed. "Er, ahem, Mummy wanted me to talk to you about something important," he said.

"Is it my cooking?" she said immediately. "Did I not put enough salt in the chicken? My daddy always complaints that I—"

"No, no, it's nothing like that. You see, Mummy has noticed that you are in your time."

"Time?" she said blankly.

He sighed. "Your menses. Period. That you are having your period. And er, um, in our house, women who have their menses sit separately. They do not touch the food in the kitchen, use separate utensils and all that."

She stared at him in disbelief. "Feroz, you're joking, correct?"

He looked annoyed. "I know it must sound old-fashioned to you, a modern-day girl." His tone was strange, and Sera couldn't help but feel that he was parroting his mother's words. "But those are the rules of this house. My mother's rules. And since we are living with her, we must follow her rules." He looked at her pleadingly. "So for everybody's peace of mind, Sera, just do as she asks. After all, it's for your own good. When a woman is bleeding, she is weak. So this tradition is just a way of conserving her strength."

This is my foreign-returned, modern husband, she marveled to herself. A big-shot executive at Tata's. Suddenly she remembered what a colleague of hers used to say—"A Parsi man will turn into a mouse in front of his mother."

"Feroz, please, this is ridiculous," she said. "I mean, I thought only those poor, old-fashioned women in Udwada sat separately during their periods. This is Bombay, janu. And people do have to change with the times, after all."

He sighed again, more heavily this time. "Look, Sera, I'm so tired today. Very long day at work and all that. Darling, just give in to Mamma about this, okay? She's an old lady, set in her ways, you know? And it's such a small point to upset her over. I want so much for all of us to get along like one big, happy family. Please, just say yes."

It was the vision of the one big, happy family that got her to swallow her reluctance and say yes. "What exactly does this entail?" she added, suspiciously.

"Oh, God, I don't know," he said, giving her a quick hug. "But really, probably all it means is you have your food served to you in your room and a few other things. Thank you, Sera, for not humiliating me in front of my family."

It felt strange having her dinner brought to her in her room, but Sera forced herself to swallow the hurt feeling that rose in her when the voices of the other three floated toward her from the dining room. She turned on the radio in the bedroom to drown out their voices, eating her dinner without relish. Feroz soon came into the bedroom and whispered how sorry he was and how much he'd missed her at the dining table. That night, he held her in his arms till dawn. Sera marveled at the easy familiarity their bodies already had with each other. And getting to know Feroz's body had allowed her to know her own body better—its desires and needs, its twitching muscles and electric nerves, its hollow places and sweet spots. "Don't go to work today," she whispered to him in the morning. "Let's spend the day together, alone."

He laughed and pulled away reluctantly from her embrace. "God, I wish I could. But I already took time off for the honeymoon, you know? And I have a big presentation this afternoon."

She stood on the balcony to wave good-bye to him, aware of the fact that Banu was standing as far away from her as she could while she too waved to Feroz. Her feelings still bruised from last night's conversation, Sera lingered on the balcony even after Feroz drove away and Banu returned indoors. She heard the thin cry of the banana vendor as he pushed his wooden cart; she noticed the two teenage boys on the terrace of the building across the street as they flew their kites. As she stood, she debated whether to talk to Banu about her conversation with Feroz; asked herself whether it would do any good to try to make her mother-in-law change her mind. Many old Parsi women had this superstition about menses, Sera knew, but so far none of those women had interfered with her life. She was the daughter of a scientist, and it humiliated her to have to give in to such primitive ideas. This is not how I was brought up, Banu mamma, she wanted to say. And if this was the condition, you should've mentioned it to me before I came into this house.

The sun was beating down on her face, making her sweat. From the balcony, she could hear Freddy Dubash's music playing on the record player, could hear Polly squawking at the high notes. A loud growl from her stomach reminded her that she was hungry. Was she supposed to ask for her breakfast, or was she to return to her room and wait to be fed like some criminal in prison? she wondered, and the humiliation that she felt made her sweat even more. She decided to return to her room.

Banu was on the couch in the living room, a white mathubanu covering her head and a prayer book in her hand. "Kem na mazda," she was praying as Sera walked past her, crossing the living room.

The next second, there was a deafening shriek. "Out, out," Banu screamed. "Acchut. Unclean girl, dirtified the whole room while I was praying. All my prayers are ruined by your unclean presence. Didn't your mummy-daddy teach you anything, you dirty girl?"

Sera stared at Banu dumbfounded. It took her a minute to realize that her mother-in-law was talking to her in this hysterical manner. The agitated woman before her was totally unlike the shy, eager-to-please woman who had encouraged her to marry her son, who had welcomed her into her home just a few weeks ago. "I . . . I," she stammered.

Freddy Dubash came running in from the dining room. "What happened? Did someone fall?"

"Oh, Freddy, thank God you are here," Banu said dramatically. "Help me, darling, help me."

Freddy looked distraught. "Banu, what is it, will you speak? Is it your heart?"

"No, no, nothing like that. Just that this whole house will have to be purified now. Sera walked across the room while I was praying and she is having her monthly cycle, you see. Still, without any consideration, she interfered with my prayers."

Sera blushed. Before she could speak, Freddy raised his voice. "You and your superstitious vhems and dhakharas. Crazy woman, you are. Harassing this poor child, scaring her for no good reason." He grew even more angry. "And worst of all, you've ruined my enjoyment of my music. A new Mozart record I'd just bought, and now your hysterical faras has made me miss the best part." He flung a sympathetic look at Sera and then stomped out of the room.

Banu narrowed her eyes and flashed Sera a look that made her heart stop. "See what you've done, getting my Freddy all upset?" she said, careful to lower her voice so that it didn't carry into the next room. "Is that why you entered my house, to create friction between my husband and me?"

Sera felt dizzy, as if she had drunk four beers one after the other. She took a step toward Banu and reached out to touch her hand. "Banu mamma, I don't know what happened—"

"She touched me," Banu screamed. "Deliberately, on purpose, she touched me with her impure hands. Oh, God, what kind of daakan has entered my house, to make me miserable in my old age?"

This time, Gulab, the Dubashs' servant, came into the living room. She took one look at the situation and pushed Sera toward her bedroom. "Baby, you go in your room for a while," she said authoritatively. "Go on, I will calm Mummy down."

In her room, Sera collapsed on the bed. If Banu had physically assaulted her she could not have hurt her more. Some part of her kept thinking that the whole scene had been an elaborate joke, a cruel but harmless initiation ceremony into the family, devised by Feroz. That any minute now, Freddy and Banu would walk into her room, wide, sheepish smiles on their faces, and confess to their role in Feroz's silly joke. But even as she waited, she remembered something her mother had said during her engagement period. "I ran into Miss Amy Smith today," her mother had said with a slight frown. "You remember her, na, your sixth-standard teacher? Seems she lived in Feroz's building until a few years back. I gave her the good news about you, and she was very happy you were finally getting married. But something she said disturbed me, beta. She said that Banu Dubash was a little strange. I got the feeling that Miss Smith didn't like her very much."

At the time, Sera had brushed off her mother's words as casually as flicking off an errant eyelash from her cheek. "All Parsis are strange and eccentric, Mummy." She laughed. "Nothing new there."

But her mother was not convinced. "Maybe we should make some discreet inquiries. You know Miss Smith is very fond of you. She wouldn't have said anything unless there was a reason."

"Mummy, please. Don't embarrass me. It's Feroz I'm marrying, not his mother. And Banu mummy has been so sweet to me. Just the other day she told me that from the first time she met me, she knew I was the one for Feroz."

Jehroo Sethna smiled. "You will learn, deekra. You never marry just a person. You always marry a family."

Now, as she sat shell-shocked by the scene that had occurred, her mother's words came back to Sera with the force of a speeding train. Please let Feroz come home early today, she pleaded. Please let me not have made a mistake by marrying him.

An hour later, Freddy Dubash knocked on her door and came in with a plate of scrambled eggs. "Sorry breakfast is so late, my dear," he said. But when she raised her teary eyes to him, he looked away.

"Sorry also about that—about what happened out there. And this menses business—I don't know what to say, my mother was like that too. Made life miserable for Banu. And now, to think she is acting like this also. Best if you stay out of her way during this time, deekra."

She nodded. She spent the rest of the day in her room, reading a novel and pacing. Time had never passed so slowly. At one point, she caught a glimpse of herself in the mirror and was shocked at the trapped, animal-like desperation she saw in her eyes. *A few months ago, I had a successful job, a good life, could come and go as I wished,* she thought. *And now I'm afraid to leave this room, all because of the idiotic beliefs of a superstitious old woman.* She blinked her eyes, as if the gesture would somehow alter this strange reality that she found herself encased in.

Her best friend, Aban, had argued with her when she'd told her she was giving up her job at Bombay House. "No, yaar, in this day and age, a woman should be independent," she'd advised. At that time, swept up in Feroz's declaration that he was more than capable of supporting his wife, she had put Aban's words down to a simple case of envy. But Aban was right, she now realized. Today, she missed the simple routine of deciding what outfit to wear to work, the grand feeling of being swept up in the tidal wave of office workers as they poured out of the morning trains, the camaraderie that came from participating in the jokes and gossip that circulated around the office like unofficial memos, the satisfaction of doing a job that earned her praise from Mr. Madan. Never in her life had she experienced the heavy, oppressive feeling that now weighed on her as she sat in her bedroom and waited for Feroz to come home.

Banu opened the door for Feroz that evening. "What's wrong, Mamma? Where's Sera?" Sera heard him ask.

His mother sighed. Then, in a loud voice, she replied, "Don't ask. Just don't ask. But if you wanted to kill your old mother, you should've just delivered me to the Tower of Silence on your wedding day. Then, I wouldn't have to die this slow-slow death. Being pecked by the vultures is better than this."

Sera waited for Feroz to burst out laughing at his mother's melodrama. She wanted him to set the old woman right with a few choice words, much as he straightened out his subordinates at work. Or, failing that, she wanted him to walk into their bedroom, scoop her up in his arms, and waltz out the front door with her while Banu stared after them openmouthed.

"Let's go in your room and talk, Mamma," Feroz said. "Tell me what's bothering you."

When he came into their room an hour later, his face was a mask. "Hi," he said. "What did you do today?"

Sera looked incredulous. What did I do today? she wanted to say. I wrote a new chapter to the Ramayana. I composed a symphony while eating lunch. I invented a device to shoot interfering mothers-in-law straight to the moon. "Nothing," she said.

He smiled weakly. "Mummy says there were some fireworks today. It's my fault. I forgot to warn you about not going near her while she prays."

It was his fake humility that set her tongue on fire. "Let's see. I'm not allowed in the living room when your mother is praying. I'm not to go in the dining room to eat. Or in the kitchen to cook. So basically, I'm to be a prisoner in this room while I'm having my period?"

"There's no need to be dramatic, Sera . . ."

She made a sound between a cough and a hiccup. "I am dramatic? I am? My dear Feroz, your mother would've won an acting award for her performance this morning."

"Keep your voice down, woman."

"Take me out."

"What?"

"Take me for a drive—Chowpatty, somewhere. Let's go eat some bhel. I need to get out of this house, get some fresh air."

"Sera, be reasonable. Mamma's cooked dinner for us. How do you think she will feel if—"

"You used to take me for bhel all the time, Feroz. Your mamma had dinner cooked then, too."

"That was different."

"Why? What was different?"

He stared at her speechlessly, and she saw the answer in his eyes: The difference was between wooing her, making sure that she chose him over every other man, and knowing that he had won her and there was no reason to impress her anymore. She turned away from him, afraid that he would see the disappointment in her eyes. Because she wasn't disappointed *by* him as much as she was disappointed *in* him, by his banality, by how, how *common* he had turned out to be.

He took her chin in his hand and turned her face toward him. "Look at me," he said. Then, urgently, "Sera, don't be like this. I told you, I'm sorry. Think of my position, please. I don't want Mamma to feel that I've turned against her just because I'm now married. I'll tell you what. On Friday, I'll come home from work a little early and we'll go out, just the two of us. Now, please. Just control yourself a bit."

Four days later she joined Banu in the kitchen after she had showered. "Okay, Mamma," she said, forcing a lightness into her voice. "All clear now. Let me prepare lunch today."

Banu looked at her and took one step back. "Did you wash your hair?" she said in a strangled voice.

Sera stared at her blankly. "My hair? No, I'm going to wash it tomorrow, so—"

"So you're still dirty, then. You can't be pure until you've washed from top to bottom. And in this state, you've walked into my clean kitchen."

Sera began to laugh. She laughed until tears were rolling down her cheeks. She heard sounds emerging from her mouth, sounds that she herself couldn't tell whether they were sobs or laughter. Out of the corner of her eye, she saw Gulab, her hands covered in flour, staring at her, a worried expression on her face. The look made Sera laugh even more. She thinks, I'm going mad, she thought. Oh my God, I *am* going mad. Somehow the thought made her laugh even more.

"Shameless." Banu's hand shot out and slapped her cheek. "Laughing at your old mother-in-law. What kind of home were you raised in that you have no shame at all?"

The slap did what it was intended to do. The hysterical laughter that had formed at Sera's mouth turned into bile. "You slapped me," she said in shock, rubbing her cheek with her index finger. "You actually hit me." Disbelief made her voice louder than she intended it to be.

"Liar," Banu said promptly. "I just shook you, to get you out of your hysteria." She turned to the servant. "Gulab, you are my witness. Did I touch this girl?"

Gulab looked from one to the other and then shook her head. "I wasn't looking, baiji," she said. "I was busy making my chappatis."

"See?" Banu said triumphantly. "Even Gulab says I'm innocent. Wicked girl, to accuse her mother-in-law of hitting her. We're not slum people, that we'd do such foul-bad deeds."

Sera backed away from Banu, afraid of what she was seeing in the older woman's eyes. Banu's eyes had grown big and shiny, and there was a mad look in them that chilled Sera. Then there was a smugness on Banu's face that alerted the younger woman to the fact that, whatever she said or did, Banu would win. That resistance was futile. Even while the outline of Banu's fingers lingered on Sera's burning cheek, she was convincing Sera that what she felt was a phantom pain, born from her imagination. Sera felt that she was up against something insidious; that Banu was assaulting both her body and her mind. So this is evil, she thought to herself. Before, she had always imagined that evil played out on a large canvas—wars, concentration camps, gas chambers, the partitioning of nations. Now, she realized that evil had a domestic side, and its very banality protected it from exposure. A quick look at Gulab's impassive face told her the servant had long ago learned what she was just learning.

"I'm sorry, Mamma," she stammered. "I . . . I'll go back to my room."

When Gulab came in with her lunch that day, she sent her away. "Eat, na, baby," Gulab said, stroking her back. "Why you're hurting yourself unnecessarily like this? In a family, a little tension-fension is to be expected."

Sera wanted to tell Gulab of the civil, gentle way in which she had been raised. I have never been struck even once by my parents, she wanted to say, and I have never had to sit locked up in my own house like I am now. But her pride rebelled against having to confide in a servant. "It's okay," she said. "I'm just not hungry."

At four o'clock, Banu left to go to the fire temple. "I may be long today, dear," she called to Freddy from the door. "I have to talk to Dastur Homjee about consecrating the kitchen, now that it has been fouled up by unclean hair."

A few minutes later, there was a knock on Sera's door. "May I come in?" Freddy said. Polly was not on his shoulder.

Freddy stood at the door and took in her disheveled hair, her red-rimmed eyes. "Come on," he said quietly. "Let's go in the living room and play some music."

His pleading face did not allow Sera to refuse. "Okay," she said. "Let me just freshen up a bit."

When she walked into the living room, the stereo was already on. "Moonlight Sonata," he said, looking up. "I thought something pensive and beautiful would be appropriate. We can leave this room and pretend we're in a place where moonlight dances on the water."

Sere smiled thinly and sat beside him on the couch. After a few minutes, she felt the music enter her body and make it relax. She closed her eyes so that she was lost in a dark and orange world, where nothing intruded except the sacred sound of a single piano. "When I was young, I used to think the piano was my favorite instrument," she said, modulating her voice so that it did not overpower the music. Her eyes were still shut, but she felt Freddy shift in place. "But now," she continued, "now, I love the deep sound of the cello. Somehow, it seems to be what most sounds like life—sad and sweet and lost. Lonely. I always think that if the heart could sing, it would sound like a cello. Do you think that's too stupid?"

Freddy made a choked sound that caused her eyes to fly open. She turned her head slightly to face him and realized with a start that the old man was crying. "Freddy pappa, what is wrong?" she cried. "Did I say something . . ."

He turned to face her, and she noticed for the first time how the skin under his trembling chin sagged, how his eyes were beginning to grow that thin film of age. With a shock, she noticed that he was folding his hands in a pleading gesture, and her eyes fell on the lines and age spots on his caramel-colored hands. "Forgive me," Freddy was saying, the tears running freely down his cheeks. "Forgive me, my dear, for not saying something earlier."

She looked at him in confusion. "No, Freddy pappa, it's okay," she said. "I just now only asked you about your favorite instrument—"

"I'm talking about her," he said harshly, pointing his head toward Banu's room. "When you first came here, when you were planning on marrying Feroz, I should've told you about her—

moods. How nasty-mean she can be at times. And about Feroz, too. But what to do, deekra? I liked you for the first moment I met you. Remember the first time you came to this wretched house? How we spoke of classical music and you played with Polly and all? Right then, I wanted you as a daughter. I wanted so badly for someone new to come into this home. Someone more like me. And you, from such a good family. Your father himself a music fan, cultured and intelligent. Bas, I decided to keep my mouth shut. Somehow I was thinking that once you came here, she would get better. But it is not to be, I see that now. Gulab told me what transpired this morning. Forgive me, deekra, for this sin I have committed."

Through the vortex of his words, Sera heard only one thing. "What about Feroz?" she said. "You said you should've warned me about Feroz."

Freddy sighed. "Oh, nothing. I mean, my dear, he's basically a good boy. But sometimes, he has a temper like his mother's. Or perhaps he is like *my* mother, I don't know. My mother was a terror, God bless her soul. Made Banu's life miserable, you know. I used to secretly call her Mrs. Chilipowder, when I was a boy."

"And . . . you said, Feroz is like her?"

Freddy stared at her intently, a pitying, sorrowful look in his eyes. "Feroz has a temper. With God's grace, you will never get to see it. When he was a boy, I used to talk to him for hours and hours about controlling his anger. But what to say, beta? Blood is blood. If something is in your blood, it is very difficult to get rid of it, no? I thought he would learn his lesson when he lost Gulnaz. But he is like his mother—speaks first and thinks later."

"Who's Gulnaz?" Sera asked, wanting and not wanting to know.

Freddy's eyes wandered the room before they came back to rest on Sera's tired face. Suddenly, he reached out and ran his fingers through her hair. "Don't look so sad, my dear," he murmured. "I feel like my talk is aging you ten-fifteen years." He sighed heavily and began again. "Gulnaz was his girlfriend. They were engaged and all. Her parents were from Jamshedpur, nice, simple people. Till today, I don't know exactly what all happened. But one Sunday, while we were eating lunch, Gulnaz showed up unexpectedly. Right in front of Banu and me, she took off her ring and threw it on the table. Threw it with such force, Sera, it bounced off the table and into Feroz's dhansak. Said that she couldn't take his temper-femper anymore and that she had heard enough stories about Banu to convince her she didn't want to come into this family. Banu immediately asked her what all she had heard, but Feroz interrupted his mother and told Gulnaz to stop insulting his family and get out of the house. Bas, that was it. If he ever saw her again, I don't know."

The record had been over for several minutes, and Freddy rose to change it. As Sera sat in shocked silence on the couch, he picked out another record. "How about this?" he said. "The New York Philharmonic, conducted by our very own Zubin Mehta."

She nodded absently, her head a junkyard of confusing, contradictory thoughts. Feroz with another woman. Someone he must've cared enough for to want to marry. Someone to whom he had given an engagement ring. So it was all a lie, his declarations about how no other woman had haunted him the way she, Sera, had; about how he had never known love until Sera had entered his life? What to make, then, of the relentless, eager way in which he had pursued her—was that merely the desperate, last-ditch effort of a middle-aged man who did not want to spend his life alone? Could any Parsi woman with reasonable good looks have caught his eye? Or had he picked her precisely because she was twenty-eight years old and was beginning to give off the scent of being desperate and unwanted? Had he sensed something about her, some vulnerability, some defect, some weakness, that he was able to exploit? Had she blinded herself deliberately to his flaws, had she allowed herself to be flattered by his obvious desire for her?

As if he could read her confused mind, Freddy said, "One thing I know, Sera. My Feroz loves you. Those looks that he gives you at dinner, the way he straightens with pride when you walk in the room—only a father can see those things. Nothing bad about Gulnaz, but he never looked like that with her."

She smiled her gratitude, but her eyes were cloudy with doubt. "Thank you, Freddy pappa. Feroz is a good—" She choked on her words. "Feroz is my life now," she cried, her voice ragged with emotion and desperation.

Banu came home that evening at six-thirty, carrying ashes from the fire temple in her embroidered handkerchief. Freddy and Sera were still sitting on the sofa, listening to music as the evening shadows fell across the room. Turning the front door key, Banu let herself in and immediately switched on the light, destroying the dark, intimate mood that they had created for themselves. They sat blinking in the sudden light, and Sera saw a slight narrowing of Banu's eyes as she took in the scene and sensed the obvious affection between Sera and her father-in-law. "My God, like a pair of gloomy owls you two look," she said, walking briskly into the room. "Or should I say a pair of lovebirds?" Seeing Freddy's outraged look, she added hastily, "In love with your Mozart-Fozart, of course."

Standing in front of Freddy, she took a small pinch of the ash and smeared it on his forehead. "Dastur Homjee sends his salaams to you," she said. "Says it's been two-three months since he's seen you in the agyari." She pinched the ashes in her handkerchief once again, and Sera prepared herself for receiving the holy ashes. But Banu relaxed her grip and turned away from her daughter-in-law, leaving Sera sitting on the couch, feeling foolish and snubbed.

"Come on, get up, you two," Banu said over her shoulder. "Turn off this sad funeral music. Feroz will be home soon."

Sera waited to ask Feroz about Gulnaz until they were alone a few days later. They had had dinner at a new Chinese restaurant at Colaba, and after dinner, Sera wanted to go to the Gateway of India. "Want to go have tea at Sea Lounge in the Taj?" Feroz asked promptly.

"No, I was thinking it would be nice just to take an evening stroll near the water," she said. "Get some fresh air."

"Okay," he said, giving her elbow a squeeze. "Whatever you say, my dear."

After the tensions of the last few days, it felt wonderful to be alone with Feroz in a public place. Sera felt closer to him than she had all week, as they strolled along Apollo Bunder in a companionable silence. So she was surprised and even dismayed to hear herself ask, "Why didn't you tell me about Gulnaz?"

He tensed. "Who told you? Mamma?" he asked.

She wavered. "Um, actually, it was your daddy."

He exhaled harshly. "I should've known. Mr. Bigmouth himself."

She felt compelled to defend Freddy. "Pappa didn't mean anything bad. Anyway, this was something you should've told me. Why didn't you?"

He stopped abruptly, so that a teenage couple walking in the opposite direction had to separate and go around both of them. The boy glared at Feroz as he passed by. "What rudeness, yaar," he muttered. Feroz ignored him. When he turned toward Sera, his face was blank and expressionless. "I didn't tell you, my dear," he said, spitting each word out as if they were stuck between his teeth, "because frankly, it's none of your business."

She felt a pain in her stomach, as if his contempt had reached her like a punch. "I'm your wife," she said weakly.

"Correct. You're my wife. Now. Today. You weren't my wife

then. And what I did then was my business. Nothing to do with you, okay?"

She gazed out at the dark sea, as big and fathomless as the grief that rose in waves in her. She blinked back her tears, trying to reason with herself, asking herself if he was right, if somehow she had violated some unspoken rules of marital etiquette. Was it really not her business that Feroz had been in love with someone else before he had met her? Was it not her place to ask?

Then she remembered how he had yelled at her the night before when she had stepped into the bathroom while he was brushing his teeth; how he always turned off the light when he changed into his pajamas. He was cordoning off his past just as he cordoned off his body to her, she realized.

"Come on, let's go," he said brusquely. "It's getting late."

The thought of entering that house again, of having Banu's restless eyes following her every move, made her voice quiver with intensity. "Tomorrow's Saturday. Please, I need to walk more. I'm not ready to go yet."

He sighed impatiently. "Okay, I've been at work all day already, but if the wife wants to walk, we will walk."

Just then she saw a Muslim couple coming toward them. The man's clean-shaven face was young and golden under the streetlights. Sera couldn't see the woman's face because she was wearing a black burqua, which covered her from head to toe so that only her eyes were visible from behind the net. Normally, the sight would've repulsed her. She would've thought uncharitable thoughts about the husband who allowed his wife to walk around in this prison of cloth, who ignored statistics that showed a higher prevalence of TB rates among women who kept their faces covered all day long. But now, she noticed that the veiled woman's index finger protruded out of the black robe and that it was linked to her husband's finger. Thus they walked, their fingers touching in a poignant connection that proved the fallacy of the veil and suggested something deeper and more eternal than human conventions.

The sight tore at Sera's heart and filled her with a sudden, hot envy. "Feroz," she said, wanting to explain everything to him— how certain notes of the Moonlight Sonata shredded her heart like wind inside a paper bag; how her soul felt as endless and deep as the sea churning on their left; how the sight of the young Muslim couple filled her with an emotion that was equal parts joy and sadness; and above all, how she wanted a marriage that was different from the dead sea of marriages she saw all around her, how she wanted something finer, deeper, a marriage made out of silk and velvet instead of coarse cloth, a marriage made of clouds and stardust and red earth and ocean foam and moonlight and sonatas and books and art galleries and passion and kindness and sorrow and ecstasy and of fingers touching from under a burqua. She turned to him, feeling feverish with desire. "Feroz," she said again. "I . . . I really love you."

Two things happened then. Feroz turned to her, his eyes warm and moist. "I love you, also, Sera," he said, his voice deep with emotion. "I'm sorry for acting like such an idiot." And even as she was grateful for his words, she was aware of a feeling of letdown, of having betrayed herself. She knew that she had taken the easy way out, that she had let the steam escape from the boiling pot of her emotions. What she had meant to say was not "I love you" at all. What she had wanted to say was "I love life," a self-declaration as naked and real and authentic as an X-ray. And then, a door slammed shut somewhere in the inner recesses of Sera's mind: If she had said what she really intended to say, she knew Feroz would not have understood. A lonely feeling swept over her like an icy wind, and she shivered.

"Are you cold?" he said immediately, his voice solicitous. "Come on, let's go to the Taj and get you a hot cuppa tea."

As he took her hand to cross the street, she hated herself for the duplicitous, betraying thoughts flapping around her mind like bats. Why should you not say "I love you" to Feroz? She fought with herself. After all, it is true, no? Even if that's not what you meant to say at exactly that moment, it's true, right? But still, the cold feeling of self-betrayal lingered.

The waiter seated them at the table, and Sera gazed out of the picture windows at the dark waters of the Arabian Sea. "I think I'll have beer instead of tea, janu," she said.

"A Kingfisher and a sherry," Feroz ordered. "And bring a bowl of cashews along."

8

Riding next to Viraf in his air-conditioned car, Bhima smiles. She treasures this Saturday morning ritual with him. She is grateful at not having to ride to the bazaar in the crowded, rickety BEST buses. She is getting too old to handle the inevitable rushing that occurs when one of the red buses appears at the stop. Just last week, Serabai had told her the story of one of her distant relatives, a bony woman of sixty-eight, who had broken her wrist when she was knocked aside by the frenzied crowd trying to board the bus. "I swear they target Parsis," Sera had muttered. "Everybody knows our bones are as brittle as Britannia glucose biscuits."

In the old days, at least the women were spared the elbowing and jostling that occurred each time a bus appeared like a mythical beast at the stop. But in today's Bombay, it was everybody for himself, and the frail, the weak, the young, and the old entered the overflowing buses at their own peril. Bhima felt as if she barely recognized the city anymore—something snarling and mean and cruel had been unleashed in it. Bhima could see the signs of this new meanness everywhere: slum children tied firecrackers to the tails of the stray dogs and then laughed and clapped with glee as the poor animals ran around in circles, going mad with fear. Affluent college students went berserk if a five-year-old beggar child smudged the windows of their gleaming BMWs and Hondas. Every day Serabai would read the newspaper and tell Bhima about some latest horror—a union organizer being bludgeoned to death for daring to urge factory workers to agitate for a two-rupee wage raise; a politician's son being found not guilty after running over three slum children on his way to a party; an elderly Parsi couple being murdered in their beds by a servant who had worked for them for forty years; young Hindu nationalists writing congratulatory notes in their own blood to celebrate India's successful test of a nuclear weapon. It was as if the city was mad with greed and hunger; power and impotence; wealth and poverty.

Bhima herself could feel the meanness course like sludge through her own veins as she waited for a bus. When the red beast arrived in a cloud of smog, she could feel her heart pounding as she eyed her fellow passengers, trying to assess who looked weak and vulnerable, and who could be elbowed out of her way. As soon as the bus rolled in, the queue disintegrated into a mob. Others came running from all directions, trying to leap onto the platform of the bus before it even came to a stop. Once, an old man with one foot on the deck and the other still on the ground was dragged half a block by the moving bus, until the cries of the other passengers alerted the conductor to stop. Bhima noticed the man's legs were shaking so hard that it was impossible for him to board. The conductor eyed the man impatiently from his imperial perch. "Coming or not?" he asked, but the poor old man merely stood there panting. The conducted clicked his teeth and rang the bell again. The bus rolled on, leaving the passenger in the middle of the road, discarded like a package with no address on it.

"Is the air-conditioning too strong?" Viraf asks, and although Bhima is slightly cold, she shakes her head no. Viraf baba gets hot easily, she knows.

Bhima looks out of the window at the streets flitting by. The city looks so much nicer out of the tinted glass of an air-conditioned car, she thinks. Even the exhaust fumes of the nearby buses and lorries are powerless to burn her eyes and throat, and she feels as if she has defeated her old nemesis, the sun. Better to be slightly cold than to feel the sun attacking her eyes and skin.

Viraf has the stereo on, some English music Bhima does not understand or like. She wonders why he always plays English songs, never the Hindi film music that is so popular in her basti. She eyes the man sitting next to her in his white cricket clothes, and he feels as alien to her as the white-skinned ferangas she sees when she and Serabai go shopping at Colaba. Serabai had once explained to her why these people had yellow hair and skin the color of a hospital wall—about how something was missing from their bodies and how they had to come to warm places like Bombay to darken their skin. She felt sorry for them then and, seeing their long hair and shabby clothes, wanted to give them some money, but Sera laughed at that and said she needn't pity them, they actually were very proud of their white skin. How can you be proud if something is missing from your body? Bhima wanted to ask, but before she could, Sera said that they didn't need money from her and that they came from places far richer than she could imagine. Now Bhima was sure that Sera was lying to her because one look at their dirty hair, faded shirts, and torn blue pants, and any fool could see that these untidy, colorless people were very poor.

Viraf is looking at her curiously. "Did you hear anything I just said?" he asks.

She jumps guiltily. "Oh, Viraf baba. Forgive me. I was just—"

"That's okay." He laughs. "I was just inquiring about Maya."

She flushes, reluctant to discuss Maya's situation with a man, even if that man is Viraf. But before she can say anything, he sails to her rescue. "Listen, Bhima," he says awkwardly. "This is not a pleasant business, I know. But it must be dealt with. Listen, I have a friend who is a doctor. After I get home from the match today, I

was going to call him to get a name of a doctor who performs—
that is, one who is—you know, someone who can help Maya get rid
of the baby. It's time to move on this, no?"

Instead of the gratitude she knows she ought to feel, Bhima is
shocked to feel a deep resentment at Viraf's words. Easy for him to
talk about getting rid of Maya's baby, she thinks. After all, he and
Dinaz baby are going to have a child of their own, a child who will
never know what it is to have adults plot its death. A child who will
be welcomed into the world. Who will never cause his parents
shame or dishonor. She feels a moment's blinding fury that is so
large it encompasses Maya, Dinaz, and Viraf. All these young people, all these children about to be born. She is tired of it all—tired
of this endless cycle of death and birth, tired of investing any hope
in the next generation, tired and frightened of finding more human
beings to love, knowing full well that every person she loves will
someday wound her, hurt her, break her heart with their deceit,
their treachery, their fallibility, their sheer humanity. Bhima feels
dried out, scooped out, as hollow and wrinkled as a walnut shell.
She has nothing left to give, no love left to spare. For this reason,
she refuses to feed a morsel of leftover food to the stray dogs in the
slum colony, who wag their tails and sigh expectantly each time she
steps out of her hut. She cannot stand the sight of their matted,
mangled, crippled bodies, their heartbreaking eagerness, the
hunger for love in their eyes.

Gopal. Their two children, Amit and Pooja. And later, her son-
in-law, Raju. She had loved them all, and one by one, they had all
left her, left deliberately or left because they lost their battle with
death. But the end result was the same—she was left behind while
the others sailed on to what Bhima imagined were greener pastures.

She blinks her eyes and forces herself back to the present. She is
ashamed of her envy at Dinaz and Viraf's good fortune. Dinaz has
grown up before Bhima's eyes, and she still remembers what a won-

derful child Dinaz was, full of hugs and laughter. A miracle that a child like that could blossom under the shadow cast by her dark mountain of a father. Once she started earning her own paycheck, Dinaz was forever slipping a ten or a twenty-rupee note into Bhima's hand. And Viraf baba—so sunny, so full of mischief and light. To punish herself for her uncharitable thoughts, Bhima digs her right thumb into the palm of her left hand until the pain makes her wince.

"You're correct, Viraf baba," she says numbly. "I was saying the same thing to Maya last evening, only."

Viraf flashes her a quick look. His hand flutters in the space between them as if he wants to comfort her, but then it comes to rest on the steering wheel. "I'll talk to my friend today," he says quietly.

When he drops her off at the market, she notices that he waits until he sees she has safely crossed the street. Bhima smiles to herself. Such a thoughtful boy, that Viraf baba. Some of his gestures remind her of Amit—the same courteousness, the same solicitousness. Amit. Her only son. Where was Amit now? Did he ever think of his mother, long for her, miss her, the way she did him?

Lost in her thoughts, she almost runs into the wooden hathgadi parked in the middle of the sidewalk. She curses as the long wooden handle of the cart digs into her left hip, sending a bolt of pain through her bony thigh. A man in his early twenties is sprawled out on the flat cart, fast asleep. Bhima marvels at how he can sleep through the noise of the crowd that jostles around them. Ever since Maya's pregnancy, Bhima's sleep patterns have gotten so disturbed, even the chattering of the mice that scuttle around their hut can keep her awake. As Bhima rubs her hip and debates whether to shake awake the sleeping youth and ask him to move his hathgadi, she notices the bulge under his loose white pajama bottom. "Saala badmaash," she mutters to herself, as she quickly averts her eyes. "Drunken lout, lying here in the open as if he owns the city. Shameless, shameless people."

A familiar voice pierces her angry thoughts. "Arre, mausi, over here," the voice calls. "I've been saving my best-of-best vegetables for you only."

Bhima waves dismissively. "I'll be over," she yells back. "But first I have to find that good-for-nothing Rajeev."

"He was here one-two minutes ago, only. Was looking for you, mausi."

As if on cue, Rajeev appears, balancing the huge wicker basket on his head. He is a tall, stooped man of about fifty, with a long, handlebar mustache. He reminds Bhima of the coolies from Rajasthan who used to populate Victoria Terminus Station in the old days, when she and Gopal used to take the train to his ancestral village. Although Gopal insisted on carrying their trunks, the coolies would follow them like a pack of hungry dogs, begging for a chance to carry their bags for them, lowering their asking price with every step that Bhima and Gopal took.

"Where were you?" Bhima scolds Rajeev in her usual greeting. "You think I have time to waste like you? I'm in a hurry."

"Ae, Bhima mausi, slow down, slow down," Rajeev says with an appeasing smile that shows the red marks of the paan he has freshly placed in his mouth. "Why for you hurry so much? Your bai is nice—she doesn't worry if you are a few minutes early or late."

But Bhima is already walking toward the vegetable vendor who had earlier called her name. On her way there, she must walk past Parvati, the old woman who comes to the market every morning and stays until she sells her total inventory of six tiny, shriveled cauliflowers. The frail old woman sits on the footpath on a filthy cotton sheet, calling out for customers in her thin, nasal voice. Ever since Bhima has known Parvati, the old woman has had a large growth the size of an orange on her throat. Once, when Parvati had fallen asleep on the footpath, Bhima happened to walk by and noticed the old woman absently fingering the lump in her sleep.

As she does every Saturday, Bhima averts her head. The sight of Parvati and her sorry-looking vegetables fills her with unbearable sadness. She knows from the gossip of the other vendors that Parvati has no husband or children. She also knows that the others help the old woman, sending her home each evening with the overripe fruit and the spoiled vegetables they are unable to sell. Still, Bhima wonders how the woman can possibly stay alive on such a meager income. And why does Parvati not increase her stock? Why does she not get better quality cauliflowers, so that she, Bhima, can buy some from her? As it is, her heads of cauliflower are so small and shriveled that even if Bhima bought her entire supply of six, it would not be enough to feed the Dubash family. Even as she asks the question, Bhima knows the answer—the old woman is so hand-to-mouth that she never makes enough profit to buy more supplies.

When Amit and Pooja were young, Gopal and she used to take them to the seaside every Saturday. There, she would insist on buying the children the animal-shaped balloons sold by the balloon-walla, a tall, gaunt Pathan from Afghanistan. Something about the man's quiet dignity, the careful, nonshowy way in which he would twist the balloons into different shapes, broke Bhima's heart. When the other balloonwallas tried to seduce the children with their flashy, nimble contortions, their agile fingers twisting the rubber into elephants and dogs, she would shoo them away and wait for the Pathan to arrive. As he worked on his creations, a slight, far-away smile on his face, she wanted to ask the old man questions—why he had left his rugged homeland, whose terrain seemed carved onto his creased, wind-battered face; whether it was hard to get used to the city's noisy and polluted streets; whether he missed the sweet mountain air of his homeland. Above all, she wanted to find out how he could make ends meet merely by selling these red and white pieces of rubber and air. The income didn't seem enough to support one tall, skinny Pathan, let alone a family. But shyness, awkwardness made her hold her tongue, so that the greatest mystery of Bombay—how an entire breed of Bombayites (such as the balloonwallas and the earwax removers and the rag collectors) clung to the promise of this great metropolis by the skins of their teeth, how they managed to feed themselves despite their pathetic jobs—that mystery remained unsolved for her.

Now Bhima steps over a castaway banana peel and stops before her favorite vegetable vendor, Rajeev a few steps behind her. The man gets down on his haunches and lowers the wicker basket from his head and onto the sidewalk. Ignoring the vegetable vendor's cries of "Ae, mausi, I've already taken out the best vegetables for you," Bhima begins to pick through the colorful, beautifully arranged selection before her. She buys six kilos of ladies fingers, carefully picking out the small, tender pieces. She looks over the purple brinjals and screws up her nose at the bruises on them until the vendor, grumbling under her breath, reaches behind her and brings out four gleaming ones. She holds the pods of garlic in her hand, trying to find the largest ones. She fingers the cilantro, breaking off the dead leaves from a bunch. She has the woman chop off a new slice of red pumpkin for her because the cut piece has flies sitting on it. As the vendor weighs the vegetables on her old metal scale—the hexagonal weights on one side, the produce on the other, and places them into the pink plastic bags, Rajeev picks up the bags and tosses them into his basket.

Bhima gets up from her haunches and removes a note from the end of her sari. She waits for her change, but the woman stares back at her. "This is the right amount, mausi," she says finally. "I gave you a good-good price today. Anyone else I would've charged extra. Such freshum-fresh produce you are getting."

Any other Saturday Bhima would've argued, would've stood her ground until she got some money back from the woman. After

all, bargaining is a time-honored tradition at this bazaar. Also, unlike most of the servants who shop for their mistresses, Bhima tries
never to waste a paisa of Serabai's money. To Bhima, it is a matter
of trust. Serabai trusts her enough to send her grocery shopping on
her own. So it is right to protect Serabai's finances as zealously as
she would if she were spending her own money.

But today she is tired and has other things on her mind. Also,
her own grief has made her more alert to the misery of others. For
the first time, Bhima notices the dark circles around the woman's
eyes, the premature traces of gray in her hair, the small hole in the
sleeve of her sari blouse. Today, she can't think of this woman as
her adversary, someone with whom she must engage in a battle of
wits. The few rupees that she will save by arguing with her suddenly seem meaningless. "Okay," she says abruptly. Then, to Rajeev, "Let's go. I need some potatoes and onions." As she leaves, she
feels the vendor's puzzled stare behind her.

She is not nearly as nice to the man who sells her the potatoes
and onions. He is a short, bespectacled baniya in a small, narrow
shop, and he treats her with less respect than the other vendors do.
And ever since she caught him placing his hand on the scale to
weigh it down, she has mistrusted him. If Bhima had things her
way, she would never patronize his shop, but Serabai likes the
man's produce and insists that Bhima shop there. So Bhima now
eyes him grumpily. "Five kilos of potatoes," she says curtly. "And
make sure none of them are rotten. Last week, two of them were
so bad we couldn't use them."

Instead of looking apologetic, the shopkeeper sneers. "Everything in Mumbai is rotten," he says loudly. "The air is rotten, the
politicians are rotten, the public transportation system is rotten.
Why should a few of my poor potatoes not be rotten?" He snickers, showing brown-stained teeth. The sickly-looking teenage boy
with the long, thin arms who works in his shop shakes his head in

admiration. "Well said, boss, well said," he says, flinging Bhima a hostile look.

"You hear this?" Bhima says to Rajeev, loud enough for the shopkeeper to hear. "Such badmaashi you have to put up with, even when you spend your hard-earned money. I've a good mind to take my business elsewhere."

The shopkeeper suddenly looks nasty. "It's not your money you're spending, it's your mistress's," he says. "You could never afford my wares and my prices, you old woman. Now stop wasting my time."

Bhima flinches from the truth of the man's words. But before she can react, Rajeev has taken a menacing step toward the shopkeeper. "You watch your tongue, you," he says. "Lots of shops here that sell potatoes and onions. I can make sure not one of my customers steps foot in your shop again."

Suddenly, Bhima wants nothing more than to be done with this. She still has to go to the fish market, and she shudders at the thought of wading through the smelly, dirty, slippery, wet floor, making sure that a fin or a fish scale does not get in between her foot and one of her rubber chappals. She hates the din of the indoor market, the shrill, insistent cries of the fishmongers as they try to lure customers to their stalls. She hates the dumb, glassy expressions on the faces of the dead, defeated fish and the slippery feel of the coins when the vendor hands her the change. While Rajeev and the shopkeeper are growling at each other, she takes the money out of her sari and puts it on top of the stacked potatoes. "Here," she says hurriedly. "Here's your payment. Now give me my change and let me go."

She watches as Rajeev places the bags into his basket. Usually, the teenage helper assists Rajeev as he squats on the ground to lift the basket on his head, but today, the boy folds his hands and watches impassively as Rajeev struggles to his feet. The basket is filling up now, and Rajeev staggers for a moment under its weight before he steadies himself. Bhima catches his faltering step, and pity slashes through her chest. She looks away, angry at herself for her uncharacteristic sentimentality. She has enough problems of her own without taking on the world's problems, without feeling the pain of every vegetable vendor and transporter she meets. Gopal always used to tell her that her heart was too soft, that the world would take advantage of that softness, and hadn't time proven her husband a genius? Hadn't he been absolutely right? And the fact that Gopal himself had been the one to leak the softness out of her heart and transfuse it with a cold, cementlike hardness, well, that had just been the final irony.

"Where to next, mausi?" Rajeev asks, and she points toward the fish market.

After they are done shopping, Rajeev sets the filled basket by her feet and says he will go find them a cab. This is their weekly ritual, but today the memory of Rajeev's coming to her defense still plays on Bhima. "Chalo," she says. "Before you do that, let us get a hot cup of tea. You have a full load to carry today."

Rajeev looks at her curiously but nods. "That will be fine, mausi. Many thanks."

They stand outside a small café and sip the light brown liquid from the short glasses. The owner, a portly man with a big belly, sits at the entrance of the café, placing spiced potatoes rolled in batter into a huge wok with oil bubbling in it. The smell of the battatawadas makes Bhima's mouth water. She thinks about how much of Serabai's money she will have left over after she pays for the cab and quickly calculates that she can afford to treat herself and Rajeev to a snack. "Two battatawadas in bread, chutney on the side," she calls out to the café owner, and when the snack is served to her on a piece of newspaper, she wordlessly hands a sandwich over to Rajeev. The basket carrier looks delighted. "Many thanks," he says and wolfs his meal down. Bhima wants to buy him a second sandwich, but she is excruciatingly aware of the fact that this is Serabai's money she is squandering. Instead, she forces herself to stop eating her sandwich and pretend as if she is full. "These battatawadas are big," she says. "I can't finish it. You want this, Rajeev?" The sandwich is out of her hands before the words are out of her mouth.

In the taxi, Rajeev rides up front with the driver while she sits in the backseat with the basket propped next to her. The meal has put Rajeev in a good mood, and he wants to talk, turning around to make frequent comments to her. But she is not in a talkative mood, and pretty soon Rajeev faces the front and strikes up a conversation with the cabdriver instead. Under the protective shield of the two male voices, Bhima is free to get lost in her thoughts, and she stares out the window. She leans over the basket and rolls up the right window, to guard herself from the exhaust fumes of the bus in the next lane. She had rolled up the left one as soon as she entered the cab. The shut windows make the vehicle unbearably hot, but even the heat is preferable to the violent convulsions her lungs have started going into when assaulted by exhaust. She misses the air-conditioning of Viraf's car, misses gazing out on the outside world while her skin is kissed by its sweet, sharp coolness.

Bombay slips past her window, quietly and swiftly, much as most of her life has slipped by her.

9

Sera wakes up with a groan. She peers at the alarm clock and feels a rush of relief when she sees that the dial reads 4:00 A.M. She can sleep for at least another hour. She feels a moment's resentment at having to get up so early this morning. In a few hours, she will be picking Bhima and Maya up at the bus stop near their home. The plan is for Bhima to continue on her way to work while she, Sera, takes Maya to the abortion doctor. Three days ago, she had been flattered when Bhima told her that Maya had requested Sera accompany her to the doctor. Now, lying awake, staring at the darkness of the room, Sera feels irritation. She had not bargained for all this when she volunteered to pay for Maya's college education. Paying Maya's fees every term is one thing; accompanying the girl to a doctor who will flush out her illegitimate baby is quite another.

But you're not doing this for Maya, she reminds herself. You're doing this for old Bhima. The thought is immediately accompanied by a dull ache below her shoulder. It is a phantom pain, she knows, a psychosomatic ache, but still she feels the hurt. After all, it has been many years since the blow that made her arm swell and ache for weeks. On the other hand, who knows? Perhaps the body has its own memory system, like the invisible meridian lines those Chinese acupuncturists always talk about. Perhaps the body is unforgiving, perhaps every cell, every muscle and fragment of bone remembers each and every assault and attack. Maybe the pain of memory is encoded into our bone marrow and each remembered grievance swims in our bloodstream like a hard, black pebble. After all, the body, like God, moves in mysterious ways.

From the time she was in her teens, Sera has been fascinated by this paradox—how a body that we occupy, that we have worn like a coat from the moment of our birth—from before birth, even—is still a stranger to us. After all, almost everything we do in our lives is for the well-being of the body: we bathe daily, polish our teeth, groom our hair and fingernails; we work miserable jobs in order to feed and clothe it; we go to great lengths to protect it from pain and violence and harm. And yet the body remains a mystery, a book that we have never read. Sera plays with this irony, toys with it as if it were a puzzle: How, despite our lifelong preoccupation with our bodies, we have never met face-to-face with our kidneys, how we wouldn't recognize our own liver in a row of livers, how we have never seen our own heart or brain. We know more about the depths of the ocean, are more acquainted with the far corners of outer space than with our own organs and muscles and bones. So perhaps there are no phantom pains after all; perhaps all pain is real; perhaps each long-ago blow lives on into eternity in some different permutation and shape; perhaps the body is this hypersensitive, revengeful entity, a ledger book, a warehouse of remembered slights and cruelties.

But if this is true, surely the body also remembers each kindness, each kiss, each act of compassion? Surely this is our salvation, our only hope—that joy and love are also woven into the fabric of the body, into each sinewy muscle, into the core of each pulsating cell?

Out of the blue fog of time, Sera remembers the blow and the balm; the tormentor and the healer: Feroz and Bhima.

She and Feroz had moved out of Banu's flat and into a home of their own by then. By the time the first blow landed, she had already forgotten how the fight began. All she could focus on was Feroz's face—the vein throbbing angrily in his forehead, his eyes bulging in fury, his skin flushed a rusty brown. And then, out of the corner of her eye, she saw the brass candleholder in his hand and the fast, furious strokes in the air before it came crashing down on her arm, the arm that she had lifted in an effort to protect herself from the gust of his anger. A sharp, bitter pain flooded her body, and a high-pitched animal scream had escaped her lips before she forced her mouth shut. She collapsed on the side of the bed, holding her bruised arm, but still Feroz would not stop, raining blows on her back, this time with his bare hands. She thought she would pass out from the pain, but the beating ended as suddenly as it had begun, as if someone had turned off the switch that had made his hands perform their violent deed.

In the past, after the torrential downpour of his anger had ceased, he would look at her uncomprehendingly. Then, the tears and the apologies and the self-recrimination would come. He would sob and beg her forgiveness; he would slap himself hard on his cheeks or hit himself behind the head. But today, Feroz simply stood looking at her, and when she finally managed to look up at him and saw his face through the distorting lens of her tears, the look of revulsion made her heart stop. He was staring at her as if he loathed her, as if the very sight of her crumpled, bruised body made him sick. "Today you went too far," he hissed. "Today, you deserve what you got. Your damn pride, your arrogance—you're a ballbuster, not a woman at all, you know that?"

They had been married for enough years for Sera to know better than to answer him. Feroz was like a man possessed when he was in one of his black moods, and the slightest provocation could make the furies within him whirl and twirl even faster, like a gathering dust cloud. So she looked away, thankful that Dinaz was at the park with Bhima, that her child was protected from having to over-hear the sounds of her parents' breaking marriage. And while she was counting her blessings, she should probably be grateful for the fact that she had the kind of skin that healed quickly, so that she was spared the humiliation of being one of those women who wore the signs of their husbands' violence on their bodies like a window dis-play for all the world to see.

But this time, the bruises didn't heal. Three days later, her arm was still black and blue, and so swollen she could barely lift it over her head to wear her sadra each morning. Even tying her kasti, the traditional Parsi sacred thread that was woven with seventy-two strands of wool and worn around the waist, caused her arm to ache. There was also the bruise on her upper lip, where she had hit the bed as she fell to her knees. But at the moment, she didn't care. She wanted to stay in bed all day long, flooding her mind with numbness, the way her body was being flooded with pain. Each morning she got up long enough send Dinaz off to her nursery school class before getting into bed again. There she stayed, until it was time for Dinaz to come home.

The day after the beating, Feroz had come into the bedroom and announced that he was leaving for Pune on a business trip. She knew he had made up the trip as a way of getting out of the house, but she didn't mind. She was thankful to have him gone. That way, there was nobody to look at her contemptuously when she went back to bed by 9:00 A.M.; there was nobody to tell her to tell her to snap out of it or else she would end up like one of those old boodhi Grant Road Parsi women if she wasn't careful; no one to criticize the way she looked or walked or smelled; no one to claim that the bruises on her body were fake, that she was deliberately clinging to them as a way to make him look bad. Still, despite her relief at hav-ing the house to herself, her heart leapt each time the telephone rang or the postman knocked on the door. She kept waiting for Feroz to apologize by mail or phone, to acknowledge her pain, to inquire about her bruised body. But when he called each night, it was only to say good night to Dinaz. This time, there would be no apology. The usual pattern of unleashed violence, followed by the flood of tears, apologies, sweet talk, kisses, and promises, would not occur this time. This time, there was simply the drought of silence and distance. She felt acutely the loss of their usual cycle of fighting and making up. It was as if another phase of their marriage had ended, and now Sera didn't even have the sweetness of being wooed back to look forward to. Feroz's indifference hurt as much as the bruises on her arm did.

On the fourth day, Bhima came to work holding a small bundle. Sera eyed it disinterestedly when she opened the door to let Bhima in and returned to her room. A little while later, Bhima came into her bedroom, holding a plate with two slices of toast. "Come on, bai, get up," she said. "You'll get more sick, staying in this bed. Anyway, today Bhima is going to fix you. All these dark spots on your arms will be gone by the time the sun sets, I promise."

Sera smiled weakly. She was too tired to pay Bhima much mind. Even when she heard her pounding something in the kitchen, Sera didn't pay it much attention. But she looked up when Bhima brought the Primus stove into the bedroom. "Bhima, what are you doing with that thing in here?" she cried.

"Shh, shh. Bai, you just let me do what I'm doing. This is my Gopal's mother's recipe, from his village. One time, when we were visiting his old mother, one of the village girls was raped and beaten by a gang of goondas. When we went to see her, bai, this poor girl was so discolored, you couldn't tell what color her skin was. Even doctorsahib didn't know what to do with her. My mother-in-law went back home and returned with these dried leaves and some hot oil and applied them all over this girl's body.

Believe or don't believe, by the next morning, the girl had skin like a newborn's."

Sera wanted to protest, but she was too tired. So she lay back and watched while Bhima took a pinch of the dark brown powder and mixed it in the oil. She turned the stove onto its lowest setting and warmed the mixture for a few seconds. Then she poured the oil on her rough, callused hands and began to rub Sera's arms.

Sera recoiled. Bhima had never touched her before. She tried to muster up some resistance but found that she couldn't come up with one good reason for why Bhima's hands should not touch her. The oil stung Sera into awakeness. Although Bhima's thin but strong hands were only massaging her arm, Sera felt her whole body sigh. She felt life beginning to stir in her veins and couldn't tell if this new, welcome feeling was from the oil or the simple comfort of having another human being touch her in friendliness and caring. Even at the sweetest moment of lovemaking with Feroz, it never felt as generous, as selfless, as this massage did. After all, lovemaking always came with strings attached—the needs of the other had to be met, so that even when Feroz was concentrating on giving her pleasure, she was always aware of his own throbbing body, of how closely he was watching her, of how he waited to see his own performance reflected in her response to it. When you got right down to it, sex was ultimately a selfish act, the expectations of one body intrinsically woven into the needs of the other. But here, with Bhima, there was none of that. Here, she could just listen to the sound of her body uncoiling, watch as the sting and venom left the bruises on her flesh, until they appeared as harmless as black butterflies on her arm.

She almost groaned in frustration when Bhima stopped for a second to make more of the mixture. Now Bhima was gently turning her on her stomach and undoing the back buttons of her dress.

"Poor Serabai," she was murmuring. "So many burdens this poor body is carrying. So much unhappiness. Give it up to the devil, give it up, don't carry this around." While her hands circled Sera's smooth back—plucking at the stringy muscles, pounding on the painful spots, her fingers moving up and down the vertebrae like piano keys, Bhima kept talking to her in words and languages Sera barely understood. As her body relaxed under Bhima's wise hands, Sera felt herself receding, moving backwards in time, so that for a moment she was a young bride sitting astride her new husband's lap as he rocked her back and forth in a sexual rhythm, and then in the next moment, she was a young child on her mother's knee, being rocked to sleep after a hot, restless night, and then she was older and younger than even that—she was a small fish floating around in a warm world of darkness and fluids, a being as formless and translucent and liquidy as her bones felt right now. And still Bhima was talking to her, her words flying out of her mouth as fast as sparrows at dusk, her tongue working as fast as her hands were, so everything was a blur of words and rhythm; of speech and motion. And Sera was fading now, caught in the undertow of an ancient, primal memory, drowning in a pool of sensation and feeling, old hurts and fresh wounds being exorcised from her body, leaving her feeling as bright and new as the day she was born. Paradoxically, as the hurt left her body, she began to weep, as if now that pain had stopped occupying her body, there was at last room for tears. The tears streamed down her face and were caught by the pillow, but if Bhima noticed the heaving of her back, she did not comment on it. Bhima appeared to be in a trance herself; the strange murmurings continued over Sera's soundless weeping, a fact that Sera was grateful for.

The last thing she remembered before she fell asleep was the smell of the oil in the room. It reminded Sera of the smell of her grandmother's apartment, and the thought of her grandmother, a stout, gruff woman with a large, pillowlike bosom, to which she would press her granddaughter's head, made Sera smile.

When she woke up a few hours later, the bruises on her arm had shrunk. If they had originally looked like the map of the world, now they were down to the size of the map of Brazil. Any other time she would've been surprised, but after the dreamy strangeness of the massage from Bhima, anything seemed possible. She rose from the bed, slid her feet into her rubber slippers, and walked into the kitchen. Suddenly, she felt unaccountably shy in front of the woman who was leaning over the sink, scrubbing dishes with the same intensity with which she had rubbed her back a few hours ago. She wanted to thank Bhima for her kindness, wanted to explain to her how hot and wonderful life felt when it trickled back into one's veins, wanted to tell her about how cold her heart had felt after this last encounter with Feroz and how Bhima had warmed it again, as if she had held her cold, gray heart between her brown hands and rubbed it until the blood came rushing back into it. But a net of shyness fell over Sera as Bhima looked up from the dishes and at her. She had long accepted that Bhima was the only person who knew that Feroz's fists occasionally flew like black vultures over the desert of her body, that Bhima knew more about the strangeness of her marriage than any friend or family member. But now, Sera felt as if Bhima had an eyeglass to her soul; that she had somehow penetrated her body deeper than Feroz ever had. "Better?" Bhima asked, unsmilingly.

In reply, Sera raised her arm so that Bhima could see the receding marks on her skin. The older woman nodded briskly. "By tomorrow morning, there will be no signs of . . . no signs, at all."

Sera felt her face flush at what Bhima had not said. No signs of Feroz's brutality, that was what Bhima had wanted to say. Mortification made Sera turn her head away, so she didn't notice that

Bhima had abandoned the kitchen sink and taken a few steps toward her, drying her hands on her sari as she walked. "Serabai," she said softly, "You are much wiser than I am, an educated woman while I am illiterate. But, bai, listen to me—do not tolerate what he is doing to you. Tell somebody. Tell your father—he will march in here and break his nose. You are trying to cover up your shame, bai, I know, but it is not your shame. It is Feroz seth's shame, not yours."

Sera's eyes welled with tears. She felt exposed under the X-ray vision of Bhima's eyes, but the relief of another human being acknowledging out loud what Feroz was doing to her was immense. "Does—does Gopal never beat you?"
Bhima snorted. "Beat me? Arre, if that fool touched me once, I would do some jaado on him and turn his hands into pillars of wood." Then, seeing Sera's shocked face, she smiled. "No, bai. With God's grace, my Gopal is not like the other mens. He would sooner cut his hands off than hurt me."

Lying in bed now, Sera remembers Bhima's confident assertion about Gopal—*He would sooner cut his hands off than hurt me*—and smiles bitterly. Time had proven Bhima wrong, had shaved off her confidence in her husband and left a raw, splintered woman in its wake. They were alike in many ways, Bhima and she. Despite the different trajectories of their lives—circumstances, she now thinks, dictated by the accidents of their births—they had both known the pain of watching the bloom fade from their marriages. Gopal had been a good man, but he had struck Bhima like a viper and stolen away the brightest, shiniest object in her life.

Well, no use lamenting the past, Sera thinks as she gets out of bed and turns off the alarm clock. Better to try to fix the future, which is what she's doing by helping Maya get an abortion. She sits at the edge of the bed and prays five Yatha Ahu Vahiriyos. Next she kisses the small picture of Lord Zoroaster that she keeps in a plastic frame on her bed stand. She heads into the bathroom, walking silently so as to not disturb the children sleeping in the other room. Thinking of Dinaz reminds Sera of how Bhima used to dote on her when Dinaz was a little girl. Bhima has done this whole family many favors, she thinks. If Maya needs my help now, how can I possibly refuse?

10

t least she is not picking them up at the slum, Sera thinks
as she gets into the cab. Thank God she'd had the presence
of mind to ask Bhima and Maya to wait at the bus stop for
her. This way, she and Maya can continue in the cab to Dr. Mahta's
clinic. Although many years have passed, Sera still shudders at the
memory of her visit to the slum.

Bhima had been sick with typhoid fever. Unable to come to
work, she had sent news of her illness with one of her neighbors,
and Sera had immediately known that it was something serious. Typhoid was nothing to be blasé about, she knew. And so she had decided to visit Bhima and Maya.

Although her apartment building was located less than a fifteen-
minute walk away from the basti, Sera had felt as if she had entered
another universe. It was one thing to drive past the slums that had
sprung up all around the city. It was another thing to walk the narrow byways that led into the sprawling slum colony—to watch
your patent leather shoes get splashed with the murky, muddy water that gathered in still pools on the ground; to gag at the ghastly
smell of shit and God knows what else; to look away as grown men
urinated in the open ditches that flowed past their homes. And the
flies, thick as guilt. And the stray dogs with patches and sores on
their backs. And the children squawking like chickens as their
mothers hit them with their open hands. Sera had wanted to turn

away, to flee this horrific world and escape back into the sanity of her life. But her concern for Bhima propelled her forward.

As Sera walked on, a group of slum dwellers—excited children hopping on one foot, curious women, and a few of the bolder men—began to follow her, making her feel even more like an alien, a space invader who had stumbled upon a different planet. The crowd behind her was festive, filled with excitement, the steady buzz of their conversations following her like a swarm of bees. But none of them talked to her except to point out the way to Bhima's hut—"Take left, madam," and "No, bai, this way." She knew that the slum people encountered well-dressed, affluent people like her every day on the streets and that many of these people must have jobs working in the homes of people like her. They were familiar with her world; the novelty was in having someone from her world step into theirs.

But the worst part of her visit—the memory that still makes Sera's cheeks flush with heat—was the reception that awaited her when she got to Bhima's house. One look at Bhima told Sera the older woman was deathly ill. Bhima's gaunt face was skeletonlike, and her eyes were bright with the high fevers that were battering her daily. Still, Bhima scrambled to her feet to welcome Sera into her humble home. Rummaging through her belongings, she pulled out a five-rupee note and asked Maya to go get a Mangola—she knew it was Sera's favorite soft drink—for their guest. Without being asked, Bhima's neighbors hastily found an old wooden chair that everybody insisted Sera sit upon. When she protested and said she could sit on the floor, they laughed as if she'd cracked a really good joke. Maya returned with the Mangola. When Sera offered her a sip, the child refused, although she licked her lips and looked away.

Sitting on the only chair in the room, surrounded by people sitting on their haunches, and sipping the Mangola while the slum children looked at her with their big, greedy eyes, Sera felt overwhelmed by guilt and sorrow. With each sip of the thick, sweet mango liquid she felt as if she was swallowing a blood clot. Several times she made like she was full and didn't want to drink anymore, but each time Bhima looked crushed. The generosity of the poor, Sera marveled to herself. It puts us middle-class people to shame. They should hate our guts, really. Instead, they treat us like royalty. The thought of how she herself treated Bhima—not allowing her to sit on the furniture, having her eat with separate utensils—filled her with guilt. Yet she knew that if she tried to change any of these rituals, Feroz would have a fit. Still, Bhima's sickly, fevered face and her spontaneous generosity had decided something for Sera. "You're coming home with me and staying with us until you're better," she said. "No, no use arguing, Bhima. You're in no position to take care of yourself, let alone Maya. Anyone can see that. Just get whatever things you need and let's go."

True to her word, she had nursed Bhima back to health, taking her to see their kindly family doctor, Dr. Porus, the next day.

But now, her mind racing along with the speeding cab, Sera feels no comfort or pride in that. What she remembers instead is the fact that, even so ill, Bhima had slept on the thin mattress on the balcony. The thought of her sleeping on one of their beds had been too repulsive to Sera. Little Maya had slept on a bedsheet next to her grandma. At the time Sera had blamed Feroz for this, had told herself that he would not tolerate anything else. But the truth was that she would've been uncomfortable with any other sleeping arrangement. The smells and sights she had encountered in the slum were still too fresh, as if they had gotten caught in her own hair and skin. Each time she thought of the slum, she recoiled from Bhima's presence, as if the woman had come to embody everything that was repulsive about that place. For many years, Sera had marveled at how clean and well-groomed Bhima was. Now, when it was time to give Bhima her pills, Sera made sure that she plopped them in Bhima's open palm without making contact. And for the next few weeks, she zealously kept Dinaz away from Bhima. She told herself it was because of the fever, but she had also wanted to protect her daughter from the sheen of dirtiness she now saw each time she looked at her servant.

Sera sighs so loudly that the cabdriver looks at her in his rearview mirror. Try as she might, she cannot transcend her middle-class skin, she thinks. Still, she has done her best for Bhima and her family. And now she must see this thing with Maya through. But for all their sakes, she will be glad when the whole sordid affair is over. This wretched business has affected Bhima terribly—just yesterday, Sera had to bite her tongue on at least five occasions while Bhima made stupid, careless mistakes.

When Sera reaches the bus stop in the cab, they are waiting for her. She sees them before they spot her, two figures almost fifty years apart and yet unmistakably linked by blood and destiny. Although they are not speaking, their bodies are leaning into each other's in an unconscious gesture of familiarity and intimacy. Sera feels her throat tighten with affection and warmth for Maya. It has been quite some time since she has seen her because a few months ago—about the time Maya had her affair, Sera now speculates—the girl stopped showing up for work at Banu's house. Banu's day nurse at the time preferred to leave by 3:00 P.M. and Sera had hired Maya to bridge the gap before the night nurse started her shift at 8:00 P.M. It was an easy job too—all Maya had had to do was stop by Banu's apartment after college and make sure that the old lady had her afternoon tea and evening meal. Sera knew she could get away with paying someone else a lot less than she paid Maya for the job, but Maya was practically a family member and Sera didn't begrudge her the extra money. The teenager probably already felt out of place around her more affluent college classmates, Sera figured. After all, not too many of them were orphans whose only surviving relative worked as a domestic servant in someone's home. If a few extra rupees could help decrease her discomfort, if it helped pay for an extra outfit that boosted her confidence, then it was worth it.

"Pull up a little past the bus stop," she directs the taxi driver. "Bas, this is good. Stop here, only."

As she steps out of the cab, the other two spot her and walk toward her. Sera is distressed to notice that Maya does not make eye contact with her and stares at the ground instead. Somehow, the girl's lack of enthusiasm at seeing her pricks at her, deflating her earlier gush of affection. "Hello, Maya," she says coldly. "How are you?"

"Fine," Maya says in a dead voice. Feeling Sera's critical gaze, she at last lifts her head and looks at her. But her look is as dead as her voice, as if her face has suddenly turned to stone.

Bhima looks from one to the other, worriedly. "She's in a bad mood today, Serabai," she explains. "Woke up all depressed, only." Her old, gray eyes silently beg Sera to understand and forgive.

Sera suddenly wishes Bhima was accompanying them to the hospital. She does not wish to deal with this new, sullen Maya. The girl that she knows, that she has nurtured and educated, is lighter, younger than this heavy, depressed girl standing in front of her. She fights the urge to remind Maya that it is she who has asked for Sera to accompany her to the doctor and not the other way around. She also feels a moment's guilt—had she, Viraf, and Bhima conspired to force Maya to have an abortion against her will? After all, she has never spoken directly to Maya about her wishes. But then she takes one look at Bhima's old, tired face and her spine stiffens. This girl is simply too young and naïve to know what awaits her if she has a child out of wedlock. The vulturelike savagery with which the world will descend upon her and tear her to bits. No, best to get rid of the baby, and then, after a few weeks have gone by, maybe she can sit down with Maya and explain to her the importance of re-suming her education. Maybe she can even help her get enrolled at a different college, someplace where she can make a fresh start. No boyfriends, no affairs this time, she will say to Maya. Just your studies. Remember, without education, you are nothing. In this city, people with law degrees and Ph.D.s go hungry. A high school degree is not enough even to get a job as a channawalla. It is the same lecture she had given Dinaz years ago. But with Maya, she will add another threat. Without at least a bachelor's degree, you will spend your life sweeping other people's floors and washing their dirty clothes. Is this what you want for yourself—the same life that your mother and grandmother had?

The thought of Maya's dead mother softens Sera's feelings to-ward the girl standing next to her. She glances at Maya, but Maya's face is as blank as a ceiling. Sera sighs. She is tempted to tell Bhima that she has changed her mind, that she wants her to accompany them to the clinic after all, but she resists the urge. There is simply too much housework for Bhima to take the time to go with them. Despite the intervention of Viraf's doctor friend, God knows how long they will have to wait. The last thing she wants to do at the end of this day is go home to a dirty house. "I've left the house keys with the next door neighbors," she says to Bhima. "They will let you in."

Maya looks at Sera sharply, and a laugh, as bitter as almonds, es-capes her. "She could've brought the house keys with her," she says to her grandmother, as if Sera is not there. "She could've trusted you with them. But she trusts the neighbor more."

Sera is shocked at the insolence. But no, that's not quite it. It's the hostility in Maya's voice that shocks her. That and—well, it has to be said—the sheer ingratitude. But before she can respond, Bhima does. "Stupid, ignorant girl," she berates her granddaughter. "Poking your nose where it doesn't belong. What business is it of yours what Serabai does with her keys? It's her house, na? See if you can get your own big-big house someday and then do what you like with your keys. Until then, you keep your trap shut, you understand?"

Such ugliness, so early in the morning. Sera is not quite sure what has brought it on. It must be the pregnancy, she thinks, the unwanted baby growing inside Maya anticipating its imminent death and unwilling to leave this world without soiling it with its presence. The thought of a dead baby makes her shudder. The sooner this day ends the better it will be for all concerned, she thinks. She has never seen Maya so angry, so defensive, so uncultured, so—low-class, really. And ever since she found out about Maya's pregnancy, Bhima has been like a madwoman—slow and absentminded one moment, agitated and prickly the next. The unwanted pregnancy had also cast a pallor on the Dubash household, so that the baby growing like a weed inside Maya was smothering the happiness they should be feeling at the thought of the child flowering within Dinaz's belly. Dinaz was probably curtailing her own shouting joy in deference to Bhima's sorrow. Now that she thought about it, Sera had detected a certain subdued quality to Dinaz in the past few weeks. And there was no reason for it. Dinaz's first trimester had been hellish, Sera knew. She had been nauseated, tired, irritable, and she and Viraf had picked at each other like crows picking at roadkill. But as the fatigue and nausea abated, Dinaz became more like her old self with each passing day. Still, somehow Maya's baby was casting a shadow over their happiness. It was hard to come home laden with new clothes for the newborn, to think of what color to paint the old wooden crib that had once been Dinaz's, to decide on which obstetrician and what hospital, all under Bhima's deadpan but watchful face. Like trying to hold a wedding reception in a funeral home.

Well, if there is to be a funeral, if the baby living in Maya's womb is to be killed—Sera winces at the word—then there is no time to waste. Best to get the show on the road. "We'll drop you off at the next street corner, Bhima," she says briskly, getting into the cab. "Then you can walk it up. Maya and I will continue to the clinic. Now come on, let's get going."

Maya hesitates for a split second before getting into the taxi. But Sera pretends not to notice.

11

D
r. Mehta is a tall, stooped man with droopy, sad eyes and
a disconcerting habit of not making eye contact with
Maya when he speaks about her. Instead, he addresses his
questions to Sera.

"So how is she feeling?" he asks.

Sera glances at Maya, who seems intent on gazing at a particular
spot on her feet. "Fine," she says at last. "I mean, all of us will feel
better when—"

"I know, I know," the doctor says hurriedly. He rises to his feet.
"Well, not to worry, Mrs. Dubash. We'll have this little matter resolved in no time." He turns to face Maya for the first time since
they have been in his office. "Um, follow me, please," he says, as he
rises from his chair. "The clinic is this way."

The girl gets up also and looks at Sera. For the first time this
morning, Maya looks scared. Her eyes are wide, and there is a film
of sweat on her upper lip. Sera's heart lurches in sympathy. She
reaches out to comfort the girl, but Maya takes her hand and holds
on tight to it. "You come with me," she whispers fiercely. "I don't
want to be in there all alone."

Sera stares at her in horror. Being in the room when the fetus is
removed is the last thing she wants to do. She feels revulsion rising
in the back of her throat. Don't put me in this position, she thinks.
This is much more than what I bargained for.

Before she can speak, Dr. Mehta sails to her rescue. "Nonsense, girl," he says. "Nobody is allowed back there except the staff and the patient. Relatives have to wait in the waiting room. And why uselessly you're getting scared and all? We'll extract this baby faster than you can extract a tooth."

Both Sera and Maya flinch at this comparison. As the two women exchange a look, Sera pats Maya on her right arm. "Don't be scared," she says. "I'll be waiting right here for you."

Sera sits in the waiting room, reading an old issue of *Eve's Weekly*. There are only two other women in the room, and neither of them tries to make eye contact with her. Both appear to be in their late forties, and their fine saris and gold jewelry tell Sera that they come from money. She wonders what their stories are. Probably here to take care of their college-age daughters. There is no limit to what money can buy, she thinks. Everything from silk sheets to an abortion in a beautiful, sunlit private clinic. Then, she catches herself. You, too, are here because you have money, she reminds herself. And she is grateful to Viraf's friend for arranging this appointment. How different things would've been if Maya had had to go to a government hospital. Sera has heard stories about doctors making lewd jokes about fallen women, slipping their hands up women's private parts for their own gratification under the guise of a medical exam. And most of those women, too ignorant to know what was happening and too poor to protest even if they did. She shudders at the thought of Maya in one of those places.

Sera glances at her watch and realizes she'd forgotten to see what time they took Maya in. She has no idea how long the procedure will take or—and here she feels a jolt of apprehension—what condition Maya will be in when they're done. Should've asked more questions, she chastises herself. But then she remembers Dr. Mehta's long, sad-eyed face. Not the kind of man you can chitchat with.

Conjuring up Dr. Mehta makes her remember the expression Maya's face as the doctor escorted her into the back room. How tiny, how scared the girl looked. Not so different from the orphan who had arrived at her doorstep with Bhima almost ten years earlier. Children today, Sera sighs. Still a child herself and here was Maya, pregnant with another. Well, at least it would all be over soon. Despite her unease at being here, Sera has no doubt that what they are doing is the right thing. If Maya is to have a chance, this is where her baby's story must end, here in this elegant clinic.

She must've dosed off, because now a nurse in a starched uniform is standing over her, softly saying her name. "Mrs. Dubash?" the nurse says. "Your patient is ready to see you."

Maya looks pale and small in her hospital bed. Her eyes glitter with tears when Sera approaches. "Well," she says before Sera can say anything, "all of you will be satisfied now. My baby is dead."

Sera flinches. She feels her temper flare and tries to check it before it turns into words she will regret. The girl has just been through a trauma, she reminds herself. Be gentle with her. When she speaks, her voice is empty of anger. "Unfortunately, there was no other option, Maya," she says. "But I can imagine that you feel sad. How are you feeling physically, girlie?"

Maya begins to sob. "I don't know," she says. "I'm hurting a lot. But the nurse said they will give me some pills for the pain. She said I will be fine in two-three days."

Dr. Mehta approaches the bed and signals for Sera to follow him out of the room. His eyes look even more droopy and sad than before. "There was a lot of blood," he says. "Happens sometimes. So there may be some cramping. And the girl may feel weak for a few days. If you think the family can afford it, I'll order a tonic."

"Please do," Sera says promptly. "Don't worry about the cost, Doctor. I want this child to have the best of everything."

Dr. Mehta smiles slightly, and Sera is amazed at how much it transforms his face. "Good," he says. "Good. Listen, Mrs. Dubash, I'm going to keep the girl here for a few more hours before I send her home. If you would like to—That is, if you have shopping to do or something, you can come back for her in a few hours. Get some lunch for yourself also."

When Sera returns a few hours later, she has purchased a new salwar khamez for Maya. She has also picked up the tonic that Dr. Mehta prescribed and bought a pineapple and some bananas and oranges. The girl will need to eat right for the next few days. And she will give Bhima money to buy coconut water daily to help Maya's insides heal.

Maya is sitting up and waiting for Sera. Her hair is combed, and perched on her hospital bed, she reminds Sera of a neatly tied brown paper package waiting for someone to claim it. "Ready?" she asks, and Maya drops off the bed with a soft grunt.

Outside, Sera notices how gingerly Maya walks and feels a twinge of sympathy. "How is the pain?" she asks, but the girl simply shrugs, her face impassive.

They look around for a taxi. "Let's go back to my place, okay?" Sera says. "I'll let Bhima out early to take you home."

Maya's blank face is suddenly animated. "No, Serabai," she says. "I would—I—that is, just drop me off at the bus stop near the basti. I'm tired. I'd rather go home and rest and wait for Ma-ma to get home."

"Maya, be reasonable. How are you going to walk from the bus stop to the basti? I can tell you're in pain." Please don't ask me to escort you inside the slum, she thinks.

"I'll be okay, Serabai. Really. I . . . I'm just anxious to go home and lie down. Please."

Sera feels something tight within her suddenly give way. She exhales. She is tired of assuming responsibility for this stubborn girl. She is tired of fighting, of holding herself against Maya's obstinacies and rudeness. Surrender feels so much lighter and lovelier.

"Okay," she says. "If that's what you want. I'll let Bhima out early, as soon as I get home."

A cab slows down near them, and Sera flags it. Maya leans against the door and stares resolutely out the window. They ride the rest of way in utter silence.

BOOK TWO

12

Two months have gone by, Bhima thinks, and still the girl won't come to life. Maya sits in their mud hut day after day, like a big stone statue of a god. But unlike a god, Maya doesn't look wrathful or vengeful or joyous. She does not scowl like Kali or smile sweetly like Krishna. Rather, she sits stone-faced, as if the abortion doctor has killed more than her baby, as if he has also cleaned out her insides, has scooped out her beating heart just as Bhima scoops the fibrous innards of the red pumpkin that Serabai puts in her daal. Whatever it is that makes human beings laugh and dance and hope and love and pray, whatever it is that separates youth from old age, life from death, Maya has lost that. And Bhima, unable to steal, purchase, or borrow it for her granddaughter, feels strongly the weight of her poverty and age and illiteracy. If I were educated, she thinks, I would know what to do. I would find the cure in a book; I would know who to consult—a doctor or a priest or a teacher. But how can I cure a disease that I can't name?

Soon after the abortion, Bhima had urged Maya to resume her education, but the girl had turned to her with such ferocity that Bhima's words had become dry leaves in her mouth. Same thing when she broached the subject of Maya's finding part-time employment. And truth to tell, Bhima didn't pursue that with the same urgency that she asked her grandchild to consider returning to college. It was too late to get the job at Banubai's place anyway.

The new day nurse, Edna, was able to work longer hours than the previous one, and Serabai had hired Edna shortly after Maya had stopped showing up for work. And the thought of Maya working in the homes of strangers made the muscles in Bhima's stomach clench. Working for Serabai, it was easy to pretend that they were simply helping out a family member in need. But the thought of her granddaughter doing the backbreaking work that she did was painful for Bhima. That had been the whole point of sending Maya to college—that she could build a different destiny for herself.

Tonight, the atmosphere in the darkened house, made oppressive by Maya's dreary presence, is too much for Bhima to take. "Did you bathe today?" she asks and is gratified to see the insulted look on her granddaughter's face as she nods yes. There is hope, she thinks. The girl is not so far gone that her vanity is crushed.

That faint hope propels her to action. She turns off the stove she had lit just a second ago. "Get dressed," she says. "We're going to the seaside. We'll eat some panipuri or bhel there. No dinner at home tonight."

Maya stares at her for a second, and then a light comes into her eyes. Watching her granddaughter scramble to her feet, Bhima feels a pang of guilt. She should've thought of this a long time ago. Sitting alone all day in this miserable place—no wonder Maya has turned to stone. Bhima curses herself for being so old that she has forgotten what a teenage girl needs—fresh air, a change of venue, the company of others, the opportunity to wear new clothes and put some kaajal on her eyes. She herself has become a machine, existing only to work and earn a salary, needing only enough food and water to keep her parts oiled and functioning. And how can a machine know the thoughts and needs of a young woman? she chastises herself. How can you know what a young, red heart, throbbing with life and desire, feels like? No wonder the poor girl sits at home like a shriveled raisin all day.

They walk to the seaside in a companionable silence. As they approach the water, they can hear the ocean pounding the rocks, and as a faint mist rises from the rocks, it kisses their faces in welcome. Maya grins, a sudden, effortless grin that reminds Bhima of the seven-year-old she had brought back from Delhi. "The sea is talking," she says, and watching her granddaughter's happy, guileless face, Bhima feels hope rising in her like sea mist.

"That's what your grandfather used to say," she replies. "We used to love coming here with your ma and your uncle Amit when they were children."

Maya's face turns wistful as it does every time Bhima mentions another member of their vanished family. "Tell me," she says. "Tell me about those days."

Bhima frowns, as she reflexively does when she remembers the past. She sifts through her memories, as if she is sifting through the rice at Serabai's house, removing the stones and the hard pieces, leaving behind what's good and shiny. "We came here every Saturday," she says. "All four of us. When your ma was little, Gopal would carry her. Not like the other mens—expecting their women to do all the work. Your da-da was not like those men."

"What was Ma like? When she was little, I mean." Maya's voice is breathless, and hearing her eagerness, Bhima's heart wobbles a bit.

"Your ma?" She laughs. "Your ma was like you when you were little—thin as a stick but as strong as one. Intelligent, too. Knew her mind from the day she was born. I remember, after I'd finish feeding her my milk, if I didn't pull her off my titties right away, she'd bite me. Even with no teeth, with those little gums, ae bhagwan, she could bite. She was a little fighter from the day she was born, that one."

They laugh. But Bhima notices that the girl is panting a bit from the walk, and she pulls her to the cement ledge that runs along the sea. "Let's sit for a minute," she says. "My legs are getting tired."

But inwardly she worries about Maya. It is not right that a girl of seventeen should be breathless after such a short walk. It is a sign that all is not right with Maya, and Bhima resolves to ask Serabai for the name of some strength tonic for the girl. No matter how much it costs, she will give it to Maya for at least a month. No amount of money is too much for this girl, Bhima thinks, and the gust of love she feels at that moment is strong enough to knock her off this cement ledge and into the sea.

Suddenly, she feels the desire to share the past with Maya. This is her inheritance after all, this currency of memories that Bhima carries around with her in an invisible sack. Perhaps the moment has come to share the inheritance with the girl, before the passage of time devalues it completely.

"There used to be a balloon seller here," she says. "An old Afghani, a Pathan. A tall, dignified man. The children loved him. He used to make the most wonderful designs out of his balloons for them. Gopal would make chitchat with him—ask him how business was, where he lived in Bombay—but, but I never did. I don't know why I never spoke to him, but I didn't. I wish now that I had. I wanted so much to ask him—things."

"What things?" Maya whispers. Her face glistens with anticipation, like it does each time Bhima throws morsels of memory at her.

"Things like, how he could bear to be so far away from his homeland, whether he missed his family, where his wife was. Because I knew he was all alone here in Bombay town. It was in his eyes, you see. Lonely as this sea, they were. I could see that in his eyes but still I didn't say anything."

Maya misunderstands. She puts one hand around her grandmother. "That's okay, Ma-ma," she says. "I'm sure the Pathani man was all right."

Bhima shakes her head impatiently. "No, that's not why. I mean, I was concerned about him, but that's not why I regret not asking."

She lowers her voice until she is whispering. "You see, I think he could've helped me . . . face what was to come later in my own life. He had the secret, see? The secret of loneliness. How to live with it, how to wrap it around your body and still be able to make beautiful, colorful things, like he did with those balloons. And he could've taught it to me, if only I'd asked."

They stare at each other for a moment, their faces naked and hungry. Then Maya begins to weep. "I'm sorry, Ma," she says. "I'm sorry to be one more burden in your life. I know what your life has been like, and I never wanted . . ."

The other people sitting on the wall are looking at them, openly curious, shamelessly eavesdropping. Bhima glares at a young man sitting next to Maya and then pulls her granddaughter to her feet. "Let's walk," she mutters. "Too many people with elephant ears here."

As they walk, Bhima takes Maya's hand in hers. The softness of her granddaughter's hand never fails to thrill her. It is a source of pride to her, this hand, because Bhima has paid for this softness with her own sweat. She remembers her own hands at seventeen—hard and callused from working as a servant from the time she was a child. Ruined from a lifetime of handling the sharp, pointed bristles of the broom, of dipping her hands in ash to scour pots and pans until they sparkled. Maya has escaped that fate. So far. Bhima rubs her thumb on the back of Maya's hand as if she is fondling a piece of velvet.

"Ma-ma, don't." Maya giggles through her tears. "It tickles."

"Always ticklish, you were." Bhima smiles. "Always. I just had to look at you and you'd wriggle like a fish. When I first got you back from Delhi, I used to take you to Serabai's with me all day while I worked. As shy and scared as you were then, it was the only way to make you smile. Serabai would tickle you and you would laugh."

"Ma," Maya says suddenly. "You never really told me. What was it like when you got to Delhi?"

Bhima tenses. A closed, guarded look falls like a trapdoor on her face. "No point in bringing up the past," she says in a choked voice. "Bad enough to have lived through it, without remembering it all over again. Anyway, it's nothing a young girl like you needs to know."

"You can't protect me forever, Ma-ma," Maya replies. "I need to know. After all, this concerns me. These were my own parents— my baba and my ma." Seeing the stubborn look on her grand-mother's face, Maya adds, "This is not just your property, Ma. This belongs to me too. Just because it's in your possession doesn't mean it's yours alone. By not telling, you're stealing something from me."

Bhima's face is set in stone. Seeing this, Maya's own face turns crafty. "I know how they died, Ma-ma," she whispers. "I know they died of AIDS."

Bhima wishes they had just stayed at home tonight. This night air, this whispering sea, this anonymity as they walk among thou-sands of strangers are making Maya ask questions she would nor-mally not ask. She looks around for a food vendor, hoping the girl will be distracted by the smell of roasted peanuts or battatawadas being fried.

"You hungry?" she asks, but the girl doesn't answer. Maya's lower chin is jutting out, and she has the look she used to get while working on a tough accounting problem. Suddenly, she asks, "Why did Ma and Baba leave you here and move to Delhi?"

"Because your baba was the best truck driver at his company. When his boss retired to Delhi, he took your baba with him to be his private car driver."

Maya considers this. "Maybe if they hadn't moved to Delhi, they wouldn't have gotten . . . sick."

Bhima is unsure how to respond to this. "God's will," she says feebly. Then, feeling the need to defend her son-in-law, "Raju was a good man. He loved you and Pooja very much."

Maya is not appeased. "I'm glad I was born in Bombay," she declares suddenly. "I'm a Bombay girl at heart. Ma missed the city, too, I remember."

Bhima nods warily, bracing herself for more questions. She doesn't wait long.

"Did Grandpa and Amit come for the wedding?" Maya now asks and, when Bhima shakes her head no, "Why not?"

"Because your mother didn't invite them," Bhima says shortly.

She skips past that long-ago argument with Pooja. "It's not as if your father is dead," she'd pleaded. "Can you imagine what people will say—a girl whose father is alive prefers to get married without him present at the wedding?"

But Pooja would not budge. "Let those same people also remember how he crept out on us," she cried. "You forget, Ma—we didn't leave him; he left us. Why should he come back now, to do all his fake herogiri for one day and charm everyone? What will he do for us besides dress like a film hero and eat our food? Besides, you yourself said—you're my mother and my father."

Remembering, Bhima picks up her pace, and Maya scampers to keep up with her. Bhima feels the girl's eyes on her, assessing her, gauging her mood. She struggles to swallow the taste of sour curds that suddenly fills her mouth. "She should've," Maya now says. "Ma should've invited Grandfather to her wedding. If I ever got married, I'd invite Grandfather. And Uncle Amit," she adds, in an appeasing voice.

Bhima hears the appeasement and knows that the girl means well. But Maya's reference to marriage reminds her again that the girl is damaged goods, and she can't keep the irritation out of her voice. "Forget about marriage," she says harshly. "You just think of college, nothing else."

Maya flinches. Bhima hates herself for hurting the girl in this manner, but she is also relieved that her words have snuffed out her granddaughter's questions. They walk in a guarded silence for a few minutes.

"Let's get some bhel," Bhima says finally. "You need to eat some food." They both know this is her way of calling for a truce.

Maya's soft hand reaches out for Bhima's. "I'm just glad you took me in, when Ma and Baba died," she says unexpectedly. "I don't know what I would've done if it wasn't for you."

This girl is like her grandfather, Bhima thinks. She can pierce my heart with words the size of a mosquito. To cover up her emotions, Bhima smacks Maya lightly on the arm. "Silly girl," she says gruffly. "Of course, I took you in. You're my blood, aren't you? What did you think I was going to do with you—sell you to the junk man? Or donate you to the circus?"

Maya smiles. "Wonder what the junk man would've paid for me."

"Five paise. And even that would've been too much for a silly girl like you."

They walk along the crowded footpath, their fingers loosely linked together. After a few minutes, Maya tilts her head and rests it on her grandmother's shoulder. "Ma-ma," she says, in her most beguiling tone, and Bhima tenses, bracing herself for another round of questioning.

But Maya says only, "Ma-ma. I'm hungry. But can we get pani puri instead of bhel?"

13

The telegram that came from Delhi said only POOJA AND RAJU SICK STOP COME IMMEDIATELY STOP.

Bhima had left for Delhi the next morning. Serabai had helped her get the train tickets.

AIDS.

Standing in the crowded, filthy hallway of the government hospital where Pooja lay on a moth-eaten cot, a young, tired-looking doctor had flung the word at her. "Your daughter has AIDS," he said briskly. "Given to her by your son-in-law. You understand? He's not even going to live past the next day or so. As for"—he looked down and consulted a clipboard—"Pooja, it's hard to tell how long she'll be among us."

"Eids?" she whispered. "Is that like food poisoning?" It was the only thing that could explain why Pooja and Raju had looked so emaciated.

The doctor sucked in his cheeks and stared at her. "You don't know what AIDS is?" When she shook her head no, he did not bother to hide his disgust. "You people," he said. "God knows why the government spends lakhs of rupees trying to educate you about family planning and all. It's a useless cause." He stared at her another minute and then swung around on his heel. "I don't have time to give you a medical lesson. Have hundreds of other patients to check on. Anyway, I'm a doctor, not a bleddy teacher." He began to walk away and then stopped. "You better go say your goodbye to your daughter, if you want my advice." And then, seeing the stricken look on her face, he added, "I'm sorry."

Bhima stood in the hallway of the hospital, unable to move. Pooja and Raju dying? Had she heard the doctor correctly? Or had she, in her usual ignorant way, misunderstood what he was saying? And why had he sounded so angry at her? She looked around her and saw hundreds of people wandering the long corridor, looking as dazed and stricken as she did. Hundreds of people around her, and yet she had never felt so alone. If she had been in Bombay, she would've known what to do. She could've called Serabai and had her talk to that young doctor. Even a neighbor from the basti would have helped her at a time like this. She would've swallowed her pride and asked for help. For Pooja, she would strip herself naked and walk on her knees to get help. Anything to have saved her from this ugly, flesh-eating illness that was killing her. Suddenly, Bhima's knees buckled under her, and her hand shot out to touch the dirty, paan-stained wall for support.

"Ae, somebody help that woman," she heard a voice say, and a pair of arms gripped her from above the elbow. "Careful, didi, careful," another voice said. "Here, come sit on this bench for a minute."

Her head felt as light as a cleaned-out watermelon. She sat with her eyes closed until the nausea and dizziness passed and then opened them because Pooja's thin and dying face was floating in front of her eyes. She turned to thank her rescuer and noticed that he was a young, lightly bearded man in his twenties. "God bless you, beta," she said.

"Hyder is the name," he said and then leapt to his feet. "Let me get you a cup of water," he said. "I have a flask." And before she could reply, he was gone.

She watched him struggle past the ever-growing crowd of relatives as he made his way back to her. "Here, didi," he said. "Cold-cold water."

She hesitated for a split second. She had never shared a utensil with a Muslim before and a lifetime of teachings spiraled like a funnel cloud into her head. Then, she looked around the hellish place she was in—took in the wasted, hollow faces of the dying patients, the haggard, aged faces of their relatives, the foul smell of urine and cheap tobacco that hung in the air like a hangman's noose. She took in Hyder's gentle, curious face and realized that, in this place of wall-to-wall people, he was the only one who had come to her assistance.

She drank. The water ran cool down her parched throat.

Hyder watched her. "You're not from Delhi town, didi," he said in a tone that was more statement than question.

She nodded. "Bombay," she said between sips. "But my daughter and her husband live here. Took the train to Delhi and came in yesterday."

Hyder nodded. "I see. And . . . is that your daughter in there?"

The tears came into her eyes unbidden. "Daughter and son-in-law, both. He's in the male ward."

She was surprised to see that Hyder didn't seem surprised. "Happens all the time," he said. "Husband does get it and passes it on to wife."

She felt a sudden flash of anger. So Raju was responsible for this? What had he done? Brought home some bad food? Or was it like a fever or malaria, where one person could make the other sick?

"What does the husband do?" she asked. "How does he pass it on?"

Hyder blushed. He looked at Bhima as if trying to decide what and how much to tell her. She stared back at him pleadingly. "Beta, if I'm to have a cure for my daughter, I must know what this Eids is," she said. "I'm an illiterate woman, knowing nothing. The doctor sahib was too busy to explain this illness to me."

"There is no cure," Hyder said, and she flinched at the hard cruelty of his words. "That's the first thing to understand, didi. Nobody lives from this wicked illness." His voice softened as he saw the devastation his words had wreaked. "What they say is, it's a blood illness. Men get it from, you know"—he blinked rapidly, trying to hide his embarrassment—"from having relations with bad girls. Whores and the like," he added, to make sure Bhima understood. "And then they come home and pass on their badness to their wives." His voice lowered. "They're saying the streets of Delhi are filled with such cases. Bombay too, probably."

Bhima was shocked. "But my Raju is not like that," she said. "He and my Pooja were happy in . . ."

Hyder chewed on his lower lip. "I'm not saying anything about your Raju, didi," he said. Then his face brightened. "They say it can be in your body for years and years before its ugliness shows. So even if your Raju had—you know—before marriage, it can still be there."

Bhima stared at the young man with fascination. "Like a curse," she whispered. And when she saw that he didn't understand, she said, "Someone does some jadoo on you—like they put cut fingernails under your mattress or they hide chilis and lime in an old rag and put it in your path—and years go by and you think you are safe. And then one day, something bad happens and you realize that the curse was with you all these years. You just didn't know it."

"Exactly," Hyder shouted. "Exactly like a curse, didi."

"Except in our case the curse was my son-in-law," Bhima said bitterly.

For the next few days, Bhima leaned on Hyder like a walking stick. In the land of the sick, his good health, his vigor, propped up her own sagging strength. Hyder raced from tending to his own dying friend—a young man of twenty-three whose parents had disowned him—to looking in on Bhima and Pooja.

He was with them the day Pooja visited her husband. Despite Pooja's own terrible sickness, she had insisted on walking the long hallway into the men's ward so that she could see Raju one last time. As always, Bhima had been helpless against Pooja's determination. It was as if that willpower was the only thing left of her daughter, the only part of her altered remains that Bhims could still recognize. So Pooja walked, her skeleton hands digging into Bhima's wrist on one side and holding on to Hyder's arm on the other. To Bhima, their slow, unsteady walk looked like a funeral procession, and indeed that was what it was, because by the time they reached Raju's bedside it was hard to tell the living from the dead. Bhima could feel a part of herself die during that walk, as if a piece of the old, creaky machine that was her heart had fallen off and been lost forever. Hyder, too, stiff with fatigue from tending to his dying friend, looked as solemn and blank-faced as a death row inmate. As for Pooja . . . Bhima winced as she noticed how much it hurt her daughter to lower herself onto a folding chair that one of the ward boys had placed next to Raju's bed. "Forgive me, Bhagwan," she said to herself. "I must've committed many-many wicked sins in my last life, to be so punished in this janam. Watching your own daughter suffer like this must be a punishment reserved only for murderers and other special cases."

Pooja lowered herself on the chair. "Raju," she whispered. "Raju, open your eyes. Look, it's your Pooja. I have kept both my promises to you, my husband. I told you that you will not die alone and that I would not leave you alone on this suffering earth. You go first, janu, and then I will follow."

Raju's eyes were open. He stared at Pooja, but Bhima was unsure if he could see any of them. His right hand, which was resting on his chest, rose a few inches off his body and shook. Immediately, Pooja took it in her own hand, wincing at the effort this cost her. She caressed Raju's hand with her own before gently lowering it back onto his chest. Raju's eyes stayed open for another minute. Then he shut his eyes, and the terrible, harsh, rasping breathing started again. Pooja turned toward her mother, her eyes opaque with fear. "Ma," she cried. "Let's take our Raju and go home. I'm frightened, Ma, of what will happen if we stay in this hellish place."

Bhima looked at Hyder for help, unsure of how to respond. Part of her would've liked nothing better than to load the two sick children into a taxi and take them home, where she could cook good, strength-giving food for them and nurse them back to health. But Hyder's emphatic words about how nobody survived this monstrous illness held her in check. Before she could think of what to say, Pooja spoke again. "No, it is God's wish that we die here, in this place of strangers," she said in a whisper. "Our fates decided before we were even born. So it is. So it will be."

Pooja insisted on sitting on that wooden folding chair in the narrow aisle between her husband's bed and the next one. Bhima tried a few times to cajole her daughter to return to her bed and then gave up. It was obvious that Raju would not make it through the night, and it was important to Pooja to keep her promise to her husband. So Bhima squatted on the floor beside her daughter, and the night filled with the sounds of hacking, groaning, moaning men. But it was the smells that bothered her more—the dull odor of the phenol with which the ward boys washed the stone floors; the sharp scent of the Flit that was sprayed in the air to kill the mosquitoes that swarmed around the damp beds; and above all, the smell of death that lingered like a dark promise. Occasionally, she mustered up the courage to take Pooja's pencil-thin hand in hers, fighting the revulsion she felt when her hand encountered bone instead of flesh. How she had worked and fought over the years to fatten up this hand. And for what? So that some man could inject an illness into her daughter that would turn her into a skeleton. She looked bitterly over to where Raju was waging a silent battle with death and found she couldn't muster up the energy that hatred called for. All she felt was pity, a bone-piercingly sharp pity for the dying man, for her Pooja, for herself, for Hyder, for every one of them trapped here in this hospital.

She felt Pooja stirring next to her. "Why didn't you send me the telegram earlier?" she whispered and then regretted the question as she saw the pained look pass like a cloud over her daughter's face.

"I don't know, Ma. Raju didn't want anyone to know. Especially you. He was so ashamed, you know? And also, for a long time, only he was sick, not me. Colds that stayed for weeks, blisters in his mouth that wouldn't heal. And stomach cramps. Arre bhagwan, those stomach cramps he used to get." She shuddered. She swallowed hard and ran her tongue over her cracked, dry lips. "But I didn't mind because I was strong. I could take care of him and Maya, both. No need to alarm you. But about six months ago, I began to get sick also. Then I—"

"Six months?" Bhima couldn't keep the indignation out of her voice. "Six months you've been sick and you didn't tell me? Daughter, I could've come and helped you—"

"I know, Ma, I know. Anyway, what's done is done. God's plan for your wretched daughter." She paused for a long time. The effort to speak had exhausted Pooja completely, and Bhima was remorseful. "Correct," she said, patting the bony hand. "No point in going over the past. Anyway, you rest now."

They were quiet for a long time. Then, as if there had been no break in the conversation, Pooja started speaking. Her voice was so low that Bhima had to strain to hear. "But see, we didn't even know what this sickness was until I got very sick about three months ago," Pooja continued. "Then, Nanavatsahib—Raju's boss—he insisted we both get a blood test. Raju was telling him how I couldn't sleep at night, how I'd wake up all shivering and sweating. So something popped up in Nanavatisahib's mind. That was the first time we ever saw this wretched hospital. Even then we were not knowing that, a few months later, we would get to know it so well. Now, of course, I see it in my dreams."

Bhima knew she shouldn't, but she couldn't help herself. "And . . . how did Raju contact this daaku of an illness?"

Pooja's face became a blank sheet. "No use in asking that question, Ma. What's done is done. He is my husband. And until all this, he kept me like a queen in his house."

As if he had heard his name, Raju groaned. Bhima leapt to her feet and stroked his feet. "Raju beta," she said gently. "It is okay. We are all with you, beta. Sleep now."

But Raju moaned even louder, a harrowing sound that carried such an awful loneliness that the hair on Bhima's arms stood up. It was the sound of a man who was truly alone, who was standing on the banks of a river where he was beyond the reach of his fellow human beings. The last of her resistance crumbled under that moan. "Raju," Bhima cried. "Look, your Pooja is here with you. I am here also. I will take care of Pooja, I promise. And Maya," she continued wildly. "I will raise your Maya as my own child. You have nothing to worry about, Raju beta. Go now. Go in peace."

Raju's jaw moved a few times. His mouth opened and shut. There was a loud, rasping breath that made his entire body shudder. His hand fluttered a few times against his chest. And then, he was gone.

Bhima and Pooja stared at each other, too numb to say anything.

Bhima was dimly aware that Hyder had come running back toward Raju's bedside and was saying something to her. But she couldn't hear him. Her mind was still seeing the footprints of death on Raju's torn body. She was still in shock at how intrusive and brutal a force death really was, how its dark breath had made Raju's frail body shudder and move under its oppressive weight.

Pooja turned her head slowly away from her dead husband and towards her mother, tears streaming down her cheeks. "My turn next," she said softly.

They came for Raju's body an hour later. Two men, who wordlessly wrapped the body, as brown and brittle as a clay pot, in a sheet and carried it down the hallway. Two men, doing their jobs in a brutally efficient manner. Bhima smelled the alcohol on their breath and was insulted by this. She wanted to protest this disrespect, but then she noticed that the relatives gathered around the hospital corridor barely moved out of the way or paused in their conversations as the men made their way with Raju's shrunken corpse. Oh, they touched their foreheads in respect when the small procession reached them, but Bhima could tell that that rote gesture was more out of habit and superstition than out of any genuine mourning for the passing of another human being. And as soon as the pallbearers passed them by, the conversations in the hallway resumed again, as if Raju's body was merely a small pebble in a pond that created a minor ripple before the calmness of the waters overcame it. It was as if this indifference to death was everywhere at this hospital. Or maybe it wasn't indifference at all but the exhausted failure of the defeated; as if so much energy went into preserving the living that there was nothing left over to mourn for the dead.

It was 6:00 A.M. by the time they got to the open field behind the hospital where a dozen funeral pyres were ablaze at the same time. Black smoke the color of despair rose from those pyres. Occasionally the fires crackled as they fed on bones. Bhima watched as Raju's body was lowered onto the carefully arranged wooden blocks. Hyder had left his dying friend and accompanied her to the site. The smoke from the other pyres made her eyes burn, but still she watched as Raju's body caught the flames that leapt high toward the heavens and against the reddening eastern sky. A terrible smell, dull and musty, the smell of wet cotton and mothballs, rose up and made her gag. Still, she watched as Raju's body turned into ash. Bhima concentrated on those leaping flames that licked Raju's body like a fiery tongue. It is right, she told herself unconvincingly. This poor boy has suffered so. This death is a release, not a punishment. You must remember that.

But then she thought of Pooja and of the little girl, Maya, for whom she would soon be responsible, and her entire body rebelled against what was happening, so that she wanted to leap into the pyre and command the flames to stop devouring this body; to demand that Raju rise from this final house of wood and ash and assume his responsibilities; to march over to Pooja and order her to grow flesh on her bones and return to her rightful home besides her healthy husband and their child. She wanted to go back to Maya's second birthday, when Pooja and Raju had invited her for dinner and she had bought a whole new outfit for her beautiful granddaughter—red and white shoes, a pink dress, and a matching pink bow for her hair. She wanted to revisit the conversation after dinner—when Raju had told her about his new job offer that would pay so much more and she had been so pleased for him until he told her that it would mean moving to Delhi. At that time, she had forced a smile on her face, had silenced her protesting heart and told Raju to do what was best for his family, had told a downcast Pooja that as a married woman her place was next to her husband and not next to her old mother. But not now. Now, she wanted to go back to that day and make her displeasure known, now she wanted to tell Raju that family matters more than money, that she would work an extra job to make up the difference in salary he would give up by staying in Bombay. Now, she would be shameless, merciless: She would remind Pooja that she was all Bhima had; that to take her only grandchild away from her was tantamount to murder; that she was an old woman, and after her death, they could move anywhere—to Delhi, to Calcutta, to the moon—but not while she was alive.

She made a gurgling sound in her throat, and Hyder put a tentative hand on her shoulder. "Didi, be brave," he said in a voice older than his years. "For your daughter's sake, be brave."

She wanted to say: For my daughter's sake, I can be anything: brave, strong, fearless. For her sake, I can walk on crushed glass, lie down on hot coals, wade through ice-cold waters. But my daughter is here on earth for a few days, I know. Soon, there will be another funeral pyre like this one. Only this time, it will be the body of the baby I gave birth to; the infant who bit my nipple each time after I nursed her; the six-year-old girl who once vomited after eating six bananas at one time; the eleven-year-old who came home crying from her job at Benifer Sodabottleopenerwalla's place because she had started her menses and thought she was bleeding to death; the sixteen-year-old who grew quiet and grave after her father left us behind like an abandoned pair of shoes. And after this second funeral, after Pooja turns into ashes before my cursed eyes, after I have witnessed the horror of my own child dying before me, I will want to melt like ice, I will want to crumble like sand, I will want to dissolve like sugar in a glass of water. I will want to stop existing, you understand? Because, Hyder, try and understand—once I had two children, and now I will have none. One dead, the other disappeared, vanished, stolen from me by my cockroach of a husband.

And a mother without children is not a mother at all, and if I am not a mother, then I am nothing. Nothing. I am like sugar dissolved in a glass of water. Or, I am like salt, which disappears when you cook with it. I am salt. Without my children, I cease to exist.

For a woman like me, Hyder, death would be a luxury. I would welcome it, as I once welcomed love. But the gods are cruel, Hyder. You are learning this lesson too, at such a young age. So this Bhima, this ugly, unfortunate, ignorant, illiterate Bhima, even now the gods will toy with her because they know she's not smart enough to fight back. And so there is Maya. Flesh of my flesh. What will happen to her if I jump into Pooja's funeral pyre like I want to? What becomes of an orphan girl on the streets of Delhi? You and I both know the answer, Hyder. A beggar child, or worse, a prostitute. Not an Indira Gandhi, that's for sure. And so I have to live. Even though I'm already dead, I know I will have to live. Because we live for more than just ourselves, hai na, beta? Most of the time we live for others, keep putting one foot before the other, left and right, left and right, so that walking becomes a habit, just like breathing. In and out, left and right. You must forgive me, beta, I know I'm confusing you. I feel confused myself . . . there is no breeze in this place, the fire has eaten up the breeze, it seems, so hot and so narrow, like the entrance to Ravan's forest, and this smell, beta, the smell of dead flowers and cobwebs and mothballs and decay, this smell that is inside my head and it will never leave me, I know, this smell that will trail me the rest of my days, I can feel it entering my bones, settling like dust into my blood . . .

Hyder caught her as she fell.

Bhima brought Maya to the hospital with her the next day, and her reward was the weak smile on Pooja's face. "Ae, chokri," she said gently to Maya, who was leaning into Bhima's hip. "Come here. Forgotten your mother in a few weeks' time, hah?"

Maya went up gingerly to her mother. "I made something for you in school," she said, handing her mother a picture of a flower.

Pooja smiled weakly, barely looking at the picture. "Good you're going to school," she said. "You must be the bestest student in the school, achcha?"

Maya smiled shyly. "I already am."

Pooja closed her eyes, exhausted. Maya turned to look at her grandmother. "She's going to sleep," she said accusingly. "I haven't even told her what the teacher said to me." She stared at her mother for a minute. "Ma-Ma, why does ma look so ugly?"

"Chup re, you bad girl," Bhima hushed her. "Your ma is as beautiful as ever. You just have to look harder to see the beauty, that's all."

Maya took a step closer and stared at her mother's sleeping face. "I'm looking hard-hard," she said. "But she still looks ugly to me." Then she began to cry.

Bhima closed the gap between them and held the sobbing child to her bosom. Just then, the sister of the woman who lay two beds away from Pooja began to wail, a high-pitched, hair-raising sound. "O Bhagwan, my sister is dead," the woman screamed. "O big sister, answer me, talk to me. O God, take me also, why have you left me alone on this lonely earth?" Listening to the woman's wails, Maya began to shake. "Ma-ma, I'm frightened," she said. "I want to go home."

Before she could control herself, Bhima turned onto the bereaved woman. "Hush your mouth," she yelled. "Scaring everybody like this. What do you think—you are the only one grieving here? That the rest of us are pillars made of stone?" Watching the woman's cowering, openmouthed face only further ignited

Bhima's rage. Her mouth tasted bitter, as if she had swallowed the ashes from Raju's pyre, and the cruel words that dropped from her lips, like ashes, were tinged with that bitterness. "Shameless woman," she went on, half aware that everyone around, patients and relatives alike, was watching her in horror. "Keep your tears to yourself. If you live to be a hundred and two years old you won't know the griefs some of us have seen. Crying like this over your sister, while I will have to watch my only child——"

"Silence." A loud male voice rang out, covering Bhima's words. "Old woman, have you no shame?" It was the same doctor she had encountered in the hallway a few days earlier, but he gave no sign of recognizing her. "What are you people, animals? Have you no respect for death or another person's grief? Fighting with each other like wild dogs." He towered above Bhima, who pressed Maya's head tightly against her bosom, as if she wanted the child not to hear the scolding she was getting. "This is a hospital, not one of your gutter homes," the doctor raged. "If you cannot respect the rules of the hospital, then take your patient and go home."

Bhima felt a single trickle of sweat start at the nape of her neck and run down her back. Her eyes filled with tears, and she glanced quickly at Pooja, to see if her daughter had witnessed her humiliation. But Pooja lay with her eyes closed. Slowly, Bhima raised her gaze so that she was staring at the collar of the doctor's white coat. "Sorry, doctorsahib," she murmured. "Maaf karo. Please to forgive me."

The doctor looked as if he wanted to say more, but then he noticed Maya, who was now cowering behind her grandmother's back, and stopped himself. He stared at Bhima for another minute and then turned away. "It's a hopeless situation," he said to himself but just loud enough that Bhima heard him. "This whole hospital— everything—it's all hopeless. Should've gone to 'Mrica when I had a chance. At least they have respect for human life there."

The doctor left a long silence in his wake. Some of the other relatives glared at Bhima in apparent satisfaction at the verbal trashing she had received; others looked away in discomfort at her embarrassment. The young woman two beds away began to sob softly to herself, resting her head on her dead sister's legs. Maya whimpered and tugged at Bhima's sari. "Let's go, na," she said. "I want to go home."

"Wait, beta," she replied. "Go sit by your mother for a minute."

"I don't want to."

"Then wait here for me. I'll come back right away."

Bhima made her way to the dead woman's cot. As she heard her footsteps, the bereaved woman lifted her head fearfully. Her wary expression made Bhima's heart twist with guilt. "I'm sorry for your loss, girl," she said. "And I beg your forgiveness for my harsh words. Please find it in your heart to forgive me. I don't know what . . . Yesterday I cremated my son-in-law. And that's my daughter over there. Anyway, my wicked words were—"

"No need to ask forgiveness," the other woman said slowly. "There is no forgiveness in this place. And your words were true. Here, we have all hit the jackpot for grief."

Maya had inched her way up to Bhima. "Ma-ma, let's go," she now cried. "I hate this room."

Bhima made a wry face. "Time to take this one home," she said. She lowered her voice. "She doesn't understand, yet." She stretched her right hand and placed it lightly over the sitting girl's head. "God look after you, beti," she said. "And remember, those who have no one, have God."

Over the next two weeks, Bhima herself began to look like one of the patients in the hospital. Every morning she woke up early, got Maya dressed, and took her over to the neighbor's home. And then she left for the hospital. Most days, she ate a banana for lunch. Once in a while, as she leaned against the bus window, she would catch a reflection of herself in the glass and notice the dark circles that had sprung up around her eyes, would be aware of the fact that her face was beginning to look as gaunt and exhausted as Pooja's. But she noticed these things idly, as if she didn't quite recognize the face that looked back at her. She was distracted. There were too many competing thoughts, buzzing around like bees in her head. She knew she should let Gopal know that his daughter was dying. No matter how dissolute the alcohol had made him, she knew he would do whatever it took to get to Delhi in time to see Pooja. But how to contact Gopal? She had an address only for his older brother and that was buried somewhere in her hut in the old suitcase that Serabai had given her. Who could she ask to dig for that address? It was not feasible to ask Serabai to go to the slum to make that request of one of her neighbors. Besides, since coming to Delhi, she had not even had the time to find someone who could write Serabai a letter telling her what she had found here. She knew Serabai would be worried, but somehow, once she stepped into the time-stopping world of the hospital, the rest of her life melted away from her. It was as if it was only in this place of disease and death that she felt alive and vital. The rest of her life became a dim memory, a blurry shadow.

Maybe Pooja's illness was her punishment for not having invited Gopal to the wedding. After all, hadn't she known that it was bad luck to marry off a daughter without her father being present to give her away? No wonder this disease had come to prey on her daughter. It was the nature of disease to prey on the weak and vulnerable. She should not have listened to Pooja's tirade against her absent father. Pooja was a silly young girl, what did she know about the trickery of the Gods, about how vengeful fate could be? But she, Bhima, knew better. She remembered the case of Seema, the woman who had moved into the ground-floor apartment of the building where Bhima lived with her parents. One Diwali festival, when Bhima was twelve years old, all the building residents were gathered in the courtyard of the building, setting off firecrackers, exchanging sweets. All except Seema and her husband. Between the sizzle and crackle of the fireworks, the other residents heard the two of them quarreling. Seema's words shot out the window of her ground-floor flat, as hot as the rockets they were firing into the air: "Useless loafer . . . good-for-nothing . . . Lying around all day. . . . Better off if you were dead, as dead as that thing between your legs." On that day, some of the celebrants had knocked angrily on Seema's door and asked her to keep her voice down. That had silenced her. But the real silencing came four months later, when Seema got home from work one evening, went straight to bed, and never woke up. All the neighbors, remembering the curses she had hurled onto her husband on that Diwali day, shook their heads at the wiliness of the gods. "They turned her own words upside down and fed them back to her," Bhima's mother had said.

Today, Hyder was sitting by Pooja's bed when she reached her daughter's side. "How is she?" she asked, and Hyder flashed her a big smile. "Doing well," he said. "Doctorji was in on his rounds, and even he said Pooja didi was looking tip-top today."

Bhima glanced at Pooja, relieved to see that Hyder's presence had indeed cheered her daughter up. "Did you sleep last night, beti?" she asked gently.

Pooja smiled. "It's all better now, now that you and Hyder are here," she said. "How is my shorty? Does she miss her mother at all?"

"She misses you a lot," Bhima lied. "All the time she is asking about you, only—when will Mummy come home, when can we go to the mela together?"

It was the wrong thing to say, she realized, as she saw the pained look on Pooja's face. "Tell her, Ma," she whispered. "She needs to understand. Tell her I'm not coming home."

154 / THRITY UMRIGAR

Hyder cleared his throat. "I'll be back later," he said.

The two women watched the youth leave the room. Pooja reached for Bhima's hand. "I'm glad he's helping you, Ma. I am so ashamed to have caused you all this trouble . . ."

"Trouble? Listen, chokri, who do you think I am? I'm not some woman from the marketplace. I'm your mother, I carried you in my stomach for nine months." Despite herself, Bhima smiled. "Even then you were a fighter cock—kicking me in my belly all the time. Baap re, I thought I was giving birth to a wrestler like Dara Singh."

Pooja turned her face away from her mother, but Bhima saw the tears rolling down her cheeks. All these tears shed in the world, where do they go? she wondered. If one could capture all of them, they could water the parched, drought-stricken fields in Gopal's village and beyond. Then perhaps these tears would have value and all this grief would have some meaning. Otherwise, it was all a waste, just an endless cycle of birth and death; of love and loss.

Pooja was in a talkative mood that day. Before Bhima's disbelieving eyes, her daughter seemed to come to life, so that despite the gaunt face and the eyes that were unrealistically shiny, she could see some trace of the old Pooja. In the afternoon she begged her daughter to sleep for a few hours, but Pooja insisted she wanted to talk instead. She reminisced about when she first met Raju and the day Maya was born; she lamented the fact that she had ever left Bhima behind in Bombay. "We should've had you move with us, Ma," she said. "Then all these years of separation would not have hurt as much as they do now. Raju was an orphan—what did he know about family love? But I should never have given you up." The thin face was flushed, almost luminous, as if lit up by an inner light.

Watching Pooja's face, Bhima felt a moment of unease. "Beti, you are tiring yourself too much with all this talking-talking. Rest, na."

But Pooja was burning like a candle. "Soon there will be nothing but rest, Ma. Today is a good day—I feel strong. Let me talk. Also, I must tell you everything about Maya. Ma, the girl is very soft-hearted. Gets hurt very easily. She's also very quick to learn. Knows how to write, already."

She was quiet for a minute while she caught her breath. Her cheeks were red, fevered. "Another thing. There is some money in the bank—our katha is in State Bank. The slip book is kept in the safe inside the metal cupboard. You remember the cupboard that Serabai gave us as a wedding present? That one. Take all the money out. I wrote some bearer checks before we came to the hospital."

"Beti, beti, this is not the time to be talking about money-foney. I will manage, I promise. I will make sure that not a hair on your daughter's head is harmed, as long as I'm alive."

Pooja's eyes glistened with tears. "Ma, I know. That is the only reason I can die in peace. Without you, I would have had to come back as a ghost to take care of my little one."

"Achcha, sleep now, beti. Preserve your strength. Sleep. I will be here when you wake up."

Pooja didn't wake up. Nor did she go without a fight. When the two men came to gather her up, her countenance showed the signs of her colossal struggle, as if her face had been trampled by the hooves of death.

Again, Bhima and Hyder stood at the funeral site, and Bhima watched as the flames did their demonic dance over her daughter's body. Maya, Bhima kept whispering to herself. Remember, you are all the little one has. Be brave, old woman, for her sake.

Three days later, Hyder came to the train station to see them off to Bombay. Under the bright light of the day, she noticed lines on his young face that she hadn't seen at the hospital. "If I live to be a hundred—" she began.

He stopped her with an embrace. "Didi," he said. "Please. Just—go in peace and try to forget all this badness." They stared at each other for a full moment, while Maya pulled impatiently on Bhima's hand.

They boarded the train and found their berth. Looking at Maya's small head, with her hair neatly parted in the middle, Bhima sighed. "I don't know how I will manage," she whispered to Hyder, who was standing on the platform outside their window. What she meant was: she didn't know this child the way she knew Pooja. She didn't know what the inside of Maya's mouth looked like, what the small of her back felt like, whether she liked sweet foods or sour, how she liked to be comforted when she was sick.

"It's okay," Hyder said. "Keep faith, didi, keep faith."

Those were the last words Hyder said to her before the train pulled out of the station. She watched his sweet, pensive face get smaller and smaller until she couldn't see it anymore.

14

era! Dinu! Welcome, welcome, welcome into our humble home," Aban Driver screams as she greets them in the doorway of her flat. "Ae, where's Viraf? Is he parking the car or what?"

Dinaz laughs as they enter the passageway that leads to the living room. She has always had a soft spot for the woman at whose home her parents first met.

"Good to see you, Aban aunty," she now says. "Viraf is coming—he got held up at work. He'll be here a little late."

"Perfectly okay, perfectly okay," Aban says. "That poor boy, working so hard. But of course," she adds, eyeing Dinaz's swelling belly, "he must, now that he will have a little one to support." She and Sera exchange a knowing look.

As they enter the crowded living room, Pervez Driver comes up to greet them. Sera is taken aback at how much he has aged since she ran into him at a friend's wedding last year. "Hello, Sera. Hello, Dinaz," he says, in the shy and tentative way he has always had around Sera. Or maybe he's like this around everybody, Sera thinks. "Please come and make yourself at home." He shoos off some of the young boys who are sitting on the couch to make room for the two of them.

"Where's Toxy?" Sera asks. After all, that is the reason they are here, to celebrate the engagement of the youngest of Aban and Pervez's three children.

"She's in the other room with her friends," Aban says airily. "You know how these youngsters are—not wanting to spend any time with us old fogies. And yes, my Dinu, you are now included amongst us oldies but goldies," she adds with a giggle. "After all, you are a married woman now and expecting your first child."

Dinaz jumps to her feet. "Nonsense," she says with a smile. "I'm going to go find Toxy and the others."

Pervez clears his throat, and the two women look up to acknowledge his presence. "Sera, what will you have to drink?" And before she can reply, he says, "Kingfisher, if memory serves me right?"

They all laugh at that. "See what a luccho he is?" Aban says. "Everybody thinks Pervez is this bhola-bhala henpecked husband, but I tell you, he's a big-big flirt, this man."

A man Sera has met at other functions but whose name she can never remember turns toward Aban. "But tell the truth, Aban, you still love this miserable husband of yours, don't you?" When he laughs, Sera notices his gums show.

"Absolutely," Aban says, taking Pervez's hand and holding it to her cheek. "Arre wah, what kind of a stupid question is that? My hubby is the best of the best."

"Oh, my God," says Meena Gupta. She is one of the few non-Parsis at the party. "Look at Pervez, he is blushing like a bride. At this rate, we won't know whether it's him or Toxy that's getting married."

Another guest Sera doesn't know slaps her knee as she laughs. "Good one, Meena, good one," she says.

Sera sips the Kingfisher that Pervez has poured for her and looks around discreetly. Despite a new coat of paint, it is amazing how much the room looks the same as it had the day she first met Feroz here, at her twenty-eighth birthday party.

She glances at Aban's round face, with its sagging, fleshy cheeks and multiple chins and marvels at how time has moved like a claw across that face, pulling it down with its harsh hand. Without the slightest hint of vanity, Sera glances at her reflection in the mirror of the Godrej cupboard that stood across the room and realizes that somehow she had been spared the ravages of time. Her middle-aged face has retained its youthful, alert vigor, and her skin is as smooth and tight as it had been when she met Feroz. In contrast, Aban's face has gotten as soft and mushy as a pudding. Her whole appearance is as shabby as this living room, with its old, unmatched furniture, the jaalas of dust under the chairs, the creaking ceiling fan that looks as if it has not been cleaned in twenty years. In contrast, Sera's living room sparkles like a jewel, with its pale, newly painted walls, the low, noiseless hum of the air conditioner, the expensive sofa set that Feroz had had specially built for the apartment, and the rosewood coffee table that Bhima polishes daily. Sera tries to remember if Aban had been this sloppy when they were younger. Even now, although she is dressed up for the special occasion, Aban's bra strap keeps slipping out from under her sleeveless sari blouse, and there is a brown stain on her bosom from where some chutney or sauce had undoubtedly fallen on it.

But if Pervez notices any of this, he does not seem to mind. Sera notices how he never strays too far from his wife and how, even when the Drivers are on opposite sides of the room, their eyes stray toward each other continually. Once, Aban blows a kiss across the room at her husband, and with a quick movement of his hand, Pervez catches it. Sera smiles when she sees that, and catching her look, Pervez smiles back sheepishly and raises his shoulders in a slow shrug.

Good old Aban and Pervez, Sera thinks to herself. Married all these years and still they act like lovebirds. She is aware of a sharp, sudden pain that she recognizes as envy. In order to bury it, she takes another sip of the Kingfisher, then looks up to see Aban making her way towards her. "Ae, come on, Sera, why such a long-tall face? The beer's not chilled enough or what?"

"The beer's fine," she says. "No, I'm enjoying myself, just sitting here thinking . . ."

"Of course, of course," Aban says, her mouth curving downward, so that she looks like a sad clown. "I am so insensitive at times, baap re baap, I could shoot myself. What a bafaat-master I am, a big, fat blunderbuss. You must be missing your dear Feroz, of course. After all, this is where you first met, na?"

Sera looks at her oldest friend, unsure of what to say. She envies Aban her innocence, her simple way of dividing the world into love and not-love; good and bad. But what she has been feeling is so much more complicated than that. Ever since Feroz's death she has had to grapple with this complicated equation, this bhelpuri of regret and resentment, of love and bitterness, of forgiveness and blame, of loneliness and relief. Does she miss Feroz? She is unsure of the answer. She does not miss the shame-inducing beatings, his clenched anger, her own cowering servility, and the hypocrisy of pretending that all is well in her marriage. No, that she does not miss. In fact, what she misses is not the marriage but the dream of the marriage. Even now, after all the intervening years, she misses the man she had thought she was marrying. She misses the aggressive courtship, the relentless wooing. She misses the fact that she will never know what it is to have a marriage like Aban and Pervez's—to be married for years and years and still blow each other a kiss across a room.

Aban doesn't give her a chance to reply. "Ho, Sera, remember the trip to Matheran? What-what fun we had there, na? I tell you,

Pervez and I still talk about trip to our kids. God, so young we were then."

This time, Sera smiles with genuine pleasure. That had indeed been a fun trip. Feroz and she had been married for only three months when Aban begged them to accompany her and her husband on their vacation. "Come on, yaar, it will double our pleasure if you two come," she'd begged. "Come on, come on, say yes, both of you."

And a smiling Feroz had agreed.

"Remember those badmaash monkeys?" Aban is now saying. "How we could never relax while eating breakfast on the veranda?" She turns to the other guests. "If you'd set your banana down for a second, they'd swoop in and run away with it. Once, one tried taking it right out of my hand. I tell you, I screamed so loudly, I think I deafened not only that monkey but its children's children." They all laugh.

"Hey, hey, you're forgetting the best part," Pervez says. "One day, I had my eyeglasses sitting on the table, and one of these red-arsed bastards comes swinging down the tree and takes off with them. And the cheek of him, he sits on a branch of a nearby tree, and what do you think? He puts on my glasses. Sits just beyond my reach chattering away in his monkey language. I was so irritated, I wanted to climb on that tree and give the bugger one-two tight slaps."

"Oh no," a guest says. "What did you do for the rest of the stay?"

"Arre, what do you mean?" Pervez says. Sera can tell by his uncharacteristically forceful manner that this is not Pervez's first drink. "After all, we had our brilliant Feroz Dubash with us. So what he did was, he sat there watching the monkey. In a few minutes, Feroz is figuring out that whatever we are doing, the monkey is doing. So Feroz went inside and brought out his own glasses. First, he put them on, just like the monkey. Then, he removed them and put them on his head. The monkey does the same thing. Then, Feroz puts one end of the frame in his mouth and nibbles on it. Same thing with the monkey. By this time, I was getting agitated, yaar. But my Aban tells me to trust Feroz. Just then, Feroz throws his glasses on the ground. And what do you know, the stupid monkey threw my glasses on the ground also. Quicker than a thief, I made a mad dash for them and picked them up. The stupid bugger sat on the tree showing us his yellow teeth and making funny-funny noises."

"But that was brilliant, just brilliant, yaar," Meena Patel says, as if the incident has just occurred. "Your husband was a smart man, Mrs. Dubash."

Sera acknowledges the compliment with a slight smile that feels forced and tight even to her. Because Pervez's recollection has unleashed another memory for her. She had forgotten the incident toward the end of their stay in Matheran, but now she remembers it in all its vividness.

They had returned to their hotel after a late dinner at Matheran's best restaurant. Earlier in the evening Feroz had been in a hearty, expansive mood. "My treat," he said to Pervez as soon as they entered the place. "I don't want you to touch your wallet tonight." Sera shot him an approving look. She was acutely aware of the fact that Aban and Pervez did not have much money, although to judge by their generosity, you'd never have guessed their rickety financial situation. Feroz signaled to the waiter. He was a handsome youth of about twenty, with large, white teeth and an eager-to-please attitude. "Listen," Feroz said to the boy. "I heard you don't have a permit room here yet. But we're from Bombay, and we're used a few drinks with our food. Understand? So see what you can do, achcha?" He slid him a twenty rupee note. "And here's some baksheesh for you," he added.

The waiter bowed. "Give me a few minutes, sahib. Let's see what I can come up with."

As always, Sera was embarrassed by this overt display of power. And given Aban and Pervez's humble means, Feroz's gesture felt even more obtrusive. But one look at her friends' admiring faces told her that she had misread the situation. Feroz winked at Pervez. "Look at her," he said, pointing his chin toward Sera. "She hates it when I do these things. But what I say is, if you can't get what you want, then you have to just take it."

Aban nodded. "Money makes the world go round," she said.

Just then the waiter returned with three cold bottles of Kingfisher. "From the owner's special stock, sahib," he said.

Feroz beamed. "Great."

The two women ordered. "Ae, darling, make sure you order meat dishes, okay?" Pervez told his wife. "No plants or leaves, please. We are men, not goats." He laughed, pleased at his own joke.

As the dinner went on, Sera noticed that Feroz grew quieter. She wanted to turn to him and ask if he had a headache, but fueled by the beer, Pervez was regaling them with stories from his boarding school days, and she was concentrating on laughing dutifully at the appropriate times. If the other two noticed Feroz's withdrawing from the conversation, they didn't say. "Let's get another plate of biryani, no?" Pervez said at one point and then looked tentatively at Aban. Before she could reply, Feroz had signaled for the waiter. "Another biryani and two more bottles of Kingfisher," he ordered. After the boy left, Feroz turned slightly toward Sera and gave her a look that she could not read. When the beer arrived, he poured himself a tall glass. Sera wanted to protest against his drinking too much, but Feroz looked as if he'd wrapped himself in a thin, cold sheet of ice. When she smiled at him, he stared back at her coldly, his face as distant as the moon.

"Su che, Feroz," Aban said finally. "All quiet-quiet you've become?"

He smiled at Aban, but Sera could see that the smile did not travel up to his eyes. "Just listening to all of you," he said unconvincingly.

Aban glanced at Pervez. "Chalo, maybe it's time to get back," she said. "It's been a long day, no?"

On the way home, Feroz participated in the conversation as all of them lamented having to leave the green, peaceful hill station and return to hot, crowded Bombay. At the hotel, he and Pervez wrestled over paying the cab fare. "Come on, yaar, fair is fair," Pervez protested. "You paid for dinner and all."

But Feroz fixed the driver a look. "Do not take money from this fellow," he said in a voice that brooked no argument. The taxiwalla accepted the note that Feroz was holding out to him.

"These menfolks," Aban said to Sera, rolling her eyes. "Always fighting about something, when everyone knows what they're really fighting about is the length of their ding-dongs."

"Aban," Sera cried out. "The things you say."

"Come on, yaar," Aban replied. "Stop acting like a virgin. This is one of the bonuses of being a respectable married woman, na?"

"Good night, Aban," Sera said, with a smile in her voice. "You are too much for me at times."

She and Feroz walked down the hallway toward their room in silence. Sera was conscious of an unspoken tension between them. She noticed that Feroz was holding himself stiffly, walking close to the wall to avoid touching her. "Are you okay, janu?" she inquired as they entered their room. "Have a headache or something?"

"I'm fine," he said shortly. He headed for the bathroom, and when he emerged, he had changed into his pajamas. He had also changed into a different mood; his face was flushed, and a vein throbbed in his forehead. Sera started at him in fascination, convinced that he was sick. She had never seen Feroz look like this. "Oh, God, Feroz, what's wrong?" she said, reaching out for his arm.

He brushed her hand away. "Do not touch me," he said through clenched teeth and it was then Sera realized that her husband was not sick, just furiously angry. Her mind went over the conversation at dinner. Had Pervez said anything that had upset Feroz? Had Aban's behavior irritated him?

"What . . . What's wrong?" she repeated.

Her turned on her then. "You. You are what's wrong." Ignoring her start of surprise, he went on, "Don't think I didn't notice your nataak during dinner. Embarrassed me in front of our friends. Flirting with a waiter young enough to be your son. Smiling at him, saying thank you every damn time he filled your glass with water. Don't think I didn't see everything that was going on. You must think I'm a total chootia, to flirt with another man—and that too a boy—while I'm sitting right there."

He was joking. He had to be joking. The whole thing was so preposterous it was surreal, Sera thought. She had barely noticed the waiter, would not recognize him if she passed him on the street tomorrow. She tried to formulate her outrage and surprise into a sentence and found that she couldn't. Her husband's preposterous accusation had left her speechless. Also, the man who stood before her, with the bulging eyes and the jaw that worked convulsively, was someone she didn't know. A perfect stranger. And part of her resented even having to defend herself against the ridiculousness of his charges. It was late; they were to get up early tomorrow for a day of sightseeing. And nobody had ever spoken to her in this tone before. She was a serious, thoughtful person, all her friends knew that. Not one of those cheap, heavily made up women who flirted with anything in pants. Didn't Feroz know this about her? And if he did not, what else didn't he know about her? After all, this was her character that he was attacking . . .

She blinked back the tears that were beginning to form in her eyes. "Your remarks are not worthy of you," she said, with all the dignity she could muster. Suddenly, she felt a spurt of anger, like a matchstick lit in the dark. "I was not even looking at that waiter. How dare you accuse me of——"

"Keep your voice down," he hissed. "You're in a hotel, not in your home."

"My voice *is* down. And you should have thought of that before you began all this . . ." A wave of remorse washed over her. "Listen, Feroz, it's late. You've probably had too much to drink tonight. Let's not spoil our trip with a stupid fight." She reached out to stroke his arm.

She did not see the punch coming. It landed on her right arm with such precision that the pain seemed to go straight through the thin layer of muscle and into the bone, where it vibrated like the silver gongs the priests rang in the fire temples. The pain was so sharp that she felt nauseated, so even while she cradled her right arm with her left hand, she drew her hurt arm over her stomach to control the nausea.

Feroz was standing over her, shuffling from one foot to the other like a boxer waiting to see if his opponent is down for the count. "I told you not to touch me," he said. "I warned you . . ."

She was conscious of a fear so large that it covered even the nausea. I have to get away from him, I have to call for help, she thought, but she was held in place by another thought—that this was no stranger she was trying to run away from, this was no dark man who had leapt at her from behind the bushes. This was her husband, the man she had married only three months ago, the one to whom she had pledged her future. She looked around the room in a blind panic, unsure of what to do next. The last time anyone had struck her had been in third grade, when she had gotten into a fight with a classmate over a stolen eraser. Raised by parents who were dead set against corporal punishment, she had escaped the physical violence that most of her contemporaries took for granted. Sera now realized she had no defenses, no strategies to protect herself from Feroz, who was still breathing heavily and had a mad, out-of-control look on his face.

She took a few tentative steps backward, until her knees hit the edge of the bed, and then she let herself down. And now the tears came, streaming down her face and landing on the hand that still cradled her stomach. Even as the pain in her arm receded a tiny bit, the pain in her heart grew. She cried at the swift brutality of Feroz's violent gesture; she sobbed at the injustice of his false accusation; and above all, she cried at the thought of spending year after year in the company of a man who thought so little of her that he could blithely accuse her of flirting with a common waiter. She, who had turned down marriage proposals from men who came from families of three generations of doctors. She, who had spent her Saturday evenings at Homi Bhabha Auditorium in the company of cultured, dignified men. She, whose father, one of the most eminent scientists in Bombay, had never so much as raised his voice at his wife.

Her heart swelled with outrage and, despite her fear, gave wings to her words. "In my whole life, no one has ever treated me like this," she said to him. "No one has ever accused me of inappropriate behavior. And nobody has ever hit me. If my father knows what you have done here tonight, he will . . ." Her voice cracked, and she was unable to finish her sentence.

And suddenly, as abruptly as the punch that had landed on her arm a few minutes ago, Feroz was on his knees before her, rubbing her arm, begging for forgiveness, his eyes shiny with tears. "Oh, God, Sera, I'm so ashamed. I'm so sorry, darling. I don't know what happened. . . . It's just that I love you so much, I can't bear the thought of losing you. And I'm so much older than you, and it makes me so nervous . . ."

She could feel the frost leaving her heart at his words, and despite herself, she was thankful. His tears were falling on her lap now, a reminder of his hot shame, and they melted the icy feeling that had come over her. She stroked his head with her hurt arm, ignoring the pain that shot through it when she raised it. Listening to his fervent apologies, his promises that it would never happen again, she felt assaulted by a million conflicting emotions—doubt, fear, apprehension, hope, shame, but above all, relief. Relief that Feroz had been restored by her tears, that he had been brought back to life by her words. "You know, it wasn't my intention to strike you, darling," he was now saying. "What happened was I just raised my hand and just then you were touching me and I don't know what happened—I think you just got in the way of my hand."

For a quick second, the memory of the well-landed punch flashed through Sera's mind, but she was as eager to believe her husband as he was to convince her. She put the memory out of her head, let Feroz hide it in the burlap sack of his soothing words. "I know you wouldn't hurt me deliberately, Feroz," she said. "And janu, why would I notice some low-class waiter when I have you?"

"I know. I know you're a respectable woman, Sera. You're right, it must have been the Kingfisher talking. Here, let me rub some Iodex on the spot where it hurts. I'm so sorry. I'm so clumsy, and you got in my way."

Now Sera grimaces at the memory. You should've left him then and there, she tells herself. The first time he hit you, you should have left. And you should never have covered up for him, never allowed his shame to become your shame. She remembers the long-sleeved, polka-dotted shirt she had worn the next morning, to cover up her bruised arm. "Goodness, Sera," Aban had said. "Why the long-sleeved dowager's clothes? It's not so cold, is it?"

And recalling her weak reply, unconvincing even to her ears, Sera feels a fresh wave of anger. You deserve what you got, she tells herself. You should've humiliated him in front of Aban and Pervez all those years back. That would've stopped his bullying right then.

Dinaz has walked back into the living room and is looking at her with a curious expression on her face. "You okay, Mummy?" she asks lightly. "Is the beer going to your head?"

For a moment, Sera feels as if Dinaz has read every dark thought that dripped into her mind like paint. Not for the first time, she wonders how much Dinaz knows about Feroz's sporadic assaults on her. After Dinaz was born, she did her best to muffle her cries when Feroz's fists rained on her body, to cover up the hurt that showed on her body and in her eyes. She had not wanted the shadow of her father's violence to eclipse Dinaz's childhood.

Sera brushes aside the cobweb of anger and forces herself to smile at her daughter. "I'd have to drink a lot more for that," she says. "How is Toxy? Did you see her?"

"Yah, she'll be out in a minute," Dinaz replies. "All the girls are back in the bedroom, doing their girl talk." She bends toward Sera and lowers her voice. "What's wrong, Mummy? You look so—sad."

Aban overhears Dinaz. "I said the same-to-same words to your mummy a minute ago, Dinu," she says. "I tell you, my Sera has not been the same since her beloved Feroz's death."

Mother and daughter exchange a quick look. Dinaz raises her right eyebrow slightly, in a gesture reminiscent of her father. And in that moment, Sera is sure that Dinaz knows. She is unsure of how that makes her feel. On the one hand, Dinaz's unspoken gesture implies a solidarity that gratifies Sera. On the other hand, she feels guilt at her inability to have spared her daughter the knowledge of her parents' frayed marriage.

Dinaz puts her arm around Sera. "Mummy's okay, Aban aunty," she says. "She's just a little tired, that's all. Our Bhima has been a little—preoccupied lately. So Mummy's had to do more of the housework."

"That's what you get when you treat the servant like the mistress of the house," Aban says promptly. "Pardon my saying so, Sera, but I've told you for years that Bhima will take advantage of you. Say what you will, these ghatis are ghatis. We Parsis are the only ones who treat our servants like queens. And it always backfires."

Sera wishes Dinaz had not brought up Bhima's name. Truth to tell, she is a little tired of thinking about Bhima. Ever since the Maya affair, she has had to think more about Bhima than about her own family. And the cold, distant way in which the girl treated Sera on the day of the abortion still rankles her. She had been looking forward to a carefree evening, but Dinaz has unwittingly launched Aban on her favorite subject.

Sera half-turns toward her daughter to give her a warning look, but it is too late. "I didn't say anything was wrong with Bhima," Dinaz says. "She just has her own problems, like we all do."

Aban stares openmouthed at Dinaz for a second and then bursts out laughing. She flings her arms around the younger woman and covers her face in a flurry of kisses. "Oh, oh, oh, this is too much," she roars. "Like mother, like daughter, I say. Oh, my God, look at this one's angry face—just like her mother she is looking. My God, their precious Bhima, they treat her like she is the Kohinoor diamond or something."

Another guest, whom Sera knows lives in Aban's building, pipes up. "I tell you, though, Aban is correct. You can't treat these people too well. Best to keep them at some distance. Otherwise they will take advantage of you, hundred percent guaranteed."

"Arre, did you see the story in last week's *Times of India*?" someone else says. "About that elderly Parsi lady who was murdered? They said she had been a professor at Elphinston College for forty years. Poor woman, stabbed in her bed by her own servant. Neighbors said the woman had worked for her for decades. But the professor kept her wedding jewelry in her house, see. And of course, the servant knew that. They are like snakes, these people. They can see in the dark, I think. Stabbed her seventeen times and took off with the jewelry. Paper said her boyfriend encouraged her."

"But really, our Parsis are also mad, if you ask me," Pervez says. "Being a professor and all, she should know not to keep jewelry in the house. That's why we have our own Central Bank. Should've had a locker there."

"But janu, that's what's wrong with us Parsis," Aban intones. "We're too trusting, you see. And honest, too. So naturally we think all other jaats will also be honest like us." Aban turns to Meena Patel. "Including the Gujaratis, of course. They are an honest community, also. But not these Maharashtrians. First-class crooks, they are."

The doorbell rings, and Pervez goes to the door. A second later, he comes back with Viraf. Aban rises from her seat with a squeal. "Ah, my Prince Charming is here. How are you, my darling? Working too hard, Dinu says. Well, what to do, as a soon-to-be father of course you have to work hard. Still, you are looking too thin, my dear," she says, pinching his cheek.

Viraf grins. "Hello, Aban aunty," he says. "You're looking as lovely as ever. And by the way, I've gained five kilos in the last few months. Except it's all going to my dimchu," he adds, patting his stomach.

Aban beams, as she usually does in the company of handsome men. "Achcha, Viraf, you be the referee. We were just saying that you can't trust these non-Parsi servants, no matter how much you do for them. So what do you say? Are Sera and Dinaz making Bhima sit on their heads, or not?"

Viraf looks around the room. "Oi, Aban aunty," he says. "Bad manners, yaar. You haven't even introduced me to Toxy's hubby to be. So where is he?"

"Very clever, very clever, changing the subject." Aban laughs good-naturedly. "Great diplomat, our Viraf. I think they're going to send him to Pakistan to negotiate with that General Musharraf—I call him General Sheriff—over Kashmir." Her face falls. "Darius and his family won't be here. His mother thinks it's bad luck for the bride and groom to see each other a few days before the wedding. God knows where our Parsi women get these ideas from."

Dinaz grabs Viraf's hand. "Come on, I'll lead you to Toxy," she says. "You can at least say hi to her."

Take me with you, Sera wants to say to her daughter's departing back. I don't want to be stuck here with these ignorant people. "Tell Toxy to come say hello to us old fogies," she calls, and Dinaz lifts her hand in acknowledgment.

Aban looks as though she is about to resume her discourse, but just then her maidservant, Jaya, pokes her head in from the kitchen. "Bai," she calls. "Come for a minute, na. Cutlets are ready."

Aban grumbles as she gets to her feet. "Can't manage for ten seconds without me," she says.

Sera is chatting with Meena Patel about the ugly new skyscrapers that are sprouting up all over Bombay when Aban reenters the room. Behind her, Jaya, a sprightly girl of about twenty, is holding a large tray heaped with mutton cutlets. "Chalo, hurry up," Aban says. "Serve them to our guests while they are hot-pot."

As Aban hands out small paper plates, Jaya trails behind her, offering the cutlets to the guests. "Leave the tray on the table," Aban directs her when she is done. She rolls her eyes behind the girl's back as Jaya sets down the tray.

"See how she walks, swaying her hips and all?" Aban says after the maid is back in the kitchen. "I tell you, such nakhras this girl does. Even if I tell her to run down to the bakery, she won't leave the house until she has her kaajal on. And she wants a new pair of clothes every Diwali. Better than my own children I treat her."

"Well, God, Aban, she is just a child," Sera says. "What do you expect?"

Aban shrieks with laughter. "What did I tell you, what did I tell you?" she yells. "Oh, Sera, you're too much. I swear, I think you're a Communist or something."

"Ae, speaking of Communists and other thugs, listen to this," another guest says. "This happened to the old woman living in my building. About a month ago, someone rings her doorbell, and the poor woman opens the door. Three goondas, big, tough fellows, push her aside and enter the flat. This is at three in the afternoon, mind you. Before she can say anything, they are asking her only one question—Where are the biscuits? So this poor innocent woman thinks they are hungry and takes them to the kitchen. There, she climbs on a stool and pulls down a packet of glucose biscuits. But for some reason, this makes the thugs even more angry. They slap her a few times—an eighty-year-old woman they are slapping, can you imagine?—and tie her to a chair. Then, they turn her whole house upside down, top to bottom, looking for something. When they are not finding it, they slap her two-three times more and leave."

The questions pile up on top of one another:

"What happened to the woman?" someone asks.

"What were they looking for?"

"Did the poor thing die?"

"Stop, stop, I'm telling you, na," the man says. "Well, it turns out they got the building number mixed up. Seems that there was a smuggler who had cheated someone else out of gold biscuits—you know, bars of gold. So that bugger had hired these goondas to go to his house to recover them. Instead, this poor woman got stuck in the middle. Only reason she survived was her neighbor, who brought her dinner every night, knocked and knocked on her door and finally let herself in. She found the poor woman strapped in the chair. Seems she had even done soo-soo in her knickers."

"Bastards should be hanged for their actions," another guest says.

"They deliberately target Parsis, I tell you," someone else cries. "They know we are small in numbers, so they pick on us."

"Well, in this case, it was not deliberate," Sera murmurs.

"Okay, but generally speaking, it's true," another woman says fiercely. "They know we are a peace-loving community, so they target us. Let them try such nonsense with the Muslims and then they'll see. They wouldn't dare—"

"Arre, yaar, we should start our own organization. Like a Parsi Shiv Sena."

Aban giggles. "And who will be our Bal Thackeray?" she asks, referring to the ferocious head of the right-wing Hindu organization. "That's our trouble, you know. My daddy always used to say, the problem with Parsis is that everyone wants to be a general and no one wants to be a soldier."

Sera sighs to herself. She has heard some variation of this conversation her entire life. She is both amused and irritated by the people around her; even as she is appalled by their chauvinism, she feels affection for their lofty ideas and bombastic dreams. And besides, she reasons with herself, they're basically good people, you know that. A little soft in the head maybe, with all that interbreeding and stuff, but lovable in their own way.

One of the younger male guests, who Sera knows is married to a Catholic girl, speaks up. "Ah, what does it matter anyway? They say there's less than hundred thousand of us. We'll all be extinct in a few generations, tops."

There is a sudden, brittle silence in the room. The unspoken message—Yes, and by marrying outside the community boys like you are hurrying up that day of extinction—hovers in the air. Sera shifts on the sofa, feeling acutely the young man's discomfort. To break the uncomfortable pause, she speaks with uncharacteristic gaiety. "Well, while we're still all here, all the more reason to live life to the fullest, no?"

"Hear, hear," Pervez says, raising his glass. "Well said, Sera."

Viraf has walked back into the living room. "Here's to extinction," he says. "But before that, here's to Toxy and Darius's long and happy marriage, and may Aban and Pervez be grandparents soon." He lifts his glass higher, swaying slightly on his feet. "In fact, here's to many, many Parsi babies—toward which effort, my wife and I will soon be making our own little contribution."

A tall, bearded man standing next to Viraf thumps him heartily on the back. "Congratulations," he says. "This is exactly what our Parsi com needs, young, healthy men like you."

Viraf grins. "And women, like my wife," he says lightly. "Let's not forget the women."

"Of course, of course," the tall man says, turning hurriedly toward Dinaz. "I meant no offense, my dear."

Dinaz glares at Viraf. "Don't pay any attention to my husband," she assures the man. "He's just being a joker, as usual."

Across the room, Aban squeezes Sera's hand. "So sweet, your Dinu and Viraf are." She sighs. "Can you imagine, Sera? I mean, when we were first working at Bombay House, who could have imagined that someday we would have all this?"

Sera feels a rush of warmth toward Aban. She and Pervez have had a tough life, she knows. It could not have been easy, raising three children on their salary. Plus, Pervez came from a poor family and also helped support his parents while they were alive, Sera remembers. Then there was Aban's mastectomy a few years ago. But despite their humble lifestyle, Aban and Pervez have succeeded in building a life together. Their apartment is old and shabby, but all three of their children have finished college and now have good jobs. She would've traded her life with Aban, Sera suddenly realizes. She would've given up the prestige and the wealth that came from being Feroz's wife to have had the devotion and love that Pervez felt for Aban. She would've preferred to slave at a job, ride the crowded trains daily, and come home exhausted and sweaty at the end of the workday rather than to live in the splendid isolation Feroz had imposed upon her.

As far as Sera knows, there are no dark secrets in Aban's life. Looking at her old friend now, Sera sees a childlike purity and clarity in her eyes that she knows comes from not living half her life in the shadows. At times, Aban had complained to Sera about the injustice of having to provide for Pervez's old parents. But in the same breath she would talk about how grateful she was for her in-laws, how well they treated her and took care of her children when she was at work. During those times, Sera would bite down on her tongue to keep from revealing how wretchedly Banu treated her. Or she would enthusiastically sing the praises of her father-in-law and hope that Aban did not notice her silence about her mother-in-law.

Now Sera takes her old friend's hand in both of hers. "You're right, Aban. We were so young then. How could we have ever imagined all this? I mean, your little Toxy getting married. God, I remember the day she was born."

Aban lowers her voice. "Every sad or happy occasion of my life, you have been part of. Don't think I will ever forget all your many kindnesses toward my family. What I would have done without you, I don't know."

Sera is shocked. They have been friends for decades, but she has never felt that close to Aban. Still, she is absurdly moved by Aban's words. "Same here," she says, hoping Aban doesn't hear the insincerity in her voice. "I feel the same way, dear."

Jaya comes up to Aban. "Bai, dinner is ready," she says.

Aban gets to her feet. "Attention, attention," she says. When the chatter in the room has died down, she gives the familiar cry that announces dinner at Parsi weddings. "Jamva chaloji," she says with a grin. "Come on, let's eat. It's buffet style—the food is awaiting you in the kitchen."

"Well, that was a fun evening," Viraf says during the drive home. His hands on the wheel are steady, and he drives swifly through the uncharacteristically deserted night streets. "An evening filled with typical Parsi chauvinism, the usual bullshitting by drunken Parsi gentlemen, and of course, let's not forget the oily, aggressively nonvegetarian food. So much for our diet."

"Wonder which one of the guests will drop dead of a heart attack tonight," Dinaz adds.

"Oh no, dear, that won't be until the actual wedding feast, when they eat the full, cholesterol-filled, five-course dinner," Viraf replies promptly. Dinaz and Sera both giggle.

"Children, children," Sera protests weakly. "Stop being so mean. Aban is my oldest friend."

"Oh, no offense to Aban aunty," Viraf says. "She's a darling, a dear, and a lamb. In fact, we're planning on running away to Switzerland first thing tomorrow morning. She'll be waiting for me at V.T. Station. We're taking the train to Switzerland."

Dinaz smacks Viraf on his thigh. "Stop with your koila jokes, yaar," she says. "I swear, your sense of humor is going from bad to worse."

But Viraf is unstoppable. "She has promised to educate me on the superiority of Parsi culture during the journey," he continues. "Did you know that the Parsis invented honesty?" Glancing at Dinaz, who is trying her best not to laugh, he says, "It's true—ask

anyone. On July sixteenth in the fourth century B.C., the Parsis—
or I should say the Zoroastrians—invented honesty. The next day,
they invented goodness and charity."

Sera groans. "Okay, Viraf, okay . . ."

"Wait, I'm not done. Aban aunty also wants to discuss with me
the possibility of starting a movement to lead the Parsis back to
their ancestral home in Iran. The great Persian empire will rise
again. Hey, if the Jews could claim Israel, why not we Iran? So,
who knows? We may give up Switzerland and go directly to Iran.
Today, Bombay. Tomorrow, Iran. Repeat after me: Tomorrow,
Iran."

Dinaz turns back to face Sera. "I swear, if this gadhera ever
drinks again in front of me, I'm going to kill him. I just hope our
baby doesn't inherit his father's stupid sense of humor."

Viraf grins happily. "Scoff as much as you want, my dear," he
says. "I'll send you a postcard from Iran."

Sera closes her eyes. It has been a long day and she is exhausted.
She is amazed at how drained she feels. Either I'm catching a cold or
I'm just not used to these big parties anymore, she thinks. Dinaz has
often told her that she has become reclusive since Feroz's death, but
until tonight, Sera had not really thought much about the subject.
She knows it is one of the reasons Dinaz insisted that she and Viraf
move into Sera's home. During those six months after Feroz's death
and before the children moved in, Sera had found little reason to
leave the house other than to go check on Banu. Finally, Dinaz and
Viraf had stopped by one evening and made their offer. "Our little
flat is too far from our jobs, Mummy," Dinaz had said. "The rush-
hour commute is just getting to be impossible these days. And you
seem so alone in this big house since Daddy has been gone. So we
were wondering—how would you feel if we moved in with you?"

She had been careful to control her first reaction, which had
been one of undiluted joy. Having Viraf and Dinaz living in this

house! Having their youthful presence chase away the ghosts of the past. Not having to spend her days unconsciously awaiting Feroz's footsteps and then feeling that strange blend of guilt and relief when she realized he was not coming home. It would be lovely to have something to look forward to at the end of the day, to cook the children's favorite meals for them and watch in satisfaction as they ate with her in the dining room.

But the memory of those wretched years in Banu Dubash's home stopped her from shouting out her joy at their proposal. "It's not easy for adults to live with each other," she said. "You know, your granna really made my life hell when I lived with her. I would hate to find myself acting like her, ever. And you are young and haven't been married for so long. You need time to build up your marriage. If things were to go wrong between us, I would never forgive myself."

"Sera mummy, stop it," Viraf said, laughing. "Please, you are nothing like Banu granna. Even seeing her now, I can imagine what a tyrant she must've been. And anyway, Dinaz worries so much about you. Besides, you would be doing us a favor—the commuting to work is too much for us, really. Still, it's your house, so you—"

"It's not my house," she interrupted. "Whatever is mine belongs to both of you, you know that, Viraf. It's not like I have six other children. This house is yours, Viraf, don't ever feel that—"

"In that case, it's settled," Dinaz said. "We're moving back into our own house."

"Just think about what I've said," Sera argued. She sighed. "Of course, it would be lovely having you two living here. Still, this is not an easy decision. Give it some thought, deekra."

Slumping in the backseat, Sera gazes drowsily at Dinaz and Viraf in the front. Thank you, God, for my children, she whispers. The joy these two have given me is my reward for staying with Feroz all these years.

The car turns onto Banu Dubash's street, and as always, Viraf slows down. "The light's still on in the flat," he says. "The night nurse is still up."

"Granna is probably throwing one of her tantrums," Dinaz says. "The poor nurse—I don't know how anyone can put up with the old lady."

You said it, Sera thinks. I certainly couldn't.

15

Four years into her marriage, Sera had woken up one morning to feel something hot and sticky in the back of her throat. For a minute, she thought it was the start of another sinus infection, but when she swallowed cautiously, her throat did not hurt.

It was hate. Hate that was lodged like a bone in her throat. Hate that made her feel sick, that gave her mouth a bitter, dry taste. Hate that entered her heart like a fever, that made her lips curve downward like a bent spoon.

It was a beautiful December day. A pigeon sat on Sera's windowsill, cooing its mindless melody. There was a slight chill in the air, a welcome respite from the hot Bombay sun. But lying there awake, Sera could not participate in the beauty of the day. She felt dull and blackened, as if hate was corroding her body. She stayed in bed, exhausted. She couldn't remember another time in her life when she had loathed anybody. But now, hate dripped in her throat, thick and ugly, making her feel diseased.

She tossed the cotton sheet off her body and leapt out of bed. Gathering up her clothes in a hurried rush, she went to the crib where Dinaz lay sleeping and shook her tiny body until her daughter's eyes finally flew open and her little mouth widened in a yawn. "Come on, wake up, Dinu," Sera whispered. "You and I are going on an adventure today." She went into the bathroom, turned on the hot water geyser, and adjusted the plastic bucket under the pouring water before she hurried the child into the bathroom with her. "We are going to take a bath together today," she said.

They were both dressed before they emerged from the bedroom. Leaving Dinaz in the living room, Sera went into the kitchen to find her mother-in-law. "I'm taking Dinaz out with me for the day today," she said, averting her eyes from Banu's penetrating ones. "We'll be back later."

"Going out of the house in the morning? What about breakfast for baby? And the lunch we're cooking? You can't waste my Feroz's hard-earned money . . ."

Sera felt the thickness in the back of her throat. She was afraid of looking Banu in the eye, afraid that her face would reflect the loathing she felt for the older woman. "I'll explain to Feroz myself," she said. "I have to leave now. I'll be home this evening. Bye."

Resolutely ignoring Banu's dark mutterings, steeling herself against the barrage of harsh words that questioned her motives, her upbringing, and her morality, Sera grabbed Dinaz's thin arm as if it were a chicken wing and pulled her toward the front door. She exhaled loudly as soon as the door shut behind her. Still, she kept up a fast clip as they headed down the hallway toward the elevator. At the last minute, she swerved. Instead of waiting for the elevator, they would take the stairs. She forced herself not to look back in fear, to see if Banu was following them. "She's just a silly old lady," she kept saying to herself, but the feeling in her stomach was identical to the one she got when watching a scary movie in a dark theater.

Once on the street, she realized that it was only 9:30 in the morning and she had no idea where to go. She thought briefly of stopping by to see Feroz at work and was shocked at the heaviness she felt at the idea. She wondered whether to drop in on Aban but the thought of her friend's endless chatter made her feel claustrophobic. And surely Aban would read something on Sera's face, surely she would pry and want to know what was wrong.

No, she would take Dinaz and go visit Mummy and Daddy. They would be glad to see them and they wouldn't ask any questions. Sera suddenly longed for the cool sanctuary of her old bedroom. Also, she had not visited them in several weeks, and she knew that her absence hurt their feelings, although they were too decent ever to say so. Yes, she would go visit her parents. Her mind made up, she abruptly changed directions and started toward the taxi stand, pulling Dinaz along. "Mummy, slowly," the girl said, and with a start of guilt, Sera slackened her pace.

She felt her heart slow down as soon as she was in the cab and had given the driver the address. She watched the streets fly by and wondered why she had not done this earlier. She was suddenly so anxious to be at her parents' home that she almost urged the cabdriver to go through the amber light. Her entire body leaned forward, propelled by a fierce desire for speed. She wanted to keep moving, keep running, put as much distance as she could between herself and Banu's gloomy, life-draining house. But the cab stopped at the light. Almost immediately, a swarm of beggars appeared at her window. She looked away, afraid that any eye contact would encourage them to linger. Dinaz tugged at her blouse. "Mummu, money," she said. Sera sighed. Dinaz was such a sensitive child. Already she knew better than to harass her father to give alms to beggars. Feroz often said that he did not believe in encouraging beggary and would prohibit Sera from tossing a coin into a waiting hand when they were out together. "Saala, lazy bastards," he would say. "I'd like that too—lazing around all day, making easy money."

Digging into her purse for a few coins, Sera suddenly laughed out loud at a memory from Feroz's birthday earlier that year. Dinaz had watched as her grandparents made Feroz stand facing east, put a red tilla on his forehead and a garland of flowers around his neck. Then Banu had gone to the coffee table and returned with an envelope of cash. "Happy birthday, my dear boy," she said, embracing him.

Suddenly Dinaz, who was sprawled on the couch, sat up. "Saala, lazy bastard," she yelled. "Making easy money." Her intonation so perfectly imitated her father's that for a second Sera thought the words came from the ever-present Polly.

Feroz's cheeks puffed, and he looked as if he was ready to chastise Dinaz for her language. But Sera was making a strange sound, and it took the rest of them a minute to figure out she was guffawing with laughter. Feroz's lips quivered, and he looked uncertain as to whether to scold his daughter or join his wife in her laughter. Sera helped him decide. With tears streaming down her cheeks, she went up to Dinaz and put her arms around her. "You naughty, naughty girl," she said, squeezing Dinaz to her side. "You mustn't talk like that, understand."

By this time, all of them were laughing. "This girl is going to follow in her grandpa's steps and become a lawyer, I tell you," Freddy said. "Will bring the High Court to its knees, this one."

Now, as the cab took off, the smile lingered on Sera's face. She glanced down at Dinaz, and her heart twisted with love. She is the only bright spot in my life anymore, she thought. She and, to some extent, Freddy pappa. The rest of them—he and his mother—they have ruined my life.

At six that evening, Sera's mother, Jehroo, glanced at her husband and then turned to Sera. "Sweetheart, we have a dinner to go to this evening. Should we cancel? Or are you going to your home soon?"

She was about to tell them to go ahead with their plans, that she and Dinaz would be leaving soon, when she realized she was not leaving. She was not going back to Feroz's house. The knowledge took her breath away, as if her mind was just catching up with what her body had already known. She stared at her mother, wondering how to put this in words that would reveal just enough, words that would conceal the full extent of the dread she felt at the thought of returning to Banu's house. "I was wondering," she began, "That is, I thought Dinaz and I would stay here tonight. I mean, you and Daddy go to your dinner. But I thought, Mummy, that we would be here when you returned."

Jehangir Sethna looked as if he was about to say something, but his wife flashed him a warning look. "Sure, Sera," Jehroo said smoothly. "You know this is your house, darling. You're always welcome here. But are you sure Feroz won't mind sharing his lovely wife with us?"

Again, that hot drip at the back of her throat. Sera swallowed hard before replying. "I think he will manage okay, Mummy. But you and Daddy should get ready for your party."

"Hey, if my darling daughter and granddaughter are staying here, I don't want to go to dinner," Jehengir said promptly. "I'm sure the Pundoles will understand."

"No, no, Daddy, don't cancel your plans, please." And seeing the familiar stubborn look come over her father's face, she added, "Actually, I . . . I need a little privacy to . . . think about things."

Jehroo nudged her husband and blinked repeatedly, averting her face from her daughter so that only he could see her. "Come on, Jehangu. Let's keep our engagement. We can come home a little early if you like. Then you can stay up and talk to your daughter till your stomach is full."

After they left, Sera phoned the Dubash residence. Please let Feroz answer the phone, she pleaded. Please, please.

"Hello?" Feroz's crisp voice sounded so clear on the phone that, for a second, Sera forgot the speech she had prepared.

"Feroz? It's me. Listen, I was just calling to say——"

"Where the hell are you? We've had dinner ready for the last hour, waiting for you to get home."

"I'm at my parents' home. Feroz, listen. I was thinking I might stay here for a few days."

She heard the harsh intake of his breath before he felt silent. Say something, she pleaded silently. Say something and remove this taste of mothballs from my mouth.

The silence held. "Hello?" she said finally.

"I'm here."

"Aren't you going to say anything?"

This time, she heard him gritting his teeth. "What's there to say? You leave the house without any warning this morning, you don't come home this evening while we sit around like chootias, waiting for you while the food gets cold, and now you tell me you're staying at your mummy's house, for no rhyme or reason. What should I do? Come crawling on my knees and beg you to come home? You've picked the wrong man for that, Sera."

For a second, she almost saw it his way. She imagined him coming home tired from work and asking for her and Dinaz; pictured the smug look on Banu's face as she told him that his wife had been gone since morning and had taken his daughter with him.

"Do . . . do you want to say good night to Dinaz?" she asked tentatively.

"How long are you planning to keep my daughter away from me?" he asked. "And you mean to say, your parents are encouraging you to neglect your duties?"

"Feroz, it's not like that. I didn't even plan any of this. I don't so much as have a pair of underwear or a sadra with me. I don't know how long I'll need to stay here. It's just that things at home are so tense right now between me and your mummy—"

"Bullshit." The words came down the phone line like a punch

and set her ears ringing. "Don't blame Mamma or anyone else in my family for your hysteria. You have made your bed, now lie in it."

She stared at the phone in disbelief, not registering the fact that Feroz had hung up on her. Still holding the receiver, she sat down heavily on the couch. Was it possible that they had gotten cut off, compliments of the inefficient Bombay telephone company? But even as she thought about the possibility, her heart told her that Feroz had deliberately slammed down the phone. She debated whether to call him back, but she knew that his pride would not let him pick up. And if Banu answered the phone, her humiliation would be complete.

Two weeks went by without any communication with Feroz. At first, Dinaz asked for her father and grandfather, but soon the questions ceased and she appeared to have adjusted to their new life. But was it a new life? Or just a temporary respite from her old one? Jehroo Sethna practically asked that question of her daughter one day. The two of them had gone shopping at Colaba, leaving Dinaz at home with her grandfather. "Let's pick up some more knickers for baby," Jehroo said as they passed a narrow shop that sold children's clothes. Then she stopped and looked at her daughter intently. "Or should we not?" she added gently. "It's so hard knowing what to do about her clothes and all without knowing—the future."

Sera knew immediately what her mother was asking. She looked away, unable to bear the gentle pity she saw in her mother's eyes. Without being aware of it, they had stopped walking, so that the other shoppers gave them dirty looks before walking around them. Sensing a captive audience in the two women, the vendors in their booths raised their nasal cries to frenzied proportions, their voices drowning one another out: "'Allo, ladies, what you looking for? Cassettes, perfume, soaps, Kraft cheese in cans fresh from Australia. Chocolates, too—Nestlé, Toblerone. Arre, take a dekho, this is aasli maal, madam, the real stuff. All phoren imported stuff, come on, good cheap price I'll give you."

Lost in their private communication, Sera and Jehroo ignored the restless rustlings their still presence was generating among the desperate vendors.

"Come on," Jehroo said, pulling Sera by the hand. "Let's go to the Irani restaurant and have a cold drink. And then we can talk."

At the restaurant, they each ordered a Thums Up and a plate of chicken sandwiches. They sat in a companionable silence for a minute. Then Jehroo turned toward Sera. "For two weeks, I've kept my mouth shut. Two weeks, hell, for two years now I've kept my mouth shut. What, you don't think I've noticed the dark chakars under your eyes, the way you never smile anymore? Deekra, I'm your mother. I carried you in my stomach for nine months. I know every inch of your skin. If a mosquito lands on you, I feel the sting."

Sera smiled. "I feel that way about Dinaz," she said.

"Exactly. The menfolk can remain blind to what's under their noses. But we women, we see everything. And so I'm asking you, Sera—what is going on with your marriage? All these months I've minded my own business, told myself you are now your husband's property, no longer ours. But now I cannot bear to watch my only child look so miserable. So I'm asking you—why are you at our house? And why hasn't Feroz called even once or come to take you home?"

He beats me, she wanted to say. And his mother makes my days a living hell. The words formed on her lips like foam at the edge of a beach and then died away. She could not burden her mother with this. She did not wish to take the dark circles from under her own eyes and place them under her mother's. She had no desire to un-burden her own heart by packing her grief on her mother's back. Besides, there was no telling what her father would do if he found out about what Feroz did to her behind closed doors and in the dark. How sometimes it was just an appetizer—a quick but hard pinch, his thumb and index finger in a scissorlike grip that pulled at her flesh and made it ache days later. How, at other times, it was a full-course meal, a banquet that included punches, slaps, and an occasional kick—a meal that left her so full she had to spend hours the next day deciding which long-sleeved dress to wear and how to explain the bruises on her face. What was worse than the actual beatings was the speculative, triumphant look she saw on Banu's face the morning after. In some way, those beatings joined her and Banu, gave the older woman an inroad into the broken, littered streets of Sera's heart.

No, there was no telling what her parents would do if they ever found this out. Violence, cruelty—these were things outside their experience. And they were too old to have to rescue her, to fight her battles for her. Besides, her mother had tried to warn her about Banu. She had offered to make inquiries, to track down rumors. And how arrogantly, how blithely, she, Sera, had dismissed that offer. How idealistic, how confident that woman who had left her parents' home had been. What was left of her now? A tremble in her right hand that she sometimes couldn't control; dark circles under her eyes, and a heart that broke like a fallen plate.

"Mummy, Feroz and I are having some difficulties, obviously," she said carefully. "I know it's an imposition on you and Daddy, having me and the little one over. But if I can stay just a little longer, I will—"

"Now you will make me angry," Jehroo said. "Darling, don't play with my words like they are marbles. You know how much your daddy and I enjoy having you with us. But that's the point—your place is not with us; it is with your husband and your in-laws. So tell me, what bothers you?"

"She interferes with us a lot." Sera said the first thing that came into her head. "You know, she's an old woman, set in her ways." She realized she was making Banu sound like an eccentric old woman, instead of the evil monster that she was.

"This joint family system is a curse on India, I tell you," Jehroo said. "Countless women have been sacrificed to its cause." She looked out of the restaurant to where a young white man wearing baggy, floral pants and a printed, loose-flowing shirt, stood talking to a woman in a cotton skirt carrying a backpack. "You know, we Indians talk about these Westerners and how they kick their children out of their homes when they turn eighteen, how they put their elders in old people's homes, how they don't have the same love for family that we do. But sometimes I wonder if we're really as superior as we think we are. What's the point of everyone living together if all it does is cause kit-pit at home? Better to go your own separate ways than always fighting-fighting.

"You know our neighbors Freny and Jamshed? Well, they are taking care of Jamshed's mother in their home. The other day I went to visit the old lady, and what do you think? The poor woman is covered in bedsores. Freny says she's just not strong enough to turn her in bed as often as she needs to. You know, Jamshed is at work all day, so it all falls on Freny. During my whole visit, that's all Freny did—complain about the old woman, about how she doesn't cooperate in turning in the bed or when they have to lift her to give her the bedpan. When everyone can see that the poor thing is all skin and bone. She can barely lift her eyebrows, let alone her own buttocks. But Freny is convinced she is doing this on purpose, to harass her. And Freny herself—what to say about her? She looks like she's aged fifty years in two months. Says she can barely leave the house for more than an hour at a time, says she smells urine and rubbing alcohol even in her sleep. Her whole life has been taken over by this problem." Jehroo raised her eyes to Sera. "Beta, I'm sure she prays for the old lady's death day and night. And yet we criticize those foreigners for warehousing their old people. I pray that when my time comes, I'm not a burden to anybody." She smiled. "Just slip some pills in custard or pudding, and one, two, three—problem solved."

Sera reached over and stroked her mother's hand, spilling a little water from one of the glasses the waiter had brought to them as soon as they'd sat down. "Mummy, don't say that. If something happened to you, I don't know what I'd ever do."

Jehroo's voice was soft and gentle. "Your daddy and I won't be around forever, darling. We're getting old, you know. Which is why I say, your place is with your husband. In every marriage there is some tension. It is unfortunate you live with your in-laws. But that's a choice you made. Just tolerate the old woman as much as you can. And with your good nature, you should be able to win her over."

Sera smiled at her mother, but her heart was cold. She felt removed from this elegant woman with the big, kind eyes. Her mother might have lived more years than she had, but at that moment Sera felt older, more jaded, more experienced. Jehroo Sethna had been blessed with kind, wealthy parents who cared for her; an erudite, gentle husband who doted on her, a daughter who loved and respected her. She had never known the impact of a man's hard knuckles bouncing off her soft flesh; she had never experienced the claustrophobic feeling of being locked in a room in her own house; she had never had her husband contemptuously tell her she was getting old, fat, and ugly, or accuse her of flirting with every man they encountered together. She had never known the ratlike swiftness of eyes that followed her every move in her own house. Jehroo Sethna had not suffered, Sera realized, and for the first time in her life, she felt distant from her mother, unable to connect with her at a level other than the obvious love they had for each other.

"Tell you what, Mummy," she said. "Let's go buy those knickers for Dinaz. That way, if I decide to stay with you a few more weeks, we won't have to go shopping again."

One afternoon three weeks later, there was a knock on the door, and Sera opened it to find Freddy Dubash leaning against the wall. Freddy had on his brown bowler hat, and his gold watch chain dangled from his pocket. "Freddy pappa," Sera cried with delight. "What are you doing here?" Her faced clouded over. "Is everything . . . is Feroz all right?"

"Everything is fine," the old man said. He pretended to frown. "Arre wah. Do I need a reason to come to see my daughter and granddaughter?"

Sera flushed. "No, of course not. Please, come on in. Daddy," she called. "Look who is here."

The two men hugged. "Kem, Freddy, how are you?" an unperturbed Jehangir said, as if Freddy stopped by his house every day. "Please, have a seat."

"Fine, fine," Freddy replied, lowering himself into a chair. "I saw in the paper that Franz Gutman is going to be conducting this Saturday. I have one of his early recordings of Haydn's Symphony Number Ninety-four. Are you going to the concert?"

"Of course. Wouldn't miss it for anything. And now that my Sera is here to accompany me . . ." He glanced at Sera and then fell silent as he realized the circumstances of Sera's presence. An awkward silence fell over them. Jehengir looked around the room for help. "I'll go wake Jehroo up," he said. "She's napping with Dinu."

"Actually, don't," Freddy said. "What I mean is, I actually wanted to talk to Sera in private for a few minutes, if that's okay with you."

Jehangir looked at his daughter for a cue. When she nodded imperceptibly, he rose to his feet with a sigh. "See you soon," he said vaguely.

Alone with Freddy, Sera felt a heavy shyness fall over her, making it difficult for her to lift her eyes toward him. When she finally forced herself, she noticed that Freddy was staring hard at her. There was a serious look on his face, a look of purposefulness that she had never seen before.

"Just like that you walked out," he said. She could hear the hurt in his voice, and she imagined what it must've been like for him, discovering that she was not returning, realizing that his only music companion had deserted him. "Not even a good-bye, not even a 'Freddy pappa, stay well, I will miss you.' Bas, just like that you are gone. Taking away all the joy out of my house." His voice had dropped and his chin was resting on his chest, so that she had to strain to hear him. She felt as if he was talking to himself.

"How is Banu mamma?" she asked, realizing as she asked the question that she really wanted to know.

His head shot up. "Banu? I wish I could say my darling missus has turned into Mary's little lamb, all meek and tender. But the sad truth is she is as mean and jabri as ever. She's driving poor Gulab mad with her do-thises and do-thats."

"Does . . . does Feroz know that you're here?"

Freddy looked at Sera, his watery eyes searching her face. "Listen, deekra," he said seriously. "I've come here on a very important mission. I want you to pay good attention to what I am saying." Suddenly he looked exasperated and addressed the room. "Will you look at this girl, with her face as long as a pineapple? I've come all this way to see her, and all she is wanting to know is whether her hubby knows I am here." He sighed dramatically. "Yes, my dear, Feroz knows I'm here. And more important, he knows why I'm here. Now will you pay attention to what I have to say?"

Sera nodded.

"Good. Two days ago, I ran into one of my old clients. Divan Shah is his name. He is a very rich man now, but a few years back he was in legal trouble and let's just say I helped him a lot. Anyway, all this is of no interest to you. The main thing is, this man is a builder. You remember Moti Mahal, the big bungalow that's at the end of our street? Well, turns out that the old woman who lived there for over fifty years has sold the building and surrounding land to Divan's company. They are going to knock it down and build a new seven-story building there."

Sera found her attention wandering. She wanted to go wake Dinaz from her nap so that she could spend some time with her grandpa Freddy. How will Dinaz respond to him? she wondered.

"My dear, are you listening? What I'm trying to say is, I spoke to Divan about buying a flat in his new building. He is willing to give it to me at a good price. And last night I spoke to Feroz. Talked to him in a way I've never talked to him before, if you are knowing what I'm saying. Man-to-man. Told him that if he lost you, his life was finished. That he would someday end up like one of those old, pathetic Parsi men, talking to themselves on the road and drooling on themselves when they eat. And for once, my bullheaded son came to his senses. And he agreed."

Freddy stopped, looking at Sera triumphantly. Noticing the expectant expression on his face, Sera knew he was waiting for her to say something. "That's good," she said vaguely. And when Freddy didn't respond, "Agreed to what?"

Freddy smacked his knee. "Now we're getting somewhere. I tell you, chokri, I'm beginning to worry about you. You look like you've been taking five calmpose tablets every morning. If you're not careful, cobwebs will start growing on your face."

Sera pulled herself up. "Freddy pappa," she said. "I'm sorry to say this, but I have no idea what you're talking about."

"How could you? I haven't told you yet." He leaned forward. "What I'm saying is, I am buying a second flat. For you and Feroz—and Dinaz, of course. Separate from Banu and me. That way, Banu cannot do her usual dadagiri, and you and Feroz can have some privacy."

She stared at him, afraid to believe her ears. "And . . . Feroz agreed to this plan?"

"Yes. Beta, I know my son. His stupid pride will never let him beg you to come back. But I tell you, he is a changed man. He comes home late, hardly eats anything for dinner when he is home. The other day, he was leaving for work and I had to remind him that he'd forgotten to shave. Can you imagine, our Feroz forgetting something like that? But without you, he has become someone I don't recognize. Even Polly has noticed."

Sera struggled against the sudden spurt of hope that burst into her heart. "Even if Feroz agrees, Banu mamma will never," she said dully.

Freddy looked annoyed. "Arre, meaning what? All of you may forget, but I am the man of the house. The head of my household. I told Banu last night that unless she wants to see her son look older than her in her lifetime, this is the only solution. Explained the situation to her and didn't give her a chance to do her yes-but-no business. Bas, told her that this was the plan and that she had to accept it, chup-chaap."

"And what did she say?"

Freddy roared. "Didn't I just tell you? There is nothing for her to say. Out of my own hard-earned money I am buying this flat. It is my gift to my son and my darling daughter-in-law, if she will have it."

She saw, for the first time, the pleading look in his eyes, heard the uncertain quiver in his voice, noticed the slight tremor in his hands. Freddy pappa is getting old, she said to herself. And still he has come here, swallowing his own pride.

"Beta," he said before she could respond. "You are the crown jewel of our family. Your place is at the side of your husband. Trust me when I say, Bombay is no place for a single woman to raise a child. In my years as a lawyer, I have seen many, many ugly things. Of course, you are having your wonderful parents, may God bless them with good health. But still, this is not your home. Your home is with Feroz. Now tell me, do you accept an old man's gift?"

She got up from the sofa and went over to where he was sitting so that she saw the top of his bald, round head, which looked so much like Feroz's. Looking at that head, she felt a pang of loss. For a moment, she missed Feroz terribly, missed the hard outline of his body as it slept against hers, missed his dark hands cupping her breasts when he came up behind her, missed his cool, easy confidence, the sense of protection and safety she felt when they were out in the city together. Besides, Dinaz needed—no, she deserved—what only her father could give her.

"Freddy pappa," she cried. "I hope I'm not making a mistake, but I accept your kind offer. I accept."

16

The salty sea air smells good, and the ocean tickles Bhima's and Maya's feet as they walk along the water's edge, zigzag-ging on occasion to avoid the people coming toward them. A slight wind plays with Bhima's tightly pulled back hair, making a few stray strands stand up at the top of her head.

As they walk, Bhima feels herself dropping her burdens into the welcoming water, so that her body becomes softer, more pliable, and she loses some of the angry stiffness that she normally carries in her. She is glad that she and Maya have taken to going to the seaside in the evenings. She listens to the rhythmic sighing of the dark sea and feels that it echoes her own. The water fights against the shore, chafing at its boundaries, leaving behind a foamy hiss of frustration as it recedes. Bhima feels her tired feet dig deep into the wet sand, looking for a place to call their own.

It has been years since she has come to Chowpatty Beach. "Your grandpa and I used to come here," she tells Maya.

"With Ma and Amit?" she asks.

Bhima clicks her tongue. "No, before. Just after our marriage. This place used to be different then." Her face softens at the mem-ory of how she and Gopal would sit on the caramel sand and eat vegetable pakodas and chew on pieces of fresh sugarcane. Then, af-ter the sun went down and the crowds receded, leaving behind only pockets of lovers, Gopal would reach for her and pull her towards him. All across the sand, couples sat together in different stages of passion, but etiquette demanded that one did not pay attention to what the others were doing. Some days it seemed to Bhima that all of Bombay was on these sands—those engaged to be married, those involved in illicit affairs, those in romances that could result in grave punishment if their parents found out. In contrast, she felt safe and respectable being here with her husband.

"Different how?" Maya is saying, and Bhima feels a moment's impatience at being disturbed in her reverie.

"The government has cleaned up the place," she says. "Before, this beach was dirty and littered. People used to do soo-soo in the sand, right in front of your eyes. And that part"—she points to the glittering half of the beach that's filled with food vendors—"that used to have many-many more pani puri and other food stalls. Now it's all regulated by the government babus."

She hopes that her explanation will make Maya recede into silence because she wants to revisit the past, spend some time again with Gopal on the golden beaches of their youth. But Maya wants to talk. "Your balloonwalla," she says. "The Afghani man you were talking about. Did he come here also?"

"I don't know," she says but feels a sudden revulsion at the thought of the man selling his wares at gaudy Chowpatty, amid the tartlike glitter of this beach. She wants to picture him in the more somber vistas of Marine Drive, where there were no crowds of teenagers and college students descending in search of the perfect plate of bhelpuri. Where someone could take the time to appreciate the man's artistry, the patient, careful way he twisted a bit of rubber and air and made magic out of it. "Probably not," she says. "He wouldn't have come here."

"I'm sure he did," Maya says. "If this is where the crowds were, I'm sure this is where the business was. So he had to have sold his balloons here. We learned that in my business class—you have to go where the demand is."

Bhima feels a sudden, hot surge of anger, and her fingers itch with the desire to slap Maya's smug, all-knowing, young face. She is unsure of the root of her anger—whether it stems from Maya's casual reference to college or whether her unthinking words have somehow desecrated the memory of the dignified Pathan and cheapened his artistry. "He wasn't a businessman," she cries. "Stupid girl, I told you. He didn't come here."

Maya looks shocked and then hurt, but some stubborn streak makes her not give in. "Well then, no wonder he was poor. No wonder you felt sorry for him."

Bhima wants to correct Maya, wants to point out that it's not clear to her whether she indeed felt sorry for him. She wants to say: But beti, it's more than that. He wasn't the kind of man you felt sorry for, exactly. Rather, looking into his fine, sad eyes, you felt a deep sorrow, the kind of melancholy you feel when you're in a beautiful place and the sun is going down. And mostly, now, when I think of him, I feel sorry for myself. Because that old Pathan had something that I need now. I don't know what it was, don't even have a name for it. All I know is that he could've taught me something, if only I had not been young and shy and afraid to ask.

But Maya is younger than she had been then, and Bhima knows it is no use trying to explain all this to her granddaughter. Besides, she feels a memory rise from the dark landfill of the past, and she needs to concentrate on helping that memory move into the present. Something the old Pathan had said once while talking to Gopal . . . What had Gopal asked him, maybe some question about his homeland? Yes, that was so. Gopal had said, "Compared to our Bombay, with the monsoons and all, your Afghanistan must seem as dried up as an old woman, no? All hills it is, dry as a bone, correct? I saw a picture of it once."

She had expected the Pathan to be insulted, but he laughed. "Nahi, sahib," he had said in his low, dreamy voice. "My Afghanistan is very beautiful. A hard land, yes, full of mountains, but toughness has its own beauty." He had paused for a long moment, his hands stilled over the balloon that he was transforming, and Bhima had the distinct impression that he was traveling down those hard Afghani roads again. "In the morning, when I was a lad, I used to wake up and run outdoors," he continued in that same deep voice that, to Bhima's ears, carried in it traces of tobacco and camphor and eucalyptus. "I would smell the clean mountain air, look at those hills that in the morning light, looked almost bluish pink. And I would think I was the happiest boy in the world." The Pathan smiled at the foolishness of that long-ago boy.

"Wah, old man, you make me wish I could see your home country," Gopal said in his usual cheerful way. "Are you sure you're not a poet instead of a balloon seller?"

Bhima was about to pinch Gopal when she saw that the Pathan was smiling. "Everybody is a poet in my homeland, sahib," he said. "The country makes you so." Then his face clouded over. "That is, everybody *was* a poet. Now the country is broken. Too many people fighting over the poor land, and the land is sick in its heart. Night and day it is weeping. Now it cannot take care of its sons and daughters." He stopped, and his eyes were like inkwells, the skin on his face like parchment paper. He looked as if he was about to speak again, but just then Amit interrupted him. "Is my balloon done?" he asked, hopping from foot to foot and impatiently looking up at the man who must've appeared as tall as a building.

The Pathan stooped down and patted Amit's head. "Sorry, baba," he said. "I'm getting slow in my trade." He finished the balloon in his usual methodical way and handed it to Amit like a flower.

"Sorry, what to do, this boy is impatient just like his father." Bhima smiled her apology. "But . . . what happened to your homeland that there is so much fighting?"

The Pathan looked at her and smiled slowly. "There is a saying in my community," he said. "They say that when something is very beautiful, the Gods of Jealousy notice it. Then, they must destroy it. Even if it's their own creation, its beauty begins to make them jealous and they are afraid it will overshadow them. So they destroy the very temples that they have built."

The Gods of Jealousy, Bhima now thinks. Was that what happened between her and Gopal? Did their happiness stick in the eye of some mean god? Was that why both her children were taken away from her? Why she had to urge her grandchild to destroy her own baby? Maybe the Pathan was right, maybe too much happiness and beauty were not good for humans. Perhaps human happiness had to be measured out in spoonfuls, like the castor oil that Banubai used to pour into a teaspoon and swallow every Sunday. Drink directly from the bottle and it could kill you.

"Ma-ma, I'm asking and asking you and you won't reply," she hears Maya say. "Are you angry with me or what?"

Bhima shakes her head to destroy the fog of the past. "I'm sorry, beti," she says. "I was just thinking and didn't hear you."

"I asked what happened to the old Pathan."

Bhima feels an icy sensation around her heart at Maya's words. "I don't know," she says abruptly. "After your grandfather's accident, we stopped coming to the seaside."

"Why?" Maya insists. "There was nothing wrong with Gopal dada's legs, was there? Why couldn't you come to the seaside?"

Bhima's face is as closed as a book. "After the accident, everything changed," she says shortly. She looks away, blinking back the tears that have formed unexpectedly in her eyes.

Maya leans her head on Bhima's shoulders. "Ma-ma," she says softly. "My poor ma-ma."

"Listen, beti," Bhima says. "I never told you what happened after the accident. But I'm going to tell you now, so you understand, once and for all, how this world treats those without an education."

She had been sick with the flu the day of Gopal's accident, which was why the man from the factory found her at home when he knocked on her door at three in the afternoon. He was a stranger to her, this dark-skinned man with the anxious, shifty eyes. "Are you . . ." He consulted a piece of paper, "Bhima? Gopal's wife?"

"Yes."

He looked toward his feet. "I'm afraid there's some bad news," he said. "You have to come quick to the hospital." He pronounced it "hispeetaal." "There's been an accident."

"Accident? Involving my Gopal?" She felt light-headed, faint from the flu and from the sudden fear that grabbed her heart like a giant hand. "Is he . . . hurt badly?"

The man shifted uneasily. "He's okay," he said. "Just a small hand injury. But still, the boss sent him to the hospital, to get tip-top care. And then he sent me here to inform you. At Godav Industries, we take care of our workers."

Gopal had been working at Godav Industries for fourteen months, after the textile mill where he had worked for years had filed for bankruptcy. Bhima had never met any of Gopal's new colleagues, including this man who stood at her door. But there was something about him that she didn't like. "And who are you?" she said.

"I'm Gopal's foreman. But come on, we should go. I have to return back to work." Bhima noticed he didn't offer his name, and she was too shy to ask. She didn't want the man to think Gopal had a forward wife.

She made arrangements with the woman next door to keep Amit when he got home from school. "Pooja will be home from her job around seven, didi," she said. "Tell her to make some rice for Amit if I'm not home from the hospital by then."

"The children can eat here," the neighbor replied. "Your children are my children."

"Many thanks." At the last minute she went to the stainless steel pot in which she kept a few rupees for household expenses and grabbed them. She wished the man would look away for a minute as she pulled out the money, but he was watching her every move.

The foreman hailed a cab and waited for Bhima to get in. He gave the driver the name of the government hospital.

"We took him to the government hospital because it was nearby," he said to Bhima. "He was bleeding, so we put him in a taxi and took him. Bara seth paid for the taxi," he added proudly.

Bhima felt faint at the thought of Gopal bleeding so much they had to hire a taxi for him. "Tell me the truth," she said. "Is my husband hurt badly?"

"He will be okay," he replied. "All depends on what kind of care he receives. Since his right hand is injured, we need you to sign some papers, allowing us to give him the treatment he needs." He reached into his plastic briefcase and pulled out a long printed form and a pen. "Sign here," he said.

Bhima felt the familiar shame rise in her like heat as her eyes fell across the page with the incomprehensible words. "I can't," she said, swallowing the sob that formed in her throat. "I can't read or write."

"That's okay," the man said immediately, digging into his briefcase. "You are in luck today." He pulled out an ink pad. "Here," he said, flipping it open and pulling her hand toward it. Just dip your thumb in the ink and place it on the paper."

For the umpteenth time, Bhima wished she were not illiterate. She would've liked to have read this long piece of paper, read it as fast and casually as she'd seen Serabai read the morning newspaper. Perhaps the paper would tell her the truth about Gopal's condition. She felt shame at the memory of how she had argued with Gopal against placing Pooja in school as he had wanted to. Now, Pooja would grow up as dumb and illiterate as her mother. "She's a girl," she'd argued with Gopal. "What does she need an education for? Before we know it, she will grow up and marry a man who will expect a wife who knows how to cook, sweep his house, wash his clothes. Better she know how to use a broom than a pen."

"These are modern times," Gopal said. "A girl should—"

"Not so modern that a man would accept a woman who was uneducated in housework. And not so modern that we could not use an extra income in the family. That way, we can pay for Amit's school fees. If he is educated, he can help his sister later in life."

As Bhima's thumb hovered over the white form in front of her, her cheeks burned at the memory. She wished Amit had been home when this man, this bearer of bad news, had knocked on her door. Her son could've made out these black words that rested like dead insects on the page. Beside her, she felt the man shifting impatiently. "Come on, we're almost at the hospital," he said. "Ink takes few minutes to dry. Press your thumb here." And before Bhima could react, he covered her hand with his, directed it to the paper, and pressed on her thumb, so that it left an impression on the form.

A strange man touching her in the backseat of a taxi. Bhima was mortified. Her dislike for the man curdled like milk. She moved in the seat of the small Fiat until she was leaning against the door. But the man's mood seemed to have changed. "Don't lean any further, bhenji," he said with a laugh. "Or else I'll have two patients to take care of instead of just Gopal."

Bhima stared straight ahead of her, ignoring his words.

But at the hospital, she was grateful for the foreman's presence. She would have never made her way around the big, chaotic building without him. He strode ahead of her purposefully. He asked a nurse the way to the operating theater, and when she heard those words, Bhima almost cried out loud. Why was Gopal in the operating theater? This man, whose name she still didn't know, had not said anything about surgery. Was Gopal sicker than she had been led to believe? But when she tried to stop him to ask, he simply clucked his tongue dismissively. "I told you. Your husband is fine," he said shortly. "Just follow me."

When they got to the cream-colored doors that said "Operating Theater," he pointed to a large wooden bench. "Sit here," he ordered. "I will return." She saw him walk away and stop when he saw a nurse. She saw him reach into his pocket and pull up a note, although she was too far away to see the denomination. She saw the nurse swiftly accept the money and shove it into her pocket. The nurse bent down to consult a chart, and then she was pointing down the hallway. "Shukria. Thank you," she heard the man say.

He came and sat down heavily next to her. "Okay," he said as if picking up a conversation. "Gopal should be out of the surgery room very soon. It seems as if he has lost three of his fingers." If he heard Bhima's anguished cry, he did not let on. "Doctor sahib has done the best he can. Now, when they take him to his bed, someone will inform you. You can go visit him there." He looked at his watch and cursed softly. "Saala, I'm very late. I have to return to my job. I am needing to report to the big boss what happened here." He looked at her scared, bewildered face and frowned. "My boss has already lost so much time and money over this. That Gopal was always a careless fellow. Many-many times I have told him to be careful. After all, a big machine is like a tiger—you don't put your hand in its mouth. But he never listens, your husband. Too much herogiri on the job."

Bhima was sobbing silently, wanting to defend Gopal, wanting to find the words that would put this nasty man in his place and not knowing how. The man looked at her for a long moment and then got up with a jerk. He dug into his pocket and peeled out a fifty-rupee note. "Here," he said, flinging the note in her lap. "Take a taxi home when you leave here." He stared at her weeping face for another second, began to walk away, and then took a few steps toward her. "I'll be back to see Gopal tomorrow morning," he said. "We'll do all our hissab-kittab then, settle all our contractual obligations. Understand?" She shook her head no, but he ignored her. "Okay then. Tomorrow morning."

When she finally got to see Gopal that evening, he was acting strange, looking at her with heavy, sleep-laden eyes and muttering rubbish. For a few minutes she had feared that the foreman had lied to her, that it was really Gopal's brain that had been damaged in the accident. But the mother of the patient in the next bed told her that it was normal; that the sleeping medicine that they gave patients before surgery made them look and talk in this manner. Also, there was the white gauze bandage around Gopal's right hand, already stained with a rusty red from his blood and the yellow-orange of an unknown substance.

The next morning, Amit refused to go to school. "I want to go see Baba," he said. "I know he needs me." Bhima didn't protest too much. At twelve, her son was already taller than she was, and she marveled at the easy, confident way in which he walked down the hospital hallways. So this is what knowing how to read and write does, she thought, and she felt a flare of pride at having provided her son with this gift.

When they reached Gopal's room, his bed was empty. Bhima felt a moment's blind panic—had he died in the middle of the night? she wondered and then dug the nails of her middle finger into her thumb to punish herself for such a thought. She spun around, wondering who to ask about her husband's whereabouts, when the elderly woman from the next bed who had set her mind at ease last evening spoke up. "They've taken him downstairs for an X-ray," she said. Bhima nodded her thanks, and this propelled the woman to get up from where she was sitting at the side of her son's bed and come to Bhima. Lowering her voice and positioning her body so that she was blocking Amit from the conversation, the woman murmured, "Your mister was having some problems during the night. Had a fever and all. And he had a cough. Kept my boy up half the night with his hawk-hawk coughing." She smiled to show Bhima that she didn't hold this against her.

Fear settled on Bhima like the dust that blew onto her stainless steel pots and pans each morning. "But why?" she whispered. "He doesn't have a cold. Why would he have a fever and cough?" She thought for a moment. "I myself have been sick the last few days. Could it be my Gopal has caught my cold?"

The woman shrugged. "That I don't know, beti. I'm just telling what I saw-heard."

Amit pulled at the bit of flesh near Bhima's elbow. "Ma, what's going on?" he whispered urgently. "Shall I go find Baba?"

"Better not to," the old woman replied, as if he had addressed her. "The doctors here are very . . ." She made a face. "Better not to have them angry with you. Just wait here and they will bring him back after his X-ray."

They sat on Gopal's bed glumly. "Is Baba hurting?" Amit said after a while, and Bhima shook her head noncommittally. She still felt unwell herself from the lingering effects of the flu. She wondered if Murti, the woman from her building, had already delivered her message to Serabai, informing her of Gopal's accident. It might be days before she could return to work. How would Serabai manage without her? And with Gopal and her both not working, they would have to get by on Pooja's salary. Then she remembered what the factory foreman had said yesterday—something about settling some business. So the company was going to give them money to live on while Gopal was sick. Good thing the foreman had thought about that—yesterday, her mind had flown away from her, like a bird from a nest, and she had given no thought to money or anything else. Bhima felt a throb of gratitude toward the man. Perhaps she had misjudged him. He must be a good man, to worry about their welfare at a time like this. She would apologize to him today for the coldness of her behavior. She tried to remember if the factory foreman had told her what time to expect him. Did he say he would come this afternoon?

A half hour later, they wheeled Gopal back into the room and transferred him onto his bed. Bhima let out a cry of apprehension when she saw his thin, shivering body. Less than twenty-four hours had passed since she had sent her cheerful, robust husband off to work, but she barely recognized the man who lay before her. Amit must've noticed the difference too, because he crept closer to his mother and stared mesmerized at his father. "Ma, what happened to his hand?" the boy cried out in a harsh whisper.

Gopal's eyes fixed on Amit and he tried to speak, but a coughing fit swallowed up his words. Listening to the guttural sounds, Bhima could barely believe her ears. When she had left Gopal last evening, his breathing had been smooth and even. Now, he sounded like those asthmatic old men who gathered in front of the bidi shop near their house each evening to while their time away. And when she touched Gopal's forehead, she pulled her hand away with a jerk, as if she had accidentally touched a pot of boiling water.

Gopal's eyes were agitated and helpless when he looked at her.

Again, he tried to speak, but the cough tore at his chest and slashed his words. "Don't speak," Bhima said, resting her hand on his chest in order to still its heaving. Under her hand, she could feel the roar and growl of his congested lungs. "Don't speak, my Gopal. We are here with you. Rest for a little while."

Gopal closed his eyes, and now Bhima could study his mutilated body. She noticed that the bandages on his hand had been changed, but fresh blood had still leaked on them; she saw the lines that had appeared on his face overnight; she saw how his brown face seemed almost reddish, as if the fever was a flashlight that shone just below his skin. And she heard the ominous sound of his ragged breathing, heard the air rattling in his chest. And along with that sound, another sound was penetrating her ears—the sound of Amit crying by her side, although it took her a second to recognize it. "Ma," the boy sobbed. "What is wrong with Baba?"

Afraid that his weeping would awaken Gopal, she turned on him fiercely. "Go wait outside in the corridor," she hissed. "Take your tears and your sourpuss face and go out there if you're going to be acting like this."

As if to punish her for the harshness of her words, a nurse came up to Gopal's bed right then. She was holding a syringe in her right hand, and Amit and Bhima stared at the long, thick needle with fearful fascination. "This your patient?" the nurse said impatiently. "Please to wake him up. He needs to lower his pajamas." Even while she was talking, the woman had grabbed the waistband of Gopal's pajamas and was trying to pull them down. Bhima tensed, waiting for Gopal to wake up, but he slept on. "Heavy sleeper, eh?" the nurse said, and the next second, she had jabbed the needle into Gopal's thigh. "Ah, ah," Amit cried in vicarious pain, but other than jerking for a moment, Gopal slept through. The nurse clucked her tongue in sympathy. "Pain from the fingers must be so great, poor chap doesn't even notice this jab," she said.

Bhima followed the nurse as she prepared to leave. "Sister," she said. "Can you please tell me—what is wrong with him? Why does he have a fever and cough?"

The nurse shrugged her shoulders. "Infection," she said. "There's infection in the body because of the surgery. Understand?"

No, Bhima wanted to say, I don't understand. I thought the surgery was to help my husband, not give him a fever. But before she could say a word, the nurse nodded curtly and walked away.

Bhima walked back to where Amit was waiting. "Stay here with Baba," she told the boy. "I have to make a phone call."

From a public phone booth, she dialed Serabai's number. She dialed slowly, in the careful way that Sera had shown her. At the time Serabai had insisted she learn how to use the phone, Bhima had resisted. Now she was grateful for this skill. Although the numbers all looked the same to her, she had memorized their places on the dial, and now she placed her index finger in each hole and turned it.

"Yes?" It was Feroz seth's voice, strong and impatient as always. Bhima wondered why he was still home.

"Feroz seth?" she yelled. " 'Allo? Yes, this is Bhima calling."

"Bhima? Stop screaming, for God's sake. Just talk in your normal voice. No, lower your voice. That's better. Now tell me, how is Gopal? Your neighbor was just here, giving us the news."

"He's not well, Feroz seth," she said, trying to remember not to raise her voice. "The nurse said he has a"—now what was the word?—"influxtion."

Feroz cursed softly. "That's not good," he said briefly.

"So I was calling for that reason only," Bhima said. "What is this thing? Is it an illness?"

There was a slight pause. "Hold on," Feroz said. "Sera is here and wants to talk to you."

"Hello, Bhima?" Sera's voice came into Bhima's ear like a comfort. "What's going on?"

"The nurse said Gopal had an influxtion." Something about Sera's familiar, kind voice melted the rigid fear that had held Bhima captive since yesterday, so the tears now came easily. "He's very sick, Serabai. Has a high fever and a cough like ten mad elephants are jumping on his chest. What is this new disease he is having?"

"What about his hand?"

"He's lost three fingers."

She heard the sharp intake of Sera's breath. "And they did surgery? Do you know what they did?"

"No, nobody has said. Nobody here talks to me, bai," she said.

"I see." Sera sounded angry. "I'm sure these gadhera doctors screwed something up during the surgery." She paused and then spoke again, more slowly this time. "Bhima, an infection is like something that enters your blood. It sometimes happens after surgery. But with good medicines they can clear it up, usually. But you have to be careful."

"Should I make him drink some narial pani?" Bhima asked. "I can have Amit run outside and buy some coconut water. They say it flushes out all illnesses."

"No, this will call for medicines that are stronger than narial pani." Sera paused. "Are you going to be at the hospital all day? Yes? Good. Okay, hold the phone for a second." Bhima heard her talking to Feroz. Then she was back. "Hello? Okay, Bhima, listen. Feroz and I are to go out today. It's our wedding anniversary, you know? But we will stop by the hospital before that. At that time we can see what can be done. What floor is Gopal on?"

Gopal had woken up by the time Bhima returned to his bedside. Amit was sitting next to his father, stroking his head and singing a song from a new film that he and Gopal had seen only last week.

"Baba asked me to sing to him," he said to Bhima. The boy's eyes were shiny with tears. Bhima nodded, and Amit went back to his singing. Watching the two of them, Bhima's heart ached with love. Until this accident, no dark shadows had fallen over their lives. Despite having two children of his own, Gopal was as playful and carefree as a child. While Sujata's marriage to Sushil had withered on the vine, her marriage had blossomed like the pink flowers that appeared each spring on the tree outside their apartment building. And from the moment of Pooja's birth, Gopal had treated his children with a degree of tenderness and love that made them the envy of the other children in the chawl.

Amit was still singing, even though Gopal had fallen asleep. Bhima rubbed the boy's bony back, her heart twisting again as she felt the familiar rise and fall of his muscles in the cup of her hand. "Baba is sleeping," she whispered. "You can stop singing now."

"He asked me to," the boy whispered. "I could tell, Ma, it was helping him."

She nodded and hugged her son. "You are the pillar in my life. Everybody should have a son like you," she said to him and watched as he picked at a pimple on his face to mask his embarrassed pride. Oh, God, restore my family to me, she prayed. Let this illness running like a darkness through Gopal's blood leave his body. Give me back my Gopal, laughing and smiling like always.

It was almost noon when Feroz and Sera walked in, Sera looking radiant in a green sari. To Bhima, it seemed as if the two of them, in their good clothes and their clean, glowing faces, were a splash of color against the black-and-white background of the dark, dingy room. They look like film stars compared to the rest of us, she thought, like gods dropped from the sky onto this mortal earth.

She noticed that the other people in the general ward, patients and their relatives alike, were staring openmouthed at the Dubashes as they made their way toward her.

"Serabai," Amit screamed with pleasure. He stood before the two of them beaming his delight, a little afraid of Feroz but unable to contain his joy at seeing Sera. "Amit," Feroz said stiffly, nodding his head in acknowledgment of the boy.

But Sera's face suffused with warmth. "How do you do, Amit?" she said, extending her hand for a handshake. Amit giggled at this familiar greeting. "Fine, thank you," he responded, in the way she had taught him. Then a worried look crossed his face. "My baba is sick," he said. "His forehead is as hot as a cup of tea."

Bhima sat with her hands folded in a gesture of gratitude. "Bai, many thanks," she said. She turned toward where Feroz was standing. "Sorry to trouble you so, seth," she added.

Feroz waved her thanks away. "Where are the doctors and nurses?" he said, scanning the room. "Who is in charge here?"

"A sister was here earlier," she replied. "Gave Gopal a big injection. She was the one who told me about the influxtion."

"Infection," he corrected her absentmindedly. His eyes darted around the room until they fell upon a ward boy who was about to give someone a bedpan. "Ae, you," Feroz called. "Come here a moment."

Mesmerized by the authority in his voice, the boy dropped the bedpan and began to walk toward them. "Mere re," Sera whispered. "You'd think he could have finished giving that poor man his bedpan before coming here."

Feroz pulled out his business card. "Listen here," he said. "Take this to the attending doctor and tell him I want to see him here in a few minutes. Hurry up, we don't have much time. We have to be somewhere else by one-thirty P.M."

The ward boy held the card as if it were an important document. But he lingered. "Doctors come only once in morning and once in evening," he said.

Feroz roared. "Listen, you. You tell that doctor to show up here in three minutes," he said. "I know the people who built this hospital, understand?"

The boy scuttled as fast as a cockroach. "Yes sir," he said. "Two minutes, sir."

Bhima watched in amazement as an older man in a white coat walked up to them a few minutes later. "Mr. Feroz?" he said. "I'm Dr. Kapur." He was a man of medium height with coarse gray hair and bags under his eyes. One end of his eyeglasses was held together with dirty-looking medical tape.

"Ah, yes, good," Feroz said, extending his hand. "I'm Feroz Dubash, senior executive with the Tata Group."

"I see." The doctor looked at Feroz and Sera curiously. "What can I do for you?"

"We just wanted a progress report on this young man here," Feroz said, glancing at the sleeping Gopal. "He had an operation yesterday after some kind of industrial accident. We were told he has an infection. I was wondering if you could explain what has happened."

Dr. Kapur looked uneasy. "Yes, there is some infection, per se. Common problem here, postsurgery," he mumbled. "You know, sometimes germs get in after surgery. We are trying to cure him."

"So when was he put on antibiotics?" Sera asked.

"Antibiotics?" Dr. Kapur looked as if he'd never heard the word. "Well, that is, he's not on those yet, per se. We were trying other measures first."

Sera flushed with anger. "What, are you feeding him paan-sopari first?" she asked sarcastically. "What are you saving the—"

Feroz squeezed her elbow to quiet her. "Sorry, Doctor, my wife is a little worried," he said. "You see, this fellow is important to our family." He leaned closer to the doctor, his black eyes scanning the man's face and his words slow and deliberate. "Anyway, what's done is done. It sounds like your hospital has made a major mistake here. But the question is, What can we do to fix this?" His voice dropped even lower. "May I speak to you a moment, man-to-man? Good. Now here's the thing. For some reason, my wife is very fond of our servant here. And if my wife is happy, then I am happy." He winked at the doctor. "If you are a married man, Doctor, then you know what I mean. For instance, today is our wedding anniversary. I took the day off to be able to spend it with my wife. Believe me, the last thing I want to do is to be here, in this—place. But my wife insisted we stop here to check on things, and here we are."

"No need to bother about anything," Dr. Kapur said testily. "This man here is getting good treatment . . ."

Feroz suddenly looked furious. The vein in his forehead bulged. Still, he kept his voice low. "Do you call not treating an infection with antibiotics good treatment?" he said. "Do you call not explaining to a wife what's wrong with her husband good treatment? Is there any explanation for this?"

Dr. Kapur looked away. "He's not the only patient here, per se." He laughed uneasily. "You can worry about just one patient. We have to worry about all our patients."

Feroz made a gruff sound that sounded like a bark. "Then, worry. Goddamnit, worry. Do something. If this man dies because of lack of care, I swear to you, Kapur, I'll have your testicles wrapped around your head so fast—"

"Now look here, Mr. Feroz. There's no need to talk so crudely. I came to see you because—"

"If you're worried about my talk, you better never see my actions," Feroz interrupted. "I work for the Tatas, you understand? Do you know what pull we have with the hospital administration?

One word from me and you will be out on the streets with not even your white coat with you. And what's more, I'll make bloody sure not one other hospital in Bombay hires you, you understand?"

Sera moved swiftly toward her husband. "Now, Feroz, I'm sure there's no need for all this," she said smoothly. "I can tell the doctor here is a good man, that he will do his best for Gopal."

"That only is what I'm trying to tell your husband, madam," Kapur said. His voice had changed, and there was a sniveling, ingratiating quality in it. "This afternoon only we will put your patient on antibiotics, per se. A few days and he will be brand new again."

Bhima noticed Sera flashing Feroz a warning look. But Feroz ignored it. "Okay," he said. "Here is the plan. You have my business card. I want you to have one of your doctors call my secretary every morning and give her a report on Gopal's progress. Tell him to call around eleven o'clock."

Dr. Kapur smiled a chastised smile, but his eyes were cold with fury. "Mr. Feroz, be reasonable," he said. "This is a hospital, not a railway station. I cannot spare one of my boys to call you daily. If you like, you can call the main office and talk to someone there."

"You're right," Feroz said thoughtfully. "Your boys have no time to call me. Okay, here's a better idea—I want you yourself"—he jabbed the older man lightly with his index finger—"to phone me each morning. Understand?"

Dr. Kapur stared at the floor. His Adam's apple worked furiously. "I am a trained doctor, sir," he started to say and then fell silent.

"Then act like one," Feroz said. "Don't tell me what you can't do. Tell me what you *can* do."

At this final insult, Dr. Kapur's face went slack, reminding Bhima of a straw hut collapsing in the monsoon rains. "Okay, sir," he said. "I will phone you every morning. And I will personally oversee his treatment, I promise."

"Good," Feroz said curtly. Kapur shuffled his feet. "Anything else I can do?" he asked.

"No, that's all. You can go now."

Kapur flushed. Keeping his eyes averted from all of them, he nodded and walked away.

Bhima looked in wonder from the doctor's retreating back to Feroz's triumphant face. To her surprise, Feroz was laughing and winking at Sera, as if his earlier show of anger had just been a performance. "Just having some maaja-masti with him." He chuckled. "Can't let these government fellows get big heads."

So this is what education does, Bhima thought. It opens doors for you. She wondered if her Amit would someday be like Feroz, able to get others to do things for him. She was thrilled and repulsed by the thought of Amit exercising such naked power over someone else. How that doctor had burst, like one of the Pathan balloonwalla's creations. A few words from Feroz sahib and he had collapsed totally. And now, Gopal would get the help he needed. Already Serabai was explaining to her that they would soon be starting Gopal on some new tablets.

"Feroz seth, if you live to be a hundred years old, I will not be able to stop thanking you for your help today," Bhima said. She walked toward him, her hands cupped together so that she could take his right hand and lift it to her head in thanks. But Feroz flinched and jerked away as her hands touched his. "It's okay, it's okay," he said hurriedly. "No thanks needed."

Bhima did not allow herself to feel the sting of his rejection. "When Gopal is home I will make you some shrikhand," she promised. She knew that Feroz often brought home the sweet yogurt paste from Parsi Dairy Farm.

Feroz smiled. "I only like Parsi Dairy's shrikhand," he said. Then, seeing the hurt look on her face, he added, "But we'll see, we'll see. Let him get home first."

After they left, Bhima gave Amit two rupees to go get himself some samosas for lunch. "And you, Ma?" he said.

"I'm not hungry," she said shortly. "You go outside and eat and then come right back, achcha?"

Watching the boy speed down the hallway, Bhima smiled. Amit was as sharp and fast as lightning. Tomorrow, she would insist he go back to school. He would argue with her, she knew, but she wouldn't listen. Watching how Feroz seth had completely dominated the conversation with the doctor had sealed her belief in the power of education. Someday, her Amit, too, would argue like this with doctors, lawyers. Perhaps he would be a doctor or lawyer himself. Bhima didn't really know what a lawyer did, but she knew Freddy seth was one and she liked him. Freddy seth was nice— once, when she had accompanied Serabai to her in-laws' house, he had allowed her to stroke his parrot, Polly. And when he came over to Sera's home, he always inquired about Gopal and the children. Yes, Amit could be a lawyer and Freddy seth would help him.

But then another thought struck her and she paused, as if she were at a busy intersection and her thoughts were cars she had to watch for. The doctor babu had to be an educated man also. Then why had he allowed Feroz seth to talk to him in that manner? Was education alone not enough? And if not, what was the missing part? She had not been able to follow the actual conversation because Feroz and the doctor had spoken in English. Still, she needed to know, for Amit's sake. Could Feroz seth talk like this because he was a Parsi? Everybody knew the Parsis were educated and rich and their women mostly wore dresses instead of saris. In other words, they were different. Different from her and Gopal and even the doctor sahib, with his frayed rubber chappals and his eyeglasses held together with tape. So was that it? Or was it some other thing? Was it because Feroz seth knew how to look angry even when he wasn't? Would her Amit be able to do that? Was that something they taught you in school also?

Bhima looked up to see another nurse, this one younger and prettier than the one who had given Gopal his injection earlier in the day, standing beside the bed.

"New medicines we are starting him on." The nurse smiled, holding out her hand. "Antibiotics."

17

opal came home after ten days in the hospital, and Bhima returned to work. The fever and cough had receded, but he complained about the terrible pain in his hand, pain that ran like hot bolts of electricity up his arm. "Wait till the wrapping comes off, Gopu, then I'll use some of our home remedies," she promised him. "We can even ask your brother to send us some herbs from the village."

"And what will those do?" he asked. "Make my fingers grow back?" He had developed this abrupt new way of talking that hurt and bewildered her.

"No, but . . . At least they will help with the pain," she said feebly, but he made a dismissive sound and turned away.

Bhima did not persist in engaging him. Something else was bothering her, something more urgent. Ever since the day of the accident, the foreman had vanished, not to be seen again. He had not shown up the next day, as he had promised, nor the day after. What had he said about coming to them with a business offer? It was time for him to contact them, now that Gopal was home. After all, they needed the money if they were to pay the month's rent. And in a few weeks, once the bandages came off and Gopal was feeling stronger, he would want to get back to his job. Even if he couldn't run the machinery now, surely there was another job for him at Godav Industries.

Bhima wanted to discuss this with Gopal, wanted to tell him about the strange man who had escorted her to the hospital on that terrible day, but her husband's face seemed to turn to stone any time she mentioned the hospital or the accident. He'll feel better in a few days, she said to herself. I'll talk to him then.

As if he had read her thoughts, the foreman knocked on their door the next evening. Bhima had just returned home from work and was kneading the dough for the chappatis. She glanced out the window at the darkening sky. Pooja should be home any minute now, she thought. She could hear the cries of the neighborhood boys with whom Amit was playing cricket in the courtyard of the building. "Sixer," a young voice shouted enthusiastically, and Bhima prayed that it was Amit who had hit the ball hard enough to score the six runs. She tried to look through the window, but the angle did not permit her a good view of the courtyard.

When the doorbell rang, she noticed that, although Gopal was nearest to the door, he stayed in his seat and looked to her to wipe the flour dust off her hands and answer it. The old Gopal would never have done this, she thought but then snuffed out the thought. Poor man, she said to herself. He hurts so. If he wants to rest, why not? It won't hurt me to walk to the door.

It took her a moment to recognize the foreman. When she did, relief made her forget the fact that she did not like this man, and she smiled enthusiastically. "Welcome, bhaisahib," she said. "I was thinking you had forgotten us." Stepping aside for him to enter, she turned toward her husband. "Gopal," she said. "You have a visitor. It's the foreman from the factory."

The man behind her cleared his throat. "Er, actually, what I said the other day was not exact-to-exact. I, er, just thought it was easier that day, given all the tamasha that was going on. Actually, I'm the accountant for the company."

Gopal stood in front of the man, looking at him with puzzled eyes. "You're the accountant?" he said.

"Namaste, ji," the man said, folding his hands in greeting. Instinctively, Gopal started to imitate his gesture, but a quick glance at his mutilated hand made him drop his hands to his side. He nodded. "Namaste," he said.

"Please to allow me to introduce myself," the man continued. "I'm Devdas. I am doing the bookkeeping for Godav Industries."

Gopal glanced quickly at Bhima, as if to reassure himself that she was in the room. "You shouldn't have taken the trouble to come here all this way," he said politely. "After all, I am planning on returning to work in a few weeks. As soon as these come off," he added with a rueful smile, indicating the bandages.

"Well, er, that all is what we are needing to talk about," the man said. He eased himself onto a chair and then opened his plastic briefcase.

"What will you take?" Gopal asked graciously. "Chai? Or something cold?"

"No, no, nothing," Devdas said, shaking his head vigorously. "I will only be taking a few minutes of your time," he said, including Bhima in the sweep of his glance. "After all, you must still be resting, no?"

Gopal shrugged. "Only so much resting a man can do."

The accountant laughed, as if Gopal had cracked a fine joke. "True, true." He paused and looked at a long sheet of paper that he had pulled out of his briefcase. When he spoke, his voice had changed. "Achcha," he said crisply. "About this contract. According to this, it says that Godav Industries will pay you one thousand rupees as a one-time, lump-sum payment. After this, you will have no more claims against us. You will be free to seek employment anywhere in this city that you like." Ignoring their dazed expressions, he leaned back in his chair and smiled benevolently. "I have come prepared to pay you the entire sum of money tonight," he said, stretching out each word. "That's why only I have come so soon after your return home. After all, the boss understands that you will have need for money at a time like this."

Gopal spoke through a fog of confusion. "Excuse please, but I don't understand. I intend to come to work as soon as I am able."

The man's face was equal parts pity and contempt. "Just think, Gopal babu," he said in a voice laced with malice. "What are you going to be doing at the factory? Can you lift the sheets of plastic anymore? Can you move them around so that the machine cuts them just so? A factory worker with three fingers missing—I don't know, baba. That's like a woman without breasts."

Gopal leapt up. "Watch what you say in this house, mister. This is a respectable house you have entered, not a whorehouse, you—"

"Calm down, calm down, Gopalji," the man drawled. "Why for unnecessarily you're getting all riled up? You need to preserve your energy, na? I meant no insult to your chaste wife here. But my main point is there is no job for you at our place. Okay?" He searched his briefcase with his fingers, all the while keeping his eyes on Gopal. He pulled out a fat, brown envelope with a flourish and then fished around some more before he pulled out his receipt book.

"So here's the thousand rupees," he said, stroking the envelope. "Not a small sum of money in these hard times." He turned to where Bhima was standing and offered the packet to her. "Here, didi," he said. "You are the mistress of the house. You count the notes and make sure I haven't made a mistake. After all, these days in Bombay you can't trust anyone."

"Don't touch that money." Gopal's warning rang out sharply, like the smack of a cricket bat against a ball. "I want a job, not the price of my three fingers. And also, what about my workmen's compensation money? That alone will be more than this measly sum."

"Ah, babu, that's what I'm trying to tell you," the accountant said softly. "While you were in the hospital, your wife here signed the terms of this settlement. According to this piece of paper, this is all you're entitled to."

Gopal's face turned pale. He turned to look at Bhima, and there was so much hurt, betrayal, and confusion in his eyes that she felt mesmerized by the look, as if his eyes were arrows that had her pinned against the wall. Those arrows pierced her chest, killing the words of explanation before they were born; they welded her to the space on the floor where she stood, so she could not take a step toward her husband and bridge this awful chasm that had sprung up between them. She wanted to explain to Gopal the panicked ride to the hospital, her distraught state of mind, and Devdas's lies about the piece of paper he had tricked her into signing, but she could mount no defense under the weight of Gopal's look.

"Liar," Gopal finally said to Devdas, who was looking from husband to wife, a strangely satisfied expression on his face. "My wife doesn't know how to read or write. How could she sign anything?"

In response, Devdas held up the sheet of paper. "Thumb impression," he said. His tone was triumphant, almost giddy, as if he was trying to suppress a laugh. He turned to Bhima, who still stood rooted to the floor. "Tell me," he said. "Is this your impression or not?"

But she was staring at Gopal, watching the single line of saliva that hung from the roof of his open mouth; noticing how he was licking his lips nervously; seeing the lines that appeared on his brow, the tears that glistened like dead stars in his dark eyes. "Woman," he said hoarsely. "What have you done?"

Devdas shifted in his seat impatiently. "What's done is done," he said. "Now, if you please, my wife is waiting for me for dinner. Please to sign this receipt on this stamp here, saying you have accepted the money. Or do you need an ink pad also?"

"I can sign my name," Gopal said, his eyes still on Bhima. He accepted Devdas's pen and scribbled on the pink government stamp with his left hand. "Here it is," he said, returning the book to Devdas. "I have just signed my life away."

Devdas dropped the receipt book in his briefcase and stood up. "Thank you," he said. "And now, with your permission, I will take your leave." He set the brown envelope on the table and looked at Gopal as if he expected something—curses, violence, threats, a display of anger, anything. But Gopal stared at him blankly, with the face of a dead man. The accountant clucked his tongue in dissatisfaction. "I tell you, Gopal babu, you brought this misfortune on yourself. You should've been more careful on the job," he said. "After all, these are big, dangerous machines, not a child's dollhouse. Next time, you will learn to be careful."

Finally he got the reaction he was after. Gopal got up from his chair with a roar of anger. "Get out of my house," he yelled. "Take your lying evil out of my sight. Telling me I should've been more careful when everybody knows that only three days earlier I had complained to the big boss about that machine. And none of you sons of whores did a thing about it. Cheaper to pay off a worker like me than to stop work for a day to get the machine fixed. Don't think I don't know what's inside this envelope—it's blood money. It's my three stolen fingers returned to me inside this brown envelope, nothing more. Saala maadarchot, who do you think you're fooling? You may fool your mother and sister and your son who still hangs from your wife's tits, but you won't fool me, understand?"

Devdas made a sound that was a cross between a snort of anger and a helpless giggle. "Now, babu, no need to act like this. After all, I'm a guest in your house." He caught the gleam in Gopal's eye. "I'm going. Good-bye," he said hastily.

The house was eerily quiet after Devdas left. Bhima went back to making her chappatis while Gopal sat in the chair where Devdas had sat just a few minutes ago, staring at the wall in front of him as if it would reveal the mysteries of his life. The envelope lay untouched on the table. Occasionally, Bhima stole a glance at Gopal, but his face was as blank as the wall he was staring at. Finally, she couldn't bear the silence any longer. Wiping her hands clean of the flour, she went to where Gopal was sitting. "My husband," she said quietly. "Find it in your heart to forgive me. I am a stupid, ignorant woman. That badmaash lied to me. He told me what I was signing was a letter to make sure you got good treatment in the hospital."

Gopal shook his head slowly. "Woman, don't you see?" he said. "It doesn't matter. One way or the other, they would've tricked us. Because they own the world, you see. They have the machines and the money and the factories and the education. We are just the tools they use to get all those things. You know how I use a hammer to pound in a nail? Well, they use me like a hammer to get what they want. That's all I am to them, a hammer. And what happens to a hammer once its teeth break off? You throw it away and get a new hammer. All they did was use you to buy themselves a new hammer."

She stared at him uncomprehendingly. She did not recognize this Gopal nor did she like him very much. Not only did this Gopal look different but he even smelled different. Her Gopal was built of sunshine and songs and laughter and jokes and smelled of mint and coriander and new rain. This new Gopal was hard as a hammer, tough as leather, and smelled of sweat and ashes and sour milk. "Gopi, listen to me," she said desperately. "Forget Godav Industries. With my stupidity, I took this job away from you, but I'll find you another one instead, I promise. And from tomorrow, I'm going to feed you a piece of chicken every day, to help you get your strength back. And I'm going to pay Pandav to write a letter to your brother, asking him to send us some herbal cures for your pain. Gopal, my husband, while you were in the hospital, I fought to keep you among the living. And now that you are home, I will take tip-top care of you, I promise."

He smiled at her, and it was then that she knew the gods had played a trick—they had kept Gopal among the living, but they had taken away that essential something that makes a man want to keep on living. Gopal was like the empty shell of a clock whose insides had been removed. There was nothing to keep him ticking anymore. She wished that he would cry, weep, curse the world, beat her, smash something, tear the envelope on the table to bits, rage against Devdas—do something to tell her that he was still alive. But instead, he smiled, this slow, sad, fatalistic smile that made him look more dead than he had in the hospital.

"Shall I turn on the transistor radio?" she asked, thinking the Hindi film music would cheer him up. But he simply shrugged. "I'm tired," he said and turned away to face the wall again. After a minute, she went back to the kitchen stove.

She heard Amit and Pooja race up the outside steps, and the next second they flew into the room. Bhima caught the worried look that Pooja flashed toward her father, a look so grown-up and cautious it tore at her heart. This girl is too young to worry about so much, she thought. Bhima saw Pooja go up to Gopal and stroke his hair as she spoke quietly to her father, and her heart ached with love for her quiet, steady, sensitive Pooja. Amit, by contrast, seemed unaware of the tension in the room, his face still flushed from the energetic cricket game. There was something about Amit that reminded Bhima of a lively, excited, eager-to-please puppy. If this boy had a tail, it would be wagging all day, she thought. And ever since Gopal had returned home, Amit's tail had not stopped wagging. He is so happy to have his baba home that he doesn't seem to notice the change in Gopal, Bhima marveled. Now Amit was doing a jig, telling his father about the match. "I hit two sixers, baba," he said. "That Vasu tried to

catch one of my shots, but he's such a fatty, he couldn't even run behind the ball. And then that new boy tried to . . ." His eyes fell on the
envelope. "What is this?" he asked, picking it up.

Gopal turned around slightly, and his and Bhima's eyes met over
the boy's head. "That is an early Diwali present," Gopal said deliberately, his eyes never leaving Bhima's stricken face. "Open it."

Amit's eager fingers tore open the envelope, and the bundle of
ten hundred-rupee notes fell on the floor. "Hah," the boy gasped.
He had never seen so much money at one time. He turned to his father in confusion. "What is this, baba? So-so much money."

"You know what this is, beta?" Gopal said. His face was as feverish as that day in the hospital. "This is your baba, inside that envelope. This is how much your baba is worth. This is the price for—"

"Chup re." Bhima swooped into the room and shot Gopal a
warning glance. She focused her gaze on Amit's bewildered face,
and something about his confused innocence irritated her. "Stupid
boy," she said, whacking him hard on his shoulder, "pick up that
money at once. Asking stupid questions and annoying everybody."
She smacked him again, this time on the back of his head.

"Ma," Amit howled. "Stoppit. What did I do?"

"Stop beating the child for your sins, woman," Gopal said to her
softly so that only she could hear.

This infuriated her even more. "What did you do?" she
screamed at the boy, who was rubbing his head. "Whiling away the
evening playing cricket like a mawali, along with all your other
good-for-nothing friends. Whereas I come home tired from work
and still—" She choked on her words as if they were pieces of hot
coal. But the anger and fear still bubbled in her chest. "Spending
our hard-earned money to send you to school while Pooja and I
slave all day. And what do you do, you shameless namak-haram?
Playing cricket with the neighborhood goondas."

Amit's face sparkled with outrage and defiance. "But, Ma, you only told me it was okay to go downstairs to play. And anyway, those are my friends, not goondas."

Suddenly her anger flickered and then died down, like the blue flame on the Primus stove. She stared at her son in pity and sorrow. "Go wash your face," she said gruffly. "Dinner will be ready soon." She turned to where Pooja was standing. Bhima had a feeling that, despite her calm exterior, the girl was cowering in fear inwardly. She sighed to herself. It was the special curse of parents, to know the insides of their children so well. "And you, chokri," she said, her voice deep with the brew of emotions she felt, "you better go wash your face too. Must be tired to the bone after working all day. That mistress of yours should be the head of the police force, the way she bosses you around."

"Actually, today she was nice to me. Gave me a piece of choco-late with my lunch," Pooja said. Out of habit, Bhima glanced at Gopal, and for a quick second, there was the old communication as they exchanged knowing looks. They both knew that Pooja was an instinctive peacemaker and that she often exaggerated or lied about things to make her parents feel better.

"Chocolate is good, but next time tell her to give you more money," Bhima grumbled, but her tone told Pooja that her mother was teasing. She smiled and quickly went into the kitchen to use the sink.

As Bhima picked up the envelope and looked for a safe place to hide the money, she could feel Gopal's eyes watching her every move. She felt the sweat run down her back, but she steeled herself against his mocking gaze. With this money she could pay the rent for a few months plus buy groceries. God knew how long it would be before Gopal could find a job. With his income gone, they needed to save every paisa that they could.

The next day, Bhima felt hope stir in her chest as she walked to work. She would tell Serabai about the accountant's deceit, she resolved. With one or two well-chosen words, Serabai would set that accountant right.

But Sera's face was grim when she entered the kitchen a few hours later. "I just spoke to Feroz on the phone," she said. "He says it's a closed case. By putting your thumb impression on that paper . . . I'm afraid nothing can be done, Bhima," she added gently.

Suddenly, Bhima's open palm flew toward her wide forehead. She began to strike herself repeatedly with the base of her hand. "Stupid, dumb woman," she cried out in between the blows. "Noose around your husband's neck. Destroyer of his life. I curse the day you were born. I curse my mother for not sending me to school. As a child, I had such a desire to read books, Serabai." As Sera watched appalled, Bhima resumed her self-flagellation. "May you repeat endless cycles of misery in this cruel world, to pay for this one sin. May your children's children never forgive you for this crime."

"Bhima. Bhima, stop," Sera shouted. "This is not the time for hysterics." She waited until the servant stopped beating on herself. "What's the use of blaming yourself, Bhima?" she said. "How could you have known of the fellow's treachery? It's true what my mother used to say—sometimes serpents walk around disguised as people."

That evening on her way home, Bhima stopped by the small shrine to Lord Krishna that someone had built inside the trunk of a tree that stood between a bakery and a clothing store. She placed some coins at the feet of blue statue and then stood staring at Krishna's happy, peaceful face. Ever since she had met Gopal, Bhima had been drawn to Krishna because something about the god's playful, mischievous manner reminded her of Gopal. Now she watched the deity's beatific face with envy. "Bring my old Gopal back to life," she whispered fervently. "Bring my Gopal back and I will distribute three kilos of pedas to all the street urchins around here, I promise."

Gopal made love to her for the first time since the accident on the day his bandages came off. All evening long, Bhima kept glancing at the stubs where her husband's fingers had been. The skin near the nubs was pinkish, lighter than the deep brown of the rest of his hand. When Gopal accidentally hit his ruined right hand against his metal plate as the family sat eating dinner, the pain was so sharp that he let out a yelp. Since the accident he had learned to eat with his left hand, but it took him so long to scoop the rice and daal with his fingers that Bhima often wondered if that was the reason he was losing so much weight. Now, as the waves of pain crashed against his battered hand, he dropped his food and got up from the floor. "I can't eat any more," he said abruptly.

"But, baba, you haven't even eaten anything," Amit protested. But Gopal flashed him a look of such venom that the boy fell silent. The three of them ate quickly and quietly as Gopal went to lie down on his cot.

But that night, Bhima felt her husband's stubby fingers running down her back. She stiffened at their unfamiliar coarseness and fought the revulsion that rose in her stomach. As if he had read her discomfort, Gopal whispered, "Does my fingerless hand disgust you, wife?"

"Of course not," she said quickly and turned around to face him. Taking her own hand, she caressed his thin, handsome face, tracing its outline with her index finger. "So much sorrow on a face so young," she whispered. "And so thin and frail."

He buried his head in her breast and, unbuttoning her sari blouse with his left hand, sucked on her breasts. She felt the familiar fire and ice run through her body, felt herself melting and burning in the same moment.

But something was wrong. They did not seem to fit together in the same easy way as before. With every motion they made, every thrust and arch of their bodies, they seemed to be aware of those three missing fingers. When he tried to loosen the knot on the drawstring of his pajamas, Gopal's severed hand rubbed up against the cloth and he clenched his teeth in pain. While he was holding Bhima's face with his left hand, Gopal's other hand fluttered and fell by his side, helpless as a ruptured wing. When Bhima arched her hips toward him, Gopal could not seal that motion of intimacy by grabbing her buttocks as he usually did. They tried; they sweated and grunted and rubbed against each other. But they kept missing each other, like dancers out of step. Finally, Gopal stopped in midrhythm and gave up. Just before he turned on his side, he said bitterly, "It seems you've forgotten how to receive your own husband."

The words stung like a slap, but Bhima was too tired and disappointed to respond. Unlike most of her married friends, she and Gopal had always been compatible in bed. Ever since her wedding night, when they had fallen into each other's arms, giggling and sweating and nudging and snuggling, there had been an ease to their sexual relations that Bhima knew eluded many of her friends. Gopal had never tried to conquer her like she was a mountain; rather he had swum in her as if she was a river. Like a river and its fish, they had existed side by side, flowed along the same charted course, both needing each other and neither seeking dominion over the other.

But suddenly, Gopal had something to prove. Suddenly, she was a river that had to be dammed, her power controlled and checked. Now that Gopal was missing three fingers, he had to convince himself that he still had that other, important digit intact. And so, night after night, he wrestled with her until their sex became humorless, mechanical, uninspired. She remained patient, aware of his pain, knowing instinctively how important this was to him. But in time, her patience turned into passivity, and Gopal, who for so many years had been so attuned to her moods and thoughts, realized this. Wanting to move her into response, he made his lovemaking more desperate, relentless, and violent. He dug his stubby fingers into her stomach, feeling electrified as the pain shot through his body like a drug; he kissed her breasts and then bit them like they were lemon rinds; he thrust his penis deep into her like a sword. She tried to fool herself into mistaking this desperate lovemaking for passion, but the grim, fearful look in Gopal's eyes prevented her from this self-deceit.

And then, the lovemaking stopped. When she came to bed that night, Gopal was already asleep. Bhima eased into the narrow cot, afraid of waking him, but his breathing remained steady and rhythmic. She lay awake for a few hours, torn between wanting to sink into a blissful sleep and being afraid that he would touch her as soon as she let her guard down. Finally, exhausted, she slept.

The next evening Bhima returned from work and immediately caught the strange, unfamiliar smell. "Smells like a daru shop in here," she joked. But the smile on her lips died a swift death as she took a few steps toward Gopal. "You've been drinking," she cried, her tone equal parts surprise and accusation.

Gopal's face became guarded, as if someone had slammed shut a window. "So?" he said defiantly. There was a crudeness in his demeanor, a swagger that he had never had before. "If I want to have a drink or two, whose business is that?"

She looked around. "Where's Amit?" she said.

"Playing downstairs with the boys." And then, as if he had read her mind, "Don't worry, he didn't see me come up the stairs. Our darling little Amit has no reason to be ashamed of his own father."

"You're drunk," she said, as if to herself. "Baap re, Gopal, you're drunk. You, who hardly ever touched the stuff once we got married."

He flung his arms wide open. "That's before I got liberated," he said, slurring his words. "Before I stopped being henpecked by my wife."

The following morning, Bhima stopped Feroz before he left for work and asked him to find Gopal a job.

Feroz chewed on his lower lip. "Nothing comes to mind immediately," he said. "But let me give it some thought."

Gopal began to drink daily. He claimed it helped with the pain. "You have no idea what this demon pain is like," he told Bhima one day. "It's as if someone is sticking knives into my hand. And here the doctor is telling me that there's no treatment for that. The only thing that gives me a few hours' peace is this brew." His face crumbled like a cheaply built wall. "Everything else has been taken from me, Bhima—my hands, my employment, my pride. Please, don't take this one thing away from me. I'm not like those other drunken fools. I know when to stop."

When Feroz at last told her he had found a job for Gopal, Bhima went home happy but apprehensive. But to her great surprise, Gopal looked pleased. Three days later, he started at the new place. Bhima woke up early that morning and made him his favorite things for breakfast. She also placed some fried okra inside two chappatis and gave him those to eat for lunch.

He came home that night so pale and weary that, for a second, she thought he was drunk. But it was fatigue, not alcohol, that was making him slur his words, she realized. That night, after the children had gone to bed, she massaged his back, untying the knots of tension that ran down his neck and shoulders. As she undid the knots, she also loosened his tongue. "I was slow, so slow," he said softly. "And so clumsy. All the other loaders staring at the cripple who is trying to do their job. I felt like telling them, 'You should've seen me just a few months ago, chootias. The pace at which I worked then, you would still be starting your engines while I got to the finish line.' But of course, nothing to do or say except to keep learning how to carry this material against my chest, using only my left hand. The boss, Deshpande, he himself is a good man. Very patient. But I felt so ashamed, Bhima."

Love and indignation formed like a lump in her throat. "Nothing to feel ashamed of, Gopu," she said stoutly. "Only shame is in sitting at home and not taking care of your family. Trying to earn an honest living—no shame in that."

"I know," he said. "Those are the words I said to myself, only. But Bhima, there was also the pain. At times it was so strong I thought I would faint. It's funny—I was not using my right hand at all, and you'd think if either hand had the right to complain it would have been the left one because it was working so hard. But it was the useless right one that hurt so. Constantly reminds me of its presence with its messengers of pain."

Still, when he brought home his paycheck that Friday, Gopal looked happy if sheepish. "It's nothing compared to what I once made, hah?" he said. "But slowly-slowly, as I manage to work faster, I will make more, Bhima."

Her eyes welled with tears. "We can manage with anything that you earn. Just to have you home with me and you happy at your job, that's enough."

He gave her a curious look. "Happy at my job?" he repeated softly.

Gopal took to stopping at the bootlegger's shop for a drink or two after work, but Bhima forced herself not to mind. "Your baba is in pain," she told her children. "The drink is like medicine for him."

But the following Tuesday, Gopal refused to get out of bed. "I'm declaring today a holiday for all the workers of Bombay," he said. Bhima could smell the stale odor of alcohol on his breath. "You too should stay home today," he continued. "There's a new Rajesh Khanna movie out. We can go to a matinee show."

"And then rub two paise together for the rest of the week?" she said bitterly. "Even if you don't care about me, think of the children, no. What am I supposed to feed them? Already, I owe the baniya money. Just the other day, Pooja was talking of taking a second job. My daughter's entire youth will go in supporting her father's drinking habit. Is that what you want?"

"There's the settlement money," he said loftily. "You forget, my dear wife—there's the money you earned us with your brilliance."

She flushed at the insult but did not let that derail her. "Gopal, that money is to pay the rent for a few more months. Without your wages, how will we keep this place, husband? Give some thought to the future, na."

Gopal rolled onto his side and went to sleep.

A week later, Amit was waiting for her at the street corner when she came home from work. "Ma," he called as soon as he spotted her. "Come home, quick. Baba has gone soft in the head."

"What is wrong?" she said, quickening her step to keep up with her son's strides.

"I don't know. But when I got home from school he was already there. He's running around the house like a mad bull, looking for something. I got so scared I left. I've been waiting and waiting for you to come home, Ma."

Gopal turned on her as soon as they walked in the door. "Where's my money?" He panted. His hair was dishevelled, and his sweaty face had a bruised, dazed look on it, as if he'd been in a fight. "Where's the money you made off of my chopped-off fingers, you whore of a woman?"

"What for you need money?" She looked around and noticed

that he had pulled the sheets off the bed, flung open and rummaged through the cupboard, and turned every pot in her kitchen upside down.

"I have to pay the bootlegger," he said. "My credit has run out and he must be paid tonight before he will give me any more of his brew. I need my money," he said wildly.

"The money's not here," she said dully. "It's with Serabai, in her safekeeping. There's only a few hundred rupees left anyway. How do you think I've been running this house since—"

He let out a howl and rushed up to her in fury, so that she closed her eyes, bracing herself to feel his hands around her neck. Was Gopal strong enough to choke her with one good hand? she wondered.

"Baba," Amit's voice stopped Gopal in his path. "Baba, what are you doing?" The boy was crying openly, and the sight of his son's tears seemed to hold Gopal in check. Besides, Amit was digging into his pants pocket. "Here," he said, holding out a crumpled five-rupee note. "I won a bet at school today. Take this money, baba, and go get your daru."

The room stood still for an infinite second. Don't take the money, Gopal, Bhima prayed silently. If you take this money from your son, I will know for sure that you are gone away from us forever, my husband. Allow me to feel some pride in you, still. Do not strip away from our family this last thread of pride.

The stillness continued, but somehow the room seemed to shimmer and vibrate with unspoken tension. It was as if each one of its occupants knew that a moment of reckoning was at hand, that this was the test they had to meet together or forever be banished into their own separate, silent worlds; that together they formed the three points of a triangle where each of them touched the other two, and that the slightest movement on any of their parts would shatter this uneasy balance.

Gopal snatched the note out of Amit's hand. "You're a good boy," he mumbled, not daring to make eye contact with Bhima. "I will pay you back, my son."

At the front door, he paused. He looked at his son's, crestfallen face and the broken, beaten look in his wife's eyes. He let out a soft cry, as if he was noticing for the first time that Bhima had lost the plumpness he had always prized so much, as if he was surprised by her pale, hollow face, where the giant thumbs of fate had pulled her cheeks downward. Bhima stared back at Gopal, expecting to see sorrow and guilt on his face. She would've been horrified to know that what he felt instead was a dark, cruel excitement, as deft and stimulating as a whore's tongue.

A look of pleasurable malice came over Gopal's face. "By the way," he announced. "A piece of good news, wife. I was let go from my job today. From tomorrow, you will have me at home all day long."

Fingerless, jobless, unproductive, Gopal had found his area of creativity—he could still produce misery, mounds and mounds of it.

When Amit brought home a terrible report card, Gopal said maybe it was time for the boy to leave school and get a job instead. Pooja put her foot down. Instead, she took up a second job washing dishes for Mrs. Sodabottleopenerwalla's neighbor. Gopal's eyes grew misty when he first heard the news, but then he yawned and turned on his side and fell asleep.

"Ma, the baniya stopped me on the way home today," Pooja said. "Says he won't give us any more credit."

Bhima's face ached with worry. "Maybe I can pay him half of what we owe," she said. She lowered her voice. "You and I will just have to eat less the rest of the week to make up for the rent money."

Gopal, who was lying on the cot, made a face at his wife. "Always talking of money, money, money. Woman, you disgust me." He rose. "Well, since you brought this subject up, I need ten rupees."

Somehow, he always found enough money for his drinks. He stole from Bhima sometimes; other times, he simply threatened her until she gave him what little house money she had. That money came wrapped in her curses, like the tobacco wrapped in betel leaves he sometimes chewed. When she had nothing to give him, when he had picked her carcass dry, he would undertake small jobs for the bootlegger to pay for his habit. "He's my only friend," he once told Bhima. "He's the only one who understands what happens to a man who has been emasculated by his own wife."

She had to bite her lips to prevent the hate from spitting out at him then. She also didn't tell him what she knew—that Munnu, the landlord's son, had stopped by yesterday and threatened them with eviction if they didn't pay the rent.

As it turned out, the older woman who lived next door had learned of her trials. "Beti, don't be offended by what I'm about to say," she said to Bhima the next time they were standing in line outside the bathroom they shared with one other family. "But Munnu, our landlord's boy, was here yesterday and mentioned your situation to me. Munnu wants to get rid of you, that much is definite. Says he already has another family all ready to move in and that they've promised him six months' rent in advance. No heart in these people, I tell you. So if you're looking for a cheaper place to move to, let me know. I can help you."

Bhima turned to her eagerly. "Where is the place, didi? And what is the rent?"

"Actually, it is closer to your work than even this place, beti. You won't have to walk as much to get home after a day's work. In Bhaleshwar Colony, there's a nice little place that's—"

"Bhaleshwar? But that's a slum area, no? I cannot take my children to a place like that."

The old woman knocked on the bathroom door. "Arre, bhaisahib, are you building your home in that bathroom?" she yelled. "I'm an old lady, show some pity and finish your business jaldi-jaldi." She took a step closer toward Bhima and looked her in the eye. "Beti, a slum is no place to raise children, agreed. But neither is the street, correct? Do you want to come home one evening to find your things out on the street? Where will you go then? If not of yourself, think of your Pooja. A young girl on the streets is no safer than a young girl in a jungle—there are wild beasts in both places."

"How do you know of this place, didi?"

The old woman looked embarrassed. "My son-in-law owns a few huts in the slum colony," she said. "Once upon a time, he lived there himself. Now, of course, he has a nice place of his own. But as a favor to me, he will give you a good-good price on the rent."

The bathroom door creaked open, and its occupant, a bald man in a lungi and a sleeveless jersey, stepped out. "Sorry, mausi," the man muttered. "What to do, diarrhea."

The old lady entered the bathroom, holding her nose in a theatrical fashion.

Bhima stood outside, feeling the pressure of her bladder and moving discreetly from foot to foot. All these years, she had fantasized about a flat with its own private bathroom, like the one Serabai had. Instead, she was now facing a descent into a place worse that what she currently had. Daily, she passed by Bhaleshwar Colony on her way home from work, holding her nose against its, fetid smells. She remembered now how dark and endless the place looked from the street, with little side alleys running like crooked tunnels into its very heart of darkness. And the women sitting inside the open huts breast-feeding babies, their breasts hanging from blouses that were as open and exposed as their homes. And the men sitting on their haunches on the sidewalk, their insolent, drunken gazes falling on respectable women like her, who hurried past on their way to steady jobs. She imagined Gopal joining the ranks of these unemployed, dissolute men, spending his days sitting idly under the boiling sun. And she imagined Amit and Pooja in that hellish place—Amit hurrying home from school, withstanding the taunts of the idle, illiterate slum boys who wished to corrupt her son into their delinquent ways; Pooja averting her eyes from the greedy, salivating gaze of the local thugs.

No. When the old lady came out of the bathroom, she would tell her no. She would take on another two jobs if need be. Maybe Amit could find a way of earning a little money on the side also. They would make it work, she and her two children. Nothing mattered except Pooja and Amit. They didn't need Gopal anymore. She would be both, mother and father to them. It was she who had carried these two in her belly for nine months, not Gopal. The children were her responsibility, not his.

But how would she protect them if they were on the street? Even if she got a new job next week, it would still be at least another month before she got paid. And what if Munna wanted her to repay the entire amount she owed him all at once?

The bathroom door opened. Bhima saw the blank expression on the old woman's face and knew she'd forgotten all about her conversation with her. See how quickly the world forgets you, she reminded herself.

Bhima felt her mouth opening but was unsure of what she would say. So when she spoke, she heard her words at the same moment that her neighbor did. "Didi," she said. "I would like to see this place at Bhaleshwar. Can you set up a time?"

She felt a start of surprise at hearing the words. She had been so sure she was about to refuse the old woman's offer.

18

Bhima entered the dark slum and wondered where the past two years had gone. Already her feet knew by rote the sinister curves of the dark, narrow lanes that led up to their hut. She no longer gagged involuntarily when the putrid smell of the slum first assailed her nostrils. And just the other day, Amit had asked her a question about their old apartment that made her realize he was already beginning to forget its details.

Thinking of Amit made her quicken her step. The boy had stayed home from school that day, fighting a high fever. "Keep an eye on the boy, you hear?" she'd said to Gopal that morning. "If the cough or fever gets worse, take him to Dr. Roy's dispensary." She hesitated before giving Gopal a few rupees. "This money is for the doctor's fees, if you need to take Amit, understood? Do not spend it on your vileness."

Gopal had nodded earnestly. "Swear to God, wife. You must think I'm an animal instead of a man. What kind of father would spend his son's medicine money on daru?"

When she got home that evening, Amit was lying on the floor, a thin sheet covering him. Alone. "How are you feeling, beta?" she asked. "Where's your baba?"

The boy's voice was hoarse and his face shiny and flushed. "A little better, Ma," he said, sitting up. "I told Baba this afternoon to go get me some medicine from the doctor's clinic, but he said I didn't need it. But I think the fever has come down a little."

Bhima saw now that her son was shivering. "Are you cold?" she cried and, without waiting for an answer, covered him in a second sheet. "Where's your baba?"

Amit glanced at her and rolled his eyes. "Where else?"

A cold fury fell over Bhima like a steady rain. "He's at the drinking place?" she said. "Even today? He left you home alone, like this?" But she didn't really need a confirmation. She looked around the small room until her eyes fell on the broom standing up in the corner. "You stay here, Amit," she said, grabbing the broom. "I won't be gone long, beta."

By the time she reached the bootlegger's den, the fury had turned into a tempest. Bhima spotted Gopal as soon as she entered the semipermanent structure that masqueraded as a restaurant, gambling den, and drinking hole for the local men. She was the only woman in the place. "Ae, missus," someone yelled. "Ladies not allowed in." Ignoring the man, she headed straight for where Gopal was sitting with five other men. He was laughing at something, his white teeth gleaming in his dark face, when he noticed her and the laugh died in his mouth. "What are you—" he began, but the next instant he got his reply as Bhima pulled out the broom from behind her back and began to beat him with it. "Saala, besharam, mawali," she panted, crashing the broom on his body repeatedly. "Cur. Mad dog with rabies. Snake born of your mother's belly. Lowest of the low. Serpent, pig. Motherfucker. The machine should've cut off your penis along with your fingers. Hijda, that's what you are, a hijda. You're a eunuch, not a man. After all, a real man doesn't leave his sick child at home while he goes drinking with the other local loafers."

She had run out of steam now, as well as the energy it took to land precise blows on the unprotesting Gopal, who did little to protect himself against her onslaught. She stopped, keeping a warning eye on her husband, who placed his arms in front of his body to deflect any further blows and moved toward her in an appeasing way. But just then, someone at the next table giggled, and the giggle stopped Gopal in his tracks. He looked around the room quickly and saw all the men there—his neighbors and his drinking companions, who were waiting to see what he would do next, how he would restore his battered manhood. He tried to signal this to Bhima. "Come on, let's go home," he said stiffly, grabbing her by the wrist, but she shook his hand away. "Don't touch me, you kutta," she said.

Gopal had not been in a fight in fifteen years. But now his body moved of its own volition as he slapped Bhima's sunken cheek with his left hand. Her head jerked back, and for a moment, something like pity came into Gopal's eyes. Then he slapped her again. This time, a stream of blood trickled out of her nose. Gopal's eyes widened at the sight of blood. Bhima saw her husband staring at her face in fascination, saw that the sight of her blood excited him, so he looked as if he could lick it, make it his. Before she could react, Gopal was slapping her again, using the back of his hand, his wrist acting as a hinge that allowed his hand to swing like a door. Finally, a couple of the men gripped him from behind. "Bas, yaar, Gopal," a man drawled. "You want something of your wife to remain for tomorrow, na? Chalo, take her out of here and go home."

Bhima walked home behind Gopal, trying to stop the bleeding with her sari and fighting the urge to pull the garment over her shame-filled face. She felt the eyes of the basti upon them. Like vultures these people are, she thought. Peck, peck, pecking away at one another's lives, feasting on one another's misery, circling over other people's dead marriages. She saw Gopal walking ahead of her, thin and lost, and for a frightful moment she thought she was seeing a shadow instead of a man. If I didn't have a sick boy at home, she thought, ae, bhagwan, I swear in your name, I would never return to that house.

At that time, she thought Gopal had extracted his revenge for her humiliation of him at the bar. But his true betrayal came five days later.

19

As she stops at the baniya to pick up some onions for dinner, Bhima wonders whether Maya will want to go to the seaside later this evening. She has grown to enjoy these after-dinner walks with her granddaughter, she realizes. The fresh, salty air, the stretching of her sore, cramped muscles as they walk, the anonymous mingling with thousands of other sea gazers—Bhima has begun to look forward to this. Above all, she likes how their evening walks seem to be restoring Maya to her, how the girl is slowly losing her defensive, cautious manner and returning to the cheerful, energetic girl she was before her pregnancy. Soon, Bhima thinks, she will broach the subject of returning to college. Now that Maya knows about her experience with the duplicitous accountant, surely she will understand even more how life treats those without an education. And although it will be awkward to ask Serabai for help to get the girl enrolled at a new college, for Maya's sake, she would ask.

Bhima picks up her pace as she reaches the entrance of the slum and begins to walk down the winding alley to her hut. The paper bag that holds the onions is wet from her sweaty grip, and all she needs is for one of her onions to roll into the gutter on her right. She has plans to make spicy potatoes and onions with hot chappatis for dinner.

She flings open the front door, and the first thing she notices is the tall shadow that Maya is casting. The shadow runs up the tin

wall and onto the ceiling, so that Maya appears like a small child below it. The girl is sitting in the corner of the hut, a kerosene lamp
beside her. As Bhima's eyes adjust to the new light, she sees the
powder blue paper in Maya's hand and knows immediately what
her granddaughter is reading. She throws a quick glance at her
trunk, and sure enough, the lid is open. Maya looks startled, then
sheepish, but as a frown begins to form on Bhima's brow and her
eyes narrow, the girl preempts her by speaking first. "I was looking
for something else, Ma-ma, I swear. My birth certificate, actually.
And when I saw this note, I picked it up and began to read before I
knew what it was."

"What do you need your birth certificate for?" Bhima's voice is
laced with suspicion.

Maya bites her lower lip and shrugs lightly. "I don't know. I
just . . . I like to look at my birth certificate sometimes. Just to,
you know, read my ma's and baba's names on it. It . . . it makes me
feel good, I don't know why. Like I'm not an orphan."

This girl will not rest until she succeeds in destroying what little is left of my heart, Bhima thinks. She, with her blessed innocence and her killer words that pierce my heart like needles. "Who
said you're an orphan?" Bhima says gruffly. "What, is your grandma
dead that you're an orphan?"

Maya smiles. But then her face grows long and worry lines
perch like stray birds on her forehead. "Ma-ma, I never knew about
this letter," she says quietly.

The letter. The letter that had turned her life upside down. The
letter that Gopal had shaped like a dagger and plunged into her
heart. The letter, with its life-destroying words that Jaiprakash—a
fellow slum dweller who, for a small fee, wrote letters for people
who couldn't read or write—had read out loud to her, his small
eyes watching her reaction to each word, his professional pride in
his craftsmanship, his rhetorical flourishes overtaking his sympathy

for the woman whose life he was destroying with his words. She had saved the letter for years and years but had heard it read only once. And yet, such was its power that she remembered most of it, heard Jaiprakash's quietly gloating voice in her dreams.

"Read it," she now commands Maya. "I want to hear it again. I've had it read to me only once before." Her voice is steady, but its effect on Maya is electric. "Ma-ma, no," the girl protests. "Why bring up the past unnecessarily?"

Bhima smiles. "Beti, the past is always present," she says. "No such thing as bringing it up. The past is like the skin on your hand—it was there yesterday and it is here today. It never goes anywhere. Maybe when you're older you'll understand this better."

"But Ma-ma, in English there is a saying: let sleeping dogs lie. No sense in waking up a sleeping dog."

Bhima considers this. "But what if you're one of those unfortunates whose dog never sleeps?" she asks. And sensing that she has silenced her granddaughter momentarily, she presses her advantage. "Beti, read me the letter."

"To the queen-of-my dreams," Gopal had dictated to Jayprakash.

For several years now, I have been a burden to you and the family. For this and other crimes, I seek your forgiveness. I have watched my plump, beautiful Bhima, the bride I brought home with such hopes and desires, get eaten up with worry and misery. My drinking has turned you into a thin, shriveled creature, and for that crime I will be condemned to repeat this unhappy cycle of life over and over again. Don't think that my drunkenness kept me from noticing how unhappy I have made you—liquor is the kiss of the angels as well as the curse of the devil. It can conceal but it can also reveal. But until five days ago, my wife, I was not knowing how low I had fallen in life, nor how low I had dragged you. To be embarrassed at the bar in such a public manner was unbearable. After that, it would be hard for me to hold my head up in this basti without hearing in my ears the snickering of the women and children and even the stray dogs. You have emasculated me in the eyes of the world, and now the world laughs in my face. And so, my Bhima, I am leaving. And I am taking Amit with me. He will be my crutch, my support, the hand that I am missing. It is my idea that we will return to my village, where there is family and some land and fresh, clean air. Perhaps even a job and a new chance for a man with three missing fingers. Once, when I was a young man, I had believed that I was in love with Bombay and wedded to her, that the city was my bride, my wife. But now I know—Bombay is mistress to many, wife to none. My real life is in the village of my youth, to which I must return with humility and the hope of forgiveness.

With Amit and me gone, your burdens will lessen. With Pooja and you both working, there should be enough money to live on. Today is the last time I will steal from you—just enough money for train tickets to get Amit and me to my village. I have told the boy that I am taking him on a trip to meet his uncle and that we will be returning in a few weeks' time. I hope the life of the village—the simple but hearty food, the hard but honest work in the fields, a life away from the distractions of this harlot city—will agree with him. I know you will never find it in your heart to forgive me for taking Amit, but Bhima, just like you, I am needing a reason to keep on living. My son belongs by my side; he will be the support of my old age and my motive to keep putting one foot in front of the other. You, in turn, will have Pooja. She will be your reason to keep breathing.

My wife, believe me when I say that when I brought you into my home for the first time, it was my intention to treat you like a queen. Sometimes, when you are at work, I sit alone in this wretched place and fight with the gods about who or what stole away our life. I look to the bottle for answers. I look to the heavens. I search my own heart. And there are no answers. There is just a white silence that *washes up to my heart, like those waves at Chowpatty. Remember those evenings at the seaside when I was still your husband and a provider for my children? Am I correct in believing that we were happy then? My Bhima, after all these years together—years of laughter and tears, bitterness and happiness—this is all I am left with, like shells on the sand after the waves have wandered away: I loved you once, and although I know I will never convince you of this truth, I still do. Despite everything, despite the ugliness of this week, I still love you. Now, with everything else—work, money, house, pride, dignity—gone, only the love remains.*

You will never believe me, I know. But wherever we may be, I will remain

Your husband, Gopal.

Maya is crying silently by the time she finishes reading. But Bhima does not notice. She is remembering the first, fatal reading of the letter years earlier—how Jaiprakash had nervously licked his lips after he looked up from the last line and saw the demonic look on Bhima's face; how she had cursed him when he informed her that Gopal and the boy had left on the 3:30 train; how she had nervously prowled the colony, waiting for Pooja to get home; how she had spent the night unable to sleep and unable to stay awake and had woken in the morning with a temperature of 104 degrees. And the days that followed—Serabai shaking her head gravely and informing her that, since Gopal was the father, there was nothing Bhima could do to get Amit back against his wishes; Bhima anxiously awaiting a letter or word of Gopal and Amit's whereabouts; the women in the slum tsk-tsking and averting their glances when they caught sight of Bhima's mad, haunted face; Jaiprakash avoiding her for weeks and then one day running into her and deflecting blame by spitting out "It's your own fault, Bhima devi. Humiliating your husband in public like that. What did you expect? A man has his pride, you know." And Bhima had turned away, vanquished by Jaiprakash's words, knowing he was right.

Bhima shakes her head at her own bad fate. She concentrates to hear what Maya is saying to her. "Ma-ma," Maya asks carefully. "Did you ever hear from my uncle Amit?"

This girl's questions are like fingernails that she uses to pick at scabs, Bhima thinks. "Amit has never written," she says finally, draining the hurt from her words before she allows herself to speak. "But Gopal's older brother used to write now and then. Said he enjoyed having Amit work beside him on the family farm."

"If I were Amit uncle, I would've run away back to Bombay, sure-for-sure," Maya says consolingly.

"And left your baba behind all alone? Only wicked children abandon their parents."

"Perhaps he will return to Bombay one of these days. What would we do, Ma-ma, if Amit uncle were to knock on our door one day?"

What would she do? I would walk on my knees to the most distant temple to offer thanks, Bhima thinks. I would fast for a week to thank the gods. I would distribute pedas to all the children in the slum. I would fly to the moon and bring it back to feed it to my child. I would cut out a piece of my liver in order to see my son once more.

Maya is talking again. "Did Grandpa know about . . . Did you inform him about my ma and papa?"

Bhima's mouth is suddenly dry with fear, and she reaches for her tobacco tin. She rolls a wad and stuffs it in her cheek before she speaks. "I couldn't at the time. Not from Delhi. There was—no time. But after we came back, you and I, I sent a letter telling him what had happened. Serabai wrote it for me."

"What did he say?" Maya's voice is breathless.

"His older brother wrote back. They blamed me for not informing Gopal in time. Accused me of keeping him away from his daughter. Said that my Pooja's soul would not—" Seeing Maya's wide-eyed look, Bhima cuts herself off. "Anyway, after this letter, I never heard from them again."

"Would Grandpa have come to Delhi if he'd known, do you think?" Bhima can hear the fear and hope that are buried in this question.

She closes her eyes and then opens them again, staring directly at her granddaughter. "He would've come. If heaven and earth had tried to prevent him, still he would've come. He would've found a way, I know this. Your grandfather loved your mother, Maya."

"Then why did he chose Amit and leave her with you?"

Bhima swallows hard before replying. "Because he knew that I needed Pooja more than I needed Amit," she says softly. "Amit was my son. But Pooja was my firstborn—she was my son and daughter, all in one."

Suddenly, Maya starts crying. "My ma loved you too, Ma-ma," she sobs. "Believe me, don't believe me, but I remember. Always she used to talk about Bombay and your old house and about you."

Bhima scoots on the floor toward the sobbing girl and enfolds her in her arms. "Silly child," she chides. "Why are you crying over long-ago things? All this happened a hundred lifetimes ago."

"But the past is with us, Ma-ma. You just said so yourself."

Bhima smacks Maya on the hand. "Too smart you are getting for a girl," she says. Her face is weary as she eyes the bag of onions on the floor. "I could've finished cooking by now if you hadn't delayed me with your hundred questions." She sighs.

She thinks for a minute and then gets up. "Come on, go wash your face. We will walk to Chowpatty today and eat snacks for dinner. Too late for me to start cooking at this hour."

20

Bhelpuri.

It's 7:45 in the evening, and Dinaz wants bhelpuri for dinner. They have just sat down to the wonderful dinner of khara chicken and mutton cutlets that Bhima had prepared earlier in the day when Dinaz pushes away the plate of cutlets—she pronounces it "cutles," in the same old-fashioned Parsi way that Banu used to, making Sera fret about the bald power of genetics. "These cutles are making me nauseated," she says, pushing them away from her. "Take them away from the table, please."

Viraf makes a face. "I thought the nausea ended with the first trimester," he says, and both the women know what he has left unspoken: I don't think I could relive the terrors of the first trimester, when hormones, fatigue, and nausea turned my wife into a madwoman.

Dinaz laughs. "Stop looking so worried, yaar," she says. "Look at his face, Mummy, all because I don't want to eat some cutles. I tell you, it's too bad men can't have babies—we'd stop India's overpopulation problem in one day, because none of them would ever get pregnant."

"Well, you have to eat something, my darling," Sera says. "The baby needs good nutrition and—"

"You know what I have a craving for?" Dinaz says. "Bhelpuri. At Chowpatty."

Viraf groans. "Come on, Dinu. I've just gotten home from work. I don't feel like going out again. And that stuff there is so filthy. I think they use toilet water to wash their dishes."

Dinaz remains unfazed. "At least I'm not craving wall plaster and cockroaches and what all, like other pregnant women do." She smacks Viraf playfully on the arm. "Gadhera. It's your fault that I'm walking around fat as a heifer. The least you can do is feed me some bhelpuri."

"Okay, okay," Viraf says. "One of the duties of imminent fatherhood, I suppose."

Sera gazes at the table of food. She had looked forward to this dinner all day. "But what about this whole meal? Bhima will be so disappointed."

"Ah, screw Bhima," Viraf says. "In fact, she'll be glad. Less work for her tomorrow." He pushes back his chair. "Okay, let's go. Mummy, go get your shawl or cardigan. It's a little cold for November this year."

In the car, Sera sighs. "It's been so long since I've been to Chowpatty. I hear the municipality has cleaned up the area. The last time I was there was just a few days before your daddy passed away. It was so filthy then."

Dinaz laughs. "Daddy was so funny—he had such silly vhems and dhakheras about personal hygiene. I remember once, he and I had gone to Flora Fountain, and this lout standing on the footpath spat out his paan juice on the street. Daddy was convinced that some of the red juice had landed on my pants, although I couldn't see a trace of it. I thought he was going to kill the poor fellow with his bare hands. And yet, he thought nothing about eating street food."

She turns toward Viraf. "When he'd come to my school for a play or a function, he always would stop at this vendor outside the school who made the best pyali. Dad would eat two bowls. You remember, Mummy? You used to always scold him because he ate it so spicy tears would roll down his cheeks."

Sera smiles. "He once told me that, when he returned from London, he used to get sick after he ate the bhelpuri at Chowpatty. So he went there every day until his stomach finally adjusted."

Viraf laughs. "That sounds like Feroz daddy all right. He was a tough guy."

They are all silent for a minute, each of them remembering Feroz. "Next month will be three years," Sera says softly. "Can you imagine?"

"No, it doesn't seem that long," Dinaz replies. There is another silence in the car. Then Dinaz says, "I didn't know you and Daddy had gone to Chowpatty a few days before he died."

"Yes. We had gone to the big fire temple in Fountain. Your Banu granna had had the stroke just a few months earlier, and your daddy was so upset about seeing his mother like that that he made a manta that he would go to the fire temple every day for month to pray for her full recovery. I used to go with him sometimes. Often, we would go to Paradise for dinner. But this day, we decided to go to Chowpatty. Your daddy was always game for bhelpuri and panipuri. In fact, before our marriage we used to go there all the time."

Viraf suddenly lets out a guffaw. "What, what?" Dinaz says, and even in the dark of the car, Sera can hear the affectionate smile in her daughter's voice.

"Nothing," he says. "I was just remembering the advice your father gave me the first time I was over at your house. It was for your birthday party, remember? There were so many other people there. But somehow he picked up on the fact that I, that we, liked each other. So he pulled me into a corner and said he had something to tell me. Some man-to-man advice, he called it. Basically, he told me that he thought I was a nice Parsi boy with the potential to make his daughter happy. But he said I should be persistent with you if I didn't want to lose you to your other suitors. 'A man should be like a raging bull when he's chasing a woman' I think were his exact words. I was so scared, all I could say was "Yes, uncle, and no, uncle.' "

Dinaz laughs. "I think Daddy was relieved that you were a Parsi, that's all. He was always afraid that I was going to bring home a Goanese Christian or a Hindu or, worst of all, a Muslim. Also, he had this strange belief that I would feel sorry for a man who was a cripple or in a wheelchair and marry him out of pity. Can you imagine? I think that's the main reason he was so opposed to my being a social worker. He was forever telling me, 'Don't marry someone because you feel sorry for him.' And I would assure him that the thought had never crossed my mind." She pinches Viraf on his thigh. "What I didn't tell Daddy was that I was waiting for a handsome cutie-pie with film star looks to come along."

"And instead you married me," Viraf says, pulling his lips downward. "Good thing Feroz daddy was so focused on keeping you away from physical cripples that he didn't notice you married a mental cripple, hah?"

"Ovaru, ovaru," Sera says crossly, clicking her fingers. "What crazy things you children say."

"Ah, don't fall for his tricks, Mummy. He's just looking for his two ladies to tell him how smart and handsome he is."

Whistling tunelessly, Viraf cruises around for a parking space. Sera smiles to herself, thinking of how different her son-in-law is from her husband. Feroz would've been swearing under his breath by now, and looking for a policeman to slip a ten-rupee note to so that he could park illegally. But Viraf is a thanda pani ka matla—an earthenware pot of cold water. "Aha," he says triumphantly upon spotting a tiny space. "Bet I can squeeze in there."

"Impossible," Dinaz says automatically, although both she and Sera know what an excellent driver Viraf is. And when her husband gets the car into the spot on the first try, Dinaz grunts. "Guess you've forgotten that your wife has a belly the size of the Sahara desert. God knows how I'm going to squeeze out of this tiny spot."

"My, how this place has changed," Sera exclaims as they approach the beach. "So much cleaner it is looking. I've heard they're punishing people for littering and doing their private business on the beach."

"Yah, downright unconstitutional, if you ask me." Viraf grins. "Littering and doing soo-soo in public are a Bombayite's birthright."

Sera tries to remember what the beach looked like the last time she was here with Feroz. But she is distracted because all she can bring to mind is how sweet and attentive Feroz had been that night. Taking her to his favorite vendor, he had insisted that she eat the first plate Ramdas had prepared even though she knew he had not eaten all day. After they had each eaten two plates of bhelpuri, he had wanted to get some milk kulfi. "Sweetu, be careful," Sera had said. "You know it's bad for your cholesterol."

"Arre, damn the cholesterol," he'd said. "It's been so long since we've come to Chowpatty. And you know what I always say—you can spend two hundred rupees getting ice cream at the Taj or some other five-star hotel, but it will never compare to kulfi at Chowpatty. Come on, just for today. I've been good with my diet, you know that."

She had acquiesced, as he'd known she would; when Feroz got that pleading look on his face, she couldn't refuse him. And since Banu mamma's stroke, Feroz had changed. It was as if seeing his domineering mother reduced to a vegetative state had made him realize something about the brutal unpredictability of life. Every evening he went to see his mother directly from work, and when he returned home, he seemed softer and more communicative than ever before.

"So much has happened in the last few years," he sighed that night after they got home from the beach. In the light of the reading lamp, Sera noticed the lines on Feroz's face and how the skin on his bald skull creased up when he was worried. Not for the first time, she was aware of thirteen years that separated her from her aging husband. "I feel like I'm still recovering from Pappa's death, and now we have to see Mamma in this state," Feroz said. "It's unbearable to watch her suffering. I tell you, the only good thing that's happened in recent years is Dinaz's wedding. If it wasn't for her and Viraf's happiness, I don't know what there would be to live for."

Sera rose and walked over to the armchair where Feroz was slumped. She sat on its arm and stroked his head. "I was thinking that we should go somewhere for a few days, janu," she said. "Take a trip, to Goa or something."

He nodded. "I know. But not yet. Let's wait till the situation with Mamma gets stabilized. I cannot bear the thought of leaving her like this." He looked up at Sera, and she was stunned to see the tears in his eyes. So much he loves that woman, she marveled. Does he have any idea how his mother's interference has ruined the chance of happiness in our own marriage? Does he ever think about that at all?

As if he had read her mind, Feroz continued, "I know you are needing a break, too. I thank you, Sera, for taking such good care of my mother in her hour of need. I know she's—you've—she's not been the easiest person to deal with. We will go out of Bombay soon, I promise. Maybe even take the children along. Just . . . not right now."

But three days later, he was dead and that promise lay in the drawer marked Unkept Promises, along with many others. Along with the unkept promise of her marriage itself. A marriage that had begun with such high hopes and expectations had fizzled out, like those firecrackers and rockets that Dinaz and her friends used to shoot into the heavens at Diwali time and that fell back to earth with an embarrassed hiss, as if pushed down by an unwelcoming God.

Feroz came home from work early on the day of his death, complaining of a general feeling of uneasiness. "Too much work," Sera said. "Too much tension you are carrying around, janu. Maybe you should join a yoga class or something, to learn how to calm your mind."

He smiled weakly. "Maybe." Then his face fell. "I didn't even go see Mamma today," he said as he pulled back the covers and climbed into bed. "She will be so upset."

Your mother can't even recognize anyone, she wanted to say. She probably can't tell one day from the next. But she kept her thoughts to herself.

"Come lie next to me," he whispered, and for the first time, the thought ran through Sera's mind that Feroz might really be sick. He had never looked so weak, so vulnerable before.

She struggled against a sudden, irrational panic. "Sweetu," she said, trying to keep her voice level. "What exactly is happening to you? Should I send for the doctor?"

"No. No doctor, please. It's probably just the flu or something. I don't know . . . I can't exactly explain what I feel. Just like something's fluttering in my chest. I think it's tension. I just need to sleep for a few hours."

Sera went into the kitchen to tell Bhima to make sure she made no noise while Feroz seth slept. "He's very tired," she said in response to Bhima's curious look. "Needs some peace and quiet."

While Feroz slept, she spent the hours making his favorite Chinese chicken-corn soup. At six o'clock she told Bhima to set the soup bowl on the table. She would go wake Feroz up—he needed to eat; he was probably weak from all the dieting he had been doing.

She tiptoed up to where Feroz was sleeping and sat down on the edge of the bed. "Sweetu," she whispered. "Wake up. I've made some hot-pot soup for you."

There was no answer. She whispered again, and she was about to shake him when she heard something. What she heard was the lack of sound in the room. Feroz was not breathing. "Feroz," she cried, her hand going for the light switch. As light flooded the room, it fell on her husband's still face. His mouth was open, as were his eyes, but even at the peak of her fear and distress, Sera knew that the peace that Feroz had searched for his whole life was finally his.

"Feroz," she screamed. "No, no, no. Please, Feroz, please. Bhima. Bhima, come here. Oh, my God, no."

Bhima came running into the room. "Serabai," she spluttered helplessly. "Arre bhagwan. What is this new tragedy that has come to us?"

It was over. Her marriage was over. Just like this, in the blink of an eye, Feroz was gone. Feroz—husband and oppressor; lover and tormentor; victim and victimizer. No man had ever made her happier or more miserable. No man had loved her as passionately; no man had done more to strangle the love she felt for him. Feroz had held the keys to her happiness, but those keys had unlocked the gates of hell. He had been a mercurial man—aggressive, brilliant, violent, jealous, but also loving, generous, and capable of largesse. Perhaps it had been her fault that she had never learned how to handle this man, how to steer through the choppy waters he left in his wake. Could another woman—more worldly, more savvy—have done it differently? Would another woman have treated Banu as a nuisance, an irritation and nothing more?

"Feroz," she sobbed. "My husband, Feroz. I'm sorry. I'm sorry for everything. Forgive me for being such a poor wife. I was so lost in my own misery that I never stopped to consider yours."

She must've been speaking out loud, because Bhima was standing at her side, lifting up her head, brushing back her hair from her hot, teary face. "Come on, Serabai," Bhima whispered. "This is the time for courage, bai. And nothing for you to seek forgiveness for. Every time the men leave, the women are the ones who ask for forgiveness. You were a good wife, bai. I saw with my own eyes, day in and day out. Now come on, we have to inform our Dinaz."

Dinaz. Sera's heart froze at the thought of breaking the news to her daughter. Still, she forced herself to think. "They must be on their way home from work by now. Better to try to catch them on the mobile. Get me the phone book, Bhima. I have Viraf's cell phone number written in there." She stopped dead in her tracks as another thought hit her. "Oh, my God, someone will have to tell the old lady that her . . . her son is dead." Sera began to sob again.

"Viraf baba can do that," Bhima called from the other room. "You don't have to go there, bai. And who knows what that poor woman will even understand? Like a stick of carrot she lies there all day."

The doorbell rang a half hour later, and Viraf and Dinaz walked in, their eyes and noses red. "We jumped off the train," an out-of-breath Viraf said. "Took a cab. Dinaz got impatient at the traffic light, so we just got out and ran the rest of the way."

The sound of Dinaz's sobbing tore at Sera's heart. She had not heard her daughter sob like this since she was twelve years old. Sure, Dinaz had cried at Freddy pappa's funeral—Sera herself had felt as if she had lost her right arm when Freddy died—but this grief over her dead father was different—searing, acidic, hot as a branding iron. "I didn't even get a chance to say good-bye," Dinaz sobbed. "What with me and Viraf living so far away in the suburbs, I hadn't even spent much time with him these past few months."

Sera went through the purse of her memory, hunting for a few gold coins. "I know, deekra, I know," she murmured as she sifted.

Suddenly, she found what she was looking for. "Do you know what Daddy said to me just two-three days back? That your marriage was the one great source of happiness in his life."

But her offering backfired, because now there was a new sound of grief in the room. It was Viraf, his slender body racked with grief, his long nose as red as a beetroot. "He was a king," Viraf blubbered. "Feroz daddy was a prince of a man."

Suddenly, Sera felt caught in a bubble of clear, objective thought, floating untouched on the churning sea of unthinking, tumultuous grief around her. So this is how history gets rewritten, she thought. This is how it begins, with exaltation. Now it is not enough for a man merely to have been a man; now the etiquette of grief demands that we change him into a prince, a king. Now the flaws of a man have to be ironed out like creases in a suit, until he is spread out before us as smooth and unblemished as the day he was born. As if the earth would refuse to receive him, as if the vultures at the Tower of Silence would refuse peck at him, unless he was restored to his original glory. In death, all men become saints, she thought, and she both welcomed and rebelled against the thought. Perhaps it was better this way—this erasing of bad memories, this replacement with happier ones, like changing a dirty tablecloth. But if this was true, what to do about this heavy, lumpen body of hers, this body that cried out its true history, this body that wanted to testify, to bear witness to what had been done to it? This battered, bruised body that had been punished for other people's crimes—for Feroz's jealous rages; for Banu's conniving and superstitious ways. Would this body—this knitted sweater of muscle and bone and nerve endings—would this body have to be dead, would its blood have to freeze into immobility before anyone sang its praises and called it the body of a princess or a queen?

"Mummy, say something, please. I feel so alone." Dinaz's voice pierced Sera's bubble, and she felt herself plunge once again into the hot, bubbling waters of grief.

"Come here, my darling," Sera said, cradling her daughter's head. "You will never be alone, not as long as I'm alive."

Three years have gone by since that day, Sera now marvels. How can that be, when the memory of that grief-filled day is still so sharp, as if someone sprinkled chili powder in my eyes? And yet, she admits to herself, I have never been as happy as I have these three years, with the children living with me and a new one on its way. She feels a twinge of regret when she thinks that Feroz won't be here to enjoy the new baby. As much as Feroz loved Dinaz, he would've adored his grandchild, she thinks. Still—she sighs—it will be lovely having the baby to myself while Dinaz and Viraf are at work. She will get to enjoy her grandchild in a way that she never got to enjoy Dinaz. After all, Dinaz was born in a house that was always darkened by the shadow of Banu's irrational behavior and Feroz's fearsome rages. Even after they moved out of Banu's home, she never quite felt rid of the old woman's presence, held ransom to every unexpected ring of the doorbell. And contrary to her hopes, Feroz's fists had not stopped flying after they moved out. In some ways, she had given him another, more permanent excuse for his rages—the forced separation from his mother.

But all that's over, she now reminds herself. The home that you never got with your husband, you now have with your daughter and son-in-law. Viraf and Dinaz have provided you with your life's dream. So, silly woman, why live anymore in the past when the present is so full of hope?

Viraf playfully digs his elbow into Sera's ribs. "Su che, Mummy?" He grins. "Why all these seductive, secret smiles?

Thinking of a new boyfriend? What's his name, Pestonji Pipyadas? Be careful, all these bhaiyas here will think you're flirting with them."

Sera bursts out laughing. "Silly boy," she chides him. "I should tell your mummy what ridiculous things come out of your mouth."

"My mummy doesn't even know what flirting means, I'm sure," he replies promptly. He winks at Dinaz and then turns to Sera. "After all, she's not glamorous, like you are. I tell you, Dinaz, if your mother was twenty years younger . . ."

"Ignore him, Mummy," Dinaz says, taking Sera's arm. She turns to her husband with a raised voice. "You saparchand. Are you going to feed your poor pregnant wife, or are you just going to feed your own mouth with your crazy words? Come on, I'm starving."

"Let's see if Ramdas's stall is still here," Sera says. "He was your father's favorite bhaiya at Chowpatty."

They look for the booth, but things have changed. "Forget it," Sera says. "Let's just eat anywhere."

They are all starting on their second plate of bhelpuri when Dinaz lets out a cry of surprise. "Look who's here," she says, her mouth full.

"Can't follow what you're saying," Viraf says. "Swallow and then talk."

Dinaz swallows. Her eyes are shiny with excitement. "Look, it's Bhima and Maya, at the booth over there. God, it's been ages since I've seen that little girl. Bhima," she yells.

"Er, we probably shouldn't disturb them," Viraf says. "After all, with Maya having lost her child, she may be . . ."

Dinaz ignores him. "Bhima. Maya. Over here," she yells, waving her hand frantically.

The two women turn in the direction of her voice.

21

Bhima spins around. Her face lights up with genuine pleasure when she sees the caller. Dinaz is waving to them, and even across this distance, Bhima can see the eager smile on her face. "It's Dinaz baby," she says to Maya, pulling her by the wrist. "Come on, let us go pay our respects."

"You go, Ma-ma," Maya protests. "I'll wait here."

"Arre wah." Bhima looks shocked. "What, have you become so bigheaded that you cannot walk over a short distance to greet your well-wishers?" Her grip on Maya tightens. "Come on, you lazy girl."

"Hello, hello, hello," Dinaz says as they approach. "Hey, Maya, haven't seen you in so long. How are you?"

"Fine," Maya mumbles, staring at Dinaz's swollen belly.

Dinaz catches the look and laughs. "Yah, I've probably grown like a fat pig since you last saw me, na?" she says, patting her belly.

A look of sudden spite crosses Maya's face. "I was looking the same way, too. That is, until your mummy fixed me," she says and stares defiantly at Serabai, whose face has turned white at the girl's inexplicable rudeness.

Bhima is mortified. What has gotten into this girl? she wonders. She stares at the ground, trying to think of an excuse for Maya's behavior, when Serabai rescues her. "That was more than a month ago, Maya," she says in her usual, measured tone. "And what happened, happened. But you need to come talk to me about what we're going to do about your college."

Maya mumbles something and looks away. Under the golden lights of the food stalls, her eyes look artificially bright, and her face is so flushed that Bhima wonders if Maya is getting sick. That would explain her strange behavior, she thinks.

Still staring at her granddaughter, Bhima catches a movement out of the corner of her eye and follows it until her eyes fall on Viraf's face. Towering behind Sera and Dinaz, he is staring at Maya. Like Maya, he has a manic, flustered expression in such a contrast to Viraf's usual cool confidence that Bhima looks at him in fascination. Viraf chews on his upper lip and his long, slender fingers pick at the stubble on his cheek. The boy looks sick . . . no, scared . . . no, guilty, Bhima thinks and notices that Viraf is actually trying to hide behind his wife and mother-in-law. Her mind flashes to an incident at the basti a few months ago when one of the residents had accused a neighbor's teenage son of stealing money from her hut. The boy had shaken his head in vehement denial, but the hot, guilty expression on his face—the way he gulped hard, the way he ran his tongue over his dry lips—told a different story. That's what Viraf looks like, Bhima marvels, as if he's a thief, as if he's guilty of something. But what?

Dinaz, too, must've sensed something, because she looks over her shoulder and reaches for Viraf's hand. "Ae, sweetu," she says. "You haven't even said hello to Maya and Bhima."

Viraf nods. "Hello," he says in a low voice, letting his eyes fall over Maya's bowed head before they come to rest on Bhima. He gives a little start as he notices the attentive way in which she is staring at him.

Dinaz laughs gaily. "It's getting to be past this one here's bedtime," she says, poking Viraf in the ribs. "He didn't even want to go back out tonight. But I just had a craving for bhelpuri. We should get going."

"I'll go ahead and get the car," Viraf says immediately. "You all just come and wait at the traffic light."

Dinaz turns to Maya. "It was so nice seeing you, Maya," she says. "I miss seeing you at Banu mamma's." She reaches over to give the girl a quick hug. "I know you will start college again when you're ready," she whispers. "And I'm so sorry for your loss."

As the two women walk away, Bhima feels rooted in place, as if she is one of those sand sculptures of Hindu gods at Chowpatty that passersby throw coins at. Indeed, she feels as though she is made of sand and one bucket of water would destroy her. The world around her also seems constructed of sand—shaky, ambiguous, and imper- manent. A world in which none of the old rules, the old taboos ap- ply. A world in which a slum girl from a poor family can seduce a clean, handsome, upper-class boy whose wife is about to have his first child. A world in which Maya and Viraf . . .

It was strange how she found out. One moment she didn't know; the next minute she did. One moment her mind was as blank as the desert; the next minute the snake of suspicion had slithered into her thoughts and raised its poisonous head. And now she must live with the earth-shattering knowledge that Viraf Davar was the father of Maya's dead child. While she, Bhima, had looked suspiciously at every youth and middle-aged man in the slum, while she had humiliated herself before those sneering boys at Maya's col- lege, while she had foolishly imagined her granddaughter in a kitchen with shiny pots and pans, it had never occurred to her to look for the snake under her very nose.

But perhaps I am wrong, she thinks. Perhaps her suspicions themselves are made of sand and one good wave would knock them down. If so, she longs for the waters of oblivion to come and wash away the misgivings that are gnawing at her heart. But even as she prays for this, certainty hardens like cement.

By her side, Maya fidgets. "Come on, Ma-ma," she says. "I want to go home."

"There is no home in our future," Bhima says enigmatically. "There is no resting place for the wicked sinners of this world. For your sins, I will do endless sounds in this miserable world. So I may as well start practicing. No, come on, I am needing to walk some more." Maya's face flushes, and her eyes widen as she stares at her grandmother's bony face. She opens her mouth as if to protest, but Bhima has begun walking toward the shoreline, and after a second, the girl follows.

They walk in total silence. But this silence is screaming, screeching, and filled with sounds—the thudding of Bhima's heart; the clawing, tearing fear that is choking Maya's throat; the scraping sound that Bhima's feet make as they dig angrily into the sand. Inside this silence the two women walk, afraid of touching its contours, because to break the dam of silence would mean to allow the waters of anger, rage, fury to come rushing, would allow the tidal wave of the recent past—the past that they have ignored, aborted, killed—to come roaring in to destroy their tenuous present.

But quiet, like love, doesn't last forever.

And so Bhima speaks. If that choked, animal-like sound that she makes can be called speaking. "Why?" she groans. "Why him?"

Maya looks at her grandmother uncertainly, as if she is unsure whether Bhima is addressing her or some invisible deity who is floating above the waters of the Arabian Sea, laughing at them. She stares out at the vast, endless water.

Maya's lack of response infuriates Bhima. The woman thumps her hard on the back, so that Maya rocks forward for a moment. "I asked you a question, shameless," she says but still Maya says nothing.

"Ashok Malhotra, hah?" Bhima taunts. "First, you tempted a decent married man, and then you lied to me to throw me off the scent of your shame. Pissing in the pot you have been eating out of. Betraying the trust that the whole Dubash family had in you. That boy's wife, Dinaz, has been like a daughter to me. How will I ever face them again? Namak-haram, every letter that you know to read, every stitch of clothing that you wear, every grain of salt in your mouth, it all comes from Serabai's generosity."

Maya's face is a battlefield on which conflicting emotions rage. Bhima braces herself for the girl to deny the identity of the father of her dead baby, to pretend that she doesn't know what Bhima is talking about. But the time for pretense is over, and the weary resignation on Maya's face is the final confirmation Bhima needs.

But before Bhima can speak, Maya does. "That's incorrect, Ma-ma," she cries out. "I was learning how to read and write before I came to Bombay. My parents were sending me to school in Delhi. Serabai just wanted to believe I was a dum-dum she could save. And as for my clothes and food—for that I am grateful to you, not to her. It is your sweat and hard work that produce them, not Serabai's generosity. If you stopped going to work for a month, let us see if she would send you your salary in the mail."

Bhima stares at her granddaughter openmouthed. "Look at her," she says softly, as if speaking to herself. "Just listen to the sinful words coming out of the mouth of this ungrateful wretch," she said. "Pissing on the woman who has built her life. And all because she has gone and done her ugliness with Serabai's son-in-law and now she must cover up the stain of her guilt. My Pooja, God bless her, must be shedding hot-hot tears of shame at this monster she gave birth to."

They have stopped walking and stand inches apart, ignoring the warm waters lapping around their feet, oblivious to the openly curious stares of inquisitive passersby. "Why are you so fast to blame me for what happened, Ma-ma?" Maya says, her chest heaving with emotion. "Why this rush to make your granddaughter into the only sinner here? What about what he did? Or must every member of his family remain a saint in your mind? Is it only your family that you must curse and blame for every act of wickedness and shame?"

Now Bhima hears the hatred in Maya's voice and recalls how the girl had tensed up when they heard Dinaz baby call their name. At that time, she had assumed that the reason Maya stiffened and refused to greet Dinaz was shame. After all, Maya had acted strange around Serabai even on the day of the abortion and had refused to visit the Dubash residence ever since. Bhima eyes her granddaughter cautiously. "Did he—did Viraf baba—hurt you?" She chokes back the murderous rage that accompanies the thought.

Maya shakes her head impatiently, as if Bhima's question is a fly buzzing around her ears. "You just assumed that I was the one who did the evil deed. Why, Ma-ma? Why do you love their family even more than you love your own?"

Bhima swallows guilt that burns like molten lava as it goes down her throat. "Never say that," she whispers. "How can you say that when you are my whole world? Why, for you I would . . ." She shakes with emotion, unable to complete her thought. She walks back to where the sand is dry and looks for a spot away from the other people who sit on the beach. She lowers herself onto the sand, pulling Maya down with her.

For a few minutes they listen to the lapping waves in silence. Then, Bhima turns to Maya, and her face is kind and drained of judgment and anger. "Tell me what happened, beti," she says gently. "Tell me the whole story."

So Maya tells.

22

Maya was in Banubai's kitchen making tea for the old lady when the doorbell rang. She looked up, startled. It was 4:30 P.M., and she wasn't expecting anyone. The night nurse, Gaya, would not be here until eight o'clock.

She opened the door to Viraf. "Hah, Viraf baba," she exclaimed. "Here so early?" Viraf, she knew, usually stopped by on his way home from work to check on the old woman. Then, taking in the agitated look on his face, her stomach lurched. "Is everybody okay at home? Dinaz baby is not sick or anything?"

"Fine, fine, everybody is fine," he said dismissively as he brushed past her into the dining room. Then, seeing the look of apprehension still on Maya's face, "No, don't worry. Dinaz is fine. The only thing wrong with her is her damn temper. Spoiled brat. By the looks of it, you'd think she was the first person in the history of the world to give birth."

Maya blanched. She could not stand for anyone, even Viraf, to talk about Dinaz in this way. Seeing the appalled look on her face, he grinned maliciously. "Oh, sorry for criticizing your precious Dinaz baby," he said. "I forgot how devoted you two are to each other. You know, I should've solicited your help in trying to take her to the movies tonight. I took a half day and came home early for that reason. But of course, she's in one of her Durga moods. Lectures *me* instead on how she'd stayed home to do some work around the house and how irresponsible I am to just come home and expect my own wife to spend a few hours with me. So of course, I'm the chootia here."

Maya flinched at the crude slang. She'd never heard Viraf swear like this as if he was one of the louts that hung around her slum. Something of her shocked disappointment must have shown on her face because Viraf's manner softened and he looked chastised. "Sorry," he whispered. "Guess I'm getting carried away." He absently pulled Maya toward him and patted her lightly on the back. "Sweet Maya," he murmured. "I forgot how loyal you are, like a cute little puppy."

Maya was amazed, flattered, confused. After Dinaz baby, Viraf baba had always been her favorite member in Serabai's family. Feroz seth had terrified her, and while Serabai was unfailingly kind to her, something about the tall, dignified woman intimidated Maya. But ever since she had first known Viraf, he had treated her playfully and teasingly, without the distance that Serabai always cultivated. And he was also capable of bursts of generosity toward Maya and her grandmother. Just last week Ma-ma had come home with a box of sweetmeats so large that they had to distribute some to the other residents in the slum. "Viraf baba gave us this," a beaming Bhima had said. "A client of his gave him three such boxes of mithai. One of them he gave us."

Still, Viraf had never touched her before, or spoken to her with such casual affection. In fact, she had never known him like this, so erratic, so agitated. So demonstrative and so obviously in need of comfort. Something softened and stirred in her, a moist, tender feeling in her chest. She felt shy and tongue-tied as she fought the urge to stare down at her bare feet. Instead, she forced herself to look at Viraf's flushed face, trying to think of a way to soothe him back into his usual good cheer.

"Chai," she said. "I'm making Banubai a nice cup of tea. I'll make a cup for you too, Viraf baba."

He smiled, so that he looked like the old Viraf again. "Okay. I'll go give my salaams to the old lady, and then I'll be in the other room, working on her accounts. That's what I came here to do anyway." His face darkened again. "As depressing as this house is, at least there's some peace and quiet here for a man to do his work. No nagging wife with raging hormones lording it over us poor males." He flashed Maya a sudden grin. "No nagging wife. Just a mean, bedridden old lady who lords it over you instead."

She had never seen him like this, so mercurial. The old Viraf, the Viraf she was used to, was flitting in and out, like the sun behind the clouds. She stared at him openmouthed, not knowing him well enough to tell whether he was joking or serious or how to respond to the blasphemous things he was saying about his family. She felt young and small and excruciatingly aware of her strange status within this family—how she was condemned to listen but not speak; how she could not rise to his bait and say what she really felt about Banubai—that she agreed with his characterization of her as a mean old woman who made everybody's life miserable.

As if on cue, Banu's gargling sounds reached them. "Urgghh, urgggh, urgghh," she spluttered.

Viraf turned away from Maya with a wink. "Doesn't miss a thing, does she?" he said. "Well, time to go pay my darshaan to Kali devi." This time, Maya could not resist her scandalized gasp at his flagrant blasphemy. "Viraf baba," she protested, but he was gone. "Kem, Banubai?" she heard him say. "How are you feeling today? You're looking good, cheeks as red as Kashmiri apples. Keeping all the servants on their toes, I hope?"

In the kitchen Maya heard Banu make a choking sound that she recognized as laughter. That Viraf baba was too much, Maya smiled to herself. When he turned on his charm, he could even make the dead laugh.

When she took him his cup of tea, he was sitting hunched over a pile of bills and Banu's checkbook. He had removed his tie, placed it neatly on the bed, and his shirt sleeves were rolled up. "Thank you," he said with a smile and then went back to his books. "A good cup of tea is exactly what I need."

The memory of his smile warmed her as she fed Banubai her own cup of tea, holding a cloth napkin under the woman's chin to catch the trail of liquid that dribbled from her flaccid, helpless mouth. As usual, she also dipped two glucose biscuits into the milky tea and then placed their soggy ghosts into the old woman's mouth. Sometimes, when she was angry at Maya, Banu spat out her tea and the mushy bits of biscuit, so that the girl had to use the napkin to wipe her own face and clothes. But Banu was in a good mood today, cheered up by Viraf's attention and flirtatious words.

"Okay, Mummy," Maya said briskly after Banu had finished her tea. "Now go to sleep for a few hours like a good-good girl. Dinner will be coming in a few hours. You get some beauty rest."

The gray, milky eyes followed her as she busied herself straightening Banu's room. But when Maya glanced at her again, the old woman was asleep, her mouth lax.

When Maya entered the room where Viraf had been working, he was sprawled out on the bed. He stretched when he saw her. "That tea was so good it made me drowsy," he said lazily. "Thought I'd take a quick nap. Dinaz is so restless at night because of the pregnancy, I hardly get a good night's sleep anymore."

She was about to leave the room with the empty cup with he spoke. "Oi, Maya. Look in the medicine cabinet and see if there's a bottle of Iodex, would you? I have a bad crimp in my neck. Too many hours at my desk."

She returned with the small, dark bottle and held it out to him, but he smiled pleadingly. "It's hard for me to reach the spot," he said. "Can you apply it?"

She hesitated for a second and then dipped two fingers into the black ointment. Viraf loosened the first two buttons of his shirt and turned onto his stomach. When her fingers touched his skin, he let out a little cry. "Your hands are cold," he scolded, but she could hear the smile in his voice.

Her fingers found the knot of muscle and worked deftly to untie it. "Dig deeper," Viraf grunted. He turned slightly on his side and undid a couple of more buttons to give her more room to work. "Oh, God bless you," he sighed as the muscle released under the pressure of her hand. "I could barely move my neck earlier today. Probably another reason I was in such a bad mood."

Something stirred in her. "My ma-ma gets these stiff necks also. But I can always fix her," she said proudly. "Ma-ma always says I give the best champi-malish."

She could feel Viraf grin. "Bet you're not as good as those massagewallas at Chowpatty Beach," he teased.

"That's not fair." She laughed. "Those bhaiyas use almond oil with masalas and what all in it."

"So go get some Johnson's baby oil," he replied, the smile still in his voice. "Then we'll see how good you are." She paused, unsure of whether he was joking or not. Sensing her hesitation, Viraf rose on one arm and gave her a little push with the other. "Go on," he said. "I could really use a back massage."

By the time she returned, he had removed his shirt. She was amazed to see how smooth and hairless his back was. And pale. So pale. The color and texture of the wheat atta that Ma-ma kneaded to make chappatis. Compared with the louts who strolled around the slum in their plaid lungis, with backs that looked as hairy as the bears in the circus, Viraf's back looked as unthreatening as a loaf of bread.

She poured the oil, trying to focus on a spot on the wall instead of on Viraf's smooth back. She had never touched a man's back before and felt shy and tongue-tied. But her eyes kept wandering to the imprint of her dark hands on his buttery skin. "Um, um, um," Viraf moaned. "Boy, you weren't kidding. One massage from you and those massagewallas at Chowpatty would go into the narial pani trade."

It felt good to be giving him so much pleasure. As her hands kneaded and caressed Viraf's back, as she rubbed out the tension from his stringy muscles, Maya felt important and strong—and powerful. The earlier Viraf of the bad temper, the teasing, blaspheming Viraf was gone. Vanquished by her fast-moving, capable, wise hands. She could move him, mold him, and renew him with these hands. Perhaps being this relaxed would allow him to be nicer to Dinaz baby when he returned home. Maya had suspected that things were not peaceful between the couple, had occasionally overheard the angry murmurings that floated from their bedroom when she went over there to pick up her grandmother, but until this minute she had not suspected that there was anything she could do about it. Now, watching Viraf's grateful muscles uncoil like snakes in the snake charmer's basket, she knew better. Maya felt something like awe as she looked down at her dark hands moving like shadows across the placid waters of his back.

"Lower," he whispered. "My lower back hurts like hell." She worked on his lower back, making sure to keep her hands above the crack of his buttocks but allowing her eyes to stray there. She felt hypnotized by the rhythmic, circular movements of her own hands, and Viraf was so quiet for a few moments that she wondered if he'd fallen asleep.

But then he spun around so that for one confusing moment her hands strummed air, and then they were massaging the dark curls on his chest, feeling the poignant delicacy of his collarbone, feeling the sad hollow of his rib cage, feeling the tension in his chest muscles, and somehow recognizing, with an ancient, primal wisdom, that she was the cause of that tension, that she was the reason for his shallow breathing. And her awe turning to pride and the pride turning to panic as Viraf half-rose from the bed and gently but firmly pushed her back on it, pinning her shoulders down, so that for one absurd moment her upper half was on the firm mattress while her legs still dangled above the floor. Her stomach dropped and then, as Viraf lowered his lips to her bosom, came a flood of other feelings, a flood that rushed into her thighs, breaking down the dam of resistance, making her legs feel heavy and weak at the same time.

She protested; she did not protest. It did not matter, because it was inevitable what was about to happen, what was happening, and they both knew it; they were like swimmers caught in the same current; they eyed each other gravely, wordlessly. The room, the world fell silent around them; they were the only two people in it, the last two people left standing, and there was nobody else, no thought of anyone else, there was no bedridden woman in the next room, there was no nurse who would soon be arriving to relieve Maya, there was no Bhima to disapprove of what was happening in this room, above all, there was no Dinaz with a baby growing in her belly.

"Oh God, oh God, oh God," Viraf was saying as he moved above her. She bit down on her lip to stop from giving in to the sharp pain that pierced her body when he entered her; she tried to grip his back as she arched her body toward his, but her hands slipped because of the oil. And then it was all friction and all movement, it was all slick and moist—the oil from Viraf's back, the blood from biting down too hard on her lip, and a different, more ceremonial blood leaking from elsewhere, the tears welling in eyes squeezed tight from pleasure and pain, the sweat fusing their bodies together like glue, and finally, the burst of Viraf's swollen, heated body into hers.

She came to her senses before he did. While she lay frozen, rigid with terror and shame, he was still glowing, still limp with warmth and release. "Been so long . . . ," she half-heard him say. "Dinaz's pregnancy . . . so frigid . . . won't let me near her . . ." But she could barely hear what he was saying above the clanging bells of her own fear.

The telephone rang. For a second they looked at each other, eyes wide with uncertainty. Then, "Go answer the phone," he ordered. She leapt out of bed and into her salwar-khamez, mortified that he was staring at her naked body. But there was no lust in his eyes, just a blank expression she could not read. The telephone ring had ended his reverie, brought him back to reality.

It was Dinaz, asking for Viraf. "Hi, my Maya," Dinaz said. "What took you so long to answer?" and Maya could've wept at the affection and innocence in Dinaz's voice. "Is Viraf there?"

He was standing behind her, ready to take the phone. "Just fell asleep for a few minutes, my dear," she heard him tell Dinaz. "You know how boring your grandmother's bookkeeping is. No, I'm okay. No apology needed. No hard feelings, honest. We can see the stupid movie any time. I'll be home as soon as I finish these accounts. Bye, darling."

Maya was in the kitchen when he got off the phone, and she had to force herself to look up at him. She felt tongue-tied, abashed, mortified. She wanted to say something, to explain that she wasn't a bad girl, that she didn't do the things she had done with him with any man, that, in fact, she had never done such things before. But the Viraf who towered over her looked as remote as a mountain.

"Is there a clean towel?" he said. "I would like to take a shower before I leave." If he noticed the hurt, cowering look on Maya's face, he did not acknowledge it. "Also, you should wash the sheets before the night nurse arrives," he continued. "There's—blood on the sheets. It may look suspicious."

She sat on her haunches in the corner, weeping softly to herself while he showered. She felt polluted, her body carrying a scent she did not recognize. She prayed that he would stay in the shower forever, that she would never have to face him again. But after a while she heard the water turned off, and then he was before her, smelling faintly of Yardley lavender soap.

"Listen, Maya," he said softly. "I was thinking in the shower. Thinking about what . . . just happened, about what you did. Yes, that was a bad thing you did, tempting me like that, taking advantage of me while I was in a weak mood."

She started to protest, but he silenced her. "Shhh. Let me finish. What I want to say is, I'll forgive you for what happened. Provided it never happens again. And provided you never tell anybody what you did. Because poor Dinaz, if she ever found out, God, it would kill her. She'd never forgive you. You understand? She would see it as the biggest betrayal of her trust in you. And with the pregnancy and all, I can't risk anything happening to her. Remember, the Dubash family has been nothing but good to you and your grandma. They've treated you like their very own, sent you to a good college. You have a bright future ahead of you. Now don't let this one incident ruin your life. You understand what I'm saying?"

Anger provided the steel in her voice. "But I didn't do anything," she said loudly. "That is . . . you were the one who jumped on me like a rabid dog."

She expected him to lash out at her, but Viraf only studied her sadly, shaking his head slightly. "Maya, Maya." He sighed. "Now don't be like this. If you tell anybody what happened, who do you think they're going to believe? You or me? First of all, I'll deny everything. Be sensible and don't do anything to jeopardize either your education or Bhima's job. Please. Promise me you'll put this behind you?"

She nodded. Her body hurt, and all she wanted was for him to go away. Before, she had felt remorse, had felt that she had acted wantonly, but she had felt like herself, like Maya. But now, his words made her feel like a prostitute. She waited silently, like a cornered animal, while he collected his papers and locked them in the Godrej cupboard in Banu's room. He stood at Banu's bedside for a moment as if debating whether to wake her up to say good-bye, but just then the old woman let out a particularly guttural snore, and he recoiled and tiptoed out of the room.

At the front door, he stopped to look at her, and she noticed that his eyes were moist and heavy with emotion. Despite herself, her heart leapt in hope and in anticipation of a kind word, of a small gesture on his part that would remove this dirty feeling coiling her limbs. Viraf stood before her, biting down on his lower lip, his eyes darting across her face. "Are you okay?" he asked, and when she didn't reply, a look of annoyance crossed his face. "Come on, Maya, control yourself," he said. "What happened was—Well, it happened. It's nobody's fault, right? Right. Anyway, the night nurse will be here soon. So if you need to, you know, clean up or something, you better do it before Banu wakes up and all. And re-member, not a word to anybody. Best if you just put it out of your mind."

He was out the door when he turned back. "Oh, one more thing," Viraf said. "Don't forget to wash the sheets, okay?"

23

Bhima had never known that hate could have such a jagged edge. That it could feel so uncomfortable, a constant, pressing thing, like a pebble in a shoe or a piece of clothing two sizes too small. Nor had she known of hate's reductive power—how it took every ancient insult, every old betrayal and gathered them all together to settle in one's stomach in a single, burning spot. How it soured everything, as if it were a lime squeezed over the whole world.

The young doctor at the AIDS hospital who had muttered a contemptuous "You people." The accountant who had practically patted himself on his back for taking advantage of an illiterate woman. The old doctor who had ignored the sick Gopal at the hospital until he had gotten a whiff of money and power. Gopal, who had left and taken with him Amit, as if the boy was a bundle of old clothes to be moved from one place to another. Gopal, who had written her a letter that was a kiss and a murder at the same time.

And then, there was Viraf. But here the roaring in Bhima's ears becomes deafening, like the roar of those planes that she once heard at Sahara Airport when she accompanied Serabai. There is a bitter taste in her mouth that even the chewing tobacco cannot wash away. The hate feels like pinpricks, like tiny needles are stuck all over her body. Her hatred for Viraf is brand new, and it is so sharp and edgy that its points have kept Bhima up all night, have left her feeling raw and bloodied and bruised this morning. The very things she once loved about Viraf—his beauty, his clean-cut, handsome face—she now despises because she sees them as a mask that hides his cynical, corrupt nature.

How does he feel, she wonders, as she gets up from her mattress, to know that one child of his has been destroyed, even as his wife is ready to give birth to another? Does he consider that a sign of ill luck, the shadow of his dead child falling across the belly of his wife's happiness? Or does he care so little about his bastard child that he sleeps undisturbed at night, seeing in his dreams only the child, the son, who will inherit his father's looks, his charm, his wealth, his power? At that last thought, Bhima's face darkens with fury. And then, from the ashes of that last thought, rises a memory: A ride to the marketplace when Viraf was telling her calmly about how important it is not waste any more time, to get Maya an abortion as quickly as possible. Child killer, Bhima now rages. What kind of father oversees the death of his own child?

Surely that is why Maya had insisted that Sera accompany her to the abortionist. Serabai, unknowingly supervising the killing of the child who was the dark shadow, the other brother (or sister) who could someday have been a challenger to the Dubash family's happiness, to its position in society, its claims to respectability. And Maya had arranged it so that Sera was there at that moment of destruction, when the challenger was silenced forever. Bhima looks over to where Maya is sleeping, and despite her revulsion, she feels a moment's admiration for the girl. Maya had made sure that the Dubash family was implicated in her child's death, that some of the dark blood stained their hands forever. Surely Serabai had gone home that day and described the horrors of the clinic; surely Viraf had listened in cold fascination to the story of the killing of his child. Perhaps he woke up in the middle of the night with guilt covering him like a shroud; perhaps in the black of the night he recognized the damned blackness of his own heart.

But maybe not. Suddenly, Bhima feels old and tired. That familiar slowness falls on her. There is so much she doesn't know and doesn't understand. Viraf baba is a man, handsome, educated, rich, and well-traveled. He is everything that she, Bhima, is not. How could she pretend to know what he thinks? Hasn't she noticed that when Viraf addresses her he talks slowly, as if he expects her not to understand the things he says? And if she couldn't read her own husband, if she could not guess at the treachery in his heart, why should she pretend to know what weeds grow at the bottom of Viraf's black heart?

She will tell him that she knows. The thought comes to her as clearly and abruptly as a matchstick lit in the dark. She will let him know that poor though she may be and female though she may be, she is not someone who has to be spoken to slowly; that she is no longer someone who can be fooled by accountants and husbands and patronized by doctors and men who rape her granddaughter. Rather, she is someone who knows him better than his own mother does because, illiterate though she may be, can she not read the corruption of his heart? She will tell him that she knows and that he must fear her now, for she has the power to destroy his current happiness as swiftly as a wind can knock down a house. She will tell him that she knows and that he must keep his hands to himself now, that she will not allow his dirty, nasty hands to pollute the life of any other young girl. She will remind him that his thoughtless pleasure has derailed her Maya's life, has blocked the path that would've taken the girl out of the slum. What she and Serabai had built together, Viraf has destroyed. Women create, Bhima thinks, men destroy. The way of the world.

Today is Saturday, her day to ride to the marketplace with Viraf. In the car, she will tell him that she knows. That Maya no longer carries his secret for him, just as she no longer carries the symbol of his shame. He will shake and beg her forgiveness, but she will not budge. Some sins are too dark for forgiveness. Even she knows that.

Her new resolution gives Bhima energy. She lifts herself off the mattress, hearing the familiar popping of her hip joint, but today she doesn't wait to see if the wave of pain will follow. She has no time to pay attention to the creaks and groans of her own body; she is ready to inflict pain on Viraf.

"Come on, beti, wake up," she says to Maya, nudging the sleeping girl with her toes. "You go fill the pots with water while I prepare the tea. Go on now, I need to be at work early today."

Is it her imagination, or does Viraf throw her an appraising look when she walks into the house? She has no time to wonder because Sera is reaching out for her hand. "Oh, thank God, Bhima, you are here," she says. "Have you forgotten about the dinner party tonight? Come on, I need to go over the list of things I need from the market."

"Er, actually, I was going to go to the maidan a little early today," Viraf says, standing in the doorway of the kitchen. "So maybe Bhima should just take a cab to the market when she's ready."

Before Sera can respond, Bhima speaks. "Hard to find a cab on a Saturday morning. I can leave now, if you so wish."

"Yah, after all, you're both going the same way," Sera says. "No point in unnecessarily spending money on a cab, no?" She smiles. "I keep telling you children, money does not grow on trees."

Viraf's face is impassive. "Okay. Whatever." He addresses Sera, although Bhima is standing right there. "Just make sure she's ready in a few minutes."

Sera turns to Bhima while the latter is gathering the cloth bags that she carries to the market. "Ae, Bhima, is Maya feeling well?

She didn't look very good yesterday. The food at Chowpatty make her sick?"

Bhima keeps her back to Serabai. "It's not that, bai. After what she's been through recently, she is still very . . ."

"I understand." Sera sighs. "Poor girl. The whole thing is just so unfortunate. Well, as long as she learns from her mistake, some good may come from it. At that age, girls are so . . . I remember, Feroz and I used to watch Dinaz so closely when she was a teenager. After all, a girl's biggest asset is her virtue. And you know how things are like in our India, Bhima. Every man wants to marry a virgin. I don't care if it's Hindus, Christians, or Parsis, men are the same, no?"

Bhima bites down on her lower lip until she can smell blood.

Sera notices her servant's stiff back. "That is, I don't mean to suggest . . . Maya is such a good girl, I'm sure we won't have any problems finding a suitable match for her. And really, no one in your community has to know about this one incident. There is a saying in English: 'What one doesn't know, doesn't hurt one.' But no marriage for Maya for many years, I hope. Bas, the best thing is for her to finish her education first. Then we can think of getting a husband for her."

Still Bhima cannot trust herself to speak. If she opens her mouth, her words will slither out, she knows. Poisonous words, which could leave Serabai with a wound she may never recover from.

Sera comes up behind her. "Chal ne, Bhima," she says in mock impatience. "How long does it take to decide which bags to take with you? At this rate, I'll be an old woman before you get back from the market."

Viraf pokes his head in. "Ready?" he says.

Bhima nods her head, making sure that her eyes focus on a spot above Viraf's right ear. She does not trust herself to look directly at the handsome face without wanting to claw it.

They wait for the elevator and descend without saying a word to each other. Instead, Viraf chitchats with the liftboy, who shyly reaches out to stroke Viraf's expensive, gleaming cricket bat. "What you think about this new West Indies team, seth?" the liftboy asks, his eyes still on the bat. He is a tall, gangly youth with protruding teeth that make him look as if he's always smiling at some secret joke.

Viraf shrugs. "Those West Indians are always great."

The boy's mouth widens as he smiles and shakes his head. "Ah, but our India's team is no less this time," he says quickly, as if he had expected Viraf's response. "I say we'll teach those black monkeys a lesson during the Bombay match." He leans forward confidentially. "They are saying to show up at the stadium with lots of banana peels. Those African monkeys like bananas. We're going to throw them on the grounds, when it's their turn to bat."

Viraf's lips tighten with displeasure. "That's not very sporting, no?" he says. "Things like that give the country a bad name."

The elevator reaches the ground floor, and the boy jumps up from his stool to open the doors. "True, true, sir," he says. "Bad idea." His eyes blink rapidly in anticipation of a tip, but Viraf ignores him and proceeds toward his car with Bhima following a few paces behind. Stupid boy, Bhima thinks to herself. Looks like a shaved rat himself, with his teeth like scissors, and calling other people monkeys.

Viraf turns on the air-conditioning immediately upon getting into the car, but today, despite the warmth outside, Bhima is cold. She leans away from Viraf, trying to keep her teeth from chattering visibly. Her hands are clammy and cold, and there is an icy feeling in her stomach that she recognizes as nervousness. She tries to remember the bold, nothing-to-lose feeling she had this morning, tries to conjure up the hate and aggression she had felt toward Viraf just a few hours ago, but she can't. It is all she can do to suppress the humiliating shaking of her body so that Viraf doesn't see it; it takes all her willpower to control her bowels, which suddenly feel as though they might betray her.

In contrast to his usual solicitousness, Viraf is ignoring her, fiddling with the radio stations. Finding one that he likes, he begins to whistle tunelessly along with a song. Bhima casts a sidelong glance at him—unlike her, Viraf looks completely relaxed and comfortable in his own skin. Even as she knows that this posture of relaxation is a pose, a coat that he has thrown on for her benefit, she admires him for being able to fake it. She decides to try to imitate him and forces her voice not to quiver as she says, "Viraf seth, something I have to tell you."

Viraf looks straight ahead, his eyes on the road. After what seems to Bhima a long interval, he says disinterestedly, "What?"

She opens her mouth to tell him that she knows; that she will never find it in her heart to forgive him for what he has done, that he has stolen away Maya's youth and innocence, that she is unsure of whether to repeat to Sera and Dinaz the tale of his dastardly deed.

She opens her mouth, and nothing happens. Her mouth is dry with fear. Her body is openly shaking now, as if she is a single sheet of discarded paper on a windy street. And despite the cold that is seeping into her bones, she feels sweat running down her face. She opens her mouth to threaten him, to curse him, to make him understand her monumental outrage, and what comes out instead is, "Viraf baba, whywhywhywhywhy oh, whywhywhywhywhywhywhywhywhywhywhywhywhywhy?" So it is not her words but the sound of them that makes Viraf step on his brakes; it is the wailing, wounded cry of her pain that sounds curious and animal-like even to her own ears, so that for a split second she looks as shocked as he does.

Viraf blanches; he brakes slightly; his hands turn white as they tighten on the wheel; a muscle in his jaw moves compulsively up and down for a few seconds. Other than this, there is nothing. He continues to drive, keeping his eyes on the road. He does not even condescend to glance in her direction. After a few seconds, his fingers drum silently on the wheel, and from this she realizes that he is waiting for her to continue, that he wants to know what will follow the outburst.

But she is done. She is spent, exhausted, broken. The animal wail sounded piteous and weak to her own ears, and she feels like a small bird who has run into a mountain. Viraf sits in the car, as impassive and impenetrable as that mountain. She cannot touch him, she realizes. Even her hatred from this morning feels puny and laughable now, the equivalent of a child stomping her feet at a parent or a suicidal person cutting herself. Doing what women have done for centuries—turning their rage on themselves.

Because the only weapon she has over him she will not use. She knows this now. The only way in which she can hurt Viraf is to share his disgrace with Serabai and Dinaz, to watch the stain of his shame spread over their faces. And this she cannot do. To do this would mean to destroy the only two people who have ever treated her like a human being, who have been steadfast and true to her, who have never despised her for being ignorant or illiterate or weak. She remembers Dinaz at age five, six, twelve, fourteen, and every memory is sprinkled with rosewater, every memory is sweet as sugar and pure as crystal: Dinaz refusing to eat a chocolate unless she can share it with Bhima; Dinaz begging Bhima to sit on the furniture with her when the two of them were alone at home; Dinaz slipping money from her allowance into Bhima's embarrassed hands. Before there was Maya, there was Dinaz, and Dinaz had loved her with an abandon that perhaps only a child could muster. She remembers Feroz seth laughingly saying to her once, "Arre, Bhima, are you a damn jadoogar or something? How is it you've completely bewitched my little girl so? Saala, at this rate you will have to supervise her school lessons and go meet with her teachers during her parent-teacher meetings."

And Serabai, tall, fair, a sentry who stood at the gates of hell and tried to keep Bhima from being snatched away by the infernal fires. Sera, who had saved Gopal's life, who had tried to give Maya a different life by sending her to college, and who had presided over the taking of an unformed life because she believed it was in Maya's best interest.

And now their destiny is in Bhima's hands. These scarred, callused hands that have combed Pooja's hair, that have washed hundreds of dishes, chopped a thousand onions, these hands now hold the reins to Sera's and Dinaz's happiness. One jerk and happiness could gallop away from them forever.

And now at last Viraf looks at her, carefully, cautiously. "Bhima," he says. "We must all find the strength to go on."

She is unsure of what he means but knows that she will not ask. This is how it will stay between them, she thinks, unresolved, unsatisfactory, a long, thin, barren silence that will replace the joking, teasing manner of the old, untainted Viraf. She has a sudden flash of prescience in which she sees Viraf as a jowly, white-haired man, fat and old before his time, a long-ago guilt making his eyelids droop and the flesh under his chin grow. He will not age well, this one, she thinks. He will look more like his father-in-law than he now imagines.

As if he can read her thoughts, Viraf's hands tighten on the wheel and he steps on the accelerator. A young woman with two small children steps out onto the street and avoids his car by inches in the casual, thoughtless way all Bombayites do. But today, Viraf is in no mood for such irresponsible behavior. "Dumb fool," he yells, rolling down the window. "How you going to raise those children if you can't even look after yourself?" He mutters to himself as he rolls up the glass. "This city is getting impossible to live in, just impossible. Motherfucking imbeciles everywhere. Driving here is a damned nuisance, not a pleasure."

Instinctively, Bhima pulls away from his anger. She has seen Viraf angry before, has overheard his quarrels with Dinaz, but those were coated with his amused love for his wife. Now there's a vindictiveness to his anger that makes it dangerous. She has unmasked Viraf, forced him to face his own shadow, peeled back the handsome, gentle face to reveal the bloody, wormy mess of contradictions and corruptions that lie beneath. Bhima tries to imagine the clammy fear Viraf must feel at what she might do next, at whether she will expose him and make him stand naked before his wife and mother-in-law. He must feel like a man sitting on top of a pile of gunpowder, she thinks. And the horrifying truth is that the woman who could light that pile, who could set off the explosion that would blast his life and family into bits, that woman is a mere servant, an old, illiterate woman, thin as a stick, ugly as a gnawed-over chicken bone. Suddenly, Bhima feels an irrational but irrepressible urge to giggle, but before she can do so, Viraf is asking in a choked voice, in a voice that sounds as if it has swallowed a liter of the diesel fumes around them: "How is Maya?"

How to answer such a question? To answer correctly, she would have to go back at least to her great-grandmother's time, would have to explain how every female member in her family has worked as a domestic servant in someone else's home, would have to tell him of how hurt she was when her own mother left her home sick to go take care of other people's homes and children. How to make him understand that when Maya left for college in the mornings, she used to feel as if everything that she had ever gone through in her life—every deprivation, every insult, every betrayal—was worth it if she could provide her grandchild with a life better than what she and her mother and her mother's mother had known. Above all, how to tell him that the simple act of abortion did not erase the past, did not set back the clock, did not allow Maya to casually pick up the strands of her life and return to college. Yes, that was her own fault, she had blocked that road for Maya in her rush to confront and persuade Ashok Malhotra to marry her granddaughter, but what could she have done? She had been bewitched by the vision of a kitchen with gleaming pots and pans and a neat, tidy little boy running around the house.

So she says nothing and stares at the car mat beneath her feet, and after a second Viraf clucks his tongue in frustration. They are almost at the marketplace now, and he slows down to look for somewhere to drop her off. "Almost there," he says, and she hears the relief in his voice.

She is fumbling with the lock on the door when she hears Viraf say, "Look, that is, I mean . . . Do you all need anything?"

She feels her face hardening to stone. "We are all right," she says stiffly. "We are poor, but every grain of rice that we eat we have earned."

Viraf exhales loudly. "All right. Okay. God, why is everybody in this city so damn dramatic and noble? All I was saying was . . ."

She is out of the car now and into the blessed commotion and heat of the street. This is where I belong, she thinks. Among the vendors and the cart pushers and the fishmongers and the ragpickers. Not in air-conditioned cars. "Thank you for the lift, Viraf seth," she says.

She sees the hurt on his face. He has noticed that she addressed him as "sir" instead of her usual, affectionate "baba," which in the way she uses it with him, means boy. She feels a pinprick of satisfaction at his disappointment.

"No mention," he says curtly. "And listen. Tell Dinaz and Sera mummy to have lunch without me. I'll be home a little late today."

24

It has been a long day, and the house is quiet because Viraf and Dinaz are out. Bhima is almost ready to leave, but Serabai asks for a cup of tea and she feels compelled to make it for her. Serabai is different when the children are gone in the evening, Bhima realizes, more pensive and solitary. She needs her daughter and son-in-law here to make the house lively, Bhima thinks and feels a twinge of pity for the younger woman. She remembers the year after Feroz seth passed away, how Serabai sometimes forgot to eat lunch until she, Bhima, nagged her to eat, and how, once or twice, she also forgot to bathe during the day. Once she had walked into the living room to find Serabai sitting in the dark and muttering to herself while she rubbed her arm furiously. Bhima wasn't sure who had been more startled, though Serabai had, of course, turned the tables on her and grumbled about the lack of privacy and how people should not sneak up on other people. But the sight of the usually elegant, dignified Sera sitting in the dark like some caged animal, looking like one of those mad old Parsi women—like Banubai, for instance—had shocked and dismayed Bhima. The next time Dinaz baby and Viraf baba came over for their Saturday lunch, she had made it a point to say something to Dinaz. "Mummy is lonely," Bhima had whispered as Dinaz brought the dirty dishes into the kitchen. "Forgets to eat-drink at times and sits alone in the house without the lights turned on." After years of protecting Serabai, of keeping her secrets and respecting her silences, it felt strange to tell on her. But the concerned look on Dinaz's face was the affirmation she needed. "I've been wondering about that," Dinaz said softly. "Thanks for telling me, Bhima."

No, it's a good thing Dinaz baby offered to move in with her mother, Bhima thinks. Having the two young people here has been good for Serabai. Bhima has known of too many Parsi women who aged before their time, who took to their beds for seemingly no reason and used a potty chair instead of walking to the bathroom, and who refused to leave the house except for the occasional funeral. Mrs. Motorcyclewalla, who lived on the fifth floor three buildings down, was one such person. But then that woman had three screws missing even years ago. After Gopal's accident, Bhima had taken on a second job, washing dishes for Mrs. Motorcyclewalla. Each afternoon the woman would stand and watch intently while Bhima worked over the kitchen sink, not saying a word but sometimes imitating the sound of the pigeons that sat on the ledge outside her window. The sound made the hair on Bhima's hands stand up. Why doesn't she wash the dishes herself if she has the time to stand here and watch me with a face like an owl's? Bhima grumbled to herself. Still, she needed the money, and Mrs. Motorcyclewalla always paid on time. But after a few months Bhima noticed that the woman was cooing at the pigeons even when none of them were sitting on the ledge. And one day, when Bhima got ready to leave, the woman turned to her with fierce eyes and said, "Did you pege paro the bati before leaving the kitchen?"

Bhima stared at her mutely. "I'm not understanding, bai," she said finally.

Mrs. Motorcyclewalla's voice grew shrill. "I'm asking you whether you paid your respects to the oil lamp that's burning in the kitchen, under the portrait of Lord Zoroaster. No one should leave the kitchen without touching the light."

"But I'm not a Parsi, bai," Bhima said carefully. "I'm of Hindu jaat and not even a Brahmin." In most of the Parsi homes she had been in, the rules were the opposite. Banubai, for instance, went out of her way to make sure that Bhima's shadow did not fall over the bati that burned day and night in the kitchen.

For whatever reason, this was the wrong thing to say. The woman flew into a tirade. "Nobody is allowed to leave this house without paying their respects," she said, clamping her hand down on Bhima's wrist. "Otherwise a hundred years of darkness will fall on this house." She fairly dragged Bhima back into the kitchen, where Bhima followed by rote whatever motions the woman wanted her to, touching the tip of her fingers to the oil lamp and then touching her forehead in a sign of respect. "Okay, bai, I must go," she said. "Serabai must be waiting for me."

Bhima saw a new flame of madness leap into the woman's eyes at the sound of Sera's name. "You tell that Sera to come over here with you tomorrow with some sandalwood sticks. We must purify this house. The pigeons have been telling me for weeks that something was wrong, and now I realize you were the culprit. From now on, you must kiss our Lord Zoroaster's picture before leaving, understand?"

"Achcha, bai," Bhima said, backing out of the front door. "I'll tell Serabai."

It was the memory of Mrs. Motorcyclewalla, who several years ago had taken to her bed and refused to get out of it although her doctors found nothing the matter with her, that had made Bhima tell Dinaz about her mother.

And now, for the first time, Bhima wishes she had not intervened. If the children were still living in the suburbs, Viraf would probably not have been at Banubai's house the day Maya was there. Yes, Sera would have spent many more evenings like this one, walking around the house as if she were seeing ghosts, but at least Maya would've been saved, at least her grandchild would . . .

Sera walks into the kitchen. "Don't forget to add the mint leaves," she says. "And make a cup for yourself, too."

Bhima goes to the corner where she keeps her things and takes out her glass while Sera pulls a mug from the cabinet for herself. The steam from the tea creates a wavy barrier between the two women as Bhima pours. Each picks up her own cup, and they walk into the dining room to assume their usual positions—Sera perched on a dining room chair, Bhima sitting on her haunches on the floor. They sip on their tea in silence. Then Sera sighs. "Good tea," she says. "I swear you make the best tea in Bombay."

"House seems quiet this evening without the children here," Bhima says. She still can't get herself to say Viraf's name out loud.

"I know," Sera says. "But it's good that Dinaz went out with her friends. Poor thing, she's having such a miserable time with her pregnancy these last few days that she almost canceled this morning. Says she hardly slept last night. But Viraf persuaded her to go. God knows, once the baby is born she'll have no time for friends-schends. And the girls from her office were so anxious to take her out."

"He didn't go with her?" Bhima asks casually, hoping Sera won't notice her reluctance to say Viraf's name.

"No, it's a girls only party. Just as well—that boy is working much too hard and needs some rest." She made a face. "Not that being over at Banu mamma's house is rest. But he should be home soon. He just went over to settle the month's accounts with the nurses and to put Banu's papers back. Stayed up till eleven last night, doing her accounts. How many sons-in-law would do that? And even if she were aware of it, that—my mother-in-law—would not be grateful."

Bhima feels a moment's panic at the thought of Viraf being over there alone with Nurse Edna. What if he tried any of his vileness with that poor woman? She shakes her head to get rid of the unwelcome pictures forming there. Edna is a grown woman, married with children. She would know how to handle Viraf if he tried any of his badmaashi on her. And besides, men like him probably preyed on young, fresh meat like Maya. What interest would he have in a tired-looking woman with a husband and children? No, Viraf and his like needed to stain something pure, like a drop of ink in a glass of milk.

"Bhima, stop scowling." Sera laughs. "My God, you look like you've seen a bhoot or something. What dark thoughts are you thinking?"

If only I could tell you, Serabai, Bhima thinks. But it would be more merciful to stab you with a knife than to kill you with the poison of my thoughts. Aloud, she says, "My whole life is a dark thought."

Sera sighs. "I know what you mean," she says. She visibly struggles with her emotions and then forces herself to sit up straight in the chair. "But Bhima, we can't give up. We women, we live for so much more than just ourselves. You for Maya, I for Dinaz and, now, the new baby. You know, I've often thought that men can afford to take more risks, fly higher and crash harder, because they always have suicide as a way out. If things just don't work out for them— bas, at least they have that final option. When I was younger, I was so jealous of men for that. You know, I had two cousins who offed themselves. Both male, of course. But women don't live for themselves. And once you have children—forget it. I don't know why we still even have bodies to walk around in once we've had children. Then you're living totally for another person. Arre, forget children even. I even worry about Banu mamma, can you imagine? Now, with Feroz gone, I often wonder what will happen to her if she outlives me."

"Why would she outlive you?" Bhima says fiercely. "It is not your time, Serabai, and I pray it won't be for a long time."

Sera smiles. "I pray it won't be, too," she says shyly. "With the baby about to be born . . . Can you imagine, Bhima? For the first time in my life, I really want to live. Before, I could honestly say I didn't care one way or the other. Even when I was a young woman, I don't know what was wrong with me but I just didn't care that much about life. All the things you had to do just to keep living seemed too complicated to me, hardly worth the effort. But now, I'm so anxious to see how my Dinu's child will grow up. And I want to be there for—"

The doorbell rings and Bhima makes to get up from the floor, but Serabai stops her. "I'll go," she says. "Must be Viraf. I'm almost done with my tea." She takes a long final sip before leaving the mug on the table for Bhima to clean up later.

Bhima sits sipping her tea, wondering what to do with Maya this evening. Ever since running into Viraf at Chowpatty, Maya has refused to go to the seaside. The evenings at home now seem long and oppressive. Bhima misses the soft evening air, the smell of the water and the closeness between Maya and her as they walked the length of the beach. She misses the pageantry at the seaside—the brightly dressed men and women in big cars, the beggars with no legs wheeling themselves on skateboards, the burly Sikhs with their red turbans, Muslim women in burquas, old Parsi couples sitting arm in arm on the stone benches, call girls in high heels looking to be picked up by guests at the nearby hotels, large groups of loud teenagers from nearby colleges. Bhima had loved leaving behind the grim isolation of her hut in the basti and melting into this amorphous, fluid crowd. Sometimes, she felt as if she didn't have to lift a muscle, didn't have to put one leg in front of the other; that, if she just stood still, the movement of the crowd would propel her forward, like the wind, like the waves . . .

She realizes with a start that Viraf is saying her name, and her brow begins to crease with anger. Time for her to go home, and the stupid boy probably wants her to run another errand. She is about to wonder what he wants from her when her mind stops going down this track, arrested by the peculiar tone of Serabai's voice. "Impossible," Sera is saying. "You must be mistaken, deekra." Her voice sounds emphatic, worried, hurt, and defensive, all at once.

There is a silence, and then Viraf's voice, low and deep, fills the silence, like the scuttling sound of mice as they race across her hut at night. "I tell you, I saw it with my own eyes," he says, his voice higher and stronger than it has been.

"Bhima." Sera's voice, still carrying that peculiar quality, calls for her, and she rises from the floor with a groan and waits a moment for her creaky bones to settle themselves.

Viraf and Sera are in the living room, sitting close to each other on the sofa. Sera's face is flushed, and it has an urgent look, a great contrast to the pensive, reflective expression from a few minutes ago. Whatever this boy has said or done has upset her greatly. For a quick second, Bhima wonders if Viraf has told her about Maya, but she quickly brushes that thought from her head.

"Ah, Bhima, good. You're here," Sera stammers. "Seems as if Viraf baba has a problem. There's er, um, there's apparently some money missing from Banubai's cupboard."

Bhima stares at Sera blankly, unsure of why this involves her. "Is it a large sum?" she asks finally. And when no one replies immediately, "Has it been missing for a long time?"

"Well, see, that's the thing. According to our Viraf here, that is—"

"The money was there day before yesterday," Viraf interrupts. His face is damp with sweat, and a muscle moves in his jaw. "I put it there myself. Then yesterday I told you to go get the checkbooks for me. I told you to get me the one envelope but leave the other, remember?"

"It was there at that time," Bhima says triumphantly, glad to be able to help. "I saw it with my own eyes."

"Did you open it?"

"That I did not do. There was no need to. I could tell which one had the slip books, just by feeling them." Bhima wonders if she did something wrong by not checking each envelope.

There is an awkward silence, and Sera glances at Viraf helplessly, hopefully. "Well, so, it's a mystery," she says lightly. "And thank God it wasn't a large rakam. Just seven hundred rupees."

"That's not the point." Viraf's words are sharp as darts. He focuses his dark eyes on Bhima. "You said you brought the cupboard keys back to me right away, correct? You didn't give them to Edna or anyone else?"

Does this boy think I am a total loss? Bhima wonders. She has been going over to Banubai's house for years before this Viraf began to take care of her money with his slip book this and deposit book that. She has carried large sums of money from one house to another, has deposited bearer checks from Feroz into his bank account, has handled bunches of keys for both houses. "Nobody had the keys except me, seth," she says sullenly.

"Well then, there's only one logical explanation. Between the time I placed the money there day before yesterday and when I went over there today, you were the only one who handled the cupboard. So you took the money."

Sera lets out a cry of—outrage? Anger? Refutation? Hearing the cry, Bhima mutely looks at her. She wants Sera to slap the man sitting next to her, to put her hand over Viraf's mouth and force his blasphemous words back down his throat. Sera catches Bhima's look, and it seems to shake her out of her stupor. "Viraf, that's rubbish," she says weakly.

"Rubbish? Why is it rubbish? With all respect, Sera mummy, are you even going to let Bhima deny it or are you going to deny it for her? I mean, she's standing here looking guilty as a thief while you're rushing to her defense."

The world goes black for a minute and then turns startlingly, blindingly white. Bhima laughs into that white void. Out of the white—which now has a red border, red as blood, red as fury—she sees Sera's upturned, questioning face; sees Viraf's devious, conniving countenance. The boy has set a trap for her, she realizes. He must have planned it for weeks. Even as he refused to look her in the eye each time she glared at him, even as he acted humble each time she was rude to him, even as he ate those fried eggs that she once spat in before she served them to him, he was laying his trap. All this time, his mind was working, planning his revenge, arranging the pieces, laying the bricks in the wall that would fence her in.

Bhima laughs again. She laughs at her foolish innocence, which has turned out to be as dangerous as Maya's. She laughs at her arrogance, which had led her to believe that she could mistreat an educated, powerful man like Viraf and not pay the price. Above all, she laughs at her foolish notion that Viraf regretted what he had done to Maya, that he was truly ashamed of his moment of weakness. Despite the fact that this boy acted like a wild beast, she had not seen him as such. She had preferred to believe that he would never strike her family again, that the knowledge that she knew about his guilt was enough to defang him.

And now he has brought her down to this moment. Even Feroz seth, with his explosive temper and arrogant ways, would never have doubted her honesty, the doglike faithfulness with which she had served this family. She remembers Maya's bitter words about how she has treated the Dubash family better than her own. The girl was right—she has slaved and worked for, protected and defended this family as if it were her own. And now this snake, this devil with a handsome face, is accusing her of stealing from Serabai.

"See what a naffat she is?" Viraf is saying. "Can you imagine, laughing when someone accuses you of committing a serious crime? One more minute and I'll call the police, I swear."

The word *police* brings Bhima to her senses. She feels the blood pounding in her head, and her words pour out of her as thick and salty as blood. "Go call the police," she says. "You tell them your story, and then I'll tell them the story about your evil. How you ruined my family's reputation, how you stained my family's honor. Just open your mouth to the police, and I'll show you what I'm made of, you dirty dog—"

"Bhima," Sera hisses, her face white with fury. "Control yourself. Have you gone mad, talking in this low-class way? Don't forget who you're talking to."

Bhima swings to Sera, her face ugly with rage. She knows she must speak fast now, before the tears begin to fall and bury her words. "I know exactly who I'm talking to, bai. It's you who doesn't know who this man is. For months, I have kept my mouth shut, out of respect for you. But now I must expose him, show you the blackness of his heart—"

"Do you see what you have created, Sera mummy?" Viraf bellows. "This is your reward for treating a servant like a family member. This shameless woman will not stop at anything to hide the fact that she is a thief. God knows how long she has been stealing from you and you didn't even—"

"May God strike me down if I've stolen a paisa from this family," Bhima says, her voice trembling with unshed tears. "And may God strike you down if you're unjustly accusing a poor woman like me just so you can cover up your foulness with my dishonor."

"You ingrate," Viraf says. "You eat this family's salt for all these years and now you curse us." He turns toward Sera. "What everyone has been telling you, you should've listened to, Mummy. This is my fault, for letting this woman sit on your head. This is what happens when you try turning a stray dog into a family pet. Sooner or later, that dog is going to bite you."

Sera sits on the sofa, a stricken look on her face. Bhima feels Sera receding from her, like a moon that climbs higher and higher into the night sky. "Serabai, maaf karo. Forgive my harsh words, bai. But you don't know what evil this man is hiding. He's the mad dog, bai, not me. I beg you to—"

Viraf lifts his hand in a threatening manner above Bhima's head. "Listen, you motherfucking woman. You say one more thing against this family and I will drag you naked to the police chowki, understand? Now get your things and get out."

As Viraf chops the air with his hand, Sera flinches. "We must all control ourselves," she says loudly. "Everything is getting out of hand much too fast." She looks at Bhima with tears in her eyes. "Bhima, tell the truth. If you needed the money, I will understand. But tell me the truth."

The plea lingers in the air for a moment, like a drop of water from a leaky roof. Then Bhima, crazed with outrage and fury, decides to make the roof come crashing down. "The truth? Ask him what he did to my Maya if you want the truth," she says bitterly. "Ask him what guilt he is trying to hide. He thinks he can buy my silence with his seven hundred rupees? If he builds me a house of gold I won't forgive him for what he has done to my—"

Sera lets out a strangled cry. For a stricken moment she turns toward Viraf in a questioning gesture, her eyes wide and apprehensive as they search his stony face. But the next second denial falls on her face like a white veil. "Enough," she says, covering her ears with her hands, the way Pooja used to do whenever Bhima and Gopal had a fight. "I've heard enough of your crazy talk, Bhima. Thank

God my Dinu isn't home to hear the filth coming out of your mouth. You'd better get out of here before I say something that I will regret later. I can excuse you stealing from me, but to challenge my son-in-law's honor, that I can never forgive you for."

"Listen to me, Serabai," Bhima cries. "I'm trying to tell you—"

"What your Maya did is her business," Sera screams. "She can be a whore with fifty men for all I care. Just don't involve my family in her sickness. I've done all I could for that girl. Now I wash my hands of the whole family. Get out," she says again, her teeth biting nervously on her upper lip. "Get out of my sight."

Bhima hears the final brick click into place. She sees the film of sweat on Viraf's face and his faint, almost invisible look of satisfaction. His eyes are bright and piercing. See? They seem to taunt her. I knew I'd get you in the end.

Sobs form like bubbles inside Bhima's throat and rock her frail body. "Serabai, don't turn me away," she begs. "After all these years, where will I go?"

But Sera's face is as stony as a wall. She looks at Bhima as if they are meeting for the first time. "Get your things and go," she says softly. "Please. Don't say anything else. Just go. Whatever money I owe you, I will send to your home."

Bhima walks the long passageway leading to the kitchen on legs that seem unable to hold her up. Viraf and Sera follow her, so that Bhima feels like they are her jailers, leading a condemned prisoner to her cell. She looks desultorily at the meager possessions she keeps in a cardboard box in a corner of the kitchen—a soap dish, Pond's talcum powder, a blue comb with a tooth missing, her metal glass, her tobacco tin. As she lifts the box, the tears fall fast and hot. She looks around at the kitchen, every inch of which she has swept and cleaned so many times. So many evenings she has entered this room without bothering to turn on the lights and still she has known where to find every fork, every dish, every pan. She takes in the cobweb that is forming in the corner near the window—she had meant to clean that web off yesterday. She feels a second's pride as she notices the shine on the pressure cooker, which she washed earlier today. She sighs as she looks at the high ceiling, such a welcome change from the oppressive weight of the low roof of her hut, which she has to bend to enter.

She is walking out of the kitchen when a thought strikes her and she turns toward Sera, who has the white, dazed look of a sleep-walker. "Dinaz baby," she says, her voice cracking. "I won't get to say good-bye to Dinaz baby."

Sera's eyes flicker with warmth for a second before they turn into ice chips. "Just as well," she says, her voice hardening as she speaks. "After the ugly things you've said, I'm glad you'll never see my daughter again."

The lump in Bhima's throat tastes like blood. "Serabai, it was never my desire to hurt you or baby," she says. "That girl is like my own—"

"Achcha, bas, enough of this drama-frama," Viraf says. "Come on, chalo, get out of here."

Viraf opens the front door and holds it for Bhima to pass through. The devil at the gates of hell, Bhima thinks. But then another thought assaults her: Hell is on the other side of this door, she thinks. Hell is trying to get another job at my age, to learn the ways of another family, to sweep and clean and cook for strangers. Hell is working for less money for a strange family and watching Maya throw her future away like rotten fruit. Hell is knowing there will never be another Serabai, no one who will take an interest in Maya's education, no one who will care if she, Bhima, lives or dies.

Gratitude tears at her throat and makes her take Sera's stiff hand and hold it up to her eyes. "Serabai, if I am doomed to take a million rebirths in this world, I will never be able to repay you . . ."

Even in the dim light of the evening, she notices the teardrop that glistens on Sera's fair-skinned wrist.

Viraf slams the front door on her before she can finish the sentence. Bhima leans against the wall for a minute with her eyes closed and then walks slowly toward the elevator. But ashamed at the thought of the liftboy seeing her in her exiled state, she decides to take the stairs. She begins her slow, tortured descent into the lower levels.

25

It is dusk when Bhima emerges from the apartment building. The sky is a dusty orange, the kind of sky that falls on the faces of the people walking below it, so that each brown, sallow face glows as if it is powered by the light of a million suns. The people on the street look golden, as if kissed by a kind, benevolent god. It is a windy evening, and the wind tongues Bhima's hair, pulling strands of it out of her bun. Cradling her cardboard box in her right hand, she tries to push her hair back with her left but gives up after a few futile attempts. Instead, she uses her free hand to hold down her sari, which is billowing in the wind. Normally, she would've been irritated by this incessant breeze, but today she is thankful for it. The cool evening air dances on her face, freezing her tears on the tracks they have made on her cheeks. Somehow, the wind makes her feel free and anonymous, as if it guards her from the inquisitive eyes of the hundreds of other people walking down the same street.

Her feet scrape against the stone pavement, knowing their way as well as those of a blind dog. She doesn't have to pay attention to where she is going; her feet will lead her home. Instead she can use her mind to sort out the bodies, to identify the charred remains, to assemble the missing limbs in the aftermath of the bomb that has just gone off in her life. Because it is more than her and Maya's lives that has been affected. She is sure of this.

The look on Serabai's face when she told her the truth. Will Serabai ever be able to forget those words, to bury them under the protective layers of forgetfulness and denial? Or will those words caw in her ears like black crows, will they peck at her fair skin like vultures, will they torment her in the middle of sweaty, sleepless nights? Will she ever be able to look at Dinaz's innocent, laughing face again and not think of her son-in-law's deceit? Will Bhima's inopportune words build a glass wall between Serabai and Viraf, a wall that no one except the two of them will be able to see, a wall that neither one of them will be able to scale, that will keep them locked up in their own frozen, guarded worlds? And the baby. The new baby whom she, Bhima, will never get to see. The baby will be beautiful, she knows, with Viraf's dark, intense eyes and Dinaz's sweet mouth. But will Serabai ever be able to see the baby's fair, unblemished face without remembering the darker half brother whose death Maya had made her witness?

Do the rich think like this? Bhima wonders. Or, along with their ABCs and 1, 2, 3s, do they also learn how not to be hounded and tormented by the truth? She doesn't know. In some ways, she knows Serabai better than she knows most of her relatives, but still, how much does she understand about this proud, dignified woman who has been a presence as powerful as God in her life all these years? She is acquainted with Serabai mostly through her actions and routines, Bhima now realizes. She knows that her mistress likes her tea light and milky; that she doesn't like starch on her laundered clothes; that she is generous, and that she believes in the value of education. She also knows Serabai through her silences—the sudden, clamped-down silence when she disapproves of something; the dignified, stony silence when she does not want to expose her wounds to the world; the shy, awkward silence when she is among a group of chattering women and has nothing to say.

But after all these years of working in Serabai's home, Bhima has no idea what she thinks, she realizes. And why should you? she chastises herself. You, an ignorant, uninformed woman. And Serabai, educated and foreign-traveled. A woman who reads the newspaper every day while you grovel for the tidbits of information that fall your way like bread crumbs. What in the world would she talk to you about? Bhima flushes as she remembers how many times Serabai has had to unshackle her mind about things. Like her fear of Muslims, for instance. She had grown up like so many others, believing that the Muslims were about to overrun India, that it was their intention to acquire gold-silver until they owned the country and chased all the Hindus out. That was the reason they had many-many children, and the government was on their side, targeting only the Hindus with its family planning messages. Serabai had laughed the first time Bhima informed her of all this. But then her face grew serious and her eyes uneasy. She had gone into the other room and come back with a thick book. At first Bhima couldn't believe what Serabai read—that most Muslims in India were dirt poor and that they were vastly fewer in numbers than Hindus. "Even if some of them have any intentions of—how do you put it?—taking over India, at this rate it would take them more than a hundred years, Bhima," Serabai had said. Still, Bhima was not convinced. But then Serabai took it upon herself to translate parts of the newspaper for her, and Bhima learned about the burning of Muslim villages by Hindu mobs and how the politicians played each group against the other. Most important, Serabai told her of how both communities had lived side by side in peace for hundreds of years, until the white sahibs had come and done their badmaashi and made each group fear the other. Then, Bhima stopped hating the Muslims and started hating the politicians instead.

But now Bhima wishes that, instead of sharing history with her,

Serabai had shared some of her own thoughts. Thoughts that she had kept locked up in her head like medicine in a cabinet, like money in a cupboard. Money in a cupboard. Seven hundred rupees. Bhima knew that when Viraf threw one of his parties for his friends, he spent more than that sum on beer and soft drinks alone. The amount was too little for him to have cared about at any other time.

But who says the money is even missing? she thinks savagely. The money is probably in his pants pocket right now. The brown envelope was that final brick, you see, with which he blocked you in. You thought that that accountant from Gopal's workplace had tricked you. But he only thought of you as an ignorant fool, which was no lie. But this boy. This boy called you a thief to your face and there was nothing for you to do. Like a hunter setting a trap for a wild animal, he laid a trap for you. Probably chose a day when he knew Dinaz baby wouldn't be home. For days, weeks, he must've planned this. Every time you scowled at him, every time you didn't go as soon as he called, every time you humiliated him in front of his wife, he was thinking, calculating, planning. And how much planning did it take, after all? How scared could he have been, knowing that an old, uneducated woman was his opponent? He was probably not even biding his time. He was probably just toying with you, just batting you around, waiting for you to think you were more powerful than you were. And then, with the flick of his index finger, he made you tumble down from your perch of power. That's how much he bought and sold you for, seven hundred rupees. That's your worth—less than a party's supply of beer.

Bhima's throat burns with the salt of injustice. She swallows the lump in her throat, but it burns a pathway down her chest until it finally settles like a smoldering fire in her stomach. Should I try to contact Serabai while Viraf is at work? she wonders. And she cries out loud as the answer forms in her head: I can't. If it had been only the matter of the stolen money, she could've approached Serabai, could've convinced her of the wrongness of the accusation. In fact, she wouldn't have needed to say a word—Serabai herself had defended her, hadn't she? In this, Viraf had miscalculated his mother-in-law's sense of fair play. If that boy had thought that Serabai would have terminated her on the basis of his pointed finger and vile accusation, he was wrong. But if Viraf had been unable to light her funeral pyre, she had done it for him. She had climbed on top of the neatly arranged pile of wood and lay down; she had lit the match that brought alive the flames that had devoured her. With her words she had birthed a fire that had scorched all of them. The fire had consumed her, turning her future and her dreams to ash; she would never know how severely it had injured the other two—whether its flames had merely licked their bodies and then been extinguished by the gusts of their denial or whether the flames had scarred them permanently.

And despite her grief and outrage, Bhima prays for denial for Serabai. She has no desire to hurt this woman who has already been through so much. "Ae bhagwan, forgive me," she prays. "You should've cut off my tongue before allowing me to say those ugly words." She closes her eyes for a second to block off the sight of Sera's bewildered, confused face and brushes up against a youth riding his bicycle on the wrong side of the street. "Ae, mausi, watch where you're going," he yells over his shoulder as he zigzags through the crowd. "Almost knocked me off my bike, yaar."

Embarrassed, Bhima mumbles an apology and quickens her pace. Suddenly, she remembers the evening that Feroz seth died. Something about this sky, inflamed with orange and purple, is reminding her of that evening. She remembers standing at the door and looking at his still, stiff body and thinking how strange it was that once the ambulance people took him away she would never see

Feroz seth again. Only Parsis were allowed in the Tower of Silence, she knew. Standing at the door, she tried to study the features on Feroz's face, tried to conjure up the sound of his voice, his short, abrupt laugh. And found that she couldn't. Dead for a few minutes and already he was gone.

That's what this break with Serabai feels like, she thinks. A rupture as sudden as death. But worse, because she will have to live with the knowledge that Serabai is alive in the city at the same time she is, that in a few weeks she will be leaning over the baby's cradle and singing to him while some other woman is washing her clothes and her pots and pans.

The thought of another woman working in Sera's house makes a jolt of anger run through Bhima, and like electricity, the anger changes paths and turns inward. Oh, you stupid woman, she chides herself. What for you care about who works in their house? Even when your husband left you didn't grieve so much as you're grieving now. What do these people mean to you, after all? Discarded you like an old, stale slice of bread when the time came, didn't they? Didn't Serabai choose her son-in-law's obvious lie over your obvious truth? Didn't she hide behind the folds of family when she had to choose? And did she slap his face when he called you a thief? Did she ask him to get out of her house when you told her what he had done? No, instead she asked you to leave. What Ma always used to say is true—blood is thicker than water. So what if Serabai did not actually birthed Viraf? He is her son, just the same—the same fair skin, the same confidence when talking to strangers, the same educated way of speaking.

Bhima is not surprised to find that, on this day of deceit and trickery, even her feet have fooled her. Instead of leading her home, as she had assumed, they have turned a sharp corner so that she finds herself across the street from the sea. The sky above the water is even more violent and bruised, slashed red and purple by the razor blade of a madman. Suddenly she has a yearning to be close to the water, to hear in its wild but controlled thrashing the violent turmoil of her own soul. The wind propels her forward, through the six lanes of traffic she must cross to get to the other side. She feels a moment's twinge at the thought of Maya waiting worriedly for her at home, but the wind plucks at her guilt and carries it away.

She sets her cardboard box down on the cement wall that runs along the shore and sits next to it. She will not take it home with her when she leaves here, she decides. The box is just a mocking reminder of days that will not come again. Someone else can pick through its contents. She imagines a young boy's delight at finding her blue comb; a poor beggar woman walking away with her soap dish; a teenage girl using her Pond's talcum powder after her bath the next morning. She sits on the cement wall along with hundreds of other sea gazers and stares at the gray water as it pounds its fists against the large boulders that separate the sea from the wall. She wills the sea to send a large wave her way, a wave that will rise majestically above the protective wall and wash over everything—the wealthy ladies who are walking their dogs, the yellow-haired foreigners with their long strides and large backpacks, the couples who sit facing the sea with their hands in each other's laps, the channawalla with his nasal whine who is trying to get her to buy some peanuts. Above all, she wants the wave to rise and wash over her thin, tired body and carry it back into the sea as if it were a twig; she wants to bob in the water as if she were a dried coconut thrown into the sea to appease the gods; she prays for the water to cleanse her sins, to wash away each burning thought in her head, and to quench the fire in her throat.

"Bai, bai." The channawalla is still at her side, nagging her to buy some of his wares. She shakes her head no, but this sign of recognition only seems to encourage him more. "Please, bai," he says, with an ingratiating smile. "Business very slow-slow today. I'm having wife and five children at home."

She looks at him with contempt, remembering the old Pathani balloonwalla and his quiet dignity. The balloonwalla would never have begged a customer to buy his wares, she thinks. He would've gone hungry, would've returned empty-handed to his lonely corner of the world at the end of the day, but he would not have lowered himself into beggary. The channawalla watches the contempt gather like sea foam on her face and flinches. He walks away hurriedly, muttering to himself about the heartlessness of city people.

Remembering the Afghani balloonwalla's handsome, quietly pensive face calms Bhima so that for a moment she believes the sea has actually listened to her request. It's strange, she thinks, how she can barely remember what Feroz seth looked like. And God forgive her, she is also beginning to forget Amit's face. That is, she can conjure him up in parts—the white spots on his fingernails, the green snot that often dripped out of his nose, the texture of his thick, dark hair, the cleft on his chin. But these days, she is having trouble seeing his face in its totality. Her clearest memory of him is from about two years before he left her. And that's only because of a photograph of him from that time, a photograph that is yellow with age and smudged from the number of times she has held it, kissed it, fondled it.

And yet she can picture the Pathan's face as if she had run into him yesterday. She can see the milky gray of his sad eyes, which she always fancied reflected the skies of his homeland. She can recall the parched brown skin on a face as rugged as the country he came from. She can see the long nose, straight as a mountain range, and the thin lips that twisted like a river when he was concentrating on his work. Above all, she remembers the beautiful brown hands, hands that created poetry out of nothing, that turned lifeless pieces of rubber into magical objects that brought stars to the eyes of children.

Bhima feels something lighten in her heart. The sky is getting darker now, losing its dazzling light show, but the wind and the comforting thrashing of the sea continue to soothe her. Amid the screams, yells, and endless chatter of the people around her, she imagines she hears the Pathan's low, deep voice, comforting her, encouraging her, urging her on. His voice has come to her, over the mountains and over the years, using the wind as his messenger. The regret that she has always felt at not speaking to him, at not asking him about his life, leaves her now. Because somehow, even without her questioning, the Pathan has spoken to her. She remembers how his sunken cheeks used to puff with the air he blew into the rubber tubing of the deflated balloons, how his long, brown fingers used to run lightly down the slick bodies of the swollen balloons, like Krishna's fluid fingers as he played his flute. Bhima marvels at the paradox: A solitary man, an exile, a man without a country or a family, had still succeeded in creating dreamworlds for hundreds of children, had entered the homes of strangers with his creations of color and fantasy and magic. A man who would never again touch or kiss the sweet faces of his own children brought smiles to the faces of other people's children. Like a musician, the Pathan had learned how to make a song out of his loneliness. Like a magician, he had learned how to use sheer air to contort limp pieces of rubber into objects of happiness. Empty-handed, he had built a world.

Everything around Bhima falls silent. The white poodles cease their barking; the car horns do not honk; the vendors do not call out the superiority of their wares. All Bhima can hear is the rhythmic sound of the lapping waves and the Pathan's gentle words, murmuring to her, weaving a melody that's equal parts loneliness and the recipe for overcoming loneliness; a melody that speaks of both, the bitterness of exile and the sweetness of solitariness; of the fear of being alone in the world and the freedom that flaps its wings just below that fear. Bhima sits still, listening to the music. And soon the shenai stops its shrill, tragic wail, and after a few minutes the sitar ceases its heart-numbing drone, and then all that's left is a tabla beat—incessant, surging, powerful. Soon, the loneliness stops its wailing, and then the fear ceases its numbing drone, and all that is left is freedom—incessant, surging, and powerful.

Bhima laughs out loud. The couple sitting next to her flinch at the sight of an old woman sitting cross-legged on the cement wall and laughing to herself. "Probably thinks she's the laughing Buddha," the man whispers to his girlfriend.

"Too skinny," she whispers back.

Bhima doesn't hear them. She is taking her orders from a different authority now, following the fluttering sound in her ears, the sound of flapping wings, the sound of learning how to fly. Freedom.

She is almost grateful to Viraf baba now, for his treachery has been the knife that has cut the thread that kept her bound for so long.

She scrambles off the wall, knowing what she must do. In her haste, she does not wait for the wobbly hip joint to find its place before she begins to walk, and her punishment is a shooting pain that runs down the dark branch of her left leg. But tonight she does not mind, and even before the fire of the pain dies down, she is fiddling with her sari, looking for the twenty rupees she knows she has there. For a quick second, she thinks of Maya before the stove, waiting for her grandmother to get home, and she feels a twinge of guilt at depriving the girl of the food that the twenty rupees would buy. But then she thinks, What is this paltry sum worth anymore in today's Bombay? What will it buy me, a few lumps of sugar? I'll just take my tea without sugar for the next few weeks. For before she can go on, before she can decide what excuse to give Maya when she gets home, and which family to approach for another job, before she must confront the terrible reality of unemployment and finding work and all the humiliations that may entail, before she can decide whether to indulge in or ignore the fluttering sounds of freedom, she must do this one thing. She must honor the Pathan babu's memory.

In her eagerness, she almost walks by the young man who is squatting on the pavement, his face obscured by the balloons he is holding up. She takes a few steps back and stops in front of him, eyeing the balloons attached to thin sticks that make them look like large lollipops. "This all the balloons you have?" she asks.

The man leaps to his feet, an eager grin on his face. "Arre, mausi, so-so many balloons I am having," he says. "All different-different colors—yellow, red, orange. What more you are wanting?"

She shakes her head impatiently. "Wanting the other kind. Any other balloonwallas here?"

He eyes her resentfully, torn between wanting to make a sale and a faint sense of loyalty to his fellow balloon sellers. "Hah," he says finally. "Farther down, if you keep walking, there's another fellow, selling gas balloons. But he's very far down," he adds as a warning.

"I'm grateful," Bhima says to him. She walks swiftly now, deftly avoiding the people coming toward her from the opposite direction. At one point, she marvels at how much faster she can move alone, compared with when she's with Maya. And again she hears the sound of fluttering wings. Freedom. It has been so many years since she's ever been alone like this.

She is almost out of breath when she finally reaches the second balloonwalla. The crowds are thinner here, and she wonders briefly why the man works out of this particular spot. But then she remembers what Serabai used to tell her about how the police and the local gang lords worked hand in hand to charge the vendors money for allotting them a spot. Probably pays less to work here, she thinks.

Her heart jumps with delight when she spots the gas cylinder. So he has the kind of balloon she wants. Bhima waits impatiently as he fills a balloon for a child who is clutching her father's hand while staring at the swelling balloon in wonder. "What if it bursts?" she asks tearfully.

The balloon man smiles. "Ah, no bursting, expert job, baby," he says.

When it is her turn, the man looks around her for a child and then stares at her with a puzzled expression. "How much for a balloon?" she asks, but before he can reply, she thrusts the twenty-rupee note toward him. "I want all the balloons I can get for this much money," she says.

The man looks at her as if he is afraid to trust his good luck. "Buying for a party for your mistress's house?" he says conversationally as he begins to fill each balloon.

"I have no mistress," Bhima says curtly. And instead of tasting as bitter as aspirin, instead of tearing her mouth like jagged pieces of glass, the words taste sweet as a Cadbury's chocolate éclair in her mouth. "Hah. No mistress," she repeats.

When he is done, she gathers in the balloons like a bouquet of flowers, holding them by their long strings as they bob and weave over her head. The sky is now black, with no hint of its earlier fire, and the balloons dance in the wind like purple and red and blue heads against the blackness of the sky. Under the glow of the streetlights, she can see the curious looks of people walking by. Occasionally, a child, overcome with envy, pulls out of his mother's arms and reaches for one of the balloons. Bhima pretends not to notice. All along the dark water, she sees the glittering

Queen's Necklace, the affectionate name given to the sparkling curve of the lights from streetlamps as they bend around the coast, all the way from Malabar Hill to Nariman Point.

The wind tries to tug the strings from her hand, but she tightens her grip against its power. She looks around, unsure of what to do next, when her eyes fall on a spot where the cement wall has crumbled, creating a gap from where to step down onto the rocks that are battered by the sea. She squats near the crumbling wall and removes her slippers. She wriggles her buttocks until she is at the edge of the precipice before gingerly dangling one foot until it makes contact with the rocks. Balancing on that foot and still clenching the strings of the balloons, which are dancing like gay ghosts above her head, she places the other foot on the rock, steadying herself briefly with her hand against the wall before letting go completely. She stands still for a second, surveying the water around her, relying more on her hearing than on her sight.

She feels an urge to get closer to the water, to feel its cool wetness on her feet. Half-crouching, using the tips of her fingers for support, she inches closer to the water, stepping from rock to rock. As she makes her way forward, the boulders become moist and slippery. The wind is whipping her like a cruel master, trying to pull the balloons out of her hands. Despite the slipperiness of the rocks, she moves more deftly now, her feet curling and flexing around the contours of the rocks. She feels the water gurgling around her feet, and the sounds of the water and the wind drown out the whisperings of the Pathan's words, drown out the sounds of the city. Bombay seems far away now, and she thinks she wouldn't be surprised if she looked back and found that the city had fallen away—that the taxicabs had vanished, the tall buildings had collapsed, the people had disappeared. In the presence of immortality—the endlessly, churning sea, the plowed fields of the sky, the loose gypsy wind—the rest of her life feels absurdly, ridiculously mortal and transient. Transient as money, fragile as love. As ethereal and ready to pop as these balloons that are dancing in the wind.

And now she finally understands what she has always observed on people's faces when they are at the seaside. Years ago, when she and Gopal used to come to here, she would notice how people's faces turned slightly upward when they stared at the sea, as if they were straining to see a trace of God or were hearing the silent humming of the universe; she would notice how, at the beach, people's faces became soft and wistful, reminding her of the expressions on the faces of the sweet old dogs that roamed the streets of Bombay. As if they were all sniffing the salty air for transcendence, for something that would allow them to escape the familiar prisons of their own skin. In the temples and the shrines, their heads were bowed and their faces small, fearful, and respectful, shrunk into insignificance by the ritualized chanting of the priests. But when they gazed at the sea, people held their heads up, and their faces became curious and open, as if they were searching for something that linked them to the sun and the stars, looking for that something they knew would linger long after the wind had erased their footprints in the dust. Land could be bought, sold, owned, divided, claimed, trampled, and fought over. The land was stained permanently with pools of blood; it bulged and swelled under the outlines of the countless millions buried under it. But the sea was unspoiled and eternal and seemingly beyond human claim. Its waters rose and swallowed up the scarlet shame of spilled blood.

The balloons are still in Bhima's hands, and suddenly she imagines that their strings are all that is keeping her tied to this sad, ruined earth; that if she let go her grip on the strings, she would rise and float away beyond these rocks, to that narrow place where the sea meets the sky. And even as the thought enters her mind, her

320 / THRITY UMRIGAR

grip on the balloon strings slackens and the footloose wind cradles the balloons and carries them away. A picture of the old Pathan's face—sad and pensive but also dignified and courageous—floats in front of Bhima's eyes for a quick second and then the image is gone, carried away by the wind, and all Bhima can see are the balloons, rising and floating over the dark water like severed heads, soaring higher and higher, ascending the sky like Arjun's chariot and heading for the stars. Bhima squints her eyes and watches their flight, watches for a long time, until the last balloon disappears from her sight. She stands on the rocks, slipping occasionally but righting herself, and stares at the sea, as if waiting for an answer. A rat scuttles from under a rock near her feet, but she does not notice. She is too intent on talking to the sea, on handing over her burdens to it, as a little girl walking home from school may hand her heavy books over to her older brother.

I could stand here forever, she thinks. She could occupy this spot that's neither land nor water, wait here until the sky and the sea uncouple their dark, intertwined limbs and separate again in the light of a new day.

A new day. She will face it tomorrow, for Maya's sake. Along with the awakening sea, along with the rest of Bombay—the street urchins and the stray dogs; the impoverished nut vendors and the woman selling six cauliflowers a day; the hollow-eyed slum dwellers and the chubby-cheeked residents of nearby skyscrapers; the office workers spilling out of the trains at Churchgate and the young children boarding creaky school buses; the old men groaning on their deathbeds and the babies tumbling forth from the dark wombs of their mothers—along with the entire gigantic metropolis, with all its residents crawling along their individual destinies like an army of ants pretending to be an army of giants—along with Banubai in her damp bed, and Serabai in her shattered world, and Viraf baba with his choking guilt, and Maya with her tentative, hesitant dreams, and yes, along with Gopal and Amit waking up in a distant land to the smell of loamy earth, like all of them, the millions of people she has not met and the few she has—she, too, will face a new day tomorrow.

Tomorrow. The word hangs in the air for a moment, both a promise and a threat. Then it floats away like a paper boat, taken from her by the water licking her ankles.

It is dark, but inside Bhima's heart it is dawn.